10$\underline{^{00}}$

One Day
Closer to Death

One Day
Closer to Death

❧

Eight Stabs at Immortality

❧

Bradley Denton

St. Martin's Press ❧ New York

"The Territory" originally appeared in *The Magazine of Fantasy & Science Fiction,* July 1992. It also appeared in the limited-edition (426 copies) volume *The Calvin Coolidge Home for Dead Comedians* (Wildside Press, 1993).

"Skidmore" originally appeared in *The Magazine of Fantasy & Science Fiction,* May 1991. It also appeared in *The Calvin Coolidge Home for Dead Comedians.*

"Killing Weeds" originally appeared in *The Magazine of Fantasy & Science Fiction,* November 1986. It also appeared in the limited-edition (426 copies) volume *A Conflagration Artist* (Wildside Press, 1993).

"Captain Coyote's Last Hunt" originally appeared in *Isaac Asimov's Science Fiction Magazine,* March 1990. It also appeared in *A Conflagration Artist.*

"The Calvin Coolidge Home for Dead Comedians" originally appeared in *The Magazine of Fantasy & Science Fiction,* June 1988. It also appeared in *The Calvin Coolidge Home for Dead Comedians.*

"We Love Lydia Love" originally appeared in *The Magazine of Fantasy & Science Fiction,* October/November 1994.

"A Conflagration Artist" originally appeared in *A Conflagration Artist.*

"Blackburn Bakes Cookies" appears here for the first time.

DESIGN BY MAUREEN TROY

EDITED BY GORDON VAN GELDER

Library of Congress Cataloging-in-Publication Data

Denton, Bradley.
    One day closer to death: eight stabs at immortality / Bradley Denton. —1st ed.
        p.   cm.
    ISBN 0–312–18150–7
    1. Fantastic fiction, American.   I. Title.
PS3554.E588O5   1998
813'.54—dc21   97–38440

First edition: February 1998

10 9 8 7 6 5 4 3 2 1

Contents

Foreword
vii

The Territory
1

Skidmore
61

Killing Weeds
83

Captain Coyote's Last Hunt
127

The Calvin Coolidge Home for Dead Comedians
151

We Love Lydia Love
237

A Conflagration Artist
267

Blackburn Bakes Cookies
279

Afterword
335

—

Foreword

I'm writing a foreword in order to avoid finishing the new story that will anchor this book. But since writing a foreword still involves sitting at a keyboard and staring at a blank screen, I'm able to feel as though I'm doing real work. And as any semiobscure fiction writer will tell you, feeling as though you're doing real work is the most important part of the job. Especially if what you're really doing is anything but the job itself.

See, my problem in this case is that the new story is about death. And like any sane person, I'm scared of death. So I'd rather do this.

But since this is a foreword to a book of my stories, I ought to say something about the stories themselves. And in looking them over, I've discovered a startling thematic connection:

They're *all* about death.

This is a revelation that explains a lot.

I mean, jeez, no wonder I write so slowly. It's because every story I try to tell scares the crap out of me.

I will say this much for myself, though. If the stories in this book are any indication, I am not morbidly obsessed with or depressed over any one aspect of death. No, in the Dentonian world, death comes in many forms and flavors—and I'm not happy about any of them.

This reminds me of a wager I once made.

In college, I had a roommate who was convinced that he was not going to die, ever. He really believed this, and whenever presented with an argument to the contrary (e.g., "You are a living thing, and every other living thing in recorded history has, at some point, expired"), he would shrug and say, "Not me, man." Then he'd go up to the attic and smoke a joint, after which he was even tougher to argue with because he couldn't understand me unless I spoke in pig Latin.

So finally, I just got him to agree to a bet. If he actually did die someday, I would inherit his car and deliver a pig Latin eulogy to his grieving relatives. And if he instead turned out to be immortal (which, for the purposes of our bet, we defined as being 278 years old and still interested in girls), he and his horde of descendants would play a game of Hacky Sack on my grave.

I've lost track of that roommate over the years, so I don't know for sure . . . but I suspect that I can't claim the pink slip to his Volvo (or Yugo) just yet. However, I did hear a rumor that he had become an income tax attorney. So you be the judge.

But regardless of his current condition, my bet with him is one I still feel confident of winning. I don't have many rock-solid beliefs, but since early childhood I've never doubted that all creatures have one defining characteristic in common:

We're temporary.

So maybe I shouldn't be surprised that all of my stories are about death. It's just that I've always hoped they were about its antithesis.

I guess the stone truth, though, is that you don't get one without the other. The universe is a surly short-order cook, and existence is a combination plate with no substitutions.

And while I'm not happy about that, I can put up with it. I don't think I could write any faster anyway.

After all, I'm scared of *life,* too.

—Bradley Denton
Manchaca, Texas
February 1997

The Territory

Introduction to

༄

"The Territory"

You don't know about me, without you have read a book by the name of *Wrack and Roll, Buddy Holly Is Alive and Well on Ganymede, Blackburn,* or *Lunatics,* but that ain't no matter. Those books were made by Mr. Bradley Denton, and he lied, mainly. There was things which he didn't stretch, but mainly he lied. That is nothing. I never seen anybody but lied, one time or another . . .

Sorry. Couldn't resist.

And I am now going to make a statement which, if I had remained in academia instead of lighting out to avoid being sivilized, would probably set off a stuffy brouhaha and threaten my chances of getting tenure:

The greatest moment in all of American literature occurs in chapter 31 of *Adventures of Huckleberry Finn* when Huck says—

"All right, then, I'll *go* to hell."

And he tears up a certain piece of paper.

Of course, to understand why I find that moment so transcendent, you have to have read the whole book up to that point. And even then, you might not get it. Some people (sivilized people, especially) don't.

But that moment sets the literary high-jump bar for me. My goal as a storyteller is to give the reader the same kind of epiphany I always experience when Huck makes that incredible decision.

I don't think I've managed it quite yet.

However, I will confess that my current favorite of my own short stories is "The Territory," and I will also confess that it's my favorite for reasons that have nothing to do with any objective standards of criticism.

I like it because it's set in a place that means a lot to me. I like it because it revolves around an incident of brutality and death that has always fascinated and horrified me. I like it because I think my father, who was fond of stories involving guns and horses, would have enjoyed it. And I like it because its protagonist (who for a short time in 1861 really did join a guerrilla band) is a man with serious flaws whom I admire anyway.

But mainly, I like it because it's about deciding to go to hell.

The Territory

∽

Sam came awake and sat up choking. His chest was as tight as if wrapped in steel cables, and his heart was trying to hammer its way out. He gulped a breath and coughed. The air in the abandoned barn was thick with dust. There was just enough light for him to see the swirling motes.

A few feet away, the skinny form of Fletcher Taylor groaned and rose on one elbow. "What the hell's wrong?" he asked.

"Shut the hell up," the man on the other side of Taylor said.

"You go to hell," Taylor snapped.

"Go to hell yourself."

"Let me sleep, or I'll send you all to hell," another man said.

"The hell you will."

"The hell I won't."

Taylor shook a finger at Sam. "See all the hell you've raised?"

Sam put on the new slouch hat that Taylor had given him, pulled on his boots, and stood, picking up the leather saddlebags he'd been using as a pillow. "I'm sorry as hell," he said, and left the barn, trying not to kick more than four or five of the other men on his way out.

The light was better outside, but the sun had not yet risen. Sam closed his left nostril with a finger and blew through his right, then closed his right nostril and blew through his left, trying to clear his head of dust. The ground was dry. The thunderheads that had formed the night before had rolled by without dropping enough rain to fill a teacup. He could have slept outside, in clean air, and been fine. As it was, his head ached. This wasn't the first night he had spent in a barn or corncrib since leaving the river, but he still wasn't used to it. At three months shy of twenty-eight, he feared that he was already too old for this kind of life.

Most of the camp was still asleep, but a few men were building fires and boiling chicory. One of them gestured to Sam to come on over, but Sam shook his head and pointed at the sycamore grove that served as the camp latrine. The other man nodded.

Sam went into the trees, and within twenty steps the smells of chicory and smoke were overwhelmed by the smell caused by two hundred men all doing their business in the same spot over the course of a week. It was even worse than usual this morning, because the leaders of other guerrilla bands had brought some of their own men into camp the day before. But at least Sam had the grove to himself for now.

When he had finished his business, he continued eastward through the grove until the stench faded and the trees thinned. Then he sat down with his back against the bole of a sycamore and opened one of his saddlebags. He removed his Colt Navy revolver and laid it on the ground beside him, then took out a pen, a bottle of ink, and the deerhide pouch that held his journal. He slid the notebook from the pouch and flipped pages until he reached a blank sheet, then opened the ink bottle, dipped his pen, and began to write.

Tuesday, August 11, 1863:

I have had the same dream again, or I should say, another variation thereof. This time when I reached the dead man, I discovered that his face was that of my brother Henry. Then I awoke with the thought that it was my fault that Henry was on board the Pennsylvania *when she blew, which in turn led to the thought that I was an idiot to ask a young and unsure physician to give him morphine.*

But I would have been on the Pennsylvania *as well had it not been for the malice of a certain William Brown, perhaps the only man caught in that storm of metal, wood, and steam who received what he deserved. As for the morphine, Dr. Peyton himself instructed me to ask the night doctor to give Henry an eighth of a grain should he become restless. If the doctor administered too much, the fault was his, not mine.*

I see by my words that I have become hard. But five years have passed since that night in Memphis, and I have seen enough in those years that the hours I spent at Henry's deathbed do not seem so horrific now—or, at least, they do not seem so during my waking hours.

A pistol shot rang out back at camp and was followed by the shouted curses of men angry at having been awakened. Someone had killed a rat or squirrel, and might soon wish that he'd let the creature live to gnaw another day. These once gentle Missouri farm boys had become as mean as bobcats. They generally saved their bullets for Bluebellies, but didn't mind using their fists and boots on each other.

The dream seems more pertinent, Sam continued, *on those nights when the man's face is that of Orion. Orion was as intolerable a scold as any embittered crone, and a Republican crone at that—but he was my brother, and it might have been in my power to save him.*

Sam paused, rolling the pen between his fingers. He looked up from the paper and stared at the brightening eastern sky until his eyes stung. Then he dipped the pen and resumed writing.

It is as fresh and awful in my memory as if it had happened not two years ago, but two days ago.

I could have fought the Red Legs, as Orion and our companions tried to do. I had a Smith & Wesson seven-shooter. If I had used it, I would have either preserved Orion's life, or fallen beside him. Either result would have been honorable.

But I faltered. When the moment came, I chose to surrender, and handed over my pistol—which one of the Red Legs laughed at, saying he was glad I had not fired the weapon, for to be struck with a ball from its barrel might give one a nasty welt.

Then, as if to prove his point, he turned it on the driver, and on the conductor, and on Mr. Bemis, and on my brother.

As Orion lay dying, the Red Leg attempted to shoot me as well. But the pistol misfired, and I ran. Two of the Red Legs caught me and took my watch, but then let me go, saying that killing a Missourian the likes of me would not be so advantageous to their cause as letting me live.

I continued to run like the coward I had already proven myself to be.

Sam paused again. His hand was shaking, and he didn't think he would be able to read the jagged scrawl of what he had just written. But he would always know what the words said.

He rubbed his forehead with his wrist, then turned the notebook page and dipped his pen.

I could not have saved Henry. But Orion would be alive today, safe in Nevada Territory, had I been a man. And I would be there with him instead of here at Blue Springs; I would be thriving in the mountains of the West instead of sweltering in the chaos of western Missouri.

I have remained in Missouri to pay for my sin, but in two years have had no success in doing so. Perhaps now that I have come to Jackson County and fallen in with the Colonel's band, my luck will change.

When this war began, I served with my own county's guerrilla band, the Marion Rangers, for three weeks. But there the actual need for bushwhacking was about as substantial as an owl's vocabulary. That was before I had crossed the state, entered Kansas, and encountered the Red Legs. That was before I had seen my brother shot down as if he were a straw target.

I have not had a letter from Mother, Pamela, or Mollie in several weeks, although I have written to each of them as often as I can. I do not know whether this means that they have disowned me, or whether their letters are not reaching Independence. I intend to go up to inves-

tigate once this coming business is completed, assuming that it does not complete me in the process.

Sam laid the journal on the ground and wiped his ink-stained fingers on the grass. Then he peered into the ink bottle and saw that it was almost empty. He decided not to buy more until he was sure he would live long enough to use it.

The sun had risen and was a steady heat on Sam's face. The day was going to be hot. Another shot rang out back at camp, and this time it was followed by yips and hollers. The boys were up and eager.

Sam slid his journal into its pouch, then returned it and the other items to the saddlebag. He stood, stretched, and walked back to Colonel Quantrill's camp.

As he emerged from the sycamores, Sam saw fifty or sixty of his fellow bushwhackers clustered before Quantrill's tent. The tent was open, and the gathered men, although keeping a respectful distance, were trying to see and hear what was going on inside. Fletcher Taylor was standing at the rear of the cluster, scratching his sparse beard.

"Morning, Fletch," Sam said as he approached. "Sleep well?"

Taylor gave him a narrow-eyed glance. "Rotten, thanks to you."

"Well, you're welcome."

"Be quiet. I'm trying to hear."

"Hear what?"

"You know damn well what. The Colonel's planning a raid. Most of the boys are betting it'll be Kansas City, but my money's on Lawrence."

Sam nodded. "The story I hear is that the Colonel's wanted to teach Jim Lane and Lawrence a lesson ever since he lived there himself."

A man standing in front of Taylor turned to look at them. "I'd like to teach Jim Lane a lesson too," he said, "but I'm not crazy and neither's the Colonel. Lawrence is forty miles inside the border, and the Bluebellies are likely to be as thick as flies on a dead possum. It'd be like putting our pistols to our own heads."

"Maybe," Sam said.

The man raised an eyebrow. "What do you mean, maybe? You know something I don't?"

Sam shrugged and said nothing. Two nights before, in a dream, he had seen Colonel Quantrill surrounded by a halo of fire, riding into Lawrence before a band of shooting, shouting men. He had known the town was Lawrence because all of its inhabitants had looked like the caricatures he had seen of Senator Jim Lane and had worn red pants. Sam had learned to trust his dreams when they were as clear as that. Several days before the *Pennsylvania* had exploded, a dream had shown him Henry lying in a coffin; and before he and Orion had left St. Joseph, a dream had shown him Orion lying dead in the dust. But it wouldn't do to talk of his dreams with the other bushwhackers. Most of them seemed to think that Sam Clemens was odd enough as it was, hoarding perfectly good ass-wiping paper just so he could write on it.

"Well, you're wrong," the man said, taking Sam's shrug as a statement. "Kansas City's got it coming just as bad, and there's places for a man to hide when he's done."

Taylor looked thoughtful. "I see your point," he said. "Calling on Senator Lane would be one thing, but coming home from the visit might be something else."

Sam stayed quiet. It didn't matter what the others thought now. They would mold bullets and make cartridges until they were told where to shoot them, and they'd be just as happy to shoot them in Lawrence as anywhere else—happier, since most of the jayhawkers and Red Legs who had robbed them, burned them out of their homes, killed their brothers, and humiliated their women had either hailed from Lawrence or pledged their allegiance to Jim Lane. And if Quantrill could pull several guerrilla bands together under his command, he would have enough men both to raid Lawrence and to whip the Federals on the way there and back.

Captain George Todd emerged from the tent and squinted in

the sunlight. He was a tall, blond, square-jawed man whom some of the men worshiped even more than they did Quantrill. He was wearing a blue jacket he'd taken from a dead Union lieutenant.

"Hey, Cap'n, where we going?" someone called out.

Todd gave the men a stern look. "I doubt we'll be going anywhere if you boys keep standing around like sick sheep when there's guns to be cleaned and bridles to be mended."

The men groaned, but began to disperse.

"Fletch Taylor!" Todd yelled. "Wherever you are, get your ass in here!" He turned and went back into the tent.

Sam nudged Taylor. "Now, what would a fine leader of men like George Todd be wanting with a low-down thief like you?" he asked.

Taylor sneered. "Well, he told me to keep my eyes open for Yankee spies," he said, "so I reckon he'll be wanting me to give him your name." He started for the tent.

"I'm not worried!" Sam called after him. "He'll ask you to spell it, and you'll be stumped!"

Taylor entered the tent, and someone pulled the flaps closed. Sam stood looking at the tent for a moment longer, then struck off across camp in search of breakfast. Why Quantrill and the other guerrilla leaders were taking so long to form their plans, and why they were keeping the men in the dark, he couldn't imagine. There shouldn't be any great planning involved in striking a blow at Lawrence and the Red Legs: Ride in hard, attack the Red Legs' headquarters and the Union garrison like lightning, and then ride out again, pausing long enough to set fire to Jim Lane's house to pay him back for the dozens of Missouri houses he'd burned himself.

As for keeping the rank-and-file bushwhackers ignorant . . . well, there were about as many Yankee spies among Quantrill's band as there were fish in the sky. Sam had talked to over a hundred of these men, and all of them had lost property or family to abolitionist raiders of one stripe or another. Sam had even spoken with one man whose brother had been killed by John Brown in

1856, and who still longed for vengeance even though John Brown was now as dead as a rock.

Vengeance could be a long time coming, as Sam well knew. In the two years since Orion's murder, he had yet to kill a single Federal soldier, let alone one of the marauding Kansas Red Legs. It wasn't for lack of trying, though. He had fired countless shots at Bluebellies, but always at a distance or in the dark. He had never hit anything besides trees and the occasional horse.

Sam had a breakfast of fatty bacon with three young brothers who were from Ralls County south of Hannibal and who therefore considered him a kinsman. He ate their food, swapped a few east Missouri stories, and promised to pay them back with bacon of his own as soon as he had some. Then he shouldered his saddlebags again and walked to the camp's makeshift corral to see after his horse, Bixby.

Bixby was a swaybacked roan gelding who had been gelded too late and had a mean disposition as a result. The horse also seemed to think that he knew better than Sam when it came to picking a travel route, or when it came to deciding whether to travel at all. Despite those flaws, however, Sam had no plans to replace Bixby. He thought that he had the horse he deserved.

Sam tried to give Bixby a lump of hard brown sugar from one of his saddlebags, but Bixby ignored it and attempted to bite Sam's shoulder.

"Sometimes I think you forget," Sam said, slapping Bixby on the nose, "that I am the man who freed you from your bondage to an abolitionist."

Bixby snorted and stomped, then tried to bite Sam's shoulder again.

"Clemens!" a voice called.

Sam turned and saw that the voice belonged to one of the Ralls County boys who had fed him breakfast.

"The Colonel wants you at the tent!" the boy shouted.

Sam was astonished. Except for his friendship with Fletch Taylor, he was less than a nobody in the band. Not only was he a new arrival, but it was already obvious that he was the worst rider, the worst thief, and the worst shot. Maybe Taylor really had told Todd and Quantrill that he was a Yankee spy.

"Better come quick!" the boy yelled.

Sam waved. "I'll be right—goddamn son of a bitch!"

Bixby had succeeded in biting him. Sam whirled and tried to slug the horse in the jaw with the saddlebags, but Bixby jerked his head up and danced away.

Sam rubbed his shoulder and glared at Bixby. "Save some for the Red Legs, why don't you," he said. Then he ducked under the corral rope and hurried to Quantrill's tent. He remembered to remove his hat before going inside.

William Clarke Quantrill leaned back, his left leg crossed over his right, in a polished oak chair behind a table consisting of three planks atop two sawhorses. He wore a white embroidered "guerrilla shirt," yellow breeches, and black cavalry boots. He gave a thin smile as Sam approached the table. Above his narrow upper lip, his mustache was a straight reddish blond line. His eyelids drooped, but his blue-gray eyes probed Sam with a gaze as piercing as a bayonet. Sam stopped before the table and clenched his muscles so he wouldn't shudder. His own eyes, he had just realized, were of much the same color as Quantrill's.

"You've only been with us since June, Private Clemens," Quantrill said in a flat voice, "and yet it seems that you have distinguished yourself. Corporal Taylor tells me you saved his life a few weeks ago."

Sam looked at Fletch Taylor, who was standing at his left. Taylor appeared uncomfortable under Sam's gaze, so Sam looked past him at some of the other men in the tent. He recognized the guerrilla leaders Bill Gregg and Andy Blunt, but several of the others were strangers to him.

"Well, sir," Sam said to Quantrill, "I don't know that I did. My horse was being cantankerous and brought me in on an abolitionist's house about two hundred feet behind and to one side of Fletch and the other boys, so I happened to see a man hiding up a tree."

"He was aiming a rifle at Corporal Taylor, I understand," Quantrill said.

"Yes, sir, that's how it looked," Sam said. "So I hollered and took a shot at him."

"And that was his undoing."

Sam twisted the brim of his hat in his hands. "Actually, sir," he said, "I believe that I missed by fourteen or fifteen feet."

Quantrill uncrossed his legs and stood. "But you diverted the ambusher's attention. According to Corporal Taylor, the ambusher then fired four shots at you, one of which took your hat from your head, before he was brought down by a volley from your comrades. Meanwhile you remained steadfast, firing your own weapon without flinching, even though the entire focus of the enemy's fire was at yourself."

Sam licked his lips and said nothing. The truth was that he had been stiff with terror—except for his right hand, which had been cocking and firing the Colt, and his left foot, which had been kicking Bixby in the ribs in an effort to make the horse wheel and run. But Bixby, who seemed to be deaf as far as gunfire was concerned, had been biting a crabapple from a tree and had not cared to move. The horse's position had blocked the other bushwhackers' view of Sam's left foot.

Quantrill put his hands on the table and leaned forward. "That was a brave and noble act, Private Clemens," he said.

A stretch of silence followed until Sam realized that he was expected to say something. "Thank—thank you, Colonel," he stammered. It was well known that Quantrill liked being called "Colonel."

"You understand, of course," Quantrill said, "that in the guerrilla service we have no formal honors. However, as the best reward of service is service itself, I'm promoting you to corporal and ordering you to reconnoiter the enemy in the company of Corporal Taylor."

14

"And a nigger," someone on Sam's right said. The voice was low, ragged, and angry.

Sam turned toward the voice and saw the most fearsome man he had ever seen in his life. The man wore a Union officer's coat with the insignia torn off, and a low-crowned hat with the brim turned up. His brown hair was long and shaggy, and his beard was the color of dirt. His face was gaunt, and his eyes, small and dark, glowered. He wore a wide-buckled belt with two pistols jammed into it. A scalp hung from the belt on each side of the buckle.

George Todd, standing just behind this man, placed a hand on his shoulder. "I don't much like it either, Bill, but Quantrill's right. A nigger's the perfect spy."

The seated man shook Todd's hand away. "Perfect spy, my hairy ass. You can't trust a nigger any more than you can trust Abe Lincoln."

Quantrill looked at the man without blinking. "That concern is why I'm sending two white men as well—one that I trust, and one that he in turn trusts. Don't you agree that two white men can keep one nigger under control, Captain Anderson?"

Anderson met Quantrill's gaze with a glare. "I have three sisters in prison in Kansas City for the simple act of remaining true to their brother's cause," he said. "I do not believe they would care to hear that their brother agreed to send a nigger to fight in that same cause, particularly knowing the treachery of which that race is capable."

Quantrill smiled. "As for sending a nigger to fight, I'm doing no such thing just yet. I'm sending him as a spy and as a guarantee of safe conduct for two brave sons of Missouri. No Kansan is likely to assault white men traveling with a free nigger. As for treachery, well, I assure you that John Noland has proven his loyalty. He's killed six Yankee soldiers and delivered their weapons to me. I trust him as much as I would a good dog, and have no doubt that he will serve Corporals Taylor and Clemens as well as he has me." The Colonel looked about the tent. "Gentlemen, we've been jawing about this enterprise for twenty-four hours. I suggest that it's now time to stop jawing and begin action. If you never risk, you never gain. Are there any objections?"

No one spoke. Anderson spat into the dirt, but then looked at Quantrill and shook his head.

"Very well," said Quantrill. "Captains Anderson and Blunt will please gather your men and communicate with me by messenger when your forces are ready." He nodded to Taylor. "Corporal, you're to return no later than sundown next Monday. So you'd best be on your way."

Sam made a noise in his throat. "Sir? On our way where?"

Quantrill turned to Sam. "Kansas Territory," he said. "Corporal Taylor has the particulars. You're dismissed."

Sam didn't need to be told twice. He left the tent, picked up his saddlebags where he'd dropped them outside, and then ran into the sycamore grove.

Taylor caught up with him in the trees. "You should have saluted, Sam," he said. "It's important to show the Colonel proper respect."

Sam unbuttoned his pants. His head was beginning to ache again. "I have plenty of respect for the Colonel," he said. "I have plenty of respect for all of them. If they were to cut me open, I'd probably bleed respect. Now get away and let a man piss in peace."

Taylor sighed. "All right. Get your horse saddled as soon as you can. I'll find Noland and meet you north of the tent. You know Noland?"

"No. But since I've only seen one man of the Negro persuasion in camp, I assume that's him."

"You assume correctly." Taylor started to turn away, then looked back again. "By the way, we were right. We're going to Lawrence. You and I are to count the Bluebellies in the garrison, and—"

"I know what a spy does, Fletch," Sam said.

Taylor turned away. "Hurry up, then. We have some miles to cover." He left the grove.

Sam emptied his bladder and buttoned his pants, then leaned

against a tree and retched until he brought up most of the bacon he'd had for breakfast.

"Kansas Territory," Quantrill had said. There had been no sarcasm in his voice. Kansas had been admitted to the Union over two and a half years before, but none of the bushwhackers ever referred to it as a state. In their opinion, its admission to the Union as a free state had been an illegal act forced upon its residents by fanatical jayhawkers. Sooner or later, though, those house-burning, slave-stealing jayhawkers would be crushed, and Kansas Territory would become what it was meant to be: a state governed by Southern men who knew what was right.

To that end, Colonel Quantrill would raid the abolitionist town of Lawrence, the home of Jim Lane and the Kansas Red Legs. And Sam Clemens was to go there first and come back to tell Quantrill how to go about the task.

Orion's ghost, he thought, had better appreciate it.

On Wednesday morning, six miles south of Lawrence on the Paola road, Fletch Taylor started chuckling. Sam, riding in the center, glanced first at him and then at John Noland. Noland didn't even seem to be aware of Sam or Taylor's existence, let alone Taylor's chuckling.

Noland was an enigma, both in his mere presence in Quantrill's band and in his deportment during the present journey. No matter what Sam or Taylor said or did, he continued to look straight ahead, shifting in his saddle only to spit tobacco juice into the road. Except for the color of his skin, though, Noland's appearance was like that of any other free man of the border region, right down to the slouch hat and the Colt stuck in his belt. He even rode with the same easy arrogance as Taylor. It was a skill Sam had never mastered.

Sam looked at Taylor again, squinting as he faced the sun. "What's so funny, Fletch?"

Taylor gestured at the winding track of the road. "No pickets," he said. "We ain't seen a Bluebelly since we came into Kansas. If the

Colonel wanted to, the whole lot of us could waltz in and raise no more notice than a cottontail rabbit." He chuckled again. "Until we started shooting."

Sam nodded, but didn't laugh. It was true that they hadn't passed a single Federal picket, but that didn't mean Lawrence was going to be a waltz. The absence of pickets might only mean that the town had fortified itself so well that it didn't need them.

"You should carry your gun in your belt," Noland said. His voice was a rumble.

Sam was startled. Until now, Noland hadn't spoken at all.

"Are you addressing me?" Sam asked, turning back toward Noland. But he knew that must be the case. Both Noland and Taylor had their pistols in their belts, while Sam's was in one of his saddlebags.

Noland looked straight ahead. "That's right."

"I thought I should make sure," Sam said, "since you won't look me in the eye."

"Your eyes ain't pleasant to look at," Noland said.

Taylor chortled. "Whomp him, Sam. Make him say your eyes are the most beautiful jewels this side of a St. Louie whorehouse."

"It ain't a question of beauty," Noland said. "It's a question of skittishness. Mr. Clemens has skittish eyes. I prefer steady ones, like those of Colonel Quantrill. Or like your own, Mr. Taylor."

Now Sam laughed. "It appears that you've bested me in the enticing-eyeball category, Fletch. Perhaps we should switch places so you can ride next to John here."

Taylor scowled. "Ain't funny, Sam."

Sam knew when to stop joking with Fletch Taylor, so he replied to Noland instead. "My gun's fine where it is," he said. "Why should I put it in my belt and risk shooting myself in the leg?"

"If that's your worry, you can take out the caps," Noland said. "But it'll look better going into Lawrence if your gun's in the open. The county sheriff might be inspecting strangers, and he won't think nothing of it if your pistol's in your belt. But if he finds it in your bag, he'll think you're trying to hide it."

Sam didn't know whether Noland was right or not, but it wasn't worth arguing about. He took his pistol from his saddlebag, removed the caps, and tucked the weapon into his belt.

"Be sure to replace those caps when we come back this way with the Colonel," Taylor said. He sounded disgusted.

"I merely want to ensure that I don't shoot up the city of Lawrence prematurely," Sam said. But neither Taylor nor Noland laughed. Sam gave Bixby a pat on the neck, and Bixby looked back at him and snorted.

When the three bushwhackers were within a mile of Lawrence, they encountered two riders heading in the opposite direction. The two men, one old and one young, were dressed in high-collared shirts and black suits despite the August heat. They wore flat-brimmed black hats, and their pistols hung in black holsters at their sides. The younger man held a Bible with a black leather cover, reading aloud as he rode.

"Well, lookee here," Taylor whispered as the two approached. "I think we got ourselves a couple of abolitionist preachers on our hands."

Sam tensed. If there was one thing a bushwhacker hated more than an abolitionist, it was an abolitionist with a congregation. Taylor had particularly strong feelings in this regard, and Sam feared that his friend might forget that they were only in Kansas as spies for now.

"Good morning, friends," the elder preacher said, reining his horse to a stop. The younger man closed his Bible and stopped his horse as well. They blocked the road.

"Good morning to you as well," Taylor replied. He and Noland stopped their horses a few yards short of the preachers.

Sam tried to stop Bixby too, but Bixby ignored the reins and continued ahead, trying to squeeze between the horses blocking the way. The preachers moved their mounts closer together, forcing Bixby to halt, and the roan shook his head and gave an irritated *whuff*.

"I apologize, gentlemen," Sam said. "My horse sometimes forgets which of us was made in God's image."

The elder preacher frowned. "More discipline might be in order," he said, and then looked past Sam at Taylor. "Are you going into Lawrence?"

"That we are," said Taylor. His voice had taken on a gravelly tone that Sam recognized as trouble on the way. He glanced back and saw that Taylor's right hand was hovering near the butt of his pistol.

"I see that you are traveling with a colored companion," the younger preacher said. "Is he your servant?"

"No," Sam said before Taylor could reply. "My friend and I jayhawked him from Arkansas three years ago, and we've been trying to help him find his family ever since. Are there any colored folks named Smith in Lawrence?"

The elder preacher nodded. "A number, I believe." He twitched his reins, and his horse moved to the side of the road. "I would like to help you in your search, gentlemen, but my son and I are on our way to Baldwin to assist in a few overdue baptisms. Sometimes an older child resists immersion and must be held down."

"I have observed as much myself," Sam said as the elder preacher rode past.

The younger preacher nodded to Sam and thumped his Bible with his fingertips. "If you gentlemen will be in town through the Sabbath, I would like to invite you to attend worship at First Lawrence Methodist."

Taylor came up beside Sam. "I doubt we'll be in town that long, Preacher," he said. "But we'll be sure to pay your church a visit the next time we pass through."

"I am glad to hear it," the young preacher said. "God bless you, gentlemen." He nudged his horse with his heels and set off after his father.

Taylor looked over his shoulder at the departing men. "You won't be so glad when it happens," he muttered.

Noland rode up. " 'Jayhawked from Arkansas,' " he said. "That's a good one." He spurred his horse, which set off at a trot. Taylor's horse did likewise. Bixby, for once, took the cue and hurried to catch up.

"I'm sorry if my lie didn't meet with your approval," Sam said as Bixby drew alongside Noland's horse.

"I said it was a good one," Noland said. "I say what I mean."

"You may believe him on that score, Sam," Taylor said. "John's as honest a nigger as I've ever known."

Sam eyed Noland. "Well, then, tell me," he said. "Where *were* you jayhawked from?"

"I was born a free man in Ohio," Noland said. "Same as Colonel Quantrill."

"I see," Sam said. "And how is it that a free man of your race rides with a free man like the Colonel?"

Noland turned to look at Sam for the first time. His eyes and face were like black stone.

"He pays me," Noland said.

Sam had no response to that. But Noland kept looking at him. "So why do *you* ride with the Colonel?" Noland asked.

"Might as well ask Fletch the same question," Sam said.

"I know all about Mr. Taylor," Noland said. "His house was burned, his property stolen. But I don't know shit about you."

Taylor gave Noland a look of warning. "Don't get uppity."

"It's all right, Fletch," Sam said. Fair was fair. He had asked Noland an impertinent question, so Noland had asked him one. "I was a steamboat pilot on the Mississippi, Mr. Noland. I was a printer's devil before that, but I wanted to be on the river, so I made it so." He grimaced. "I was a cub for two years before I earned my license, and I was only able to follow the profession for another two years before the war started. I had to leave the river then, or be forced to pilot a Union boat. So here I am."

"How'd you come to be on this side of Missouri instead of that side?" Noland asked.

"I was going to Nevada Territory with my brother," Sam said, angry now at being prodded, "but the Red Legs killed him north-west of Atchison. I went back home after that, but eventually realized there was nothing useful I could do there. So I came back this way and fell in with one bunch of incompetents after another until I joined the Colonel." He glared at Noland. *"So here I am."*

"So here you are," Noland said.

"That's about enough, John," Taylor said. He looked at Sam. "I didn't know you were a printer, Sam, but I'm glad to hear it. It'll make one of our tasks easier. Marshal Donaldson's posse tore up the *Lawrence Herald of Freedom*'s press and dumped the type in the Kansas River back in fifty-six, but the *Lawrence Journal*'s sprung up like a weed to take its place. So when we raid Lawrence, the *Journal*'s to be destroyed. But we'll need to know how well the office is armed, so I suggest that you go there and ask for employment. You'll be able to get a look at things without them wondering why. After you've done that, you can help me count Bluebellies, Red Legs, and Lawrence Home Guards, if we can find out who they are."

"What if the *Journal* wants to hire me?" Sam asked.

Taylor grinned. "Tell them you'll be back in a week or so." He looked across at Noland. "John, you're to fall in with the local niggers and see whether any of them have guns. You might also ask them about Jim Lane, since they love him so much. Find out where his fancy new house is, and how often he's there."

Noland was staring straight ahead again, but he nodded.

They were now skirting the base of a high, steep hill. Sam looked up the slope. "One of the boys at Blue Springs told me that the hill rising over Lawrence is called Mount Horeb," he said. "It must be named after the place where Moses saw the burning bush."

Taylor chuckled. "If Moses is still here, he'll see more burning before long, at closer range than he might like." He pointed toward the southeast, at another hill that was a few miles distant. "That might be a safer place for him to watch from. The Colonel says it'll be our last stop before the raid, so we can see what's what before it's too late to turn back." He spurred his horse, which galloped ahead. "Come on, boys! We've reached Lawrence!"

Noland spurred his horse as well, and he and Taylor vanished around the curve of the hill.

"Now that I think of it," Sam yelled after them, "he said Mount Oread, not Horeb. Moses doesn't have anything to do with it."

He kicked Bixby, but the horse only looked back at him and gave a low nicker. It was the saddest sound Sam had ever heard.

"Do you have a stomachache?" he asked.

Bixby looked forward again and plodded as if leading a funeral procession. Sam kicked the horse once more and then gave up. The sadness of Bixby's nicker had infected him, and he felt oppressed by the heat, by his companions, and by his very existence on the planet.

They followed the road around the hill, and then Lawrence lay before Sam like a toy city put together by a giant child. Its rows of stores and houses were too neat and perfect to be real. Small wagons rolled back and forth between them, and children dashed about like scurrying ants. Taylor and Noland were already among them.

Sam closed his eyes, but then opened them immediately, crying out before he could stop himself.

He had just seen the buildings, wagons, and children burst into flame.

Sam shook himself. Here he was having nightmares while wide awake. The ride had been too long, the sun too hot. It was time for a rest.

But maybe not for sleep.

Early Friday, Sam awoke in sweat-soaked sheets. He fought his way free, then sat up with his back against the wall. He had just spent his second night in Lawrence, and his second night in a real bed in almost three months. The dream had come to him on both nights, worse than ever. He was no more rested than if he had run up and down Mount Oread since sundown.

The dream always began the same way: He and the other Marion Rangers, fifteen men in all, were bedding down in a corncrib at Camp Ralls, fourteen miles south of Hannibal. They had to chase the rats away, but they had to do that every night. Then a Negro messenger came and told them that the enemy was nearby. They scoffed; they had heard that before.

But they grew tense and restless, and could not sleep. The sounds of their breathing were unsteady. Sam's heart began to beat faster.

Then they heard a horse approaching. Sam and the other Rangers went to the corncrib's front wall and peered out through a crack between the logs. In the dim moonlight, they saw the shadow of a man on a horse enter the camp. Sam was sure that he saw more men and horses behind that shadow. Camp Ralls was being attacked.

Sam picked up a rifle and pushed its muzzle between the logs. His skull was humming, his chest tight. His hands shook. The enemy had come and would kill him. The enemy had come and would kill him. The enemy had come and would—

Someone shouted, "Fire!"

And Sam pulled the trigger. The noise was as loud and the flash as bright as if a hundred guns had gone off at once.

The enemy fell from his saddle and lay on the ground. Then all was darkness, and silence. There was nothing but the smell of damp earth.

No more riders came. The fallen man was alone.

Sam and the others went out to the enemy. Sam turned the man onto his back, and the moonlight revealed that he was not wearing a uniform, and that his white shirt was soaked with blood. He was not the enemy. He was not even armed. And his face—

Was sometimes Henry's, and sometimes Orion's.

But just now, this Friday morning in Lawrence, it had been someone else's. It had been a face that Sam did not recognize. It had been the face of an innocent stranger, killed by Sam Clemens for no reason at all . . . no reason save that Sam was at war, and the man had gotten in the way.

Fletch Taylor, in the room's other bed, mumbled in his sleep.

Sam could still smell the whiskey. One of Taylor's first acts of spying on Wednesday afternoon had been to hunt up a brothel, and he had been having a fine time ever since. He was counting Bluebellies too, but it had turned out that there weren't many Bluebellies to count.

Sam had visited the brothel with Taylor on Wednesday, but hadn't found the girls to his liking. So he'd spent most of his time since then trying to do his job. He had applied for work at the *Lawrence Journal,* as planned, and had been turned down, as he'd hoped—but had learned that the *Journal* was a two-man, one-boy operation, and that they didn't even dream of being attacked. A carbine hung on pegs on the wall in the pressroom, but it was kept unloaded to prevent the boy from shooting rabbits out the back door. The *Journal*'s type would join the *Herald of Freedom*'s at the bottom of the Kansas River with little difficulty.

From the purplish gray color of the patch of eastern sky visible through the hotel-room window, Sam guessed that it was about 5:00 A.M. He climbed out of bed and went to the window to look down at the wide, muddy strip of the town's main thoroughfare, Massachusetts Street. Lawrence was quiet. The buildings were closed up, and no one was outside. Even the Red Legs and Home Guards slept until six or six-thirty. If Colonel Quantrill timed his raid properly, he and his bushwhackers could ride into Lawrence while its citizens were still abed.

The Union garrison shouldn't be much trouble either, Sam thought as he looked north toward the river. The handful of troops stationed in Lawrence had moved their main camp to the north bank of the Kansas, and the only way for them to come back across into town was by ferry, a few at a time. Two small camps of Federal recruits—one for whites, the other for Negroes—were located south of the river, in town; but those recruits were green and poorly armed. The raiders could ignore them, or squash them like ladybugs if they were foolish enough to offer resistance.

Sam left the window, pulled the chamber pot from under his bed, and took a piss. Then he lit an oil lamp, poured water from a pitcher into a bowl, and stood before the mirror that hung beside the window. He took his razor and scraped the stubble from his throat, chin, cheeks, and sideburns, but left his thick reddish brown mustache. He had grown fond of the mustache because it made him look meaner than he really was. The dirt that had been ground into his pores had made him look mean too, but that was gone now. He'd had a bath Wednesday evening, and was thinking of having another one today. Lawrence might be a den of abolitionist murderers, but at least it was a den of abolitionist murderers that could provide a few of the amenities of civilization.

When he had finished shaving, he combed his hair and dressed, then put out the lamp and left the room. Taylor was still snoring. Whiskey did wonders for helping a man catch up on his sleep.

Sam went downstairs and out to the street, opening and closing the door of the Whitney House as quietly as possible so as not to disturb the Stone family, who owned the place. Taylor had told Sam that Colonel Quantrill had stayed at the Whitney when he'd lived in Lawrence under the name of Charley Hart, and that Mr. Stone had befriended "Hart" and would therefore be treated with courtesy during the raid. So Sam was being careful not to do anything that might be interpreted as discourtesy. He wanted to stay on the Colonel's good side.

The wooden sidewalk creaked under Sam's boots as he walked toward the river. It was a sound that he hadn't noticed on Wednesday or Thursday, when he had shared the sidewalk with dozens of Lawrence citizens. Then, the predominant sounds had been of conversation and laughter, intermingled with the occasional neighing of a horse. But this early in the morning, Sam had Massachusetts Street to himself, save for two dogs that raced past with butcher bones in their mouths. Sam took a cigar from his coat pocket, lit it with a match, and drew in a lungful of sweet smoke.

He had to admit that Lawrence was a nice-looking town. Most of the buildings were sturdy and clean, and the town was large and prosperous considering that it had been in existence less than ten years. Almost three thousand souls called Lawrence home, and not all of those souls, Sam was sure, were bad ones. Perhaps the raid would succeed in running off those who were, and the city would be improved as a result.

Sam paused before the Eldridge House hotel. The original Eldridge House, a veritable fortress of abolitionist fervor and free-state propaganda, had been destroyed by Marshal Donaldson in 1856, but it had been rebuilt into an even more formidable fortress in the service of the same things. It was a brick building four stories high, with iron grilles over the ground-floor windows. Quantrill might want to destroy the Eldridge House a second time, particularly since the Lawrence Home Guards would probably concentrate their resistance here, but Sam's advice would be to skip it. A mere fifteen or twenty men, armed with Sharps carbines and barricaded in the Eldridge House, would be able to kill a hundred bushwhackers in the street below.

"Hello!" a shrill voice called from across the street. "Good morning, Mr. Sir!"

Sam looked across and saw a sandy-haired boy of ten or eleven waving at him. It took a moment before he recognized the boy as the printer's devil from the *Lawrence Journal.*

Sam took his cigar from his mouth. "Good morning yourself," he said without shouting.

The boy pointed at the Eldridge House. "Are you staying there, Mr. Sir?" he yelled. "You must be rich!"

Sam shook his head. "Neither one. But if you keep squawking like a rusty steamboat whistle, I imagine you'll be meeting some of the inhabitants of the Eldridge House presently." He continued up the street.

The boy ran across and joined Sam on the sidewalk. Sam frowned at him and blew smoke at his face, but the boy only breathed it in and began chattering.

"I like the morning before the sun comes up, don't you?" the boy said. "Some days I wake up when it's still dark, and I ride my pa's mule out to the hills south of town, and I can look down over

27

Lawrence when the sun rises. It makes me feel like the king of the world. Do you know what I mean, Mr. Sir?"

"I'm sure I don't," Sam said.

The boy didn't seem to notice that Sam had spoken. "Say, if you aren't at the Eldridge, where are you at, Mr. Sir? I'll bet you're at the Johnson House, is what I'll bet. But maybe not, because the Red Legs meet at the Johnson, and they don't like strangers. So I'll bet you're at the Whitney, then, aren't you, Mr. Sir?"

"Yes," Sam said. "The Johnson was not much to my liking."

"The Red Legs seem to like it just fine."

Sam nodded. "I have made note of that." And indeed he had. If the Red Legs could be punished for their crimes, he would be able to sleep a little better. And if the specific Red Legs who had killed Orion could be found and strung up, he would sleep better than Adam before the Fall.

"Those Red Legs, they have a time," the boy said. "I just might be a Red Leg myself, when I'm old enough."

"I would advise against it," Sam said, gnawing on his cigar. "The profession has little future."

The boy kicked a rock off the sidewalk. "I guess not," he said. "They say they'll have burned out the secesh in another year, so there won't be nothing left to fight for, will there, Mr. Sir?"

"Stop calling me 'Mr. Sir,' " Sam said. "If you must speak to me at all, call me Mr. Clemens." He saw no danger in using his real name. The self-satisfied citizens of Lawrence clearly didn't expect bushwhackers in their midst, and wouldn't know that he was one even if they did.

"I'm sorry, Mr. Clemens," the boy said. "I listened to you talking to Mr. Trask at the *Journal* yesterday, but I didn't hear your name. Would you like to know mine?"

"No," Sam said.

They had reached the northern end of Massachusetts Street and were now walking down a rutted slope toward the ferry landing. Before them, the Kansas River was dull brown in color and less than a hundred yards wide; hardly a river at all, in Sam's opinion.

28

But it would be enough to protect Quantrill's raiders from the soldiers on the far bank, provided that the soldiers didn't realize the raiders were coming until it was too late. To assure himself of that, Sam wanted to see how active or inactive the Bluebellies were at this time of morning. If they were as slumberous as Lawrence's civilians, he would be able to report that there was little chance of any of them ferrying across in time to hinder the raid. There weren't many soldiers in the camp anyway. Taylor had counted only 112, and some of those weren't soldiers at all, but surveyors.

"How come you're heading down to the river, Mr. Clemens?" the boy asked. "Are you going fishing?"

Sam stopped walking and glared down at the boy, taking his cigar from his mouth with a slow, deliberate motion. "Do you see a fishing pole in my hand, boy?" he asked, exhaling a bluish cloud.

The boy gazed up at the cigar, which had a two-inch length of ash trembling at its tip.

"No, sir," the boy said. "I see a cigar."

"Then it is reasonable to assume," Sam said, "that I have come to the river not to fish, but to smoke." He tapped the cigar, and the ash fell onto the boy's head.

The boy yelped and jumped away, slapping at his hair.

Sam replaced his cigar between his teeth and continued down the slope.

"That wasn't nice!" the boy shouted after him.

"I'm not a nice man," Sam said. He didn't look back, so he didn't know if the boy heard him. But he reached the riverbank alone.

A thin fog hovered over the water and began to dissipate as the sun rose. The sunlight gave the tents on the far bank a pinkish tinge. The camp wasn't dead quiet, but there wasn't much activity either. At first, Sam saw only two fires and no more than five or six men up and about. As he watched, more men emerged from their tents, but military discipline was lacking. Apparently, these Bluebellies could get up whenever they pleased. That would be good news for the Colonel.

Sam threw the stub of his cigar into the river and heard it hiss. The sun was up now, and the soldiers began emerging from their tents with increasing frequency. From old habit, Sam reached for his pocket watch. But he still hadn't replaced the one that the Red Legs had stolen two years before.

He heard a scuffing sound behind him and looked over his shoulder. The boy from the *Journal* was close by again, twisting the toe of his shoe in the dirt.

"Say, boy," Sam said, "do you have a watch?"

The boy gave Sam a look of calculated contempt. "Of course I have a watch. Mr. Trask gave me his old one. I got to get to the paper on time, don't I?"

"Well, tell me what time it is," Sam said.

"Why should I tell anything to someone who dumped a pound of burning tobacco on my head?"

Sam grinned. The boy was starting to remind him of the boys he had grown up with in Hannibal. "Maybe I'd give a cigar to someone who told me the time."

The boy's expression changed. "Really?"

"I said maybe."

The boy reached into a pocket and pulled out a battered time-piece. He peered at it and said, "This has six o'clock, but it loses thirty-five minutes a day and I ain't set it since yesterday noon. So it might be about half past."

Sam took a cigar from his coat and tossed it to the boy. "Much obliged, boy."

The boy caught the cigar with his free hand, then replaced his watch in his pocket and gave Sam another look of contempt. "Stop calling me 'boy,' " he said. "If you must speak to me at all, call me Henry." The boy jammed the cigar into his mouth, turned, and strode up the slope to Massachusetts Street.

Sam turned back to the river. The fog was gone, and most of the soldiers were out of their tents. To be on the safe side, Sam decided, the raid would have to begin no later than five-thirty, and a detachment of bushwhackers would have to come to the river to train their guns on the ferry, just in case. He didn't think he would have any trouble persuading Colonel Quantrill to see the wisdom in that.

He started back up the slope, but paused where the boy from the *Journal* had stood.

"Henry," Sam murmured. "God damn."

Then he went up to the street and walked to the livery stable to check on Bixby. Bixby was in a foul mood and tried to bite him, so Sam knew that the horse was fine.

That evening, Sam was in his and Taylor's room at the Whitney House, writing down what he had learned so far, when he heard the *Journal* boy's voice outside. He went to the open window, looked down, and saw the boy astride a brown mule that was festooned with bundles of newspapers. The boy dropped one of the bundles at the Whitney's door, then looked up and saw Sam at the window.

The boy shook his finger at Sam. "That seegar was spoiled, Mr. Clemens!" he shouted. "I was sick all afternoon, but Mr. Trask made me work anyway!"

"Good," Sam said. "It builds character."

The boy gave Sam yet another contemptuous look, then kicked the mule and proceeded down the street.

As the boy left, four men wearing blue shirts and red leather leggings rode past going the other way. They all carried pistols in hip holsters, and one had a rifle slung across his back. They were unshaven and ugly, and they laughed and roared as they rode up Massachusetts Street. They would no doubt cross the river and make trouble for someone north of town tonight. Sam didn't recognize any of them, but that didn't matter. They were Kansas Red Legs, meaner and more murderous than even Jennison's Jayhawkers had been; and if they themselves hadn't killed Orion, they were acquainted with the men who had.

"Whoop it up, boys," Sam muttered as they rode away. "Whoop it up while you can."

He came away from the window and saw that Taylor was awake. Taylor had gotten up in the afternoon to meet with Noland, but then had gone back to bed.

"What's all the noise?" Taylor asked.

"Newspapers," Sam said. "I'll get one."

Taylor sneered. "Why? It's all abolitionist lies anyway."

But when Sam brought a copy of the *Journal* back upstairs and began reading, he found news. Horrifying, sickening news.

"Sons of bitches," he whispered.

"What is it?" Taylor asked. He was at the mirror, shaving, preparing for another night out in Lawrence's less respectable quarter.

"A building in Kansas City collapsed yesterday," Sam said.

"Well, good."

Sam shook his head. "No, Fletch. It was the building on Grand Avenue where the Bluebellies were holding the women they suspected of aiding bushwhackers. The paper says four women were killed, and several others hurt."

Taylor stopped shaving. "That's where they were keeping Bloody Bill Anderson's sisters," he said. "Cole Younger and Johnny McCorkle had kin there too. Does the paper give names?"

"No. But of course it suggests that the collapse might have been caused by a charge set by guerrillas 'in a disastrous attempt to remove the ladies from Federal protection.' "

Taylor's upper lip curled back. "As if Southern men would endanger their women!" He shook his razor at the newspaper. "I'll tell you what, though. I was worrying that the Colonel might have trouble riling up some of the boys for this raid, especially since Noland has found out that Jim Lane's out of town. But this news will rile them like nobody's business. And if Bill Anderson's sisters have been hurt, you can bet that he and *his* boys will shit blue fire. God help any Unionists who cross their path." He dipped his razor in the bowl and turned back to the mirror. His eyes were bright. "Or mine, for that matter."

When Taylor had finished shaving, he asked if Sam would like to go out and have a time. Sam declined, and Taylor left without him.

Then Sam read the rest of the newspaper, most of which he found to be worthless. But he admired the typesetting. There were few mistakes, and most of the lines were evenly spaced and straight. He wondered how many of them the boy had set.

He put the newspaper aside and wrote in his journal until the evening light failed. Then he undressed and got into bed, but lay awake for so long that he almost decided to join Taylor after all. But he had no enthusiasm for the idea. Spy work wasn't physically strenuous, but it took a lot out of him mentally.

When he finally fell asleep, he dreamed that he was a printer's devil for Orion again. This time, though, their newspaper was not the *Hannibal Journal,* but the *Lawrence Journal.*

He was setting type about a fire in which over 150 people had been killed, when a man burst into the pressroom. The man was jug eared, greasy haired, narrow faced, and beardless. His thick lips parted to reveal crooked, stained teeth. Sam had never seen him before.

The jug-eared man pulled a revolver from his belt and pointed it at Orion.

"Henry!" Orion shouted. "Run!"

Sam, his ink-smeared hands hanging useless at his sides, said, "But I'm Sam."

The jug-eared man shot Orion, who shriveled like a dying vine.

Then the stranger pointed his revolver at Sam.

Sam tried to turn and run, but his feet were stuck as if in thick mud.

The revolver fired with a sound like a cannon going off in a church, and the jug-eared man laughed.

Then Sam was floating near the ceiling, looking down at two bleeding bodies. Orion's face had become that of Josiah Trask, one of the editors of the *Lawrence Journal.* And Sam's face had become that of the boy, Henry, to whom he had given a cigar. The cigar was still in Henry's mouth.

Sam awoke crouched against the wall. He was dripping with sweat.

Night had fallen, and Lawrence was quiet. Taylor had not yet returned to the room. Sam crept away from the wall and sat on the edge of the bed, shivering.

"Henry," he whispered. "God damn."

At noon on Wednesday, August 19, Sam and Taylor were sitting on a log in southern Jackson County near the village of Lone Jack, in the midst of their fellow bushwhackers. They and Noland had returned to the Blue Springs camp two days before, and Colonel Quantrill had received their report with satisfaction. Then, on Tuesday morning, Quantrill had ordered his guerrillas to move out without telling them their objective. In order to fool any Federal scouts or pickets that might spot them, the Colonel had marched the bushwhackers eastward for several miles before cutting back to the southwest. En route, the band had been joined by Bill Anderson with forty men and Andy Blunt with over a hundred, almost doubling the size of Quantrill's force.

The men all knew something big was at hand. And now, finally, the Colonel was going to tell them what. Sam thought it was about time.

Quantrill, flanked by George Todd and Bill Anderson, sat before the bushwhackers astride his one-eyed mare, Black Bess, and gave a screeching yell. Over three hundred voices responded, and a thrill ran up Sam's spine. The sound was both the most magnificent and most terrifying thing he had ever heard. If he were the enemy and heard that sound, he would be halfway to Colorado before the echo came back from the nearest hill.

The Colonel nodded in satisfaction. He was wearing a slouch hat with one side of the brim pinned up by a silver star, a loose gray guerrilla shirt with blue and silver embroidery, and gray trousers tucked into his cavalry boots. His belt bristled with four Colt pistols, and two more hung from holsters on either side of his saddle.

"Well, boys," Quantrill shouted, "I hope you ain't tired of riding just yet!"

He was answered by a loud, ragged chorus of "Hell, no!"

Quantrill laughed. "That's good," he cried, "because come nightfall, we're heading for Kansas Territory to see if we can pull its most rotten tooth: Lawrence!"

A moment of silence followed the announcement, and for that moment Sam wondered if the men had decided that the Colonel was out of his mind. But then the bushwhackers exploded into another shrieking cheer, and at least a hundred of them rose to their feet and fired pistols into the air.

Taylor clapped Sam on the shoulder. "Are these the best damn boys in Missouri, or ain't they!" he yelled.

"They're sure the loudest," Sam said.

Quantrill raised a hand, and the cheers subsided. "Save your ammunition," the Colonel shouted. "You've worked hard to make it or steal it, so don't waste it shooting at God. There are plenty of better targets where we're going!"

Another cheer rose up at that, but then Quantrill's expression changed from one of glee to one of cold, deadly intent. The bushwhackers fell silent.

"Boys," Quantrill said, no longer shouting, "there's more danger ahead than any of us have faced before. There could be Federals both behind and in front of us, coming and going. Now, we sent some men to spy on Lawrence, and they say the town's ripe to be taken—but there might be pickets on the way there. So we could have General Ewing's Bluebellies down on us from Kansas City, and some from Leavenworth as well. I doubt that we'll all make it back to Missouri alive." He straightened in his saddle, and it seemed to Sam that his metallic gaze fell on each bushwhacker in turn. "So if there's any man who doesn't want to go into the Territory with the rest of us, now's your chance to head for home. After we leave here tonight, there will be no turning back. Not for anyone."

Beside Quantrill, Bill Anderson drew a pistol. Anderson's hair was even wilder than it had been when Sam had seen him in Quantrill's tent the week before, and his eyes were so fierce that they didn't look human. "Anyone who *does* turn back after we've started," Anderson cried, "will wish to God he'd been taken by the Yankees before I'm through with him!"

Taylor leaned close to Sam and whispered, "I think Bloody Bill's heard about the building in Kansas City."

Sam thought so too. In the face of Bill Anderson he saw a hatred that had become so pure that if Anderson ever ran out of enemies against whom to direct his rage, he would have to invent more.

"But although we'll be going through hardships," Quantrill continued, "the result will be worth it. Lawrence is the hotbed of abolitionism in Kansas, and most of the property stolen from Missouri can be found there, ready and waiting to be taken back by Missourians. Even if Jim Lane ain't home, his house and his plunder are. We can work more justice in Lawrence than anywhere else in five hundred miles! So who's going with me?"

The shrill cheer rose up a fourth time, and all of the men not already standing came to their feet. Despite Quantrill's warning to save ammunition, more shots were fired into the air.

Quantrill and his captains wheeled their horses and rode to their tent, and Sam left Taylor and went to the tree where he had tied Bixby. There, after avoiding Bixby's attempts to bite him, he opened one of his saddlebags, took out his revolver, and replaced its caps.

When he looked up again, he saw John Noland leaning against the tree, regarding him with casual disdain.

"You ain't gonna shoot something, are you, Mr. Clemens?" Noland asked.

"I'll do my best if it becomes necessary," Sam said.

Noland gave a sardonic grunt. " 'If it becomes necessary,' " he repeated. "Why do you think we're goin' where we're goin'?"

"I should think that would be obvious," Sam said. "To retrieve that which belongs to Missouri, and to punish the jayhawkers and Red Legs who stole it."

"You'll know a jayhawker on sight, will you?" Noland asked.

"I'll know the Red Legs on sight, I'll tell you that."

Noland pushed away from the tree. "I reckon you will, if they sleep in their pants." He sauntered past Sam and tipped his hat. "Hooray for you, Mr. Clemens. Hooray for us all."

"You don't sound too all-fired excited, Noland," Sam said.

Noland looked back with a grim smile. "You want to see me excited, Mr. Clemens, you watch me get some of that free-soil money into my pocket. You watch me then." He tipped his hat again and walked away.

Sam watched him go. How, he wondered, could two men as different as Bill Anderson and John Noland be riding in the same guerrilla band on the same raid?

Then he looked down at the gun in his hand and remembered that he was riding with both of them.

Bixby nipped his arm. Sam jumped and cursed, then replaced his revolver in the saddlebag and gave Bixby a lump of sugar. The horse would soon need all the energy it could get.

At dusk, the Colonel had the bushwhackers mount up and proceed toward the southwest. Only thirteen men had left the raiders after Quantrill's announcement of the target, and only two of those had been members of Quantrill's own band. Sam marveled. Here were more than three hundred men going to what might be their deaths, just because one man had asked them to do so. True, each man had his own reasons for becoming a bushwhacker in the first place, but none of them would have dreamed of attempting a raid so far into Kansas if Quantrill had not offered to lead them in it.

In the middle of the night, the guerrillas happened upon a force of over a hundred Confederate recruits under the command of a Colonel John Holt. Holt and Quantrill conferred for an hour while the bushwhackers rested their horses, and when the guerrillas resumed their advance, Holt and his recruits joined them.

At daybreak on Thursday, August 20, Quantrill's raiders made camp beside the Grand River. They were only four miles from the border now, and this would be their final rest before the drive toward Lawrence. Late in the morning, fifty more men from Cass and Bates Counties rode into the camp and offered their services. Quantrill accepted, and by Sam's count, the invasion force now consisted of almost five hundred men, each one mounted on a strong horse and armed with at least one pistol and as much ammunition as he could carry. A few of the men also had rifles, and many carried bundles of pitch-dipped torches.

If Federal troops did attack them, Sam thought, the Bluebellies would get one hell of a fight for their trouble. They might also become confused about who was friend and who was foe, because almost two hundred of the bushwhackers were wearing parts of blue Union uniforms.

At midafternoon, Captain Todd rode among the dozing men and horses, shouting, "Saddle up, boys! Lawrence ain't gonna plunder itself, now, is it?"

The men responded with a ragged cheer. Sam got up, rolled his blanket, and then carried it and his saddle to the dead tree where Taylor's horse and Bixby were tied. He had spread his blanket in a shady spot and had tried to sleep, but had only managed to doze a little. Taylor, lying a few yards away, had started snoring at noon and hadn't stopped until Todd had ridden past.

"How you could sleep with what we've got ahead of us, I can't imagine," Sam said as Taylor came up to saddle his horse.

"I wasn't sleeping," Taylor said. "I was thinking over strategy."

"With help from the hive of bumblebees you swallowed, no doubt."

Taylor grinned. "We're gonna be fine, Sam," he said. "You know they ain't expecting us. So there's no need for a man to be afraid."

"No, I suppose not," Sam said. "Not unless a man has a brain."

Taylor frowned. "What's that supposed to mean?"

Sam took his Colt from his saddlebag and stuck it into his belt.

"Nothing, Fletch. I just want to get there, get it done, and get back, is all."

"You and me and everybody else," Taylor said.

As Sam and Taylor mounted their horses, a cluster of eleven men rode past, yipping and laughing. They seemed eager to be at the head of the bushwhacker force as it entered Kansas.

The man leading the cluster was jug eared, greasy haired, narrow faced, and beardless.

Sam's heart turned to ice. Slowly, he raised his arm and pointed at the cluster of men. "Who are they?" he asked. His throat was tight and dry.

"Some of Anderson's boys," Taylor said. "Full of piss and vinegar, ain't they?"

"Do you know the one in front?" Sam asked.

"Sure do," Taylor said. "I've even ridden with him a time or two. Name's Frank James. You can count on him in a fight, that's for sure." Taylor clicked his tongue, and his horse started after the cluster of Anderson's men.

Bixby followed Taylor's horse while Sam stared ahead at the man from his dream. The man who had entered the *Journal* pressroom, killed an unarmed man and boy, and then laughed.

At six o'clock, Quantrill's raiders crossed the border into Kansas. Ahead, the Territory grew dark.

By eleven o'clock, when the raiders passed the town of Gardner, the moonless night was as black as Quantrill's horse. Gullies, creeks, and fences became obstacles, and some of the bushwhackers wanted to light torches to help them find their way. But Quantrill would not allow that. They were still over twenty miles from Lawrence, in open country, and could not afford to be spotted from a distance. Besides, the torches were supposed to be reserved for use in Lawrence itself.

Soon after midnight, Quantrill halted the bushwhackers near a farmhouse, and the word was passed back along the column for the men to keep quiet.

"What are we stopping here for?" Sam whispered. He and Taylor were riding near the middle of the column, and Sam couldn't see what was happening up front.

"Shush yourself," Taylor hissed.

A minute later, there was a yell from the farmhouse, and then laughter from some of the raiders.

The tall form of Captain Bill Gregg came riding back along the column. "All right, boys, we can travel on," he said. "We got ourselves a friendly Kansan to guide us!" He wheeled his horse and returned to the head of the column.

"Wonder what he means by that," Sam said.

Taylor chuckled. "What do you think?"

The bushwhackers started moving again and made rapid progress for a few miles, zigzagging around obstacles. Then Quantrill called another halt. The men began muttering, but fell silent as a pistol was fired.

Bixby jerked his head and shied away from the column. Sam had to fight to bring the horse back into place. "What in blazes is the matter with you?" he asked. Bixby had never been spooked by gunfire before. In fact, he had hardly noticed it. "It was just somebody's pistol going off by mistake!"

At that moment, Captain Gregg came riding by again. "No mistake about it," he said, pausing beside Sam and Taylor. "Our friendly Kansan claimed he didn't know which side of yonder hill we should go around. So the Colonel dispatched him to a hill of his own, and we're to wait until we have another friendly Kansan to guide us. There's a house ahead, and some of Anderson's boys are going to see who's home. We'll be on our way again before long." Gregg spurred his horse and continued back along the column to spread the word.

"Well, good for the Colonel," Taylor said. "Now that Kansan is as friendly to us as a Kansan can be."

Sam was stunned. When the raiders began moving again, they passed by the corpse. Bixby shied away from it and collided with Taylor's mount.

"Rein your goddamn horse, Sam!" Taylor snarled.

The dead man was wearing canvas trousers and was shirtless and barefoot. Even in the dark, Sam could see that his head was nothing but a mass of pulp.

It made no sense. This man wasn't a Red Leg or a Bluebelly. He might not even be an abolitionist. He was only a farmer. Colonel Quantrill had shot a farmer. Just because the man couldn't find his way in the dark.

Just because he was a Kansan.

Sam began to wonder if the preposterous stories he had read in abolitionist newspapers—the stories about Quantrill's raids on Aubry, Olathe, and Shawneetown—might have had some truth in them after all.

The column halted again after only a mile, and there was another gunshot. Then another farmhouse was raided, and the bushwhackers continued on their way. But soon they stopped once more, and a third shot was fired.

The process was repeated again and again. Each time, Sam and Bixby passed by a fresh corpse.

There were ten in all.

Sam felt dizzy and sick. This was supposed to be a raid to punish the Red Legs, destroy the newspaper, burn out Jim Lane, and recover stolen property. Some Kansans were to be killed, yes; but they were supposed to be Red Legs and Bluebellies, not unarmed farmers taken from their wives and children in the night.

At the tenth corpse, Taylor maneuvered his horse past Sam and Bixby. "Scuse me, Clemens," Taylor said. "My horse is starting to make water."

Taylor stopped the horse over the dead man and let it piss on the body. The bushwhackers who were close enough to see it laughed, and Sam tried to laugh as well. He didn't want them to see his horror. He was afraid of them all now. Even Taylor. Especially Taylor.

"Have your horses drink deep at the next crick, boys!" Taylor chortled. "There's plenty of men in Lawrence who need a bath as bad as this one!"

"Amen to that!" someone cried.

The shout was echoed up and down the line as Taylor rejoined the column next to Sam.

Captain Gregg came riding back once more. "I admire your sentiments, boys," he said, "but I suggest you save the noise until we reach our destination. Then you can holler all you want, and see if you can squeeze a few hollers from the so-called men of Lawrence as well!"

The bushwhackers laughed again, but then lowered their voices to whispers. To Sam, it sounded like the hissing of five hundred snakes.

He saw now that what was going to happen in Lawrence would resemble what he had imagined it would be only in the way that a volcano resembled a firefly. He had let his guilt over Orion's death and his hatred of the Red Legs blind him to what the men he was riding with had become. He wanted to turn Bixby out of the column and ride hard and fast back to Missouri, not stopping until he reached Hannibal.

But he knew that he couldn't. Anderson had told them all how deserters would be dealt with. Sam and Bixby wouldn't make it more than a hundred yards before a dozen men were after them. And there was no doubt of what would happen to Sam when they caught him.

Besides, his and Taylor's report from their trip to Lawrence was part of what had convinced Quantrill that the raid was possible. That made Sam more responsible for what was about to happen than almost anyone else. To run away now would make him not only a coward, but a hypocrite.

Another farmhouse was raided at about three in the morning, and this time the entire column broke up and gathered around to watch. By the time Sam was close enough to see what was happening, the farmer was on his knees in his yard. Captain Todd was standing before him holding a pistol to his forehead and telling him the names of some of the men waiting for him in hell.

Quantrill, on Black Bess, came up beside Todd. "We're too close to Lawrence to fire a gun now, George," he said.

Sam could just make out Todd's expression. It was one of fury. "God damn it, Bill," Todd said. "This man's name is Joe Stone. He's a stinking Missouri Unionist who ran off to Kansas to escape justice, and I'm going to kill him no matter what you say."

Stone, wearing only a nightshirt, was shuddering. Sam looked away from him and saw a woman crying in the doorway of the house. A child clung to the woman's knees, wailing. An oil lamp was burning inside, and its weak light framed the woman and child so that they seemed to be suspended inside a pale flame.

Quantrill stroked his stubbled face with a thumb and forefinger. "Well, George, I agree that traitors must die. But we're within six miles of Lawrence now, and a shot might warn the town."

Todd seemed about to retort, but then took his pistol away from Stone's head and replaced it in his belt. "All right," he said. "We'll keep it quiet." He strode to his horse and pulled his Sharps carbine from its scabbard. "Sam!" he called. "Get over here!"

Taylor nudged Sam in the ribs. "Go on," he said.

Sam, almost rigid with terror, began to dismount.

"I mean Sam Clifton," Todd said. "Where is he?"

Sam returned to his saddle as Clifton, a stranger who had joined the guerrillas while the spies had been in Lawrence, dismounted and went to Todd.

Todd handed the rifle to Clifton. "Some of the boys tell me you've been asking a lot of questions, Mr. Clifton," he said. "So let's see if you know what you're here for." He pointed at Stone. "Beat that traitor down to hell."

Clifton didn't hesitate. He took three quick steps and smashed the rifle butt into Stone's face. Stone fell over in the dirt, and his wife and child screamed. Then Clifton pounded Stone's skull.

Sam wanted to turn away, but he couldn't move. This was the most horrible thing he had ever seen, more horrible even than his brother Henry lying in his coffin or his brother Orion lying in the road. He watched it all. He couldn't stop himself.

Only when it was over, when Clifton had stopped pounding and Stone was nothing but a carcass, was Sam able to look away. Beside him, Taylor was grinning. Some of the others were grinning too. But there were also a few men who looked so sick that Sam thought they might fall from their horses.

Then he looked at Colonel Quantrill. Quantrill's eyes were unblinking, reflecting the weak light from the house. His lips were pulled back in a tight smile.

Todd took his rifle back from Clifton and replaced it in its scabbard without wiping it clean. Then he looked up at Quantrill with a defiant sneer.

"That suit you, Colonel?" he asked.

Quantrill nodded. "That suits me fine, Captain," he said. Then he faced the men. "Remember this, boys," he cried, "and serve the men of Lawrence the same! Kill! Kill, and you'll make no mistake! Now push on, or it'll be daylight before we get there!"

"You heard the man," Taylor said to Sam.

"That I did," Sam said. His voice was hoarse. He thought it might stay hoarse forever.

The raiders pushed on, leaving Mrs. Stone and her child to weep over the scrap of flesh in their yard.

As the column re-formed, Sam found himself near its head, riding not far behind Gregg, Todd, Anderson, and Quantrill himself. It was as if God wanted to be sure that Sam had another good view when the next man died.

The eastern sky was turning from black to purplish gray as Quantrill's raiders reached the crest of the hill southeast of Lawrence. Colonel Quantrill raised his right hand, and the column halted.

Below them, less than two miles ahead, Lawrence lay as silent as death.

Fletch Taylor cackled. "Look at 'em! Damn Yankees are curled up with their thumbs in their mouths!"

Sam nodded, sick at heart.

Quantrill brought out a spyglass and trained it on the sleeping town. "It looks ripe," he said. "But I can't see the river; it's still too dark." He lowered the glass and turned to Captain Gregg. "Bill, take five men and reconnoiter. The rest of us will wait fifteen minutes and then follow. If you spot trouble, run back and warn us."

Gregg gave Quantrill a salute, then pointed at each of the five men closest to him. "James, Younger, McCorkle, Taylor, and—" He was looking right at Sam.

Sam couldn't speak. His tongue was as cold and heavy as clay. He stared at Frank James.

"Clemens," Taylor said.

"Right," Gregg said. "Clemens. Come on, boys." He kicked his horse and started down the hillside.

"Let's get to it, Sam," Taylor said. He reached over and swatted Bixby on the rump, and Bixby lurched forward.

Despite the steep slope and the trees that dotted it, Gregg set a rapid pace. All Sam could do was hang on to Bixby's reins and let the horse find its own way. He wished that Bixby would stumble and that he would be thrown and break an arm or leg. But Bixby was too agile for that. Sam would be in on the Lawrence raid from beginning to end.

Halfway down the hill, Gregg stopped his horse, and James, Younger, McCorkle, and Taylor did the same. Bixby stopped on his own, almost throwing Sam against the pommel of his saddle.

"What's wrong, Captain?" Taylor asked.

Gregg put a finger to his lips and then extended that finger to point.

A few hundred feet farther down the hillside, a mule carrying a lone figure in a white shirt was making its way up through the trees. The mule and rider were just visible in the predawn light.

"What's someone doing out here this early?" Taylor whispered.

"Doesn't matter," Gregg whispered back. "If he sees us and we let him escape, we're as good as dead."

"But—but a shot would wake up the town, Captain," Sam stammered.

Gregg gave him a glance. "Then we won't fire a shot that can be heard in the town." He turned toward Frank James. "Go kill him, Frank. Use your knife, or put your pistol in his belly to muffle the noise. Or knock his brains out. I don't care, so long as you keep it quiet."

James drew his pistol, cocked it, and started his horse down the hill.

The figure on the mule came around a tree. He was alone and unarmed. Sam could see his face now. He was the printer's devil from the *Lawrence Journal.*

Henry.

Frank James plunged downward, his right arm outstretched, pointing the finger of Death at an innocent.

And in that instant, Sam saw everything that was to come, and the truth of everything that had been. He saw it all as clearly as any of his dreams:

The boy would be lying on his back on the ground. His white shirt would be soaked with blood. Sam would be down on his knees beside him, stroking his forehead, begging his forgiveness. He would want to give anything to undo what had been done. But it would be too late.

Henry would mumble about his family, about the loved ones who would never see him again. And then he would look up at Sam with reproachful eyes, and die.

Just as it had happened before.

Not when Sam's brother Henry had died. Henry had given him no reproachful look, and all he had said was "Thank you, Sam."

Not when Orion had died, either. Orion had said, "Get out of here, Sam," and there had been no reproach in the words. Only concern. Only love.

Frank James plunged downward, his right arm outstretched, pointing the finger of Death at an innocent.

An innocent like the one Sam had killed.

It had been more than just a dream.

He had told himself that he wasn't the only one of the Marion

Rangers who had fired. He never hit anything he aimed at anyway. But in his heart he had known that wasn't true this time. He had known that he was guilty of murder, and of the grief that an innocent, unarmed man's family had suffered because of it.

All of his guilt, all of his need to make amends—

It wasn't because of his dead brothers at all.

It was because he had killed a man who had done nothing to him.

Sam had tried to escape that truth by fleeing west with Orion. But then, when Orion had been murdered, he had tried instead to bury his guilt by embracing it and by telling himself that the war made killing honorable if it was done in a just cause. And vengeance, he had told himself, was such a cause.

But the family of the man he had killed might well have thought the same thing.

Frank James plunged downward, his right arm outstretched, pointing the finger of Death at an innocent.

And Sam couldn't stand it anymore.

He yelled like a madman, and then Bixby was charging down the hill, flashing past the trees with a speed no other horse in Quantrill's band could equal. When Bixby came alongside James's horse, Sam jerked the reins. Bixby slammed into James's horse and forced it into a tree. James was knocked from his saddle, and his pistol fired.

Henry's mule collapsed, and Henry tumbled to the ground.

Sam reined Bixby to a halt before the dying mule, leaped down, and dropped to his knees beside the boy.

Henry looked up at him with an expression of contempt. "Are you crazy or something?" he asked.

Sam grabbed him and hugged him.

Henry struggled to get away. "Mr. Clemens? What in the world are you doing?"

Sam looked up the slope and saw Frank James picking himself up. James's horse was standing nearby, shaking its head and whinnying.

Gregg, Taylor, McCorkle, and Younger were riding down with their pistols drawn.

Sam jumped up and swung Henry into Bixby's saddle. "Lean down close to me," he said.

"What for?" Henry asked. The boy looked dazed now. He was staring down at the dead mule.

"Just do it, and listen to what I say," Sam said. "I have to tell you something without those men hearing it."

Henry leaned down.

"Ride back to town as fast as you can," Sam said. "When you're close enough for people to hear, yell that Charley Hart's come back, that his new name is Billy Quantrill, and that he has five hundred men with him. And if you can't remember all that, just yell 'Quantrill!' Yell 'Quantrill!' over and over until you reach the Eldridge House, and then go inside and yell 'Quantrill!' at everyone there. If they don't believe you, just point at this horse and ask where the hell they think you got it. Now sit up!"

Henry sat up, and Sam slapped Bixby on the rump. Bixby turned back and tried to bite Sam's shoulder.

"Not now, you fleabag!" Sam yelled. He raised his hand to swat the horse again, but Bixby snorted and leaped over the dead mule before Sam could touch him. The roan charged down the hillside as fast as before, with Henry hanging on tight.

Sam took a deep breath and turned as he exhaled. Frank James was walking toward him with murder in his eyes, and the four men riding up behind James didn't look any happier. Sam put his hand on the Colt in his belt, but didn't think he could draw it. He feared that he was going to piss his pants. But he had to give Henry a good head start. And if that meant getting himself killed—well, that was just what it meant. Better him than a boy whose only crime was setting type for an abolitionist newspaper.

"You traitorous bastard," James said, raising his revolver to point at Sam's face.

Sam swallowed and found his voice. "Your barrel's full of dirt," he said.

James looked at his gun and saw that it was true.

Captain Gregg cocked his own pistol. "Mine, however, is clean," he said.

Sam raised his hands. "Don't shoot, Captain," he said. He was going to have to tell a whopper, and fast. "I apologize to Mr. James, but I had to keep him from killing my messenger, didn't I? I would've said something sooner, but I didn't see who the boy was until James was already after him."

"Messenger?" Gregg said.

Sam looked up at Taylor, whose expression was one of mingled anger and disbelief. "Why don't you say something, Fletch? Didn't you recognize the boy?"

Taylor blinked. "What are you yapping about?"

Sam lowered his hands, put them on his hips, and tried to look disgusted. "Damn it, Fletch, that Missouri boy I met in Lawrence. The one whose father was killed by jayhawkers, and who was kidnapped to Kansas. I pointed him out to you Saturday morning, but I guess you'd gotten too drunk the night before to retain the information."

Gregg looked at Taylor. "You were drinking whiskey while you were supposed to be scouting the town, Corporal?"

Taylor became indignant. "Hell, no!"

"Then why don't you remember me pointing that boy out to you?" Sam asked.

"Well, I do," Taylor said uncertainly.

Sam knew he couldn't let up. "So why didn't you tell Captain Gregg that the boy promised to come here and warn us if any more Federals moved into Lawrence?"

Taylor's eyes looked panicky. "I didn't recognize the boy. It's dark."

"What's this about more Bluebellies in Lawrence?" Gregg asked.

"That's what the boy told me," Sam said. "Six hundred troops, four hundred of them cavalry, came down from Leavenworth on Tuesday. They're all camped on the south side of the river, too, he says."

Frank James had his pistol barrel clean now, and he pointed the gun at Sam again. "So why'd you send him away?"

Sam was so deep into his story now that he almost forgot his fear. "Because he said the Bluebellies have started sending fifty cavalrymen out between five and six every morning to scout the plain between here and Mount Oread. I told him to go keep watch and to come back when he saw them."

Cole Younger, stern faced and narrow lipped, gestured at Sam with his revolver. "Why would you tell someone in Lawrence who you were and why you were there?"

"I already said why," Sam snapped. "Because he's a Missouri boy, and he hates the Yankees as much as you or me. Maybe more, because he didn't even have a chance to grow up before they took everything he had. And I didn't just walk up and take him into my confidence for no reason. Two Red Legs were dunking him in a horse trough until he was half drowned. When they left, I asked him why they'd done it, and he said it was because he'd called them murdering Yankee cowards. My opinion was that we could use a friend like that in Lawrence, and Fletch agreed."

John McCorkle, a round-faced man in a flat-brimmed hat, peered at Sam through narrowed eyelids. "So how'd the boy know where we'd be, and when?"

"He knew the where because we told him," Sam said. "The Colonel used to live in these parts, and he picked this hill for our overlook when he planned the raid. Ain't that so, Fletch?"

Taylor nodded.

"As for the when of it," Sam continued, "well, Fletch and I knew we'd be here before sunup either yesterday or today, so we told the boy to come out both days if there was anything we needed to hear about."

Younger looked at Taylor. "That true, Fletch? Or were you so drunk you don't remember?"

Taylor glared at him. "It's true, Cole. I just didn't tell you, is all. There's five hundred men on this raid, and I can't tell every one of you everything, can I?"

Younger started to retort, but he was interrupted by the sound of hundreds of hoofbeats from the slope above. Quantrill had heard James's gunshot and was bringing down the rest of his men.

Gregg replaced his pistol in its holster. "All right, then," he said, sounding weary. "Let's tell the Colonel what the boy said." He looked at Taylor. "You do it, Fletch. He knows you better than he does Clemens."

Taylor nodded, then shot Sam a look that could have melted steel.

There was a promise in that look, but Sam didn't care. Gregg had believed his story, and for now, at least, he was still alive.

And so was Henry.

Taylor told Colonel Quantrill that a Missouri boy had come to warn the raiders about six hundred new Bluebellies in Lawrence, all camped south of the river, and that a scouting party of fifty of the Federals was likely to spot the bushwhackers before they could enter the town. Quantrill listened without saying a word. He stared straight ahead, toward Lawrence, until Taylor was finished. Then he looked down at Sam, who was still standing before the dead mule.

Quantrill's eyes were like chips of ice, but Sam didn't look away. He was sure that if he flinched, the Colonel would see him for the lying traitor that he was.

A long moment later, Quantrill turned to Captain Todd. "What do you think, George?" he asked.

Todd looked as if he had eaten a bad persimmon. "You didn't see six hundred Federals through the glass, did you?"

"No," Quantrill said, "but I couldn't see the river. If they were camped close by its banks, they would have been invisible."

"Then let's go back up and take another look," Todd said.

Quantrill shook his head. "By the time the sun has risen enough for us to see the river, the people of Lawrence will have risen too. We must either press on now, or give it up."

"But if there are that many more troops down there," Gregg

said, "we won't have a chance. I say we fall back to the border, send more spies to take another look at the town, and come back when we can be sure of victory."

Quantrill looked at the ground and spat. "Damn it all," he said, "but you're right. Even if there aren't that many troops, the town might've heard the pistol shot."

The men behind Quantrill murmured. Many looked angry or disappointed, but almost as many looked relieved.

Sam tried hard to look disappointed, but he wanted to shout for joy.

Then Bill Anderson shrieked, drew one of his pistols, and kicked his horse until it was nose to nose with Black Bess.

"We've come too far!" he screamed, pointing his pistol at the Colonel. "We've come too far and our people have suffered too much! This raid was your idea, and you talked me into committing my own men to the task! God damn you, Quantrill, you're going to see it through!"

Quantrill gave Anderson a cold stare. "We have received new intelligence," he said. "The situation has changed."

Anderson shook his head, his long hair flying wild under his hat. "Nothing has changed! Nothing! The Yankees have killed one of my sisters and crippled another, and I won't turn back until I've killed two hundred of them as payment! And if you try to desert me before that's done, the two hundred and first man I kill will be named Billy Quantrill!"

Quantrill turned to Todd. "George, place Captain Anderson under arrest."

Todd drew his pistol. "I don't think I will," he said, moving his horse to stand beside Anderson's. "We've come to do a thing, so let's do it."

The murmurs among the men grew louder.

"What's wrong with you?" Gregg shouted at Todd and Anderson. "Colonel Quantrill is your commanding officer!"

Todd sneered. "No more of that 'Colonel' bullshit. Jefferson

Davis wouldn't give this coward the time of day, much less a commission."

At that, Frank James, John McCorkle, and Cole Younger moved to stand with Anderson and Todd. Bill Gregg, Andy Blunt, and John Holt moved to stand with Quantrill. The murmurs among the bushwhackers became shouts and curses. A few men broke away and rode back up the hill.

Sam decided that he didn't care to see the outcome. He began edging backward, but came up against the dead mule.

Quantrill looked as calm as an undertaker. "All right, boys," he said. "I guess you're right. We've come this far, and we've whipped Yankee soldiers before." He pointed toward Lawrence. "Let's push on!"

"That's more like it," Anderson said, and he and his comrades turned their horses toward Lawrence.

As soon as they had turned, Quantrill pulled two of his pistols from his belt, cocked them, and shot Bill Anderson in the back. Anderson slumped, and his horse reared.

The hillside erupted into an inferno of muzzle flashes, explosions, and screams.

Sam dove over the mule and huddled against its back until he heard pistol balls thudding into its belly. Then he rolled away and scrambled down the hill on his hands and knees. When there were plenty of trees between him and the fighting, he got to his feet and ran. He fell several times before reaching the bottom of the hill, but didn't let that slow him.

The trees gave way to prairie grass and scrub brush at the base of the hill, and Sam ran straight for Lawrence. He couldn't see Henry and Bixby on the plain ahead, so he hoped they were already in town.

Thunder rumbled behind him, and he looked back just in time to see the neck of a horse and the heel of a boot. The boot struck him in the forehead and knocked him down. His hat went flying.

Sam lay on his back and stared up at the brightening sky. Then the silhouette of a horse's head appeared above him, and hot breath blasted his face.

"Get up and take your pistol from your belt," a voice said.

Sam turned over, rose to his knees, and looked up at the rider. It was Fletch Taylor. He had a Colt Navy revolver pointed at Sam's nose.

"You going to kill me, Fletch?" Sam asked.

"Not on your knees," Taylor said. "Stand up, take your pistol from your belt, and die the way a man should."

Sam gave a low, bitter chuckle. He was amazed to discover that he wasn't afraid.

"All men die alike, Fletch," he said. "Reluctantly."

Taylor kept his pistol pointed at Sam for another few seconds, then cursed and uncocked it. He looked toward the hill. "Listen to all the hell you've raised," he said.

The sounds of gunshots and screams were wafting out over the plain like smoke.

Taylor looked back at Sam. "You saved my life," he said, "so now I'm giving you yours. But if I ever see you again, I'll kill you."

Sam nodded. "Thank you, Fletch."

Taylor's lips curled back from his teeth. "Go to hell," he said. Then he spurred his horse and rode back toward the hill.

Sam watched Taylor go until he realized that the fighting on the hillside was spilling onto the plain. He stood, found his hat—the hat that Taylor had given him—and ran for Lawrence again.

When he reached Massachusetts Street, staggering, exhausted, he saw men in the windows of every building. Some wore blue uniforms, but most were civilians. Each man held either a revolver or a carbine. The sun was rising, and Lawrence was awake. One of the men came outside and pointed his rifle at Sam, but the boy named Henry appeared and stopped him. Then Henry grabbed Sam's arm and pulled him into the Whitney House.

Fifteen minutes later, Sam was watching from the window of a second-floor room when a magnificent black horse came galloping up Massachusetts Street. The horse's rider, wearing an embroidered gray shirt, gray pants, and black cavalry boots, had his arms tied behind his back and his feet tied to his stirrups. His head and shoulders had been daubed with pitch and set ablaze. He was screaming.

"It's Quantrill!" someone cried.

A volley of shots exploded from both sides of the street, and the horse and rider fell over dead.

Within seconds, a hundred Missouri guerrillas led by George Todd charged up the street. Fourteen of them were cut down in a hail of lead balls, and the rest turned and fled, with soldiers and citizens pursuing. A company of Negro Federal recruits led the chase and killed three more bushwhackers at the southern edge of town.

When the gunfire and shouting had ceased, a cluster of townspeople gathered around the carcass of the black horse and the charred, bloody corpse of its rider. The crowd parted to let two men in black suits and hats approach the bodies. Sam recognized them as the preachers that he, Taylor, and Noland had encountered the week before.

The elder preacher held a Bible over Quantrill's corpse. "Earth to earth," he intoned.

The younger preacher raised his Bible as well. "Ashes to ashes," he said.

In unison, they chanted, "And dust to dust."

Then they lowered their Bibles, drew their revolvers, and shot Quantrill a few more times for good measure.

"Amen," said the crowd.

Sam closed his curtains.

Senator Jim Lane had returned to Lawrence on Wednesday for a railroad meeting, and he sent for Sam at noon on Saturday, one day after the failed raid. Lane was thinner, younger, and had more hair than Sam had guessed from the caricatures, but his fine house on the western edge of town was all that Sam had supposed. It was packed with expensive furnishings, including two pianos in the parlor.

"How did you come to acquire two pianos, Senator?" Sam asked. He had not slept the night before and did not care if he sounded accusatory.

Lane smiled. "One was my mother's," he said. "The other belonged to a secessionist over in Jackson County who found that he no longer had a place to keep it." The Senator picked up a pen and wrote a few lines on a piece of paper, then folded the paper and pushed it across the table. "Kansas is grateful to you, Mr. Clemens, and regrets the mistake of two years past when members of the Red-Legged Guards mistook your brother for a slaveholder. Had they known of his appointment as secretary of Nevada Territory, I'm sure the tragedy would not have occurred."

"He told them," Sam said. "They didn't believe him."

Lane shrugged. "What's done is done, but justice will be served. General Ewing has ordered his troops to arrest all Red Legs they encounter. He believes that such men have been committing criminal acts in the name of liberty, and I must concur." He tapped the piece of paper. "I'm told that Governor Nye of Nevada Territory is again in need of a secretary. I cannot guarantee you the appointment, but this should smooth your way." He leaned forward. "Frankly, Mr. Clemens, I think your decision to continue to Nevada is a good one. There are those in this town who believe that the burning man was not Quantrill at all, and that you are here not as a friend, but as Quantrill's spy."

Sam stared at the piece of paper. "A ticket on the overland stage from St. Joseph is a hundred and fifty dollars," he said. "I have ten."

Lane stood and left the parlor for a few minutes. When he returned, he handed Sam three fifty-dollar banknotes and a bottle of whiskey.

"This was distilled from Kansas corn," the Senator said, tapping the bottle with a fingernail. "I thought you should have something by which to remember my state."

Sam tucked the money into a coat pocket and stood, holding the whiskey bottle by its neck. *My state,* Lane had said. What's done is done.

"Good day, Senator," Sam said. He started to turn away.

"Don't forget my letter of introduction," Lane said.

Sam picked up the piece of paper, tucked it into his pocket with the money, and left the house.

Henry was standing outside holding Bixby's reins, and twelve Bluebellies waited nearby. They had an extra horse with them.

"Mr. Clemens," one of the soldiers called. "Our orders are to escort you to St. Joseph. We're to leave right away." He didn't sound happy about it. All of the Bluebellies in the escort were white, and Sam suspected that this was their punishment for failing to chase the bushwhackers with as much vigor as their Negro counterparts.

Sam nodded to the soldier, then looked down at Henry. "I suppose you want to keep the horse," he said.

"Well, *I* don't," Henry said. "He's mean, if you ask me. But my pa says he'll either have Bixby as payment for his mule, or he'll take it out of somebody's hide. And since you're running off, I reckon my hide will do him as well as any."

"A hiding would probably do you a considerable amount of good," Sam said, "but since I no longer have a use for the animal, you may keep him and the saddle as well. I'll take the bags, however." He removed the saddlebags from the horse and put the bottle of whiskey into one of them. A few lumps of brown sugar lay at the bottom of that bag, so he fed one to Bixby. Bixby chewed and swallowed, then tried to bite Sam's hand. Sam gave the rest of the sugar to Henry and took his saddlebags to the soldiers' extra horse.

"Good-bye, Mr. Clemens," Henry said, climbing onto Bixby. "I won't forget you."

Sam swung up onto his own mount. "Thank you, boy," he said, "but I shall be doing my best to forget *you,* as well as every other aspect of this infected pustule of a city."

Henry gave him a skeptical look. "Mr. Clemens," he said, "I think you're a liar."

"I won't dispute that," Sam said. "I only wish I could make it pay."

The Bluebellies set off, and Sam's mount went with them. Sam looked back to give Henry and Bixby a wave, but they were already heading in the other direction and didn't see him.

On the way to the ferry, Sam and the soldiers passed by the Eldridge House, where eighteen bodies had been laid out on the sidewalk. They were already beginning to stink. A number of townspeople were still gathered here, and from what Sam could hear, they were curious about the dead black man, who had been one of the three raiders killed by the Negro recruits. Why on earth, they wondered, would a man of his race ride with Quantrill?

Sam started to say, "Because he was paid," but the words froze in his throat.

The last four bodies on the sidewalk were those of George Todd, Cole Younger, Frank James, and Fletcher Taylor.

Sam looked away and rode on.

He spent Saturday night camped beside the road with the soldiers and Sunday night in a hotel in St. Joseph, and did not sleep either night. At daybreak on Monday, he carried his saddlebags to the overland stage depot, paid his money, and boarded the coach. Two other passengers and several sacks of mail soon joined him, and the coach set off westward at eight o'clock.

As the coach passed the spot where Orion had been killed, Sam took out the whiskey that Lane had given him and began drinking. He offered some to his fellow passengers, but they each took one swallow and then refused more, saying that it was the vilest stuff they'd ever tasted. Sam agreed, but drank almost half the bottle anyway.

At the next station stop, he climbed atop the coach with his saddlebags while the horses were being changed. When the coach started moving again, Sam drank more whiskey and stared at the fields of green and gold. Soon, his head warm with sun and alcohol, it occurred to him that the corn and grass shifting in the breeze looked like ocean swells after a storm. He was reminded of a holiday he had spent near New Orleans, looking out at the Gulf of Mexico after piloting a steamboat down the Mississippi. He wondered if he would love anything in Nevada half as much.

The thought of Nevada reminded him of the letter that Jim Lane had written for him, so he took it out and read it:

> *My dear Governor Nye:*
>   *You will recall that your intended Secretary of two years past, Mr. Orion Clemens, was unfortunately killed before he could assume his duties. This letter will introduce his younger brother Samuel, who has provided service to his Nation and is a loyal Republican. I trust you shall do your utmost to secure for him any employment for which he might be suited.*
> > *Yours most sincerely,*
> > *James Lane, Senator*
> > *The Great and Noble State of Kansas*

Sam tore up the letter and let its pieces scatter in the wind. If Nevada held "any employment for which he might be suited," he would secure it without any assistance from a self-righteous, thieving son of a bitch like Jim Lane.

Nor would he drink any more of Lane's abominable whiskey. He leaned over the coach roof's thin iron rail and emptied the bottle onto the road. Then he opened one of his saddlebags, took out his Colt, and stood. He held the whiskey bottle in his left hand and the pistol in his right.

The coach conductor glanced back at him. "What are you doing, sir?" he asked.

Sam spread his arms. "I am saying farewell to the bloody state of Kansas," he cried, "and lighting out for the Territory!"

He looked out over the tall grass. It rippled in waves.

He missed the river.

He missed his brothers.

But killing men for the sake of a world that was gone wouldn't bring it back. It was time to make a new one.

"Half-less twain!" he cried.

Both the conductor and driver stared back at him.

"Quarter-less twain!" Sam shouted.

Then he brought his left arm back and whipped it forward, throwing the bottle out over the grass. As it reached the apex of its flight, he brought up his right arm, cocked the Colt with his thumb, and squeezed the trigger.

The bottle exploded into brilliant shards.

The coach lurched, and Sam sat down on the roof with a thump.

"God damn it!" the conductor yelled. "You spook these horses again, and I'll throw you off!"

Sam held the pistol by its barrel and offered it to the conductor. "Please accept this," he said, "with my apologies."

The conductor took it. "I'll give it back when you're sober."

"No," Sam said, "you won't."

Then he threw back his head and roared: *"Maaarrrrk Twaiiinn!"*

Two fathoms. Safe water.

He lay down with his hat over his face and fell asleep, and no dead men came to haunt his dreams.

For Sam Clemens, the war was over.

Skidmore

Introduction to

᠅

"Skidmore"

Linger in "The Territory"'s part of the country for 120 years or so, and you'll find that there's still blood in the soil. Step outside barefoot, and it'll ooze up between your toes. Some is left over from the days of the border wars, but some is fresh. And none of it will ever quite seep away.

This is where I grew up, and it's not far from Skidmore, Missouri, where something happened in 1981.

Similar incidents occur all the time, and the persons involved usually manage to keep them hidden from those outside their communities. But the media found out about this one, so it became the subject of a couple of TV movies, several magazine articles, and a book or two.

But that incident per se is not really what "Skidmore" is about. Instead, it's a story about the living dead.

Don't expect any flesh-eating zombies, though. I admire a good flesh-eating-zombie story as much as the next guy, but flesh-eating zombies have never scared me much. See, in order for something to scare me, I have to believe in it . . . and in my heart, I just can't buy the notion that when the dead come back to life, they're going to want to consume any more red meat.

I do believe the dead can return. But it takes more than cannibalistic hunger to pull them from the bloody earth.

It takes the even bloodier desires of the living.

And what the dead require from us once they're back makes being devoured by zombies look like an attractive option.

So be careful what you wish for. You may get it forever.

Skidmore

~

For a long time I wanted to kill a certain man of my acquaintance. He was the sort of man who professed peace, love, and liberal viewpoints, but treated people like shit. If my conscience had been that of an infant, I could have blown him away and suffered not an hour of guilt.

And I wouldn't be caught. I've never owned weapons, but it's an easy thing to steal a firearm and replace it without detection. I'm a good shot, too, but few know it. Certainly no one would suspect me. This is because I have the reputation of being a good boy. And so, by upbringing and training, I am.

But upbringing and training can be overcome.

Let me tell you about Skidmore.

Skidmore, Missouri. Population 447.

In Nodaway County, in the northwestern corner of the state. Farm country.

On Friday, July 10, 1981, a forty-seven-year-old coon-dog

breeder named Ken Rex McElroy climbed into his pickup truck in front of the D & G Tavern in Skidmore, on Missouri Highway 113. His wife, half his age, sat beside him.

More than thirty people, the moral heart of the community, stood nearby. They had all been part of a meeting at the American Legion hall that morning. The topic had been What to Do About McElroy.

McElroy, five foot eight, 260 pounds.

McElroy, said to have cut off one of his wife's breasts.

McElroy, thief, arsonist, and rapist.

McElroy, convicted of second-degree assault for shooting the grocer.

McElroy, free on bond, with twenty-five days to file a motion for a new trial.

But the new trial had been held.

As McElroy sat in his pickup, a .30-30 steel-jacketed bullet shattered the rear window and caught him under his right ear. Then a .22 magnum slug took off the back of his skull. More bullets followed, but they weren't needed. Somebody pulled McElroy's wife from the truck and took her into the bank. She was unhurt. Outside, the truck's engine raced. McElroy's foot was jammed down on the accelerator.

No killer was ever named. No one was arrested.

Justice.

I thought about Skidmore every day for the next six years, drawn there by an urge that was like an instinct. The parallel between McElroy and the man I wanted to kill was inescapable. Their methods of abuse differed, but they were of the same mold and spirit.

Nevertheless, when discussing McElroy's execution, as everyone in my part of the country did for a while, I expressed the horror of vigilantism that I believed was proper. This was a result of my upbringing and training.

I had always been a good boy.

· · ·

Let me tell you what that means.

I have never been in a fight. As a child I was often beaten up, but that isn't the same thing. It is, in fact, the furthest thing from it. I took the blows, believing what my parents and church had taught me. When my lips bled and eyes swelled, I told myself that I would, as Jesus might say, inherit the earth.

I also told myself that I would behave no differently if I were stocky and tough instead of skinny and weak. My size had nothing to do with my values. Violence was wrong. Violence solved nothing. I knew this because I watched the TV news. I grew up during the war that was scored by body counts. I swore that I would never strike another person.

For several months during grade school, an older kid pounded me and my brother after we got off the bus to walk home. He threw us down in the ditch, then kicked us. Running did no good; he was fast. Fighting back did no good; he was stronger. Once, I gave in to my brother's insistence that we defend ourselves, and this taught me the price of betraying my convictions. We were beaten and trampled as we had never been beaten and trampled before.

Some weeks later, a friend invited me to spend a Friday night at his house. My parents said it was all right, and for the first time, I didn't get on the bus after school. I sent my brother off alone.

My friend lived near school, so we walked. On the way, we encountered a kid who didn't care for my friend. He shoved my friend; my friend shoved back. The kid then knocked my friend to the ground and punched him until blood ran from his nose. Then he punched him some more.

I stood by.

I was a good boy.

On the morning of Friday, July 10, 1987, I kissed my wife good-bye and watched her drive away down the gravel road. We were living in a crumbling farmhouse in the hills south of a Kansas college town, and she had to make the long trip in every day. I worried about her.

She worried about me, too. Things had not happened for me the way they were supposed to, and this had made me bitter. Worse, I had been lied to, used, and ridiculed. The man I wanted to kill had been instrumental in these events.

My back ached. I slept little, and awoke scowling. I shouted at my wife. I refused to speak to friends when they telephoned. Worst of all, I couldn't work. In my profession, being unable to work is the same as being dead.

And so it was that as the profitless days stretched to weeks, my desire to kill that man of my acquaintance intensified. At the same time, my other instinct urged me toward Skidmore with increasing insistence.

On July 10, as I watched my wife drive away, I knew that I could resist no longer. I would have to answer one call or the other before the day was out. After a few minutes of indecision, I made the choice that I believed would be the easier to reconcile with my upbringing and training. I made sure that my dog had food and water, and then I climbed onto my motorcycle and left. The dog chased me down the road, and I had to stop and yell at him. He slunk back to the yard.

The trip would be 150 miles, give or take 10. I had checked the atlas and memorized the roads. The day was hot and bright.

I took the most direct route: north on U.S. 59, then northeast across the Missouri River into St. Joe. North again on U.S. 71 to Maryville. West 11 miles on Missouri 46.

South 4 miles on 113.

Skidmore.

It was a few minutes before noon. The trip had taken four hours. My back hurt worse than ever, and I was hungry.

Skidmore: two service stations, a grain elevator, church, post office, bank, café, and tavern. A few parked pickup trucks. Peeled paint and a rusty stop sign. No human being in sight.

The instinct that had brought me there was gone. Skidmore had been revealed as nothing more than a podunk town after the pattern of all the other podunk towns I had ridden through on the way. If anything, it was even less alive. It was worn down, decayed. Silent. The only thing Skidmore had to distinguish it was the killing of McElroy, and that had happened six years ago.

I ate a greasy cheeseburger at the café. The air-conditioning was weak, and my hair stayed sweaty. When the burger was gone, I nursed a Coke until my back felt better. A couple of stoop-shouldered farmers came in, and one asked if that was my bike out front. I said it was, and he said it looked sharp. Then they sat down across the room and ignored me. I left three quarters on the table, used the rest room, and went out. The waitress nodded. Her mouth was a dry pink line. She looked a hundred years old.

What had I expected?

I put on my helmet, got on the bike, and headed south. I would take a less direct way home, cutting west through the southeastern corner of Nebraska. Unfamiliar territory. I hoped it would be distracting. Since the urge that had brought me to Skidmore was gone, there was only one thing I wanted to do.

I was less than a mile out of town when the motorcycle died. I let it roll to a stop on the dirt shoulder of 113 before realizing that it was out of gas. I glanced down and switched the fuel valve to the reserve so I could return to Skidmore and fill the tank. As I looked up again, I glimpsed something to my right. I turned to see it.

In the ditch, Ken Rex McElroy was waiting.

A ragged, gaping hole took up most of the left side of his face. He climbed up from the ditch, and I saw that the back of his skull was gone.

"Welcome," he said.

Some of his teeth had been shot away. He was bloody.

"Welcome to Skidmore."

McElroy was big. Redneck big. His tattooed arms were like tree trunks.

I knew men like this. I had grown up with men like this. Men like this had beaten me up for practice when they were kids. He stood on the highway shoulder, staring at me with his dead eyes, and I was afraid of him. But even more, I hated him. I hated him as much as the man I wanted to kill.

"Get away from me," I said.

McElroy didn't move. "Ready to go?" he asked. His voice was flat. Stark.

I knew then that he wouldn't leave. "I have to get gas," I said. He returned to the ditch. "I'll wait."

I was shaking, but I managed to start the bike and ride back to Skidmore. I bought gas from an old man who wanted to talk. The weather, the crops, the goddamn politicians and courts, all in a dull monotone. I left as soon as I had my change.

I would go home the way I had come. I would ride fast.

Just north of the Skidmore city limits, a right turn took 113 between two soybean fields. As I came out of the turn, I saw McElroy standing in the road ahead.

I stopped. McElroy waited. After a while, I let the bike idle up to him. He got on behind me.

The ride home was hard. McElroy was heavy, and I wasn't used to riding with extra weight. Once I lost control on a curve, and the bike veered into the left lane in front of a semi. I went off onto the shoulder, and the semi rushed past, blaring.

I was still more than seventy miles from home. I didn't think I would make it.

Then the mirror showed me a flash of silver in McElroy's eyes, and I didn't think I wanted to.

Let me tell you about a flash of silver.

One day during my eleventh summer, my grandfather, my father, my uncle, three of my male cousins, and my brother and I went tramping in my grandfather's pasture. The day was hot and bright. The adults had beer. Once in a while we kids were given a sip. My uncle carried a new .30-06 bolt-action rifle with a scope. It was a heavy weapon with a kick.

We gathered on one side of a pond that was maybe seventy yards across. On the far side, near the top of the dam, my uncle had placed a flattened beer can. It shone like a mirror. If I looked straight at it, my eyes hurt.

The others took shots at the can, and the dust that flew up showed where the bullets struck. The men each shot within two feet of the target. My cousins and brother did less well. No one hit it. I hung back, hoping they would forget to give me a turn. I had a terror of guns.

When everyone but me had fired, they started to walk around the pond. I hurried to join them, and my uncle saw me. He made them all stop, then handed me the rifle and grinned. The men and boys shaded their eyes and gazed across the water.

The weapon was even heavier than I had imagined. The barrel wavered as I brought the stock to my shoulder. My arms were white twigs.

But when the rifle was in place and I was squinting through the scope, everything felt different.

I let out my breath. The stock was smooth and warm against my cheek. The trigger nestled within my curled finger. My vision was sharp. I had become a thing of metal and wood, of crystalline sight. A thing of power.

The stock crunched against my shoulder. A crack of thunder numbed my ear. My power was gone, and I strained to see.

There was no puff of dust. I had fired over the dam.

"Pretty big gun for a little guy," my grandfather said. My father said nothing. I handed the rifle back to my uncle, and he winked at me. It was a consolation wink.

We walked around the pond and started across the dam. Then my uncle stopped above the beer can, and we all stared at it. A round hole had been punched through the middle. My uncle winked at me again.

One of my cousins said that it must have been his shot. But his bullet had sprayed dust, as had everyone's but mine. He had to know, as my uncle knew, that it was the runt, the white-armed bookworm, who had hit the target. Dead center.

My uncle gave me the can, and we headed back toward the

house. I was proud. I put my thumb through the hole. Then I felt sick, and I dropped the can in the dirt.

As I had put my thumb through the hole, the beer can had changed. It had become the face of a kid who had taunted me throughout the preceding school year. It had become the face that had called me "Muskrat."

It had become the face that I had seen through the rifle scope, in the flash of silver across the pond.

It was after five when I made it back from Skidmore. McElroy was with me. My wife would be home soon.

My dog came running at the sound of the motorcycle, then saw McElroy and stopped. The hair on his back rose, and he growled.

McElroy stood in the driveway. "I liked dogs," he said.

I took off my helmet. "Well, this dog doesn't like you."

McElroy looked at me then, and I was scared.

"You don't have to be afraid," he said. "I don't get mad now. I don't feel nothing. I don't need nothing."

Hate suppressed fear. "Then why did you want to come here?"

"You're the one wants something."

McElroy walked toward the house. He moved stiffly. Wet stains smeared his brown shirt and pants. His suede cowboy boots were speckled with dark spots.

"What in hell would I want from a corpse?" I yelled. My voice echoed from the barn.

He stopped on the porch. Something dripped from his face and spattered on the cement.

I could hear my wife's car coming up the road, so I went around McElroy and unlocked the door. He went inside.

I put him in the basement. It was mud floored, dank, and cluttered with piles of junk that a previous tenant, long since deceased, had left there years ago. These were infested with mice. I had also seen a five-foot blacksnake down there once. I doubted that McElroy would mind.

He stayed in the basement whenever my wife was home. If we needed frozen food brought up, I made sure I was the one to go down and get it. He always stood in the corner beside the freezer. Spiders built webs on him. He didn't speak unless I did.

In August, I went to a weeklong conference on the West Coast. I knew that I should skip it, but I had bought my plane ticket before McElroy came home with me, and it was nonrefundable. So I talked my wife into staying with a friend in town, and I asked a neighbor to stop by and feed my dog. My wife would have known something was wrong if I'd spent money on a kennel. The poor dog would be scared the whole time, but McElroy wouldn't hurt him. I didn't think.

As it turned out, McElroy came with me.

I didn't know it until the plane was in the air. There had been two empty seats beside me, but when I returned from a trip to the lavatory, McElroy was in one of them. I had to squeeze past, sucking in my breath so as not to touch him. His wounds never dried.

I sat down. "Go back," I said. "People will be watching me this week."

McElroy gave me his stare. "You want me here."

A flight attendant came by and asked if I would like something to drink. She didn't ask McElroy. Her eyes avoided him. Blood smeared her sleeve when she reached across him to hand me a beer, and she didn't even notice.

A few days into the conference, I discovered that one of the attendees was very much like the man I wanted to kill. He was a master of ridicule, and he made it clear that he didn't consider me worthy of anything but contempt. During his most scathing comments, I had to suppress a laugh. What would he consider me worthy of, I wondered, if he knew what waited in my room?

I thought then of what McElroy had done to the people of Skidmore, and of how they had reached a point beyond which they could take no more. I wondered how much I would be able to take before I reached that same point.

More, I believed. Much more. My upbringing and training had steeled me. I accepted my colleague's contempt and gave back a smile. I had higher limits than he could reach.

I was, after all, a good boy.

Let me tell you what that doesn't mean.

I've already said that I've never been in a fight, and that's true. But that doesn't mean I've never hurt anyone.

After the day that I saw a classmate's face as a rifle target, I had an even greater terror of guns than before. I knew now what they could do to me. What I didn't know was that a gun wasn't the only weapon that could do it. I didn't learn better until my nineteenth summer.

I had graduated from high school and was working for wheat cutters to earn money for college. One of my duties was to drive truckloads of grain to an enormous elevator on the east side of Wichita. This is what I was doing when I committed my first true act of violence.

The day was hot and bright. I had been working hard, and my shirt was stuck to my back with sweat and dirt. Grain dust grated under my eyelids. The truck cab was hot enough to bake biscuits. A single narrow alley led to the elevator's scales, and it was marked One Way.

I drove to the scales, transacted my business, and helped the elevator employees auger the grain from the truck bed. My swollen eyes itched, and my chest ached from inhaling dust. As soon as the truck was empty, I jumped into the cab and continued down the alley. When I was thirty yards short of the street, a loaded truck turned in. In front of me. Going the wrong way.

I hit the brakes and blared the horn. The other truck slammed to a halt and spilled part of its load. The red-faced driver leaned from his window. "Get out the way, asshole!" he yelled.

And I could have. I could have put the truck into reverse and backed up an eighth of a mile to the entrance. I could have let him come in the wrong way. I was supposed to be a good boy.

But I was tired and hurting, and I forgot. I yelled back at him, using the same word he had used against me. I added that he was going the wrong goddamn way.

I had never done anything like that before.

He yelled something again, but I didn't hear what it was. I was revving my truck's engine. I popped the clutch and lurched forward.

He backed out fast. Even so, I nicked the corner of his bumper. My truck rumbled onto the street at ten miles an hour, and the other guy jumped from his truck and ran after me. I saw him coming in my side mirror.

I couldn't believe it. He had left a loaded truck on the street to chase me on foot. He was screaming obscenities, demanding that I stop and let him kick the shit out of me. I leaned out the window and told him to go fuck himself. Another first. I was almost as mad as he was.

But I wasn't as stupid.

He was running behind the left rear wheel of my truck. His face was at the level of the bed. The bed was metal-edged hardwood. I sped up a little, and he kept coming. I let him gain on me until he was about four feet from the tail of the bed.

He screamed, "Stop, you little cocksucker!"

So I stopped. Hard. I heard the *whunk.*

I waited a few seconds, then shut off the engine. The street was quiet.

I got out and went to the rear of the truck. The guy was lying on the pavement with his hands over his face. He rocked from side to side. When he heard my boots scuff beside him, he uncovered his face. It seemed to swell as I watched. There was only a little blood, but it was from both nose and mouth. I saw the result of rage.

"Muffa*fucchhah,*" he said. He had bitten his tongue.

I pointed at the alley. "The entrance," I said, "is at the other end."

I got back into the truck and left. In the mirror, I saw the guy stand and stagger back toward his load. I felt better than I had all day. At the first red light, I adjusted the mirror so I could see myself laugh. My face looked familiar, but not like me.

That night, I dreamed that I was the one running after the truck, that I was the one struck down. After I fell, the truck backed over me. I awoke clutching the sheet, choking. I stumbled to the bathroom and retched up phlegm and grain dust. When I was finished, I avoided looking at the medicine-cabinet mirror. I swore that I would never again retaliate against one who had attacked me.

I still have that dream. Sometimes, after I've been run over, it's as if I'm looking down at my own dead face.

Ever since going to Skidmore, I look like McElroy.

On Thursday, July 7, 1988, my wife came home crying. Hours passed before she would say what was wrong. As I held her, waiting for the words to come, I heard thumps from the basement. McElroy was doing something, but I couldn't go down to find out what. My wife needed me.

At last, she told me what had happened. It involved the man I wanted to kill. His words and actions had been cruel and insidious. He was always careful to camouflage his behavior to everyone except his victims. I knew. I had been one of those victims. But while I had sworn to endure attacks upon myself, I had not sworn to endure any upon the one person I loved. I didn't tell my wife, but at the moment she revealed what he had done, I knew that I would finally do it.

After my wife had fallen asleep, I went down to the basement. My fear and hatred of McElroy were still strong, but I had to tell him what I was going to do. Who better to consult about death than one already dead?

McElroy stood in his usual corner, shadowed. The basement's single bulb wasn't bright enough. I could see his eyes and part of his ruined face, but the rest was hidden. Hideous as he was, I preferred seeing his entire form, as I had in the sunshine outside Skidmore.

I stopped under the bulb. "I understand now why those people had to kill you," I said. "And I think I know why you said I wanted something. Since you came here, I've become less afraid of death. So now I can use it against someone who deserves it. What do you think of that?"

McElroy stepped into the light. A long plastic-wrapped bundle was cradled in his arms. He held it out to me. I took it, careful not to touch him. The plastic, speckled with mouse droppings, was secured with duct tape.

I set the bundle on the floor to unwrap it. Beneath the plastic was a layer of canvas, and beneath that was a zippered leather case. Inside I found a .30-06 bolt-action rifle with a scope. It was in perfect condition. Someone had cleaned and oiled it before wrapping it up. A box of cartridges nestled in a pocket of the case.

McElroy pointed toward a pile of junk against the wall. "I found it under there."

That pile had been undisturbed for years, and I was certain that neither my landlord nor any other living soul knew the rifle had been there. I could use the weapon the one time I would need it, rewrap it, and replace it under the pile. Unless I was caught in the act of pulling the trigger, many more years would pass before anyone else even knew of its existence.

I sighted down the rifle and checked its action. The sensation was just as it had been on that day at my grandfather's pond. I would hit my target on the first shot.

"This," I said to McElroy, "is what I wanted from you." I held up the gun. "*This.*"

It would happen tomorrow. I would have to ride my motorcycle, but transporting the weapon wouldn't be a problem. McElroy would carry it.

I knew he would be joining me.

We left for town at 11:00 A.M. on Friday, July 8. The day was hot and bright. My dog didn't follow us. McElroy rode behind me, holding the rifle across his chest. No one would see it because no one would see him.

Earlier, after my wife had driven away, I had tested the rifle behind the barn. I had shot at a sheet of typing paper fixed to a bale of hay. From seventy yards I had hit dead center. From eighty I had blown off a corner. Close enough.

As the bike accelerated, I shuddered with the knowledge that I was about to do something wonderful. The man I wanted to kill had crushed my upbringing and training to scar tissue. I had entered a higher plane of morality. This act would be easier than hitting the brakes on the truck had been, and would do more good. Even knowing that McElroy sat behind me gave me no qualms. Death was nothing to me now but a tool to be used to improve existence. I had to struggle to keep my speed below sixty.

In town, I left the motorcycle on a side street and walked to the college. McElroy followed with the rifle. Several people passed us on the sidewalk when we reached campus, but none acknowledged me or noticed McElroy. We proceeded to the grove of maples below the campanile. A few students were picnicking, but they didn't look up. We entered a clump of bushes beside the street, and I crouched. McElroy did likewise. A bicyclist went by without giving us a glance. We were hidden.

The man I wanted to kill had his office on the third floor of the building across the street. He ate his lunch there, alone, every day. His desk and chair were beside the window, which was open. He wasn't there yet, but I knew he would be soon. I took the rifle from McElroy, then settled onto my knees and peered through the scope. I estimated the range to be about seventy-five yards. The gun barrel protruded only a few inches from the bushes. I loaded the rifle and then laid it across my thighs to wait.

The dirt under the bushes was damp, but I'd expected that. I would launder my jeans as soon as I got home, and I was wearing old sneakers that I would burn. Hate doesn't make one stupid. Rage does, but I had been careful to avoid rage. I checked my watch. It was three minutes to noon. I looked at McElroy. He stared back.

Up in his office, the man I wanted to kill sat down and opened his briefcase. I had a clear view of both chest and head.

He unwrapped a sandwich and started to eat. I wondered if they would find some of it still in his mouth. I brought up the rifle. The stock was smooth and warm against my cheek. The barrel quivered, and then was steady. In the scope, the man smiled as he chewed. He was reading something. Probably a story of pain or humiliation. The spiderweb-thin crosshairs intersected below his left eye.

The campanile chimed to announce the hour. I flinched at the sound, and the rifle twitched. I brought it back true and waited for the big bell to begin tolling. I would remain still through the first two knells to get the rhythm. On the third I would fire, blending the noise of my shot with the rumble that filled the grove.

The ground vibrated with the first deep tone, and my teeth hummed. I let out my breath. At the second tone, the man above laughed.

My finger tightened.

At the third tone, the man I wanted to kill became a bleeding wound. The rifle stock hit my cheekbone. I dropped the weapon and sat on my heels.

Before me stood McElroy, a new hole bubbling under his throat. "Take me back," he said.

The bell tolled a fourth time, and a fifth. Blood crept down the front of McElroy's shirt like syrup.

I lunged sideways to see around him, branches scratching my face. In his office, the man I wanted to kill was still chewing and chuckling. My bullet had stayed inside McElroy. I picked up the rifle and reloaded, then saw that the barrel was clogged with dirt. I tried to clean it out with my shirttail. The bell tolled a sixth time, and a seventh.

On the eighth I raised the rifle and sighted. Again, McElroy stepped into the way. I shouted, asking him why. My voice was swallowed by the ninth toll.

"You don't want me here anymore," McElroy said.

At the tenth knell I scrambled around him, crashing through the bushes, and aimed my weapon. At the eleventh the crosshairs centered on my target's grinning mouth. I saw a flash of silver.

The twelfth knell sounded.

The man I wanted to kill went on eating. I lowered the rifle and looked back at McElroy.

"Home?" I asked.

He stared down at me.

"Skidmore," he said.

It wasn't the town we had left the year before.

The buildings had been painted. The windows gleamed. Old men in denim overalls sat outside the gas stations and chewed tobacco. Women in polyester pants gathered in front of the grocery store while their toddlers sucked on Popsicles. A banner announcing a community barbecue hung over the entrance to the American Legion hall. Children rode bicycles up and down the side streets. A young farmer sauntered into the tavern, whistling.

I parked the motorcycle in front of the café and killed the engine. McElroy and I got off.

Silence.

I pulled off my helmet and looked around. The old men were staring down the street at us. The women stared too, then gathered up their babies and hurried away. The barbecue banner came loose in a gust of wind and blew onto Missouri 113. A child stopped his bicycle, let it fall, and ran. The door to the tavern opened and the farmer peered out, his lips still pursed.

McElroy handed me the rifle, then walked to the center of the street. The banner tumbled past him. He stopped and raised his hands as if in benediction.

People began disappearing into buildings.

McElroy stood there until I was the only one left outside. Then he continued down the street, his hands still raised. He left a red trail on the asphalt.

The café door opened, and the waitress ran out and grasped my arm.

"Please," she said. Her eyes begged. "Don't leave him here."

McElroy turned a corner and vanished. His blood remained.

I looked at the waitress. "I'm sorry," I said.

I leaned the rifle against the wall beside the café door, then went inside with the waitress and bought another cheeseburger. It was all I could do. Afterward, I rode up the street and filled the bike's tank at the same station as before. This time, the old man didn't want to talk. He just gazed off down the highway.

I called my wife from the pay phone there, catching her before she left work, and told her I'd be home late. Then I got on the bike and headed south. When I passed the café, I saw my rifle leaning against the wall. I slowed, then went on past.

South of Skidmore, the ditches were empty. I left the dead town behind.

The man I wanted to kill is still alive, though my upbringing and training have nothing to do with it. Someone will kill him someday . . . but it won't be me.

Let me tell you why.

I won't live with a hated man forever, as the people of that small Missouri town must live with Ken Rex McElroy. A year was enough. I've seen the price of justice, and it's a higher price than I can pay.

So I've again sworn that I will, as Jesus might say, inherit the earth. It isn't an easy vow to keep. After all, there are always those who treat people like shit, and there are always weapons available. But whenever I find myself filled with hate, I repeat these words:

"Welcome.

"Welcome to Skidmore."

As a result, I have not killed anyone.

Yet.

Which is the most, I think, that any good boy can say.

Killing Weeds

❧

Introduction to

⤜

"Killing Weeds"

I'm trying not to say too much about the individual stories in these introductions, because the stories had better be able to speak for themselves. But since I've selected these particular stories for this particular collection, it would be disingenuous not to say anything at all. After all, this is a book of stories in which death, dying, and/or the dead figure prominently—but if all of my stories deal with those things, why did I choose these eight tales instead of some of the others?

For one thing, I wanted to include stories from all stages of my career to date. I've been publishing short fiction for about thirteen years now (a fortuitous number for a book about death), and my attitudes have changed over time. So stories from various years should provide different and therefore refreshing perspectives on my themes of dissolution, disintegration, and mortality.

In addition, I wanted to be sure to include stories about several different kinds of death . . . because human beings aren't the only things that die.

With those criteria in mind, I will tell you that "Killing Weeds" is an early story (written in 1985, published in 1986) about more than one kind of death.

And other than that, I have only one thing to say about it:

In recent years, a few friends and critics have speculated that my own life experiences might have provided some of the material for my fiction. I'll speak to that general speculation in more detail at another time, such as when hell freezes over—but as far as *this* story is concerned, I want to emphasize that my own experience with farmwork has been mostly positive.

For example, mowing and baling prairie hay with my uncle in the summer of 1974 was one of the best times of my life.

And if it hadn't been for the UFO I saw toward the end, and the 150-mph windstorm that followed the UFO and destroyed most of our work, it would have been perfect.

Killing Weeds

Monday. Dad bangs on my bedroom door at five-thirty and calls, "Up an' at 'em, Phillie." I'm already dressed, though, and sitting on the edge of the bed to put on my oldest pair of tennies. The smell of bacon told me it was time. It's Dad's first full day back from summer camp, and we have a lot to do. Knowing him, I'll bet he's already fed and watered the calves in the lot behind the barn.

I go to my dresser to get the birthday presents he brought me— a camouflage jacket and a mother-of-pearl-handled four-blade pocketknife. I turned twelve last week while he was out in western Kansas teaching guys how to shoot howitzers. Seems like my birthday always falls during summer camp.

I complained about that to Mom, and she laughed, saying it was "an appropriate tradition."

"After all," she told me, "he was off being a soldier when you were born, too."

That started her on the story about how they got engaged just before Dad was drafted, and how after a year Grandma gave her the money to fly to Manila so she could marry him while he was on leave. "And that's how we picked your name," she always says at the end. It's her favorite story, and I've heard it at least a thousand times. Dad rolls his eyes every time she tells it when he's around.

This year he called from Fort Riley and told me that 1980 is a turning point for me. Whenever he's gone now, he says, I'm the man of the family.

Mom smiled her that's-nice-dear smile when I told her that. She thinks I'm still her baby, and won't even let me run the old John Deere 50 unless Dad's here to watch.

I heard them arguing about that last night, just two hours after he got home. I listened at the furnace vent in my bedroom floor.

"Most twelve-year-olds have been running tractors by themselves for three years already," Dad said.

"Most twelve-year-olds aren't as small as he is," Mom said.

"What does that have to do with it?" Dad asked, almost yelling. "Hell, he's damn near as good with the Allis as I am, and all I'm suggesting is that he could run the Deere with the weed wiper or bean bar once in a while."

"The bean buggy, maybe, since somebody else has to be there anyway, but not the pipewick. I don't want him out in the field by himself."

"Yeah, and that's why we've got this weed problem."

"No, dear, that's because your wonderful cousin didn't take care of it two weeks ago like he said he would."

There was a long stretch of silence then, and finally Dad said, "You sound like you think that's my fault."

"I can't count how many times you've called Billy unreliable," Mom said. "We've got to face facts, Loren—if we want the farm to work, you'd better quit the Guard."

"You know damn well the only reason we haven't gone under is my Guard pay."

"Then maybe we should get jobs in town."

"Just like that, huh? They're handing them out like candy at a parade, are they?"

"We could try. We can't hold on to the farm forever, and you can't pretend everything'd be all right if only I'd let poor little Philip drive the tractors while you're out Guarding."

I was so mad at Mom that I got into bed and put the pillow over my head so I couldn't hear her anymore.

It's not my fault I'm not built big, like Dad is. Maybe I would be if Mom would get me that Olympic weight set I keep asking for.

But, hell, I don't need muscles to run a tractor. On a tractor I'm as strong as anybody.

"Get down here and eat your breakfast, you lazy kids," Dad yells from downstairs. I slip my new knife into my back pocket and put on the camouflage jacket. It'll be too hot for it in a few hours, but I want to wear it while I can.

I beat Jodi downstairs, and she screams that I pushed her. Mom is busy trying to get Crissy to stop crying, though, so she tells Jodi to shut up, sit down, and eat her eggs. Jodi whines, but Mom gives her the no-back-talk-or-else look. Jodi is eight, but she acts like as much of a baby as Crissy, who is three.

Dad is already sitting at the head of the kitchen table, chewing a mouthful of bacon and listening to the morning news and farm report on WIBW-Topeka. He winks at me when I sit down, and I dig in to catch up.

"Where's Patricia?" he asks after a minute.

I swallow a big glug of milk to wash down a lump of toast. "Still in bed, I guess. Want me to go get her?"

He shakes his head. "No, Jodi'd better do it."

Jodi whines, "Oh, Daddeee, I just sat dowwwwwn."

"You get upstairs and get your sister, or you won't be able to sit down at all, young lady."

I stuff a bunch of scrambled eggs into my mouth so I won't laugh.

Jodi stomps upstairs, clomp clomp clomp on the wooden steps, and the noise makes Crissy cry louder.

"Jodi Lee Bundy, you straighten up or you'll wish you had!" Mom yells.

Mom is in a bad mood. I think it's because of the argument.

Or maybe it's just because Crissy is screeching her stupid pink head off.

Dad and I finish our breakfasts, and then we grab our Co-Op hats and walk out across the packed dirt of the barnyard to the west shop. The sun is just coming up, all orangy over the thick band of trees down in the Coal Creek valley a mile east, and the eighty-acre soybean field just this side of the creek looks like a giant, dark green carpet. There's some low, wispy fog down by the trees, but it looks like the field itself will be fairly dry. It's been five days since the last rain, and that wasn't much.

The calves in the pen behind the barn start bawling when they hear us. Dad says, "Sounds like your sisters," and makes me laugh.

He shoves open the west shop's big sliding door, and the corrugated metal rumbles like thunder. The six-row planter, the chisel plow, the pipewick rig, and the bean buggy—the bar folded in the middle so that the two pairs of fiberglass seats are facing each other—are lined up against one wall, and most of the rest of the shop is taken up by the John Deere and the big diesel Allis-Chalmers, its front-loader raised high.

I notice for the first time that the collapsed sunshade-umbrellas on the bean buggy look like furled flags.

Dad stands with his hands on his hips for a few seconds, "sizing up the situation" like he always does.

"Tell you what," he says, hitching up his jeans a little. "You check the fifty's oil and gas her up. By the time you've done that, I'll have the Allis out of the way so we can manhandle the bean bar and hook 'er up."

"You got it," I say, like I imagine his troops saying when he gives them an order, and I run over to the old green John Deere. The oil is fine, so I climb up into the seat, pull the hand clutch, and hit the starter. It takes the engine a half minute of cranking, but then it fires up, blup-blup-blup-blupblupblupblupblup. I put it in first gear, cut back the throttle, and ease out of the shop nice and slow. I hope Mom's looking out the kitchen window.

I keep the tractor in first as I drive past the barn toward the east shop. The sun is up over the trees now, and I have to squint.

I fill the 50 from the three-hundred-gallon gas tank outside the east shop, and it makes me feel good when I glance back and see that Dad isn't bothering to keep an eye on me. A few months ago, even, he would've watched to make sure I didn't use the diesel tank.

I feel the vibration in my chest when he starts the Allis and backs it into the barnyard. It's as big as an armored personnel carrier.

It takes Dad a while to get the buggy coupled to the Deere—the hookup's more complicated than most, because the buggy has to stick out in *front* of the tractor—and then he's got to mix the herbicide and water in the buggy's seventy-five-gallon plastic tank. After that he has to tinker with the compressor and test all the wands, so by the time we're finally ready to go, it's after eight o'clock. I've been playing mumblety-peg in the barnyard with my new knife, but now I put it back into my pocket and run to the house to see if the others are ready.

Dad drives the 50 with the folded-up buggy a half mile south down the dirt road to the bean-field gate, and the rest of us follow on foot.

Patricia is complaining. She's a year younger than me, and as far as I can tell she's not good for much except teaching Jodi how to whine. "If we weren't going to have to be ready until *now*," she says, "why'd we have to get up at *five-thirty?*"

"You didn't get up at five-thirty," I tell her. "Everybody else did, but not you."

"Oh, well, you're *per-fect,* aren't you, Phil-ip?" she says, mostly through her nose.

"Both of you shut up," Mom says. She's carrying Crissy to keep the kid from crying, and she isn't happy about it.

By the time we catch up to Dad at the edge of the field, he's got the halves of the bean bar folded out and locked in place. Now the tractor-plus-buggy rig is shaped like a T, with the bean bar forming the crosspiece. A couple of the hoses to the wands are tangled, so I straighten them out.

"Attaboy," Dad says, talking loudly so I can hear him over the idling tractor.

Patricia gives me a dirty look.

Mom puts a cutesy little sunbonnet on Crissy, and Dad takes the kid up onto the tractor seat with him. The rest of us take the four bean-bar seats—Mom and Jodi on the left side of the tractor, Patricia and me on the right. Mom and I have the outside seats, the best ones, and we both open our sun umbrellas.

"Okay!" Dad shouts, idling the Deere down a little further. "Be sure to aim low for the cockleburs. Don't get any on the bean plants if you can help it. Forget about the volunteer corn; I'll have to get it with the wiper after I take care of the milo."

"Okay, Dad!" I answer, and pop the four-foot wand out of its bracket on the side of my seat. It feels good in my hand. Broadleaf weeds, prepare to die.

"Patricia Kay and Jodi Lee, put up your sunshades!" Mom yells.

"Oh, Mo-ther!" Patricia whines. "It's chilly out here as it is."

"Put up your sunshades *now*," Mom says.

"But I want to get a tan!" Patricia whines.

"Me too!" Jodi says, like an echo.

"I'll tan both your butts if you don't do what your mother says," Dad hollers, and I can't help laughing.

"You be quiet," Mom tells me.

Brat One and Brat Two finally open their umbrellas, and Dad cranks up the Deere and takes us into the beans.

I aim the wand carefully and squeeze the trigger. A faintly purplish, fan-shaped spray shoots from the nozzle, spitting death onto the nutrient-sucking cockleburs and morning glories that are trying to take over our field.

The soybean plants are over a foot high, which means we're doing this about three weeks later than we should be. But all through the second half of June the big Angus steers kept getting out of the north pasture, and Dad and I had to fix over a quarter mile of fence. By the time we finished that, it was time for Guard summer camp, and another two weeks were lost. Dad's cousin Billy was supposed to weed-wipe the milo, at least, but, like Dad says, counting on Billy is like a legless man trying to count on his toes.

It ought to be all right, though. We might lose a little yield in both the beans and milo, but it's not going to be a disaster. Just like everybody else, Dad says, we do the best we can—and you can't do any more than that. In about a week, we'll have 160 acres of prairie hay ready to mow a few miles west of here, but if this spraying isn't done by then, the hay'll have to wait.

The beans really need the help. There are so many cockleburs crowding up against the stems of the plants that I have to keep my spray going constantly. It's not hard, since I can switch hands, but the job was more fun last year. Then the weeds weren't as thick, and I had more opportunity to develop my aim. It became a game to see whether I could hit the cockleburs without getting any of the spray on the bean plants or the ground. I had to stay alert.

This year, though, there's no variety, and the grumble of the tractor and the perpetual hiss of the wands combine into a monotonous hum that makes me drowsy. As the sun rises higher and the air gets warmer, the smells of gasoline, herbicide, and bean plants swirl together and almost put me over the edge into sleep.

But then the rig jerks and stops, and even though we've been going real slow, I have to grab my chair to keep from falling off. I hear Jodi shriek, and I see that she's taken a tumble. She isn't hurt, because it's only two and a half feet to the ground, but she's plenty mad. If I'd been driving, I'd be getting an earful about now.

I look back at Dad as he cuts the tractor engine.

"What is it, Loren?" Mom asks, and she sounds so worried that I begin to feel worried myself, even though I don't know why I should.

"Quiet," Dad says, and stands up, holding Crissy against his chest. She yowls, and he puts his hand over her mouth.

"What for?" Patricia asks.

Dad takes his hand away from Crissy's mouth and points toward the north end of the field. "There," he says. "Do you see something moving down there?"

All I can see are soybeans.

"What am I supposed to be looking for?" Jodi asks, sounding really hacked off.

"Don't speak to your father in that tone of voice," Mom says.

Dad is squinting, searching the field. "Somebody's in the beans."

"I don't see anything, dear," Mom says.

Dad shakes his head. "You don't know how to look."

"Maybe it was a coyote," I say.

Dad doesn't answer.

"Philip's probably right," Mom says. "A coyote could be staying low, or could even be in the trees by now."

Dad frowns, then sits down and restarts the tractor.

We continue spraying the rows of beans. Crissy continues bawling.

It's after ten-thirty and we're working about sixty yards from the trees when Dad kills the engine for the second time.

"Listen," he tells us, and this time we all hear it. Someone is shooting a rifle down by the creek, on our land. The sharp cracks come quickly, one every eight or nine seconds.

I feel like hitting something. We've posted signs on all the fences: No Hunting; No Trespassing. Yet some illiterate fools, as Dad calls them, are down there anyway, looking to get us or our cattle killed.

"God damn it," Dad says, and gets down from the tractor, leaving Crissy squalling on the seat.

"Loren, I've asked you not to curse in front of the children," Mom says.

"Yeah, Dad," Patricia says, smirking. "After all, Jodi and I have Bible School this afternoon. And then we're going to see Aunt Sue, and you know what she always says about swear words."

I was through with Bible School last year, thank goodness. I don't care if I never see construction paper or hear another verse of "This Little Light of Mine" for the rest of my life.

Mom glares at Patricia, and if she weren't so far away, I think she'd smack her. "When I want a comment from you, young lady, I'll ask for it," Mom says.

Dad begins walking toward the trees.

"Loren," Mom says, "just what do you think you're doing?"

Dad slows and half turns back toward us. "I'm going to politely tell them to get the hell out. Be right back."

I hesitate for a second, knowing that I'll get in trouble with Mom, and then I jump down from the bean buggy and run after Dad. Mom yells for me to come-back-this-instant, but I pretend I don't hear her. She has to take the girls to Topeka in a few hours, and by the time she gets back she won't be mad anymore.

I catch up with Dad at the edge of the field. He asks, "Who invited you?" but doesn't tell me to go back, so I head into the trees with him.

It's shady and shadowy in here, a jungle of walnut and hedge apple trees, climbing ivy, and gooseberry bushes. I remember that Mom promised to make gooseberry pies if I can ever get my sisters to help pick.

The gunfire sounds really close now. Dad yells "Heyyyy!" between each shot, to let the illiterate fools know we're looking for them, but no one answers.

We find the three of them on an old cow path near the creek. They're standing in a patch of shade that half hides their faces, but it looks to me like one is ancient, one is about Dad's age, and one is only a few years older than me. They're all dressed alike, in hunting vests and caps of such a dark brown that they almost look black. You'd think the illiterate fools would wear something bright to keep from shooting each other. Each one carries a rifle.

Now that we've stopped moving, I realize for the first time how steamy it is down here. My camouflage jacket feels hot and itchy. Gnats are trying to fly into my ears, and when I slap them away it sounds like a bomb has gone off in my head.

"Howdy," Dad says to the strangers, being polite just like he said he'd be.

The oldest one is chewing snuff, and he spits before answering. "Howdy," he says, but he doesn't sound friendly. I don't think he has any teeth. "How're y'all doin' today?" His voice gives him away as being from Texas or somewhere else south of here.

"Just fine," Dad says, stepping a little closer to them. I hang back, not because I'm scared, but because Dad's in charge. "My family and I are spraying our beans, and we heard your guns."

"Uh-huh," the old man says, shifting his snuff. "What you sprayin' 'em with?"

Dad doesn't answer for a few seconds, but then he says, "Two, four-DB."

The old man makes a snorting noise and spits again. "Why don't y'just use sugar water? Ain't gonna stop nothin' unless you use somethin' with some kick to it."

Dad seems to grow a few inches. "I use what most folks around here use for cockleburs."

"If you say so, Joe. Sorry if we made too much noise."

"Well, that's all right," Dad says, "but I'm afraid I'll have to ask you to go somewhere else."

"We're hunting whitetails," the one Dad's age says. "Cain't seem to find any, though."

Dad's super mad now; I can tell by the way his jaw sticks out farther. "In the first place," he says, "it ain't deer season, and in the second place, you don't have permission to hunt here. You've blown off at least thirty rounds in the last minute and a half, and that's too damn dangerous with people so close."

"Thought we might as well shoot some squirrels," the youngest says.

Dad takes a deep breath. "I hear any more of it, I'm calling the sheriff."

The old man swallows loudly, and grunts. "Everybody round here as unfriendly as you, Joe?"

Dad stiffens. "My name ain't Joe," he says, and turns to look straight at me. I can see in his eyes that he wants me to get back to the field *now.*

I turn and head back, fast.

"Nice-lookin' boy," I hear the oldest hunter say. "What is he—eight, nine?"

I'm smashing through bushes now, but I can still hear Dad say, "I want your names."

"Charlie," the old man answers.

I find another cow path and head toward the field. My run slows to a walk, but my heart still feels like a sledgehammer hitting stone. Something moves in the weeds at the edge of the path, and I remember Dad saying that there are copperheads down here. I wish I were wearing something tougher than almost-worn-out tennies.

An oval piece of tire tread, about nine inches long and four wide, is lying in the middle of the path. I pick it up with my right hand and slap the tread against my left palm. I *left* my job, I *left* my wife, I *left* my friends, I *left* for life—

I'm worried about Dad, and I think maybe I should go back to him, but I don't know what I could do if I did. I'm too goddamn small. A twelve-year-old should weigh more than seventy pounds.

I step out into the field about thirty yards north of where Mom is standing with her arms crossed. Patricia, Jodi, and Crissy are still on the bean buggy.

"Where's your father?" Mom demands as she walks toward me.

"Talking to the hunters," I say. My voice sounds high-pitched and thin.

"What's he saying to them?" Mom asks. "What are they doing here? What's that in your hand?"

I don't try to answer everything. I just say, "A piece of tire I found."

Mom frowns at the chunk of rubber. "How on earth did a tire get into all that brush?"

Then, as if by magic, Dad is with us. I didn't even hear him coming out of the trees.

"Let me see that," he says, and I hand him the piece of tire.

He looks at it for a long time, and the longer he looks, the madder his eyes get. I feel like something is my fault, and I have to look away from his face. My eyes focus on the tire chunk, and I notice for the first time that there are four dirt-clogged holes near the edges of the rubber, two toward each end of the oval.

"What happened in there?" Mom asks.

Dad doesn't answer. After another couple of seconds, he turns and throws the piece of tire back into the trees.

After we've had lunch and Mom has taken the girls to town, Dad mixes glyphosate herbicide in the pipewick's two fifty-gallon tanks, then hitches the wiper to the back of the big orange Allis. He's put new ropes through the grommets in the twenty-foot horizontal plastic pipe, and he lets me use my birthday knife to trim the ends. You have to be sure that enough rope sticks out of each hole so that you get most of the Johnsongrass, but not so much rope that you're dripping a lot of poison onto the milo—sorghum, some people call it.

When Dad kicks up the idle on the Allis, thick black smoke spurts from the exhaust, making the barnyard smell "like a truck stop." Then he touches one of the hydraulic-control levers, lowering the front-loader a few feet so he can see where he's going.

"Ought to take the damn thing off," he says, "but it's too much trouble. Besides, I've been thinking that I might spread some new gravel on the driveway."

Everything that needs doing around here, Dad can do. And does.

I ride on the tractor with him, sitting on the built-in toolbox (which Dad welded into place himself) beside the right fender. As we roar down the road past the soybean field, I can see waves of heat jiggling over the beans nearest the trees. I take off my camouflage jacket and tie its arms around my waist.

The road curves around Bald Hill, which blocks my view of the bean field, and then we chug down into the creek valley and across the low-water bridge. Dad slows the Allis way down and stares off down the creek as we cross the bridge. I think his mind's still on the hunters.

The canopy of trees over the muddy little strip of water reminds me of a tunnel. There is a stink of something dead here. A muskrat, maybe.

The trees thin out again a few dozen yards past the bridge, and the first of our two sixty-acre milo fields comes into view. It seems less orderly than the bean field, because the beans are all in neat rows, while this looks like a prairie of thick-stemmed, foot-and-a-half-high grass. Actually, the milo is planted in rows, too—it's just not so obvious from the road.

A lot of taller, scroungier-looking grass is scattered throughout the field, sticking up from six to ten inches above the crop. This stuff is Johnsongrass, and if we don't get rid of it, it'll rob the milo of nutrients just like the cockleburs are robbing the soybeans.

Dad sizes up the situation and shakes his head. "Hope we aren't too late," he says, and eases the tractor and weed wiper across the shallow ditch into the field.

Once he opens the tank valve so that the herbicide will drip off the ropes, there isn't much to do except drive slowly up and down the field over and over again, making sure we don't miss anything or overlap the previous strip too much. Grasshoppers fly up in front of us like tiny helicopters trying to escape the enormous, crushing wheels.

After turning to start the fourth pass, Dad takes a thin cigar from his shirt pocket and lights it with a butane lighter, filling my nose with the smell of sweet tobacco. Mom won't let him smoke anywhere near her. I watch the slim brown stick burn all the way down until there's less than an inch left, and I can tell that Dad really enjoys it. He stubs it out on the left fender and tosses it into the field, then winks at me.

I know what he means: This is our little secret.

The afternoon gets to be a "real steamer" the closer we get to the creek, but we've got a three-gallon cooler of iced tea with us. If you tossed back enough iced tea, Dad says, you could march across the Sahara Desert with a full pack and come out the other side ready to put a fence around the whole thing.

I wish I could think up the kind of stuff he can.

I also wish I could be more help. All I'm doing is riding up here beside him, as if that were work. I could run the Allis and weed wiper well enough to do the whole field myself if I had to, leaving Dad free to finish the beans—but with the women in town, we don't have enough people to ride the bean bar. Dad considered hiring some kids for a couple of dollars an hour, but decided that we can't afford it. We'll get it done ourselves, he says, or we won't get it done at all.

We'll make it. We'll wipe every goddamn weed off every goddamn acre, and come fall we'll bring in the best crop we've ever had. Wait and see.

About two o'clock, Dad stops the tractor and stands up, staring off toward the trees, which are about a hundred yards away.

"You see that?" he says, and points.

I climb up to stand on the right fender. I look where he's pointing, and I see a movement in the milo.

"Think it's another coyote?" I ask, and then I see something rise above the green. It looks like a flattened cone made of straw.

I give a yell, but it's already gone. We keep watching for a few minutes, but the only motion in the milo is from a weak puff of west wind.

Dad sits down again and looks at me, his eyes serious. "What did you see?" he asks.

I tell him, and his jaw widens and sticks out the way it does when he's just about mad enough to break something. For a minute I'm afraid that I'm in trouble, but then he says, "Okay, Phillie. You keep an eye out, and if you see anything else, you holler."

He starts the Allis moving again, and I watch carefully, imagining myself as an army scout. The wind picks up a little. About three o'clock I think I see someone in black clothes running beside the trees, but then I decide that it's a shadow caused by the wind moving a bough.

I don't see anything else the rest of the afternoon. Except the grasshoppers.

We have one breakdown, a flat tire on the weed wiper a little after four. The wiper's three tires are the same size as the Allis's front two, though, and Dad keeps a spare bolted behind the seat. We change the flat and keep working for another three hours.

We show up for supper about a quarter to eight, and Mom's upset because she *told* us she'd have the roast ready at seven. Usually, she wouldn't think anything of Dad's being a little late— breakdowns happen, and things almost always take longer than planned, and she knows that. The only thing I can figure is that she's still mad because of their argument over me.

I'd still be wearing a diaper if she had her way.

Patricia is whining that she wants to go "swim-ming" tomorrow, and Jodi won't shut up about the Walls of Jericho, which was her Bible School lesson today. When I ask her to please be quiet, she takes the red plastic trumpet they gave her and blows it in my face. Dad takes it away and tells her that even Joshua wasn't allowed to blow his horn at the table.

Crissy giggles, although I doubt that she understood a word of it, and burbles mashed potatoes down her front. Mom yanks her out of the high chair and drags her to the bathroom by one arm.

The kid starts screaming. I hate it when stuff like that happens at a meal, because then I don't even want to eat anymore.

Dad cleans his plate and gets up from the table.

"Going to wipe some more?" I ask, scooping my corn and potatoes into a pile so I can wolf them down. I figure he'll want to go back to the milo for at least another two hours, working by the bright lights on the Allis.

He puts on his Co-Op hat and shrugs. "I'd better fix that tire first. I won't have time in the morning, and we might need a spare before the day's out. You go ahead and finish your supper, then take care of the calves. Patricia, you can give him a hand."

"You got it," I say.

"Oh, Dad-dee," Patricia whines. "I told Tee-na I'd call her after sup-per."

Dad heads for the back door. "You can still do that if it's not too late after you help with the calves."

"But Dad-deee—"

Dad turns around and comes back to the table. He grabs Patricia by the shoulders and shakes her.

"Not . . . one . . . more . . . God . . . damn . . . word," he says. It scares me a little even though I'm not the one he's mad at.

You better believe Patricia shuts up. If Mom would only crack down on her like that, the brat might actually turn into a decent human being.

Dad goes out to fix the tire, and Jodi sings, "Patti got in trouble, Patti got in trou-ble—"

Patricia hits her on the head, and Jodi shrieks.

"Behave out there or you'll wish you had!" Mom yells from the bathroom.

Patricia gets up from her chair, goes behind Jodi, and clamps her left hand over the younger brat's mouth while using her right hand to yank on Jodi's ponytail.

"Stop it," I tell Patricia.

She sneers at me. I get up, go around the table, and pull her hand away from Jodi's mouth. Jodi bellows for Mom.

"That's enough!" Mom yells from the bathroom.

Patricia swings at me, but I block it with my left arm. She's almost two inches taller than me, but I'm older and she's just a girl. If she keeps trying to fight, I'll pound her into the floor.

"I hate you!" she whispers. "I hate you, you little Phillie-baby!"

I walk away from her and get my Co-Op hat from its nail. "Let's feed the calves," I say.

"You're not the boss of me," Patricia says. "You're not the boss of *any*thing!"

I give her the look I've practiced in my mirror, Dad's don't-mess-with-me-now look.

"I'm going to feed the calves," I say. "You can help like Dad said or you can get your butt spanked." And then I head out the door.

She comes out to the barn after I've already filled two buckets with grain. She gives me a dirty look, but then she picks up one of the buckets and lugs it out toward the pen. She looks bowlegged and funny, and I laugh at her.

After taking care of the calves, I find Dad in the east shop. The sun is going down, so he has the lights on inside.

The weed wiper's tire is one of the old kind, with a tube, and Dad already has it taken apart. He's holding the tube in a rusty fifty-five-gallon barrel half-full of water, and when I come close I see several streams of bubbles breaking at the water's surface as fast as machine-gun fire. A section of the tube as big as one of Dad's hands is riddled with holes.

"What the heck could've done that?" I ask.

Dad doesn't answer me, or even look at me. His eyes are fixed on the froth of exploding bubbles.

"I mean," I say, feeling nervous, "could it've been a knot of barbed wire?"

Dad lets go of the tube, and it pops to the surface, hissing. Then he turns away and goes to his cluttered workbench, water dripping from his fingers to form a dotted trail on the concrete floor.

"Can you patch it?" I ask.

He wipes his hands on a dirty red shop rag and then takes an old, torn inner tube from one of the hooks above the workbench. He tosses it toward me, and it lands at my feet.

"We'll give it a try," he says. "Cut a patch big enough to cover those holes, plus about a half inch extra on every side."

I take out my birthday knife, open the second-biggest blade, and sit down on the floor to get to work. While I'm cutting, Dad takes the punctured tube from the water and dries it.

By the time I bring the patch to the workbench, Dad's buffed the rubber around the holes and is brushing on the cement. He takes the patch from me, nods—meaning that I did a good job—and presses it down over the holes with the heel of his right hand. Then he takes two small pieces of scrap lumber, puts one over the patch and the other on the other side of the tube, and clamps the whole mess in the vise on the end of the bench.

"That ought to do it," I say.

Dad looks at his watch and says, "Twenty to ten, Phillie-boy. Better take your bath and read your Bible verses before your mama comes out and hauls you in by the left ear."

I shuffle backward toward the shop doorway. "You gonna go back out to the milo?" I ask.

Dad is standing by the barrel and looking down at the water, even though there's nothing in it now.

"No," he says, his voice real quiet. "No, I've got some shop work."

"What?" I ask, because I can't think of anything besides the tire.

He looks up from the barrel and frowns at me. "Didn't I tell you to get to the house?" he says, and this time his tone of voice says I'd better hurry.

After my bath, I sit in my pajamas in the living room, and Jodi reads tonight's verses. She has to raise her voice because the box fan is roaring in the doorway, trying to dilute the heat the house has built up over the day.

The verses Mom has Jodi read are the ones about the woman named Rahab who helped the Israelite spies escape from Jericho, and I guess the point must be that if you do a good deed, you'll be rewarded. The spies promised Rahab that the Israelites would spare her and her family if she kept the scarlet escape cord in the window as a sign, and she followed their instructions. That turned out to be the smart thing to do, because everybody else in the city was slain "with the edge of the sword."

I glance at Mom when the story is almost over. She's looking at the dark picture window instead of at Jodi, which is strange. Usually she's real attentive when we're reading Scripture, so as to correct our pronunciation. When Patricia asks a question about why the Israelites wanted to attack the city in the first place, Mom says something about Communism, then tells us that we've read enough for tonight and had better go to bed.

I use my flashlight to read comics under the covers until my eyes itch, and then I lie awake and listen to night sounds. Frogs are chirruping somewhere close.

After a while, I hear a buzz-buzz-buzzing that isn't like the sound insects make, so I sit up and pull back the curtains from my window. If I peer between two branches of the cedar tree, I can see the east shop from here. Yellow light spills from the shop's doorway into the barnyard, and as I watch, white flashes wash out the yellow for a split second at a time.

Dad is arc-welding something. I lie back and wonder what it could be.

Something to make work more efficient, I'll bet. He's good at stuff like that.

Tuesday. There are no gunshots today, so for a long time nothing interrupts the monotony. After a few hours of riding on the bean bar, I feel as if the entire world is made of soybeans, weeds, sunlight, and bugs.

Still, the work seems to go faster than it did yesterday, even though the weeds are just as thick. If all goes well, we should be able to finish spraying the beans by early afternoon, or by midmorning tomorrow at the latest.

Of course, all doesn't go well. Dad likes to quote what he calls Old MacDonald's Corollary to Murphy's Law: "If anything can possibly go wrong, it'll go wrong on a farm." Today, Old Mac-Donald's Corollary attacks us a little after eleven and clogs up a valve on the sprayer's compressor. Dad tries to fix it, but a hose splits when he reclamps it. So it's a job for the shop, and we have to abandon the soybeans until tomorrow.

But Mom has brought along some grocery sacks, so the morning won't be a total loss. By the time my sisters and I have picked enough gooseberries for a couple of pies, she says, she'll have lunch ready.

That sounds great to me, but naturally, Patricia and Jodi start whining.

"Moh-um," Patricia says, "I'm not wearing any bug spray. I'll get bit-ten. And I'll get poison i-vy, toooo."

"Meeee tooooo," Jodi pouts.

"So go home," I say, disgusted. "I can pick enough for five pies all by myself."

Dad stands up from where he's been squatting beside the compressor and wipes his hands on his jeans. "Take the girls on back to the house," he says to Mom. "I can't mess with this piece of junk until tonight anyway, so I'll help Phillie pick berries until lunchtime."

Crissy is bouncing up and down on the tractor seat. "Me pick! Me pick!" she yelps, spit bubbling at the corners of her mouth.

"You're too little," I tell her, and she glares at me and screams.

So Mom and the two older girls walk back to the house, and the three-year-old, who will only be in the way, comes with Dad and me to pick gooseberries. She rides on Dad's shoulders, looking down at me triumphantly and chewing on one of her bonnet's ribbons.

I begin sweating the instant we enter the creek's miniature jungle, and I think back to yesterday, when Dad and I found the hunters. I was sweating then, too, but the three trespassers looked cool and calm, as if they were copperheads in human form.

We find a clump of heavily laden gooseberry bushes surrounding a walnut tree, and I reach in carefully to pluck the marble-sized green fruit while avoiding the prickles. I pop the first berry into my mouth and burst it with my back teeth. The juice that squirts over my tongue is so sour that it makes me shiver.

Dad puts Crissy down beside me, then goes to the other side of the tree to work on a different bush. "Looks like we done struck the mother lode, Phillie-boy," he says as he begins to pick.

Crissy reaches for a cluster of berries and immediately gets stuck by the prickles. She shrieks as if she'd just been bitten by a snake.

Dad comes back around and picks her up, then bounces her in his arms until she stops crying. Once that's accomplished, he puts her down again, spreads his handkerchief on the ground several feet away, and tells her to sit on it. She grins and plunks her rump down, more or less on the handkerchief.

Dad and I pick gooseberries, and he whistles a tune he says is from a movie called *The Bridge on the River Kwai*. I've never seen it, but he says he'll let me stay up the next time it comes on. It sounds like fun.

We pick and pick and pick, until the world becomes gooseberries and thorns in the same way that it became beans and weeds earlier this morning. I eat about every tenth berry, and feel as though I'm at the center of a ball of sourness.

Then Dad's hand is on my shoulder, shaking me back to the trees and the heat.

"Where's your sister?" he asks.

I look at the spot where he left her. The handkerchief is still there, but Crissy is gone.

I open my mouth to yell for her, but Dad tells me to stay quiet and listen.

For several long moments I hear nothing but birds, bugs, frogs, and rustling animals. Then, so faintly that I think I might be imagining it, I hear a faraway baby-giggle. Dad takes off running between the bushes and trees.

I leave my sack of gooseberries and follow him, but I can't keep up. After a few seconds I can only see flashes of his blue cotton shirt among the leaves and shadows. He's heading for the creek.

Sweat stings my eyes, and my chest hurts. I'm afraid of stepping on a copperhead, and I wish Crissy had never been born.

At last, I stumble through a clot of weeds and thistles, scratching my arms and face, and find myself standing on a flat, mossy rock on the bank of Coal Creek. Dad is several feet in front of me at the edge of the water, his boots sunk to the eyelets in mud.

Crissy stands in the center of the shallow creek, dark water halfway up her baby-fat thighs. She's grinning proudly and using both hands to hold a broad, shallow straw cone on her head. Her bonnet is gone.

"Daddy!" she yelps in delight. "See Cwissy's hat!"

Dad stands perfectly still, his arms at his sides. I can't see his face.

"Where did you find that?" he asks in a voice that's almost a whisper. It's only because the air is so still that I can hear him at all.

Crissy dances in the water, splashing.

"Pajama man!" she cries.

It's as if the words break a spell. Dad strides toward her, murky waves rippling out before him, and when he reaches her, he yanks the hat away and throws it. It lands upside down in the water fifteen or twenty feet away.

I expect Crissy to throw a fit, but instead she laughs and claps her hands.

"Boat!" she shouts. "Daddy make a boat!"

The upside-down hat floats lazily downstream. I imagine it going all the way to the Wakarusa River, and from there to the ocean, where it will be eaten by a shark.

Dad grabs Crissy and carries her under his right arm as if she were a bag of grain. When he comes back up the bank with her, I can see his face, and I know it's time to go home.

On our way out to the field, we go by the gooseberry bushes that surround the walnut tree. Dad's sack of berries is gone, and so is mine.

. . .

After Mom and the girls leave and we've got the pipewick ready for more weed-wiping, Dad brings out his Remington twelve-gauge pump shotgun from the "off-limits-to-kids" closet in the upstairs hallway. We take it to the milo field with us.

I feel better now that we're away from the house again. During lunch, Crissy kept babbling about "pajama man" and boats, while Dad just stared at his plateful of casserole. He only ate a couple of bites.

All through the meal, Mom watched him with her face set in the expression that means she wants to talk to him but can't because kids are around. She didn't have a chance after lunch, either, because she had to take the girls to town again. All she had time to do was call out, "Be sure to phone the sheriff if those hunters come back," as she was driving the station wagon down the driveway.

Dad didn't answer her. He was already heading toward the east shop to put the patched tire back together.

Now, as we enter the field and begin wiping where we left off yesterday, Dad tells me to keep a lookout again. If I see anything move anywhere, I'm to shout and point.

So I watch, and it isn't long before I see something about a hundred yards away, just south of the bulge of trees where the creek curves.

This time I know it's no shadow, because a broad, conical hat rises above the milo.

"There!" I yell as loud as I can.

Dad stomps the clutch and takes the tractor out of gear, then stands to look where I'm pointing.

The hat rises a little more, and now I see the head and shoulders of the man wearing it. He's too far away for any features to be clear, but I have the impression that his face is leathery. His shirt is of loose black cloth.

"Do you see him?" I yell. "Do you see him?"

Dad reaches for the Remington, which is beside the toolbox,

but my legs are in his way. By the time I move and he grabs the shotgun, it's too late. The only things visible between here and the bulge of trees are milo stalks, Johnsongrass weeds, and grasshoppers.

"Fucking bastards!" Dad yells, and his voice is so loud that the tractor engine seems quiet in comparison. I've never heard him use that one word before.

His face is flushed so that it's far redder than his usual sunburn, and veins stand out on his forehead and neck. His hands are clutching the shotgun as if he wants to break it in two.

I don't want him to have to feel the way he does. I hate the goddamn fucking trespasser who did this to him.

"You want me to run home and call the sheriff?" I ask. It's the only thing I can think of that might help.

Dad's hands relax a little, and he looks down at me. His face shows his rage, but I know it isn't directed at me.

"You stay right here," he says. "You're my lookout. Hold the gun, and if you see anything else, give it to me."

I know down inside—I *feel* it—that this is the most important thing I've ever had to do.

"You got it," I say, and he gives me the shotgun. It's even heavier than I remember from when he let me shoot it last fall.

I stand on the toolbox and hold the gun. Its stock rests beside my feet on the lid, and its barrel, taller than I am, points at the sky.

Dad puts the tractor in gear again, and we continue killing the weeds that are trying to ruin our crop.

After an hour, we see three more of the men in strange hats and black clothes. Dad spots the first two; I spot the third. They can't be the same person, because they all pop up in different parts of the field within the span of a minute.

Dad fires the Remington at the third even though we're too far away. It seems to do some good, though, because we see no more of them this afternoon.

When we leave the field at seven o'clock, my head is still humming with the vibration of the blast.

As the Allis chugs up the road toward the house, Dad grins at me and pulls the bill of my Co-Op cap down over my eyes. I'm glad he feels better.

"O Lord my God," Patricia reads from the Book of Psalms, "in thee do I put my trust; save me from all them that persecute me, and deliver me . . ."

Patti's trying hard to do a good job, but tonight, again, Mom doesn't have her mind on the reading. Instead, she's staring at the picture window even though there's nothing to see but our reflections. Her fingers are twisting at the hem of her bathrobe as if she's trying to unravel it.

Jodi is sitting in a corner looking unhappy. She's holding Crissy, who is fidgeting and giggling, on her lap.

"Lest he tear my soul like a lion," Patricia continues, "rending it in pieces, while there is none to deliver."

Mom was in a weird mood this evening to begin with, but it got worse when Dad left the supper table without eating a thing.

"Are you sick, Loren?" she asked, and her tone made me want to sink down in my chair.

"Gotta fix the sprayer," Dad said, and went out. I didn't try to go with him, because I hadn't cleaned my plate yet.

Then, when I finally finished my potatoes, Mom told me to go upstairs and straighten my room. As I was going, I heard her tell Patricia and Jodi to do the dishes and look after Crissy.

My room didn't need straightening. I knew that the real reason Mom had given us those jobs was so she could be alone outside with Dad. After a few minutes of rearranging the stuff in my closet, I heard her yelling at him. I had to wait to feed the calves until she was back in the house.

I wish she wouldn't make things so hard.

"O Lord my God," Patricia reads, "if I have done this; if there be in—in—" She looks at Mom.

Mom just keeps on staring at the dark window and twisting the hem of her robe.

I look over Patti's shoulder. "Iniquity," I tell her, pronouncing the word carefully.

Patti looks miserable. Mom told her to read all seventeen verses.

"If there be in-i-qui-ty in my hands," she continues, "if I have rewarded evil unto him that was at peace with me;—yea, I have delivered him that without cause is mine enemy . . ."

There is a clang of metal striking metal outside, from the direction of the east shop, and my muscles jump. Patti's voice falters.

"Pajama man!" Crissy squeals.

"Shhhhhh," Jodi whispers.

Mom doesn't say anything, doesn't move.

"Let the enemy persecute my soul, and take it," Patricia reads. "Yea, let him tread down my life upon the earth, and lay mine honor in the dust."

I think Mom must be the one who's sick. Take tonight's Bible reading—I mean, what does it have to do with anything? Usually she picks a passage about Jesus, or forgiveness, or being grateful, or something like that.

"He made a pit," Patricia reads, sounding confused, "and is fallen into the ditch which he made. . . . His mischief shall return upon his own head, and his violent dealing shall come down upon his own pate."

Crissy giggles. I don't think she understands any of this. I don't think I do, either.

The last verse, at least, is a little more like what I'm used to: "I will praise the Lord according to his righteousness, and will sing praise to the name of the Lord most high."

We all say, "Amen."

"Very nice, Patricia," Mom says without looking at her, or at any of us. "You children run along to bed, now, and don't forget your prayers."

In my room, I kneel and pray for God to make Mom feel better. As I finish, I hear the buzz-buzz-buzzing like I did last night, and I look out to see the white flashes.

I was in the east shop after lunch today, but whatever Dad's been welding was covered with a tarp. Maybe, instead of something for the farm, he's making a surprise, like when he made the swing set out of three-inch pipe.

Maybe this time it's a present for Mom, a planter or something. That'd cheer her up, I'll bet.

"Pajama man!" I hear Crissy squeal down the hall.

I'll be glad when she's old enough to know what she's talking about. Then she can let the rest of us in on it.

Wednesday. At breakfast the radio predicted rain for tonight, but the morning is clear and dry. We should be able to finish spraying the bean field today, provided everybody does what they're supposed to. I don't know about Mom, though; she might be too upset to pay attention to the work. I wish there had been some way for Dad to bring the shotgun along without her seeing it. She keeps looking back at it like it's a snake.

Well, like Dad says, we can't very well call the sheriff and ask for a deputy to guard our fields for us. It's our responsibility. So I'm going to keep as sharp an eye out as I can, while still blasting the goddamn weeds.

As we move down the rows of beans, the poison spraying from our wands like transparent fans, I can almost see the cockleburs dying. They're sneaky bastards, and they think they can get away with what they're doing by hugging the ground and hiding up against the stems of the bean plants, but we'll teach them better.

I hear Dad shout, and I turn my head to see where he's pointing.

A black-clad, cone-hatted illiterate fool has popped up about twenty rows away. He's so close that I see his rotten-toothed grin before he drops flat again.

Dad stops the Deere, and both Patricia and Jodi fall off their seats.

"Loren!" Mom shrieks. "Dear God, what—"

Dad has brought the shotgun up to his shoulder.

"Did you see where the fucker went, Phillie?" he yells.

113

"Straight down!"

Dad fires a blast at the spot where the fucker dropped, and a couple of soybean plants are shredded. Bits of torn leaves explode upward.

"Loren, *stop it!*" Mom cries. "You're going to hit one of the children!"

But even as she yells, I see another fucker stand up, closer to the trees. This one is holding a rifle.

"Dad!" I scream, and point.

Dad turns and fires again, but the figure has already vanished.

Mom jumps off her bean-bar seat and runs back to the tractor. She grabs Crissy, who is laughing, and yells at the rest of us kids.

"Philip! Jodi! Patricia! Come quick, we're going home!" Her eyes look wild.

Jodi and Patti go to her, but they move slowly and shakily.

Dad lowers the Remington and squints off toward where the second fucker popped up. "It's all right, Kath. They're gone for now."

Mom grabs Jodi's arm with her free hand and glares up at Dad. "There was *nothing there,* Loren!"

Dad stares at her. "Are you blind? There were two of them, right over—"

"Patricia, Jodi!" Mom says sharply. "Did you see anyone?"

Jodi says, "No," and Patricia shakes her head.

My face feels hot. "Then they're blind, too," I say, not caring that I'm sassing Mom.

Mom looks at me, and her expression is one I've never seen before. The only way I can describe it is as love and fear mixed together. I don't like it.

"Philip," she says, her voice quavering, "you're coming home with me this instant."

Dad lays down the shotgun beside the tractor seat. "We've still got beans to spray," he says.

"Philip," Mom says, ignoring Dad, "you get down from that bar and come home *now.*"

I don't know what to do for a few seconds, but then I see how unhappy Dad looks. That makes up my mind.

"I can't, Mom," I say. "We've still got beans to spray."

"Philip, you—," Mom begins, but Dad interrupts her.

"You heard the boy," he says.

Mom stands there for a moment, her face puffy and splotched with pink, and then she and the girls walk off across the field.

We watch them until they're on the road. Then Dad sits down on the tractor seat again.

"Women have no eyes," he says.

I raise my spray wand. "Can we do it with just one stream?"

Dad shrugs his shoulders. "We'll do the best we can. We can't do any more."

So we start up again, spraying one row at a time. We see the trespassers five more times, but they stay near the trees, out of shotgun range. Dad fires into the air a couple of times to scare them.

I can't tell whether it does or not.

We finish the field and go to the house for lunch at two o'clock. No one else is home, so we make bologna and cheese sandwiches. Fifteen minutes later, we're taking the Allis and pipewick to the milo, once again carrying the shotgun beside the toolbox.

This is the hottest afternoon we've had this week, but there's more wind, so our sweat evaporates fast and keeps us cool. We work for over four hours and don't see any trespassers, so we begin to think that we've finally run them off.

Then we hear two popping noises over the rumble of the tractor. Dad takes the Allis out of gear, idles down the engine, and looks back.

"God fucking damn," he says softly.

Two of the weed wiper's three tires have burst.

We jump down to investigate, and Dad's Co-Op hat is blown off by a gust. It sails thirty or forty feet, so I run after it while Dad goes back to take a look at the flat tires.

I'm plunging through the milo, planning to yank up the stalk of Johnsongrass that's snagged Dad's hat, when a sharp pain burns up along the outside of my right ankle.

Simultaneously, I hear Dad yell, "Phillie! Stay still!"

But my shoe is caught, and I fall, smashing some milo. My ankle twists.

Dad's here instantly, picking me up.

"I should've known," he says. "God damn it, I should've known."

I look down and see a tight group of at least twenty barbed nails sticking up out of the ground. I've never seen nails quite like them before.

One of the outside nails has stabbed into the edge of my right shoe's sole. Dad borrows my pocketknife and cuts the side of the shoe so I can get my foot out.

A barb has opened a two-inch cut just in front of my heel. It's bleeding, but I can see that it's not bad. My ankle doesn't even hurt much from having twisted.

"Lucky grunt," Dad says.

He scrapes dirt away from the cluster of nails, and I see that they're set into a small piece of board, which in turn is set into a buried chunk of cement. If my foot had landed squarely on the nails so that the barbs had dug in, my momentum would have ripped the bottom of my foot off.

Dad carries me back to the Allis, examining the ground before each step. As we come close to the tractor, I look behind the weed wiper and see the glint of more nails.

Once we're finally there, Dad climbs up and sets me down on the toolbox. Still standing, he turns to face the trees along Coal Creek.

"All right, Charlie!" he cries. "You fucked with the wrong boy this time!"

Then he sits down, throttles up the Allis, and turns us toward the gate. As we pull out onto the road, I look back and see the weed wiper wobbling behind us, limping on its flat tires.

. . .

Mom is sitting in the kitchen, obviously ready for some kind of showdown. But before she has a chance to say anything, she sees the blood on my shoeless right foot and hustles me into the bathroom, where she makes me sit on the edge of the tub. I hear the kitchen door open and close, which means that Dad's gone back outside.

Mom splashes alcohol onto the cut, and I have to grit my teeth so I don't cry. The sting goes all the way up into my chest.

When it subsides a little, I ask where the girls are. It's hard to keep my voice steady.

Mom begins to clean the wound with a cotton ball. "In town with your aunt Sue," she says.

"Why?"

She throws the cotton ball into the can under the sink and uncaps a bottle of Mercurochrome. "Because."

"That's no answer, Mom," I say, not caring how it sounds.

She tries to give me her don't-back-talk-me look, but she can't hold it. Instead she looks at my ankle and dabs red stuff onto the cut.

"Your father needs help," she says.

The way she says it, like she feels sorry for him, makes me madder than I've ever been.

"I'm all the help he needs," I say. "You just haven't figured it out yet."

Now she looks at me like she feels sorry for *me*, too. "No, honey," she says. "*You* haven't figured it out yet. You're too little."

I stand up. "Are you finished?"

"Yes, honey. Does it sting much?"

"I don't feel a thing," I say, and it's not really a lie, because I'm so mad I can't think of anything else. I head for the bathroom door, planning to get my second-oldest pair of tennies and go back outside.

"You're to stay in your room tonight, Philip," Mom says. "I'll bring you a sandwich in a little bit."

I stop in the bathroom doorway. My impulse is to argue, but I know how much good that'll do. So instead I say, "Yes, ma'am," without looking back, and go on to my room.

Once there, I close the door and put on my tennies and camouflage jacket. Then I pull back the window curtains and peer between the cedar branches toward the east shop.

The Allis is parked just to the west of the building, its front-loader scoop lowered to the ground. The sun is low in the sky, beneath the clouds that are moving in from the south, and the tractor's orange paint glows with the same intensity as the sinking star. The Remington is still in its place beside the toolbox.

As I watch, Mom leaves the house and goes across the barnyard toward the shop. Before she gets there, Dad comes out, pushing a barrel that's sitting in a framework of two-inch angle iron. The barrel is the same one he used the other night to check the leaky inner tube. It blocks my view of the bottom of the framework, so I can't see the wheels that must be there.

Mom is saying something, but even though my window's open I can't make out her words. Dad ignores her and pushes the barrel over to the gasoline and diesel tanks, where he unhooks the gas tank's nozzle and begins pumping fuel. The barrel must be nearly full by the time he stops.

Then, with Mom still talking—maybe crying a little, too—Dad walks back into the shop and emerges again with a barrel lid and a hammer. Once he has the lid pounded down tight, he pushes the barrel-and-framework contraption into the front-loader scoop. Full of gas, the barrel must weigh hundreds of pounds, but Dad moves it like it was no big deal.

Mom screams now, and I hear every word: "For Christ's sake, Loren, *stop!*"

Dad wipes his hands on his jeans and climbs up to the tractor seat. He starts the engine, and the loader rises, lifting the barrel and framework off the ground.

Mom has her face in her hands. I feel embarrassed for her.

Dad puts the Allis into gear, and it rumbles out of the barnyard and down the driveway.

I wait until Mom has come back into the house, and then I take the screen off my window.

Creeping across the sloping kitchen roof is the hard part, because I have to be super quiet. But then I only have to jump a few inches to grab a cedar limb, and from there it's a piece of cake to climb down to the ground.

There's just enough daylight left for me to see the Allis down the road, turning into the bean field. I don't know what Dad's working on tonight, but I'm going to help.

I run down the driveway, bending low in case Mom happens to glance out a window.

By the time I've run across the bean field to where the silent Allis sits, the clouds have moved in and I can hardly see where I'm going. The trees of Coal Creek are a black mass in front of me. Night insects are whirring and clicking so loudly that I can't hear my own footsteps. I feel light-headed, worn out.

Dad isn't here.

The front-loader scoop is down, and empty. As I walk around it, I nearly trip over a shallow trough in the soft earth. Dad must have had to drag the barrel from here, so all I have to do is follow the track.

Once I get a few yards into the trees, though, I have trouble. It's so dark that I'm practically blind, and the ground is harder. I can't find any more drag marks.

But I've got my breath back, so I yell. I get no answer, but Dad has to be in here somewhere.

Something flaps away from the upper branches of the nearest tree, and it startles me. Then, as I'm gathering breath to shout again, I smell something horrible. The stench is just like the one at the low-water bridge two days ago, only stronger, closer.

It chokes me, and I have to let out my breath without yelling. I have the feeling deep in my throat that means I'm about to throw up.

A shrimpy twelve-year-old is little enough use without being sick, too.

So I clench my teeth and force the feeling away, then breathe in deep to try to yell again.

A callused hand clamps over my mouth, but I'm not scared, because I recognize the mingled smells of oil, herbicide, and soap.

"Quiet, God damn it," Dad whispers, so softly that I can barely hear him. "Dead quiet, understand?"

I nod, and he takes his hand away from my mouth. I turn to face him, but all I can see is a dark man-shape. I can just make out something across his chest that must be the shotgun.

He squats so that his head is at the same height as mine. "Is your mother here?" he asks in the same super-quiet voice.

I shake my head, but I'm not sure he can see it, so I whisper, "She'd be yelling for me if she were."

He's silent for a few moments—listening, I think—and then says, "I'll carry you." He turns, and I get on him piggyback.

Even though the insects become strangely quiet and the brush gets thicker the farther we go, I can hardly hear his footsteps. The sound of my own breathing is much louder.

We come out onto a cow path, and the stink of the dead thing is worse than ever.

My night vision has improved, but only a little. That's all right with me, because I don't really want to see whatever has died here.

We follow the path for several yards, then cut left and climb a slight rise. As we enter a clump of brush—probably gooseberry bushes—I hear the plop of a frog jumping into the creek.

There's a bare patch of ground at the center of the clump, and Dad stops here, squatting again so I can slide off his back. My tennies crunch dry sticks, and I shudder, afraid of making too much noise.

Dad puts his mouth close to my ear and whispers, "Sit down and be still." Then he's out of the bushes with hardly a rustle.

I do what he says, and I even hold my breath to be quieter. Then I hear a drumlike sound, and I know that Dad has taken the lid off the barrel. A few seconds later, he's back, and I start breathing again.

He lays the shotgun on the ground, then squats in front of me so close that I can see his eyes despite the darkness. He whispers even more softly than before.

"Keep your fingers on this," he says, and guides my left hand behind me to what feels like a strand of monofilament fishing string about three inches off the ground. It's been here all along, tied to the base of one of the bushes, and I didn't even know it.

"What's it for?" I whisper.

Dad starts to chuckle, then stops. "To give ol' Charlie a surprise. When you feel it go tight and then slack, like a one-two punch, you slap me on the arm. All right?"

"You got it," I whisper.

He takes his handkerchief from his back pocket, then reaches under a bush and pulls out what looks like a ketchup bottle. When he unscrews the cap, the smell of gasoline overpowers the dead-animal stink.

He stuffs the handkerchief into the bottleneck.

"What's that for?" I ask.

He grasps my neck with his free hand and squeezes, not quite hard enough to hurt. "Hush. Supply fucked up, so we don't have the mix or igniter. We're improvising." He lets go of my neck, reaches into his shirt pocket, and brings out his butane lighter. "If the trip wire screws up, I'll slap *you*, and you yank on the line. But if one of ours comes through, I'll tell you to cut it. Have your knife ready."

I start to say, "You got it," but make myself stay quiet instead. I don't want to fuck up.

Still squatting, Dad turns to face the cow path. He holds the bottle in his right hand, the lighter in his left. The Remington is beside him on the ground.

I get onto my knees as quietly as I can. The fingertips of my left hand are touching the monofilament line, and my right hand reaches into my back pocket for my knife.

One-handed, I open the biggest blade. Then Dad and I wait.

Chiggers are eating me alive, and I'm afraid of copperheads, but I don't move. I don't even flinch.

I won't let Dad down.

When it happens, I've been here so long that I think I must be asleep and dreaming. I hear soft, weird chattering down on the cow path, and then the fishing line jerks taut against my fingers.

Almost immediately, it goes slack and drops. I hear a loud clang and a whooshing sound. My left hand reaches up to slap Dad on the arm, but hits his leg.

He's standing, and the handkerchief in the bottle blazes with fire. It lights his face and gleams in his eyes.

Then he throws, and the flame tumbles over the bushes and down to the path.

As it flies, I think I hear Mom calling me from far away.

A brilliant yellow-and-orange wall leaps up from the path, and my eyes close from the sudden pain of the light. The insides of my eyelids are red, red, red, with dancing bluish purple flames tumbling across them.

A tremendous roar follows, washing over the distant sound of Mom's voice. I feel as if I've been thrust into the nozzle of an acetylene torch.

"Wienie roast!" Dad shouts. "Gonna have a wieeeeeee-nieeeeee roast!"

I open my eyes and see him leap out through the burning bushes like a ghost. He holds the Remington thrust out in front of him, and he's pumping and firing, pumping and firing, pumping and firing. The blasts are tiny pops punctuating the roar of the world.

The air is full of jumping light.

I look down. My pocketknife has snapped closed over the soft skin between my thumb and forefinger. Blood oozes out over the mother-of-pearl.

Now that I see it, I feel the pain, and it brings me to my feet. The heat of the fire beats at my face, and I start to run through the bushes.

Before I'm free of them, I drop my knife. I stop and get down on my hands and knees to search for it.

"Cook 'em up *hot!*" Dad yells. "Throw 'em in yellow, take 'em out *red!*"

I've lost my knife.

Wanting to cry, I stand and stumble through the crisping weeds. I have to get to Dad.

I find him on the cow path, flaming trees all around. He's reloading.

The fifty-five-gallon barrel is lying on its side not far away, still held at the bottom end by the framework Dad made. The barrel is on fire, the rusty old gray paint hissing and crackling.

I run to Dad, who is raising the Remington to his shoulder again, aiming down the path toward the bean field.

Twenty yards from us, a burning figure is running away. Another comes from the trees to join it, and then another, and another, and they meld together into a single mass of fire.

Dad shoots.

The mass flares, and is gone.

Dad fires the shotgun four more times, then lowers it. His face is dotted with beads of sweat, and they reflect the hundred fires a thousand times. He turns to look down at me, and grins.

His left arm is on fire.

I grab his right wrist. He drops the Remington, but no matter how hard I pull, he just stands and smiles at me.

I feel heat on my legs, and look down to see that my jeans are burning.

Before I can think of what to do, the air is rushing past so quickly that I almost feel cool. And then I'm in Coal Creek, in the mud, and Dad is rolling me onto my side. My face goes under, and I come up coughing.

"You're gonna be okay, Phillie-boy!" Dad shouts.

As I come to a sitting position and look up again, I see that his entire shirt is on fire.

I grab him around his legs, trying to pull him down, but I'm too small. I'm too goddamn fucking small.

Dad looks proud and happy.

Thursday. Mom won't leave the hospital, so Aunt Sue volunteers to take care of us kids. That's fine, but I refuse to stay at her house.

She tries to soothe, then argue, and then force me, but I won't listen. Every time she leaves me alone for a moment, I go out the front door and begin walking the twenty-seven miles home. My legs sting, but I don't care.

Eventually, Aunt Sue gives up and takes us where we belong. On the way, she stops at the hospital to tell Mom, who is in a waiting room I can go into.

Mom nods to us, but doesn't say anything.

She wasn't burned, even though she ran into the center of the fire to find us, but she's still in shock. I'm not mad at her anymore, because she was the one who finally pulled Dad into the water, whether she knew what she was doing or not.

"We men," Dad said to me as Mom and I helped him into the front-loader scoop, "we *know* what to do."

It was then, just as I began to feel that everything would be all right, that Mom started crying. I had to push her to make her get into the scoop with him.

Then I drove us home and called the ambulance.

Home. Aunt Sue is bustling about with lunch like a mother hen. She's the take-charge sort, or thinks she is, but with Dad in the hospital, I'm the man of the family. He said so, and nobody can change it.

After lunch, I put on my camouflage jacket and Co-Op hat and go outside.

I fill the Allis's fuel tank, then back the tractor into the east shop and hitch up the chisel plow. It takes a long time, because I can't manhandle the hitch like Dad can, but I finally manage. While I'm connecting the hydraulic hoses, Aunt Sue comes out and asks me what I think I'm doing.

I tell her what I *know* I'm doing, and if she doesn't like it, she can go back to Topeka.

Patti, Jodi, and Crissy are standing in the barnyard as I'm driving out. They look sad, so I smile and wave. I keep telling them that Dad's going to be okay and that I'll take care of them until he is, but they're still scared and worried.

When I get to the bean field, which is damp from the rain that came too late, I drive the tractor to the far edge and put it into neutral. Then I dismount and walk into the midst of the blackened trees.

It's a lot brighter in here now than it was with all those leaves and bushes, so I don't have much trouble finding my knife. It's dirty and a little warped, but it's still a damn good knife.

On the way back out, I pat the barrel to hear the booming sound, and my hand comes away smeared with orange-brown and black. All I need is some green to make camouflage paint.

Once I'm in the field again, I don't waste any time. I climb up onto the Allis, lower the chisels, and get to work.

After ten minutes, I see something ahead on the ground and stop the tractor to investigate.

I climb down and stare at the thing for a long time. Despite the smell, I don't feel sick. I kick what's left of the hat, and it crumbles.

Then I take out my knife, bend down, and cut a long strip of scorched black cloth.

As I return to the Allis, I tie the cloth around my Co-Op cap so that the loose ends will blow out behind me. If Charlie comes back, he'll see it, and he'll know what it means.

I settle into my seat, crank up the throttle, and plow the rest under with the burned crop.

Captain Coyote's Last Hunt

Introduction to

"Captain Coyote's Last Hunt"

Sometimes readers write to fiction magazines to comment on the stories, and sometimes the magazines forward those letters to the stories' authors. I've received a few such letters, and it's always a tremendous surprise. It's unexpected proof that something I made up and put down on paper actually affected a real live human brain out there. It's evidence of unseen worlds. It's like being handed the horn of a unicorn.

Occasionally, though, a magazine will refrain from forwarding a letter if the letter writer is, shall we say, less than pleased with the story in question. This is an act of kindness on the part of the magazine staff. After all, who needs bad news when it's too late to do anything about it? Who needs to know that the unseen worlds think of you as an ugly asteroid? Who needs a unicorn horn stuck between your ribs?

But once in a while the author finds out about such letters anyway.

There was no mass protest when "Captain Coyote's Last Hunt" was first published, but I did learn that there was at least one letter of outrage. I never saw it, but I was told that the letter writer was angry because he or she believed the story promoted and/or condoned cruelty toward animals.

Now, I try not to dismiss any criticism out of hand. The reader's response is paramount. And if a reader doesn't "get" a particular story, it's possible that it might be my fault.

But in this case—

No, God damn it. No, no, no, no, *no.*

And while I'm at it, I'd like to point out that:

Pulp Fiction does not promote or condone heroin addiction and gangsterism.

The Collector does not promote or condone kidnapping women to make them fall in love with you.

Romeo and Juliet does not promote or condone teen sex and suicide.

Brittle Innings does not promote or condone ripping out a base runner's tongue if he spikes your shortstop.

And the Holy Bible does not promote or condone nailing itinerant preachers to oversized T-squares. (Okay, maybe just one . . .)

Do I make myself clear?

Do you *get* it?

Captain Coyote's Last Hunt

On the night before a hunt, I would lie awake and listen to them. Even in the oven-hot bedroom, I shivered. Their quavering howls and yips echoed so that it became impossible to guess whether there were two or two hundred of them. They had come close to our houses to dare us.

And so, in the morning, we went after them.

Sometimes when the greyhounds had almost overtaken a coyote, it stopped running. Just stopped, like that. The lead dog, usually Widower, whizzed past and crashed, his legs windmilling, throwing grass and dirt. The other dogs became a tangle. During that moment of chaos, the coyote took off again.

One time, though, it didn't take off, but stood there with its tongue hanging out, laughing at the sight of Widower flailing to a halt. "Don't *you* look stupid!"

But Widower never looked stupid for long, because when he and the other dogs caught a coyote, they ripped it to pieces. Most times they stayed on it until it died, but once in a while they lost interest when it quit struggling. Then the Captain got out of the truck. If the animal was still conscious, he put a few rounds into its belly before the head shot. Sometimes he let me do it.

A hunt on open prairie always ended with a coyote mangled and dead.

Always, except once.

*

I became the apprentice of Captain Coyote after he dropped out of El Dorado High. This was several months before his mother kicked him off her property, so he had neither a job nor a reason to get one. Nor, at sixteen, did he have a chance of being drafted yet. What he did have was a .22 caliber pistol, a '61 Chevy pickup, and eleven greyhounds.

I was fourteen. My dad worked as an oil rigger, but not often. My mom would have gotten a job to fill the gaps, but she was already overworked at home. I had two brothers, both younger, both brats. We lived seven miles northeast of El Dorado, Kansas, in a house that was sixty years old and falling apart. Living there in the summer meant eating dust.

My dad had always been strict, but he really started getting after me that summer. He was home most of the time, and if I was home too, I was in trouble. Sometimes he'd knock me around.

So I spent a lot of time with Captain Coyote.

The Captain lived three miles north of us, on the edge of the treeless Flint Hills. Thousands of rolling acres spread out to the north, east, and west, broken only by flash-flood gullies and infrequent barbed wire. That summer, those acres were brown.

The Captain's mother and five of his cousins lived in a house that was even more of a shack than my family's was. When I went to the place, though, my first thought was never that the house was junk. My first thought was *dogshit*. If I stayed more than twenty minutes, my hair and clothes would smell like the stuff all day.

The Captain himself lived in a fourteen-foot aluminum trailer behind his mother's house. Beyond that were the dog pens. Ten of the greyhounds stayed in the biggest pen, and the meanest male,

Widower, stayed in a smaller one. The third and smallest pen was reserved for any bitch ready to whelp, but the Captain hadn't needed to use it since spring. The dirt in each pen was packed hard as a sidewalk. Even when the dogs were quiet, the hum of flies was constant.

I arrived for our twelfth hunt on a Friday morning in August. The previous hunt hadn't turned up any coyotes, so the Captain had decided that today we would go farther into the hills than ever before. If we were challenged by a rancher, we would pretend that we each thought the other had taken care of getting permission.

The Captain appeared in the doorway of his trailer as I steered my bike around the chuckholes beside his mother's house. He stood under his baling-wire string of coyote ears and eyed me. "You're late, punk," he said, tugging his shirt over his gut. "Thought you said you'd make it before sunup." The morning was already so bright and hot that the dogshit stank like it was cooking.

I hopped off the bike and let it fall. "Sorry, Captain. My old man's on the warpath. Had to wait until he got pissed at somebody else before I could cut out."

The Captain grunted. "You ever want to borrow my gun to kill that son of a bitch, you let me know." He squinted up at the sun. "I damn near took off without you." But his eyes were crusty, and his strawlike hair was smashed flat on the right side and sticking up on the left. He was wearing greasy jeans, a gray muscle shirt, and dirt brown boots, but that didn't mean anything because he slept in his clothes.

"Glad you waited," I said.

He grunted again and started for his pickup, which was parked beside the dog pens. I followed. When the greyhounds saw us coming, they went nuts. They were always eager to cram into the boxes, because it meant they would get to kill something. The Captain unbolted the chicken-wire door that covered the four boxes on the left side of the truck bed, and I unbolted the one on

133

the right. The doors were hinged on the bottom, so when they fell open, they made the pickup look as if it had stubby wings growing out of the bed walls.

The Captain got his rubber billy club from the cab and went to the pen where Widower waited. Widower stood almost waist-high to the Captain, and his shoulder and haunch muscles were like boulders under a coat the color of a storm cloud. His name had once been Ralph, but the Captain had changed it after Ralph killed the first bitch he mated with.

Widower rose on his hind legs and clamped his jaws onto the club when the Captain put it over the gate. Then the Captain brought him to the truck, where the dog let go of the club and leaped up into the first box on the left, smacking his head on the back wall. He turned to face outward and hunkered down, drooling. The Captain told me to load up seven more, my choice, while he stayed ready to use the club if Widower decided to attack any of them.

I grabbed the three choke chains from the cab and went to the big pen. The first dog to put his front paws on the gate was my favorite, a brindle male named Hacksaw. I let him out so he could run to the truck on his own, and then I chained the next three. They almost yanked my arms out of their sockets as they pulled me to the pickup. Hacksaw was waiting beside the right rear tire, so I helped him up first. When I'd boosted the others as well, I took off their chains and bolted the door. The four dogs grinned out at me, their eyes bright, their tongues dripping.

"Get a move on, punk," Captain Coyote called from the other side. "Widower wants meat."

I ran back to the pen, chained up three more, and then had to chase down a fourth that slipped out. Two of the Captain's snot-nosed cousins appeared as the dog escaped, and they did all they could to get in my way. It took me ten minutes to get the stray back into the pen and bring the others to the left side of the truck.

"Pretty dumb-ass thing to do," the Captain said. I got the dogs loaded as fast as I could while he smacked Widower to keep him from lunging out at them. The two cousins stood back by the trailer and made faces at me.

When the left door was bolted, the Captain told me to attach the release cables while he went into his mother's house. He returned with a loaf of bread, a package of bologna, and a twelve-pack. The cousins became big-eyed, and they ran into the house. The Captain and I got inside the pickup and headed out. As the truck bounced down the driveway, I looked back and saw the Captain's mother, dressed in a pink ribbed robe, standing on her porch. She was yelling. The Captain had taken her food and beer without asking. A couple of the dogs barked at her, and then we were on the road, leaving billows of brown dirt behind us.

At midday, among scorched hills far north of home, Captain Coyote let the truck crawl beside a gully that lay to our left. He was drinking a beer, but his eyes were intent on the brush at the bottom of the gully. His little revolver waited on the seat between us. I was eating a sandwich and trying to watch the gully as intently as he was. Behind us, the dogs were whining. I thought they must be thirsty, but I knew better than to say so.

"There," the Captain said, dropping his beer and taking up the pistol. As he stopped the pickup, the dogs shifted, rocking us. A few of them yipped.

I peered past the Captain. On the far wall of the gully was a clump of brush with an extra shadow that might have been a den. I never would have spotted it on my own.

The Captain aimed his pistol and fired two shots while he honked the truck horn and yelled. I yelled too, and the dogs went berserk. Two puffs of dust flew from the brush, and then, as if coalescing from that dust, two yellow-brown streaks shot out. They bounded up the wall and dashed into the prairie.

"God damn, *two!*" the Captain yelled. He dropped his gun and yanked on the cable looped around his outside mirror. The left bolt came free with a ping, the chicken-wire door fell, and four greyhounds leaped into the gully. Two of them tumbled as they hit the bottom, but they were up in an instant and racing after the others. Widower, in the lead, was thirty yards into the grass before the fourth dog was out of the gully.

I knotted a fist around the cable on my right. "Want me to cut the others loose? Since there's two?"

The Captain popped the clutch. "Don't touch it until I say!" He drove a few hundred yards to a shallow part of the gully, and we bounced across, almost high-centering on the far side. The dogs in back yelped.

Once past the gully, the Captain drove over the prairie at bone-rattling speed. My beer foamed into my lap. The truck was vibrating so much that I couldn't even see the running greyhounds until we almost hit the dog bringing up the rear. The coyotes were still ahead of the chase, but Widower was closing the gap with every stride.

"Chomp their asses, Widower!" the Captain cried.

The second coyote was trailing the first by a dozen yards, and Widower caught it as the Captain yelled. Widower's favorite takedown was to come up alongside and lock his jaws on a coyote's neck, but this one kept zigzagging, so he clamped onto its tail instead. The coyote pulled away, leaving him with a mouthful of fur and skin, but he had slowed it enough for the other dogs to catch up. The coyote kicked and snapped, but they piled on and forced it down.

When the Captain stopped beside them, the air already smelled of sour fur and blood. The dogs in the truck were wild with frustration. I looked back and saw them biting the chicken wire. Hacksaw, especially, was hurting himself, and I wished I could let him out. On the ground, one dog was tearing at the coyote's throat, and two were ripping into its side and belly. It was screaming the way that only a coyote can scream.

Widower stood apart. He still had a mouthful of fur, but he seemed unaware of it. He was staring northward, his muscles rigid, his ears pricked.

The first coyote stood atop a hill an eighth of a mile away. It watched as its companion was killed.

"They're okay," the Captain said, nodding at the bloody-muzzled dogs on the ground. "Let's get the other son of a bitch."

When the pickup started moving again, Widower sprinted ahead. He didn't care about the coyote that was already dying. He wanted the one that was still free, and he wanted it before the Captain had me release the rest of the dogs.

The coyote on the hill remained motionless, waiting, as we came within a hundred yards.

"Why don't he run?" I asked.

The Captain didn't answer, but slewed the truck sideways and yelled for me to yank the cable. I did, and the second wave burst out. Hacksaw led the charge.

The coyote waited until Widower was within twenty yards, and then it disappeared over the crest of the hill.

"Bastard's quick," the Captain said as the pursuing greyhounds went after it. He reached for the gearshift, then looked back. The downed coyote wasn't moving at all now, but the dogs who had tackled it were still ripping into it. They would be busy for a while yet.

On the far side of the hill we found a wide bowl webbed with gullies. Widower, Hacksaw, and the coyote were already out of sight in the maze, and the other dogs vanished as we spotted them. The Captain slammed his fist on the dash. Letting the greyhounds run in and out of gully after gully was a good way to get them hurt, and the coyote would probably escape anyway. We drove down to the edge of the nearest gully and got out to call the dogs even though we knew they wouldn't come until they had either killed their prey or given up hope of finding it.

The greyhounds popped up here and there and were making plenty of noise, so the Captain left me to keep track of them while he drove back to collect the other three. That was fine with me, because I'd been sweating in the truck, and it felt good to stand out in the hot breeze and listen to the grass whisper. Besides, my least favorite part of a hunt was getting the dogs off the coyote at the end.

The Captain had been gone less than a minute when one of the dogs in the maze shrieked. It was one long, piercing cry—and then silence. No more yips, no more barks. Nor could I hear the truck on the other side of the hill. I yelled for the Captain, but there was no answer. My voice had been swallowed by the prairie.

I jumped into the gully, climbed out the other side, and ran toward the spot where I thought the shriek had come from. I imagined a trap closing on a dog's ankle, a hole breaking his leg, a rattler sinking its fangs into his face. I plunged into another gully and ran down its length, crashing through brush and stumbling over rocks. The walls were as high as my shoulders, and when I looked back toward the hill to see if the Captain was coming, I saw land and sky through rushing brown stems. It was as if the world were lit by a sun-colored strobe. The Captain wasn't coming. I was alone when I found Hacksaw.

He was lying on his side on a bare patch of ground. There was no trap, no hole, no snake. His belly was open.

He was still a little bit alive, and he looked at me as if I should do something. I squatted and put my hand on his head, and he died. I looked away then and saw his three companions from the right side of the truck. They stood a short distance down the gully, staring at us and shifting as if they were caged. One of them whined.

We stayed that way until the Captain arrived. I don't know how he found us. He stood above on the lip of the gully, his pistol in his hand and his club in his belt, his broad face speckled with sweat. "God damn," he said. "Is he dead?"

I nodded, turning so he wouldn't see my eyes. I rubbed my hands on my jeans.

The Captain jumped into the gully, his boots setting off a tumble of rocks and dirt. "What happened?"

"Don't know." I thought my voice sounded almost okay. "I heard him squeal, and I ran over, and I found him like this."

The Captain nudged the body with a boot, and it moved like it was put together with string. He cocked his pistol, squatted, and put the muzzle behind Hacksaw's ear. I watched while he pulled the trigger. The gun went *snap*. Hacksaw's head didn't even twitch. The other three dogs approached, sniffing, and the Captain took his club from his belt. He yelled, "Truck!" and two of them obeyed, jumping out of the gully and trotting to the pickup. The third came all the way to Hacksaw's body and growled. I went to put the first two into their boxes and to fetch a choke chain.

I returned to find the Captain beating the third dog. He was telling her that she was worthless and that she ought to be shot and fed to the others. I moved to where he could see me, and he stopped. "Don't just stand there, punk," he said. "Get her into the goddamn truck."

I put the chain on the cringing dog and began tugging her up the wall.

"Where the hell's Widower?" the Captain asked.

"Still after the coyote, I guess," I said. "He don't give up."

The Captain's expression softened. "No, he don't."

I hated Widower. I had never heard of a lone coyote doing anything like what had been done to Hacksaw, but I knew that Widower had already killed at least one other dog. I figured that when Hacksaw got close to the coyote, Widower got pissed off. Or maybe the coyote had already gotten away when Hacksaw showed up, and Widower took out his frustration on him.

I hoped that when Widower returned, there would be evidence of what he had done, and the Captain would use the pistol on him.

It was a stupid hope. The Captain would never shoot Widower, not even to put him out of misery.

When the clubbed bitch was in her box, the Captain came up and began honking the truck horn. After a while, Widower appeared atop a ridge across the bowl and trotted down toward us. The Captain met him as he came out of the gully where Hacksaw lay. Widower clamped onto the billy, and they came to the pickup. There were dark smears at the corners of the greyhound's mouth, and a tuft of brindle fur.

"Look at that," the Captain said. "Traipsed over half the Flint Hills, and he still has some of that coyote's tail in his mouth."

"Uh-huh," I said.

Widower jumped into his box, and the Captain bolted the door. Then he looked at me, narrow eyed. "We'll come back tomorrow and kill the son of a bitch that done that to Hacksaw." He got into the truck and started the engine.

I looked at the gully. "Ain't we going to—"

"It'll be back for the meat," the Captain said. "That's how we'll nail it."

I got in and saw that he had cut off the dead coyote's ears to add to his string. He drove us back over the hill.

At supper that evening, my dad slapped me in the mouth. I don't remember why. My brothers were acting rotten, but they didn't get smacked. I did.

In the night, I heard the coyotes.

Before sunrise, I got up and dressed quietly so that I wouldn't wake my brothers. One of them woke up anyway, but he watched me without saying anything.

When I was dressed, I went into the kitchen and snuck bread and cheese from the refrigerator. I also took some quarters and dimes from my mom's purse. Then I left the house and rode my bike to Captain Coyote's, carrying the bread and cheese in my left hand while I steered with my right. Halfway there, two deer loped across the road in front of me and jumped a fence. In the predawn gray, they were like floating shadows.

The Captain was loading the dogs when I arrived. He was pleased that I'd brought food, and he said we could buy pop with the money. When we drove away, the two dogs we left behind looked after us with longing. Widower was in his usual box behind the driver's side of the cab.

By the time we reached the hilltop overlooking the maze, the sun had burned the sky to the color of pale slate. My strawberry soda was warm, so I took one of the Captain's beers from the styrofoam cooler at my feet. I drank half of it in one long pull as we descended into the bowl.

The Captain kept his right hand on his pistol as he maneuvered the truck between the gullies to the place where Hacksaw had been killed. There he stopped and got out, taking the gun. He motioned for me to follow, and we walked to the edge of the gully and looked down.

Hacksaw's body had been stripped of fur and flesh, and his bones were scattered over the gully floor. Flies had gathered on his head.

"God damn," the Captain said.

I couldn't blame Widower for this.

The Captain went into the gully. He kicked a few of the bones and then squatted to examine the ground. "The sons of bitches dragged off the whole back half," he said. "Ain't many tracks, but there had to be at least four or five of 'em." He stood and climbed back up the wall. "They ain't so smart, though. I can see the drag marks."

We got back into the truck, and the Captain drove slowly, following marks that I couldn't make out. As we wound our way farther into the maze, the day became hotter, and the dogs whined. I finished my beer and then sucked on ice from the cooler. The Captain wiped his forehead with the back of his gun hand. Near the center of the bowl, I saw that while he watched the gully on our left, another was angling toward us on the right. We were driving on a wedge of prairie that was becoming smaller and smaller.

"We're running out of land," I said.

"Shut up. I know it."

We reached the end, and the Captain stopped the pickup. The front tires were on the edges, and dirt crumbled into both gullies. The dogs rocked us.

The Captain killed the engine and opened his door, telling me to stay put. Outside, he checked to be sure that all six chambers of his pistol were loaded. "If I yell, or if you hear more than one shot," he said, "cut Widower's bunch loose."

"Even if they can't see the coyote?"

"They'll hear the shots. If I keep on yelling, cut the others loose too." He pulled his billy from under the seat and stuck it in his belt, then closed the door and tightened the release cable. "When the second bunch is out, you can come along." He jumped down into the big gully where the two smaller ones joined.

I watched him walk away. He held his pistol ready at his side. When he was about thirty yards distant, he went around a curve. The gully was so deep that I couldn't even see his head now.

I took another beer from the cooler, scooted to the driver's side, and waited. Behind me, the greyhounds scratched and whined. They were ready. I was afraid that the coyotes that had eaten Hacksaw would be torn up or shot before I could be there.

Between the sun and the beer, I dozed off. Widower's growl brought me awake. When I opened my eyes, I saw the coyote.

It stood in the grass on the far side of the gully, watching me with yellow eyes. It was scrawny, and its fur was mottled and mangy, but it held itself as if it were perfect. It wasn't all that interested in me. Just looking. Having nothing better to do at the moment.

At its feet lay part of a brindle haunch.

I sat stock-still. The dogs were barking and clawing at the chicken wire. I didn't know what to do. The Captain had ordered me to wait for his signal. I thought of honking the horn to alert him, but that might scare off the coyote. Anything I did would be wrong.

Slowly, as if the air were syrup, I took my left hand from the armrest. My eyes stayed locked with the ones across the gully. As my fingers closed on the cable, the coyote yawned.

The bolt came free, and the dogs hit the door. Three of them landed on the ground beside the truck before plunging into the gully, but Widower leaped all the way to the gully's center. Another leap took him halfway up the far wall. The coyote was still watching me as Widower exploded into the grass.

But when the greyhound lunged, the coyote was suddenly two feet to the right of where it had been. Widower shot past, his jaws closing on air.

The coyote was still looking right at me. But now, instead of mild interest, I saw something else in its eyes.

Don't you look stupid!

I punched the horn.

The coyote wheeled and ran, becoming a blur. Widower changed direction and raced after it. The other three dogs came out of the gully and paused, sniffing at the part of Hacksaw that the coyote had left. Then one of them took off, and the rest followed.

The chase went into and out of gullies, heading in the direction that the Captain had taken. When the coyote came in view of the dogs on the right side of the truck, I leaned across and yanked that cable too. Then I blew three more blasts on the horn and shoved my door open.

I fell going down the wall, but scrambled up at the bottom and ran, shouting a warning to the Captain. I couldn't see any of the the greyhounds now, but I heard sporadic barking. I was sure that they were all in the same gully as I was, running somewhere ahead in its twisting path.

The barking stopped and was replaced by wild snarls. The dogs had caught the coyote.

Then came a shriek like the one I'd heard the day before. Then another. Then a shouted curse and two snaps like firecrackers. The Captain was calling for help. There were more shrieks. I tried to run faster. The gully widened before me.

When I found them, five of the dogs were dead. The coyote stood in a circle of torn bodies, its muzzle shining with blood. The Captain and his three remaining dogs were backed against a wall.

The two smaller ones were cringing, but Widower still snarled. He strained to attack, but the Captain held him by the back of the neck. The Captain's free hand gripped his pistol. It was pointing at the coyote.

The coyote regarded them with the same look of semiboredom with which it had regarded me. It wasn't snarling. All it did was twitch its tail a little. It showed no interest in the bodies of the five greyhounds.

I had stopped several yards away, and it was only when I took a step backward that the Captain saw me. "Throw me a choke chain!" he yelled. "If Widower gets loose, that thing'll kill him! It's got rabies!"

I looked back at the coyote. It wasn't rabid. It grinned at the Captain, letting its tongue loll.

My chest tightened. "What are you?" I whispered.

The Captain glared at me. "A chain, God damn it! Throw me a chain, punk!"

But I didn't have one. I had run from the truck in a blind frenzy, and I hadn't thought of anything. I tasted sweat. "I'll have to go back," I babbled. "I'll hurry, Captain, I'll—"

His look froze me. "It's too late," he said. Then he squinted at the coyote, and his pistol arm stiffened.

Widower broke free, and the Captain fired. A red streak ripped down the coyote's shoulder. It didn't flinch. But as the greyhound reached it, it dodged, and Widower hit the opposite wall. He spun and charged again.

His rage had infected the other two dogs, and they charged as well. For a moment, I thought they had a chance because the coyote was facing Widower, but as they jumped, it whirled. When they hit the ground, they were screaming. Their bellies had been torn open.

As the two died, Widower landed hard on the coyote's back and sank his teeth into its neck. His momentum forced it to the dirt, and the Captain roared.

Widower weighed over a hundred pounds, and the coyote couldn't have weighed more than fifty. Yet the coyote stood and began a mad dance, flinging Widower about like a whip. But Widower held on, and below his jaws, the coyote's fur turned dark.

"Break its neck, God damn it!" the Captain yelled. "Break it, break it, break it!"

My eyes and throat burned. I wanted to go stand with the Captain and add my voice to his, but I couldn't. I was afraid.

Abruptly, the coyote stopped. For several seconds, it looked at the Captain while Widower tried to snap its spine. No matter how hard the greyhound strained, the coyote neither moved nor showed any sign of pain.

The Captain started toward them. He had taken only a few steps when the coyote grasped Widower's left foreleg and bit down. I heard the bone crunch before Widower shrieked.

The Captain rushed forward, crying out with his dog, and put the pistol against the coyote's head.

But even as Widower shrieked, he kept his teeth in the coyote's neck, and when the Captain pulled the trigger, the coyote moved. The bullet hit Widower in the right shoulder, and he let go and fell.

The coyote trotted away, hopping over one of the dead greyhounds, and then turned to look at the Captain again.

The Captain was staring down at Widower. The dog lay on his left side, writhing. His shoulder was bleeding.

"Oh please," the Captain said.

At last, I was able to start toward him.

But I was too slow. He looked up from Widower, faced the coyote, and began walking. The coyote waited for him. I began to run.

The Captain stood before the coyote and pointed his pistol, and the coyote rose on its hind legs and snapped at his hand. The Captain jerked, and the gun flew from his grasp. It landed at the base of the gully wall, and I turned toward it.

The Captain yanked his club from his belt and lunged. But the coyote dodged again, and the Captain lost his balance. His club tumbled away. As he hit the ground, the coyote took his ankle in its mouth.

My hands closed on the gun, but as I fumbled to aim, Widower stood, holding his crushed leg in the air. He leaped onto the coyote for the second time, and they rolled away from the Captain.

The Captain looked up. His cheek was scraped.

Widower couldn't stay on top. The coyote got out from under him in an eyeblink, and then it started nipping. It nipped at his neck, his ribs, his legs, his tail. It opened a dozen wounds, moving too fast for the crippled greyhound to defend himself, and giving me no clear shot.

The coyote stripped the fur and skin from Widower's tail, and then from his right foreleg. Widower collapsed again, his snarl melting into a cry like a puppy's.

I was about to shoot when the Captain crawled between me and my target. "That's enough, you son of a bitch," he said to the coyote.

The coyote eyed him for a moment, then lowered its head and bit off Widower's left ear. Widower yelped.

"God," the Captain said. "God damn."

The coyote dropped the severed ear and tore off the other one. This time, Widower only whimpered.

The coyote took both ears in its mouth and began trotting off down the gully.

The Captain got to his feet and lurched forward. I was afraid that he would attack the coyote again, but he only went as far as Widower. He knelt beside the dog and stroked his head, murmuring words I couldn't hear.

The coyote continued on, without looking back.

I had never hated anything so much.

Suddenly I was past the Captain, past Widower, past the seven dead greyhounds, and coming up behind it. It turned to wait for me. I slowed to a walk and held the pistol before me with both hands. There were two rounds left. One for each yellow eye.

When I stopped, the coyote and I were separated by less than four feet. It looked at me with the same expression as before. It was bleeding, and flies were already buzzing around the wound on its shoulder. It was only a coyote.

I squeezed the trigger. There was a loud snap, and dust flew up on the coyote's right. I squeezed again, and dust flew up on its left. It hadn't moved.

I pulled the trigger again and again, as if something more than a click would happen by magic. When I finally quit, the coyote grinned at me around Widower's ears.

Don't you *look stupid!*

And then I knew it. It was the thing that hardly noticed us, and hardly cared when it did. It was the thing that came close in the night and taunted, knowing we could never catch it.

It was why my dad was what he was. It was why Captain Coyote set his dogs on things that were free.

It was what the Captain called on when he swore.

The coyote's grin faded. It regarded me for a few more moments before turning and trotting away again. I watched until it was gone, and then I lowered the pistol. I spotted the billy club on the ground and retrieved it. My arms and legs were numb.

The Captain was still cradling Widower's head when I went to him. He didn't respond to my voice, but he looked up when I held out his pistol and club. He accepted them, and then he stood. Together, we carried Widower to the truck. The dog had stopped whimpering, but he was still breathing. We left the others behind.

I didn't get home until after midnight. Luckily, my dad was out somewhere. My mom just gave me one of her sad looks and told me that I had almost worried her to death.

I lay awake for a long time, listening to the sounds of my brothers sleeping. A few hours before dawn, those sounds mingled with distant yips and howls that echoed forever. There might have been two of them, or two hundred.

Maybe there were as many as they wanted.

*

Thanks to the Captain and the antibiotics he stole, Widower
lived. I visited them often during the convalescence, but it was a
hard thing to do, because the dog looked like hell. The ear ridges
were ragged and ugly. The last wound to heal was the stripped
right foreleg, which stayed pink and raw long after the left foreleg
was fine again. In the evenings, it gleamed in the weak light inside
the trailer. Widower was an indoor dog now. He became fat and
dull eyed.

On each of my visits, the Captain told me how lucky he was to
have a dog like this. "Those coyotes would have torn out my goddamn throat," he said, "but Widower took on the whole pack."
After the greyhound was healthy again, the Captain was going to
breed him. Then, when there were enough dogs, they would go
back into the hills and have their revenge. I was invited.

The Captain had not seen what I had.

After school started, my trips to the Captain's became less frequent. By Thanksgiving, I wasn't going at all. At Christmas, I heard
that his mother had run him off, and that he had moved his trailer
to Hutchinson. Later, someone said he'd gone into the service. No
one mentioned his dogs.

I didn't see him again until last month. I was walking through
the plant on my way to a meeting, and there he was, punching
rivets. I almost went past, but then he saw me too, and I had to
stop.

I shook his hand and called him Captain. His face locked up as
if I'd knifed him, and I knew that sometime, somewhere, he had
met it again. And had seen.

I would have left then, but I'd been to college, and I knew how
to be polite. So I asked him the safe questions you ask when you
haven't seen someone in twenty years, the questions that can be answered with generalities or lies. He'd been in the Marines. Then
he'd worked in a machine shop in Texas. Then he'd moved back to

home ground, to Wichita. He'd hired on at the plant just two days before.

I didn't ask about Widower.

He didn't ask about me.

I started to tell him that my father was dead, then decided not to. I shook his hand again and went to my meeting.

I try not to go through that part of the plant anymore, but sometimes I have to. On those occasions, I wave and say hello, and he nods.

When I say hello, I call him Duane.

The Calvin Coolidge
Home for Dead Comedians

Introduction to

༄

"The Calvin Coolidge
Home for Dead Comedians"

I have to force some stories into being, but others force *me*. "The Calvin Coolidge Home for Dead Comedians" was one of the latter. I wrote it in the summer of 1985 while I was supposed to be working on my first novel, and I didn't have any choice. I had just read an amazing autobiography, and this story was simply *there* afterward, hammering away at the inside of my skull.

Even now, almost ten years after it was first published, I get more letters, comments, and questions about this story than about any other.

And that's all I have to say about "Calvin," except for this:

If I were writing the story today, the Home would have one more important inmate. His name was Bill Hicks, and he was one of the most shockingly truthful and slashingly funny sons of bitches to ever walk this earth.

I first saw Hicks onstage in Raleigh, North Carolina, in the summer of 1987—and I didn't know whether to hide under the table, or laugh until I couldn't breathe.

I saw him for the last time in Austin, Texas, in the fall of 1993.

This was about the same time that a segment he had done for *Late Night with David Letterman* was cut from the broadcast because his material was, well, just too *pointed.* (In other words, it actually had a point. And who wants to see anything like that on TV?)

At that last live performance I attended, Hicks knocked the audience to the floor with Olympian thunderbolts of rage and laughter. And then, just to make sure he'd wiped us out, he came back with a finale that was the verbal equivalent of a thermonuclear device. It was, at the same time, the most stunningly offensive and the most drop-dead hilarious string of words I had ever heard a human being say out loud. I was hiding under the table, *and* I was laughing until I couldn't breathe.

I never got to be in the same room while Jimi Hendrix played guitar, but I did get to be in the same room while Bill Hicks played language and ideas. That makes me one of the lucky ones.

Hicks died of pancreatic cancer in February 1994 at the age of thirty-two.

And if there really is an afterlife, I have no doubt that he, like Leonard, is now giving the masters of creation one hell of a hard time.

The Calvin Coolidge
Home for Dead Comedians

~≈~

"The what-*should*-be never did exist. . . .
There is only what *is*."

1

The author of *How to Talk Dirty and Influence People* couldn't remember his own name, so he decided to ask the driver of the pickup truck in which he was riding.

Red stitching over the right breast pocket of the driver's blue overalls spelled out "Ol' Pete."

"Excuse me, ah, Pete," the author said hesitantly. "Who am I?"

Ol' Pete, an elderly man with a creased, suntanned face and a white beard, adjusted his blue baseball cap and scratched his scalp.

"Yuh," he said. "That's typical."

"Typical of *what?*" the author asked.

Ol' Pete grimaced. "Take a look at yourself, sonny."

"Sonny" looked down at himself and saw that he was dressed in a brown jacket, tie, and slacks; brown shoes; and a white shirt. The belly threatening to pop the shirt buttons was too big for the rest of his body.

Gotta get on a diet, he thought.

Then he saw the thin copper band encircling his left wrist. LEONARD was stamped into the bracelet in capital letters.

"That's me?" he asked.

"Yuh, unless somebody made a mistake."

Leonard rubbed at the bracelet with his right thumb.

"It doesn't feel right," he said. "Is it my first name or my last?"

"Yuh, that's typical, too."

Leonard wanted to ask "Typical of *what?*" again, but Ol' Pete began whistling "Camptown Races," and Leonard decided it would be a shame to interrupt.

Instead he looked out the open window on his right. The pickup truck—a dusty, battered red International Harvester—was chugging along a narrow dirt road that wound through a forest of thick-trunked trees. Leonard guessed that most of the trees were cottonwoods, but he wasn't sure.

He made a mental note: He was not a botanist. Or at least not a botanist who specialized in trees.

What kind of botanist would write a book called *How to Talk Dirty and Influence People,* anyway?

He took a deep breath. The warm air smelled wonderful, like sunshine on mown grass. The season was spring, he guessed, but late spring, because the trees were fully leaved. The gently swaying branches created an ever-changing pattern of sun dapples on the road.

"Nice area," Leonard said. His voice, at least, was familiar. "Where are we going?"

Ol' Pete stopped whistling long enough to say, "Ain't there a one of you willing to think for yourself?"

Leonard wanted to say something sarcastic but didn't know what, so he searched his mind for a memory that would help him.

In brief flashes, he remembered—

—*crowds, laughter, drugs, sex, cops*—

—but he couldn't imagine what any of that had to do with

being in an International pickup with a man he had never seen before.

He twisted the mirror attached to the outside of his door and looked at his reflection.

The pale, smooth-shaven face had brown, wavy hair; blue eyes surrounded by dark, slightly puffy circles; and an ordinary, medium-sized nose. Although he thought the face would look better with a beard, it was definitely his—a good face, a face practiced in attracting women. But it didn't look like the kind of face that would go with the name Leonard.

Without trying to recall the information, he remembered that he was forty years old.

He turned back toward Ol' Pete. "Hey, do I look forty to you?"

Ol' Pete shrugged his shoulders. "Y'all look alike to me."

Leonard began to feel irritated.

"Look, pops," he said, "I don't know where I came from or how I got here. I'm one hundred percent confused, and you're not helping, which is making me one hundred percent pi—pi—pi—"

Leonard frowned. There was a word he wanted to use, but he couldn't think of more than its first two letters.

"You mean 'angry,' right?" Ol' Pete said, the corners of his eyes crinkling in amusement.

"Yeah," Leonard said, looking first at his hands, then at the cracked leather seat, and then at the dashboard, as if he might have misplaced the unknown word. "Yeah, I'm angry, but . . . that isn't the way I was going to say it."

Ol' Pete adjusted his baseball cap and chuckled. "Well, I can see why you've been assigned to Mrs. Vonus."

Leonard stopped trying to think of the word. "Mrs. Vonus?" he said.

"She'll be your Housemother."

"Housemother?"

Ol' Pete clicked his tongue. "You got yourself a bad case of echolalia, boy."

157

Leonard wanted to punch Ol' Pete in the nose, but restrained himself. He had enough trouble with the cops without adding battery to the list.

He made a mental note of that, too.

"How about some compassion, pops?" he said. "Something weird's happened to me, and all I'm getting from you is 'That's typical' and enough whistling to make Jiminy Cricket toss his cookies. I didn't ask for this, you know."

Ol' Pete laughed and beat on the button in the center of the steering wheel. The horn blared out derisive honks, and panicked birds flew up on both sides of the road.

Leonard glared. "Just what's so funny, you smug coc—coc—"

Again, he knew there was a word he wanted, but was unable to remember it.

Ol' Pete raised an eyebrow. "Got in trouble for that one, I'll bet."

Leonard experienced another flash of memory, like a hot rush of blood, and the force of it suppressed his anger.

"Yeah," he said. "Yeah, I did. I don't know why, but the cops took me in for it."

Ol' Pete patted him on the shoulder. "Don't worry, sonny. It'll come clear in a bit. We're almost there." He pointed.

A few hundred yards ahead, a three-story redbrick mansion sat in a fenced clearing at the base of a huge hill. Half-hidden golden buildings shimmered at the top of the hill, but it was the brick mansion toward which Ol' Pete pointed.

"That's the Calvin Coolidge Home," Ol' Pete said.

Leonard rubbed his forehead, which was starting to hurt. "I thought you said I was assigned to a Mrs. Vopis."

"Mrs. Vonus, boy. She runs the Coolidge Home. And it ain't Calvin Coolidge's; that's just what she calls it."

"Don't call me boy," Leonard said. "I'm forty god—go—forty years old."

The old man pounded the horn again. "A babe in the woods!" he chortled.

Leonard was beginning to think that Ol' Pete was more than a little crazy. He was glad the ride was almost over.

Even though he had no idea where it had taken him.

2

Leonard had to cross a narrow plank over a deep ditch to get to the brick walk that led to the mansion's front door. He was halfway across when the International's horn blared behind him, and he windmilled his arms to keep his balance.

"So long, sonny boy!" Ol' Pete bellowed. "Hope to see you on the Hill one o' these days!"

Leonard didn't look back to acknowledge the farewell. He was too busy trying to avoid falling into the ditch, which was half full of murky water.

He did turn around when he'd finally made it to the other side. The truck was gone, without even a puff of dust to mark its passage.

He hadn't heard it drive away. He couldn't even remember when he'd stopped hearing the engine noise.

"Holy sh—sh—," he said, and began to see a connection between the words he couldn't remember.

He walked slowly up the path, staring down at the chipped bricks. He tried to mutter obscenities as he went.

"Sh—sh— Excrement," he said. "Fuh—fuh— Sexual intercourse. Genitalia. Scion of a golden retriever. Immoral congress with a chimpanzee. Guano cranium."

It was the best he could do.

He was so preoccupied that he stumbled over the step at the end of the walk. His palms came up just in time to keep his face from impacting on the wall to the right of the door.

His eyes were five inches from a bronze plaque bolted to the bricks:

THE CALVIN COOLIDGE MEMORIAL REHABILITATION FACILITY

VISITORS WELCOME

THANK YOU FOR NOT SMOKING

"What the coitus," Leonard muttered, and pushed away from the wall to face the dark wooden door, which was intricately carved with depictions of bored-looking cherubim.

A black iron knocker shaped like a microphone dominated the center of the door. The flat piece of metal the knocker was to strike had been forged in the shape of a laughing face, but Leonard only knew this because of the open mouth. The rest of the face had been beaten smooth. He didn't want to knock, so he kicked at a loose brick in the step for several minutes, waiting for something to happen. A blue jay landed in a mimosa tree and scolded him.

What am I afraid of? he thought. *Any place named after Calvin Coolidge, for crying out loud, can't be too horrible. Besides, they might have something to eat.*

The knocker felt hot in his hand. He brought it up quickly and let it fall.

The sound was like a thunderclap.

Startled, Leonard jumped backward off the step and fell, landing on his buttocks on the sidewalk.

"Fornication with one's maternal parent," he said. It was distinctly unsatisfying.

The massive door swung inward. Leonard wanted to run into the woods, but before he could stand, he saw the woman in the doorway. She was a blue-haired little old lady in a dark gray dress.

It would be hard, he thought, to imagine a more unthreatening figure. Yet he was frightened, and he thought he knew why when he noticed that the woman's right hand was curled into a veined, bony fist.

If there's a balled-up handkerchief in there, he thought, *I'm at the mercy of somebody's Jewish mother.*

Not his, though. His mother had been larger. . . .

Another mental note. Sooner or later, he'd have enough clues to know who he was.

The woman in the doorway looked down at him and pursed her lips in displeasure.

"So much for first impressions," Leonard mumbled, and stood. His legs felt rubbery.

The woman gave a short sigh and said, "I am Mrs. Vonus. You must be Leonard. We've been expecting you." Her voice was high, thin, and dry.

"Who's 'we'?" Leonard asked.

Mrs. Vonus stepped back and gestured with her left hand. "Come in, come in. We might as well get started."

"Get started on *what?*"

Mrs. Vonus sighed again. "Rule Number One, Leonard, is that it's rude to question your Housemother in such a belligerent tone. Please come inside now, or I'll be forced to give you a minus for your first day."

Leonard walked, a little shakily, up the step and into the dark, cool mustiness of the Calvin Coolidge Home. The worn, wine-colored carpeting in the foyer felt spongy under his shoes.

Mrs. Vonus shut the door, and the dim foyer became even dimmer.

"Saving on electricity?" Leonard asked, trying to keep his voice from quavering.

The woman appeared out of the dimness and looked up at him. She sighed a third time.

"You sure kvetch a lot," Leonard said.

The Housemother shook her head. "We have our work cut out for us."

Leonard backed away a few steps. "Speaking of cutting," he said, "I'm cutting out if somebody doesn't give me a good reason to stay. For one thing, it's too dark in here, and for another, it smells like moldy bread."

Mrs. Vonus placed her right hand on his forearm.

No handkerchief, he thought. *Must've stuffed it down her dress when I wasn't looking.*

"Your eyes will adjust to the light," Mrs. Vonus said, "and you will become accustomed to the scent of age. As for your questions—this is your Orientation Day, and I shall answer those questions that are appropriate."

Leonard tried to pull away from her grip and found that he couldn't, even though she wasn't holding him tightly. He began to suspect that he was dreaming.

"You are not dreaming," the Housemother said.

"Which is exactly what I'd expect a dream character to say," Leonard said quickly, before he had a chance to panic. "On the count of three, I'm going to wake up." He closed his eyes. "One, two, three."

When he reopened his eyes, he could see a little better. But he was still in the foyer of the Calvin Coolidge Home, and still in the grip of Mrs. Vonus.

"Three and a half," he said.

"Come into the Front Parlor," Mrs. Vonus said, and pulled him to the left. His feet shuffled along against his will.

They passed through a wide, arched entranceway into a large room with the same wine-colored carpeting as the foyer. Tall windows with gauzy drapes let in just enough sunlight for Leonard to see clearly. Ornate sofas and chairs were arranged neatly throughout the room, and huge bookcases loaded with black-spined volumes hulked against the walls. The wall space between the bookcases was covered with blue paisley paper.

Leonard shuddered. It was hideous stuff.

It wasn't quite as awful, though, as the massive mantel around the fireplace. It was carved from the same dark wood as the front door, and more bored cherubim flapped morosely across it in suspended animation.

Over the mantel, illuminated by two kerosene lamps in wall brackets, was the painted portrait of a clean-cut, Presbyterian-looking man.

Mrs. Vonus pulled Leonard close enough for him to read the brass plate at the bottom of the painting's frame. The words engraved into it were JOHN CALVIN COOLIDGE.

"Who's that?" Leonard asked. "I've heard of Calvin Coolidge, but—"

"John was his first name," the Housemother said reverently.

Leonard forced himself to smile, pretending to love the painting. Maybe if he was nice, she'd let go of his arm and he could split.

"You shan't go anywhere," Mrs. Vonus said.

She released his arm, and he found that his feet were stuck to the carpet.

Giving in to panic at last, he twisted his body painfully in an effort to escape. "Lord curse this mightily!" he yelled, and realized that he sounded ridiculous.

"You're heading for a minus," Mrs. Vonus said.

Leonard stopped flailing and tried to calm himself. He didn't know what a "minus" was, but the Housemother obviously had some sort of arcane power, and it wouldn't do to upset her. A "minus" might involve his liver escaping via his belly button.

He wondered why the idea that this little old lady had supernatural powers didn't strike him as meshugge.

The answer came floating up from his brain's lower layers:

Man, I've been dragged before people whose only power came from the word "Judge" in front of their names. What I'm dealing with here doesn't make any less sense than that.

"You must learn how to behave toward those who have been placed over you," Mrs. Vonus said.

"Yes, ma'am," Leonard said, trying to sound meek.

The Housemother pursed her lips. "You don't fool me. You're telegraphing a great deal of unhealthy defiance. Sooner or later, though, you must accept the order of the universe if you want to exist in a state of spiritual peace."

Leonard, to keep himself from responding sardonically, looked up at the portrait again and asked, "Is this the same Calvin Coolidge who was president during Prohibition?"

Mrs. Vonus reached up and buffed the brass plate with a wrinkled lace handkerchief.

Aha! Leonard thought, and was immediately afraid. But the Housemother didn't seem to have "heard" him.

"Yes, this is he," she said. "The finest man to have ever served in public office. I find it ironic that you, one of the least fine men to have ever existed, were born during his administration."

Leonard made yet another mental note. If he had been born during Prohibition and was now forty years old, then this must be nineteen sixty-something-or-other. . . .

"Time has no meaning here," Mrs. Vonus said. "We have days and nights, but only for convenience. A day is as a thousand years, a thousand years as a day."

Leonard couldn't stand it anymore. "Where the he—he—heck *am* I, then? You keep giving me this mystical shtick, but you're not telling me anything."

Mrs. Vonus sighed for what Leonard was sure must be the hundredth time since he'd entered the building. "Very well," she said in a tone of voice that clearly said *You'll be sorry.* "I prefer to give new residents more adjustment time before their screenings, but if you're impatient, we'll do it now. Come along." She began walking back toward the foyer.

Leonard found that he could move again, but before he followed the Housemother, he took a last look at the portrait.

"What a goyisher face," he muttered, and then remembered not only who Calvin Coolidge had been but who John Calvin had been:

Predestination. Purity. Punishment of sinners. Burnings at the stake. No sense of humor.

Leonard turned away from the mantel. He didn't think he was going to enjoy working this dump, but there didn't seem to be anything he could do about it.

3

Mrs. Vonus led him through the foyer, past a staircase that she said went up to "the dormitory," and down a wide hallway lined with glass cases. She walked like an overfed duck.

Some of the glass cases were in shadows so dark that Leonard couldn't make out the contents, but every thirty feet or so, a skylight let in diffused sunshine that revealed dusty medals and trophies. One case was full of china dinner plates painted with portraits of presidents and biblical figures.

"I never saw so much dre—dre—natural fertilizer in my life," Leonard said.

Mrs. Vonus sighed.

She paused under one of the skylights and gestured at the wall. Leonard stopped beside her and looked where she pointed.

Here, instead of a glass case, was a white plastic-coated board, ten feet high and eight wide, marked off in a grid of perpendicular black lines forming sixty rows of two-inch squares. Many of the squares, particularly on the right half of the board, were blank, but each of the others held one of three black symbols: +, =, or −. Hanging on a long string to the right of the board was what looked like a capped felt-tipped marker.

To the left of each row of squares was a single name. Leonard found his and saw that every square in that row was blank.

"This is the Progress Board," Mrs. Vonus said. "Each day, I shall evaluate your attitude, composure, manners, posture, and language. A plus sign means that you are making great progress, and you shall receive a silver dollar. Since there are only forty spaces in each row, the Board cannot display a record of a resident's entire stay—however, all that matters is the total number of pluses. Each resident's total appears at the end of his row. When the total reaches two hundred, the resident may ascend to the top of the Hill."

"What's at the top of the Hill?" Leonard asked.

Mrs. Vonus gave him a severe look. "You'll know when you have two hundred pluses."

Leonard looked at the column of numbers and saw that only three of the sixty residents had more than a hundred pluses.

"An equal sign," Mrs. Vonus continued, "indicates that you are equivocal. You are not rewarded, but neither are you penalized. For each minus, however, you must pay a dollar to the Dessert Fund. If you have no dollars at the time, you must pay double when you do."

Leonard cleared his throat. "What's the Dessert Fund?"

For the first time, the hint of a smile flickered at the corners of the Housemother's mouth. "Every day at dinner, those residents who have received plus signs are given a special dessert at the expense of those who have received minuses."

Leonard kept his eyes riveted on the Progress Board. *The old bat has power,* he thought, *but she's as crazy as an eighty-year-old stripper.*

"You'll soon know better," Mrs. Vonus said.

Leonard gritted his teeth. "If you don't mind," he said, "I'd appreciate a little privacy in my own brain."

"If you think dessert is crazy, Leonard, that's fine. From the looks of you, though, you take dessert quite seriously."

Leonard glared at her. "I've been planning to go on a diet, you rotten old set of external sexual characteristics!" he yelled. He didn't know what it was that he really wanted to call her, but he hoped she did.

Mrs. Vonus stepped closer to the Progress Board, uncapped the marker, and put a minus sign in the first box to the right of Leonard's name. Then she recapped the marker, dropped it so that it bounced on its string, and began waddling down the hall again.

"Please follow me," she said.

Leonard looked at the Progress Board and grinned. A quick vertical stroke could change a minus into a plus. . . .

166

He grabbed the marker, and a jolt of white-hot pain stabbed up his arm into his head.

When he could see again, he was on his back on the worn carpet. His arm and head throbbed. Mrs. Vonus stood over him, her helmet of bluish hair framed by the rectangular halo of the skylight.

"Come along, Leonard," she said. "You said you wanted answers. It's time for you to get them."

4

The hallway ended in a movie-theater lobby, complete with a popcorn machine and candy counter. The wine-colored carpet of the hall gave way to thick, plush scarlet, and velvet ropes strung between brass posts defined a path leading to a pair of wide doors on spring hinges.

Leonard ached, but he almost forgot about the pain when he saw where he was. His first thought was that the place had to be an illusion, but there was no way to fake the smell of hot buttered popcorn.

What was a movie theater doing in an old mansion?

"It serves a purpose," Mrs. Vonus said.

Leonard was about to yell at her again—he already had a minus, so what could it hurt?—but then he spotted the two young women behind the U-shaped glass candy counter.

Both were wearing red-and-white striped blouses and short blue skirts. One was tall, blue-eyed, and blonde, with hair so long that its end was hidden behind the display of Milk Duds. The other, a brunette, had dark eyes and the most sensual mouth Leonard had ever seen. So far as he remembered, anyway.

He felt that there ought to be a redhead, but two out of three wasn't bad.

"Excuse me," he said to Mrs. Vonus without looking at her, and hopped over a velvet rope.

It was only when he leaned far forward over the counter that he noticed that the women, although extraordinarily beautiful, looked as if they never smiled.

"Hey, why so depressed?" Leonard asked. They didn't look depressed, exactly, but it was the closest word he could come up with on short notice. "It's a beautiful day outside. Lots of sunshine, birdies singing, green leaves all over the place. When do you two get off work, anyway? We could go for a picnic."

The blonde looked at him with a complete lack of interest. "May I help you, sir?" she said flatly.

"You bet, babe," he said, grinning. "You can tell me how much a smile costs."

The brunette said, "We have Goobers, Sno-Caps, jujubes, Milk Duds, Junior Mints, licorice whips, red or black, Hershey bars, and Jordan almonds. We also have popcorn, with or without butter, and Royal Crown Cola. What will you have, sir?"

"A phone number," Leonard said. "A look, a smile, a touch, a wink."

"We don't have any of those, sir," the blonde said.

So that was the way they wanted to play it. Okay, fine—he knew the game as well as they did.

He straightened and shook his head in exaggerated dejection. "Some Goobers and Milk Duds, then. And your biggest tub of popcorn. Better give me a soda, too."

The brunette reached for the candy.

"Five dollars," the blonde said, moving toward the cash register.

Leonard's mouth fell open. "Five bucks? I've been places where I could've bought *you* for that!"

Something touched his right elbow, and he jumped. Then he looked down and saw Mrs. Vonus standing beside him.

"This isn't World War II," she said, "and you aren't in a French brothel. These ladies are my employees, and they do not fraternize with residents."

Leonard leaned down and whispered, "I don't wanna fraternize. I wanna boink their brains out." He was pleased to discover that he remembered the word "boink," and wondered if the reason he was able to remember it was that it wasn't really a word at all.

The Housemother grasped his arm again. "You will be going to bed without dinner tonight, and there will have to be a considerable improvement in your demeanor before I will consider allowing you to come to dinner tomorrow."

Leonard tried to pry her fingers loose. "Hey, who d'you think you are, my mother? I don't have to stick around, y'know—"

"Yes, you do," Mrs. Vonus said, and yanked him away from the counter so hard that he thought his shoulder had dislocated.

"Hey, what about—ow!—what about my Milk Duds?" he cried.

"You don't have any silver dollars with which to buy them. At the rate you're going, it will be some time before you do."

The Housemother stopped before the double doors and released Leonard's arm.

"I'll bet your kids hate you," he said, rubbing his shoulder. "I'll bet you've never gotten a Mother's Day card in your life."

Mrs. Vonus pulled open the left-hand door, revealing darkness. Cool air rushed out and made Leonard shiver.

"Go in," the Housemother said. "Take any seat you like."

Leonard tried to step forward, but a tingling sensation in his spine stopped him.

Whatsa matter, schmu—schm—

Yet another word he couldn't remember. What kind of stupid dream was it where a man couldn't even call himself an obscene name in Yiddish?

He compromised:

Whatsa matter, schnook? Movie theaters are always dark inside. Otherwise you can't see the film. So go on in, because if you don't, Grandma Goering is gonna break your arm.

"You're going to be awfully hungry in a day or two," the Housemother said grimly.

169

Leonard wanted to beat his head against the wall. "Are you gonna spy on me when I go to the john, lady?"

Mrs. Vonus gestured toward the darkness with her free hand. "Please, Leonard. I'm tired of holding the door."

He took a step toward the darkness and then paused. "Are you coming?"

"No, thank you," she said. "I must turn on the projector."

Leonard looked back at the unsmiling goddesses behind the candy counter.

"If I'm not back in two hours," he called, "better come revive me. Nude massages with baby oil often seem to be effective."

Then, before Mrs. Vonus could admonish him, he walked into the theater.

5

The door swung shut behind him, and he paused at the top of the aisle to let his eyes adjust. A dim yellow light burned at the end of each row of seats, and the screen on the wall ahead glowed a dull gray. Leonard estimated that there were two hundred seats, all of them empty.

He was amazed at how clean the place was. "What's a movie house without trash?" he said aloud, then walked down to the fifth row and sat in the third seat left of the aisle.

The screen brightened and the face of Mrs. Vonus appeared, ten feet tall and in ludicrously overtinted color.

Leonard wished he had a popcorn box to throw. He had to content himself with booing and hissing, and the sounds echoed eerily.

"Welcome to the Calvin Coolidge Memorial Rehabilitation Facility," the amplified voice of Mrs. Vonus said from the ceiling and walls. "This facility specializes in the purification of those who have spent their lives trying to gain earthly rewards through the practice of so-called humor, which, rather than evoking the laughter of joy, instead appeals to the listeners' prurient interest—"

"What's wrong with that?" Leonard yelled.

"—thus leading to the deterioration of the moral fabric of society."

"Moral fabric?" Leonard shouted. "One hundred percent cotton denim, maybe? Rayon? Dacron? The weak, frayed elastic in most of my shorts?"

"Our therapy," Mrs. Vonus said, "consists of teaching our residents those things their parents and peers failed to teach them— patience, politeness, obedience, reverence, decorum, piety, and chastity."

Leonard jumped up and waved his right index finger at the screen. "Oh, no, you don't! The Constitution says I don't have to be obedient, reverent, or chaste—especially chaste—as long as I don't abridge the rights of others, which I've never done! Furthermore, you wear too much makeup! I've spent decades in burlesque palaces, and I never saw so much rouge in my whole life!"

His last three words reverberated in his skull:

My whole life.

His legs felt rubbery again, and he collapsed into his seat. He was beginning to feel uncomfortably warm despite the theater's coolness.

What was the last thing he could remember before the ride in the red International pickup truck?

. . . something hot and delicious coursing through my body . . .

Orgasm?

No; it had been hotter, faster, more like falling into a volcano—

"And now," Mrs. Vonus was saying, "a short feature to clarify the meaning of your presence here, after which you shall meet our other residents and enjoy a heartwarming and spiritually uplifting cinematic masterpiece. You shall return to this theater every day when you feel you must, which is the only way we have of telling time here. You shall come to the theater, eat dinner, and gather for house meetings . . . according to when you feel you must."

"Whenever nature calls, huh?" Leonard mumbled.

The giant Mrs. Vonus disappeared and was replaced by the black-and-white image of a toilet.

"A toilet," Leonard whispered. His head felt as if it had been soaked in gasoline and lit with a match. "The villainous source of all those 'dirty toilet jokes' . . ."

An overweight, pale man with dark hair and a beard appeared on the screen and sat on the toilet. He was nude.

Leonard tried to stand again, but his seat held him with the same irresistible force with which Mrs. Vonus had held his arm.

The two-dimensional phantom tightened a strap above an elbow.

Leonard tried to turn away from the screen, but his head wouldn't move. Nor would his eyelids close. His eyes began to sting.

The man on the screen held a syringe. With the tip of his tongue touching his upper lip, he slid the needle into the bulging vein on the inside of his elbow. He loosened the strap.

After a moment, he looked happy.

Then something happened to his eyes, and he fell off the toilet. He lay awkwardly on the tiled floor, as if frozen in the act of rolling from his back to his side. His bearded cheek was against the tiles. His eyelids closed.

Leonard wanted to scream, but his throat and tongue were paralyzed.

The cops came into the bathroom.

They looked at the naked man on the floor and talked. Through the roar of his fever, Leonard could only hear a fraction of what they said, but that was more than he wanted to hear.

"What'd I tell you?" one of the cops said.

A second cop said something else. A third laughed.

You sons of bit—bit—, Leonard thought. But the word, the right word, the only word, wouldn't come.

Then, two by two, like animals trooping into Noah's ark, the photographers and television cameramen came in. They shone bright lamps onto the body and popped flashbulbs at it as if to purify it with white light.

The tightness in Leonard's throat broke.

"Vultures!" he cried. "Can't I have some peace in my own bathroom?"

Two by two, they came and went.

"Bound to happen sooner or later," one of them said.

Leonard wanted to run to the screen and rip it with his fingernails and teeth.

"You drove me to it!" he shouted. "You and the cops who wouldn't have gotten out of their cars to keep a black man from getting beaten up but were ecstatic to come after me for telling the truth! I had to do something to get away! Sickest of the sick, huh? You bet I am! Sick of you self-righteous coc—coc—genital lickers!"

The last photographer finished shooting, then said, "Bye-bye, junkie," and walked out of the bathroom. Other people came in, but the picture was fading.

Leonard slumped, staring at the fading image of his own body.

"I'm not a junkie," he said weakly. "I just needed to get away from the tapes and papers for a while. I just needed . . ."

The screen went black.

Leonard wanted to cry, but his tear ducts wouldn't work. All he could do was dry-sob.

This is what I get for getting a tattoo, he thought bitterly.

But when the lights brightened and he rolled his shirt and jacket sleeves up from his left forearm, he saw that the tattoo was gone.

For a moment, he had been sure of who he was, but now he knew that he could never again be sure of anything.

6

As Leonard's fever began to break, the double doors opened. Leonard turned and saw dozens of men, all dressed in brown slacks and jackets with white shirts, coming down the aisle. Some were barely out of their teens, and some were painfully old; yet they all looked alike. All were Caucasian, and all walked as if they were afraid of the floor. None of them were smiling.

Leonard used them as an excuse to try to forget the film he had just seen.

These guys told jokes for a living? So why do they look so . . . unfunny?

A shrunken, ancient man took the aisle seat on Leonard's right. Tremulously, he reached into a jacket pocket and withdrew a box of jujubes.

"Hey, pops," Leonard said, leaning to the right and trying to keep his voice steady. "What's going on here?"

The old man looked at Leonard with a puzzled expression. "It's—," he began uncertainly, as if trying to remember something he was always forgetting. "It's the afternoon movie," he said finally.

"Yeah? You know what it is?"

The old man stared with grayish, red-rimmed eyes. "Same as always, I suppose," he said, as if Leonard had been foolish to ask the question, and then opened his box of jujubes.

Leonard's stomach rumbled.

Dead or not, he was hungry.

"Mind if I have a few?" he said, leaning closer.

The grayish eyes regarded him curiously in the fading light. "You're new, aren't you?" the old man asked.

"Yeah, yeah," Leonard said, becoming impatient as the screen lit up and music rang from the speakers. "C'mon, can I have some?"

"Up to you," the old man said, extending the box.

Leonard held out his hand, and several jujubes slid into his palm.

"Thanks, man," he said, and turned to look at the screen. He had already missed the title, but he recognized the credits, which were flipping past on what looked like Christmas cards.

JAMES STEWART, he read, and then DONNA REED.

He popped one of the candies into his mouth, and it crawled across his tongue.

He choked and spat it out, then felt the jujubes in his hand crawling too. He could just make out their shapes in the flickering light from the movie screen.

Cockroaches.

Leonard yelped and shook his hand violently, scattering the roaches in all directions. One landed in his hair, and he began to hyperventilate as he frantically brushed it out.

"Real—," he began, shuddering and gasping. "Real—real funny, pops."

"Not to me," the old man's voice answered from the darkness.

Leonard felt cold. Why was the air-conditioning in a movie theater always strong enough to freeze meat?

Shivering, he drew up his knees and hugged them to his chest.

He had seen his own death.

He had put a cockroach into his mouth.

On the movie screen, Jimmy Stewart, as good old George Bailey, was about to discover that *It's a Wonderful Life*.

Leonard leaned to his left and threw up into the adjacent seat.

7

Seventeen "days" later, Leonard lay on his hard, narrow mattress and stared at the gray ceiling of his room. The cubicle had no window, so the only thing to look at besides the ceiling was the framed print on the wall above the foot of the bed. He refused to do that, because he hated it.

The print was a reproduction of a painting depicting a female saint being sliced to death by a huge wooden wheel studded with knives.

Earlier that day, Leonard had decided he couldn't stand the thing anymore, and he had tried to take it down. It hadn't budged, so he had tried to break the glass with his shoe. That had also failed, and he had received yet another minus for his efforts.

He didn't think he'd mind the print so much if the saint hadn't looked overjoyed about her impending filleting.

"It's perverse," he had told Mrs. Vonus after she'd called him down to the Progress Board to answer for his attempted vandalism. "Nobody should be happy about something like that. Talk about sick—*that's* sick!"

The Housemother had sighed, then pursed her lips.

"Why is it so difficult for you to understand, Leonard," she had said while uncapping the felt-tipped marker, "that sacrificing oneself for something greater is the highest achievement of spirituality?"

"Oh, I understand, all right," Leonard had said. "I just don't think she should be so pleased with the method. I mean, she looks like she thinks she's about to make it with Omar Sharif, for crying out loud."

Mrs. Vonus had dutifully marked the minus in the seventeenth box after his name.

As Leonard stared at the ceiling, he thought he understood what the Housemother had said about the nature of time here. The sun had set only sixteen times since his arrival, but he felt as if he'd been in the Home at least five years.

He had considered trying to escape, but even when the house let him go outside, the ditch bounding the front yard and the high wooden wall bounding the grounds on the other three sides kept him trapped. He hadn't been able to find the footbridge he'd crossed the first day.

He had also tried to befriend some of the other residents, hoping that together they might find a way out, but none of them would even talk to him. It was as if they were too preoccupied with trying to earn pluses to think about what might lie beyond the mansion's seven acres.

Leonard, though, was curious about the world outside the grounds, particularly the golden buildings on top of the Hill. He could just see them from the yard, glimmering between the trees high above like the sun peeking through gaps in green clouds.

Mrs. Vonus had told him that he might someday be allowed to go up the Hill, but that he had a great deal of work to do first. Living on the Hill was a reward, she said, a privilege to be bestowed only upon those who proved themselves worthy.

"Who wants to live there?" Leonard had said. "I just want to check it out for chicks."

That had been his fifth minus.

Let's see, he thought, still staring at the ceiling. *Seventeen days with a total of fourteen minuses, three equal signs, and no pluses. That means I need twenty-eight straight pluses just to pay off what I owe the Dessert Fund. Then still more pluses if I want to buy anything for the movies . . . that is, the Movie.*

Seventeen days at the Coolidge Home meant that he had seen *It's a Wonderful Life* seventeen times. He didn't think he could bear to sit through it more than three or four more times if he didn't at least have something to eat to take his mind off it.

The fingers of his right hand plucked at the loose fabric of his shirt where his belly had tightened it two weeks earlier. Seventeen days without sweets—six of them without anything to eat at all—had helped him begin to lose the weight he'd been wanting to take off for months before his death. He supposed he ought to thank the Housemother for that, at least.

Maybe that would get him a plus. Unless, of course, she caught him thinking that it would. Mrs. Vonus wasn't an easy woman to please. He thought he'd go nuts trying to figure out how to get along with her, or at least how to avoid her.

He also thought he'd go nuts if he didn't get into the pants of at least one of the candy-counter women, which was one of the reasons why he couldn't get along with Mrs. Vonus.

"Desires of the flesh," she had told him over and over, "must be overcome if you are to reach the goal of spiritual purification."

"I agree," he had said on Day 9. "However, to overcome desires, they must be eliminated, and the only way to eliminate them is to supply what is desired. Ergo, the only way for me to reach spiritual purification is to spend several weeks bouncing up and down on each of those young lovelies."

He had missed dinner two days in a row for that.

Then he had behaved himself relatively well, he thought, until this afternoon's campaign against the masochistic saint.

Now he lay with his stomach growling, mourning his lack of tact and wishing he could curse Ol' Pete for schlepping him to this dive in the first place.

No one he had known in all his forty years had tsuris like he did now, because the Calvin Coolidge Memorial Rehabilitation Facility was hell. It was the place where Jewish boys who got tattoos, slept with shiksas, and told dirty toilet jokes went. Not all of the residents had been Jewish boys in life, but they had all become Jewish boys in death because they had a Housemother who expected nothing less than perfection.

The fact that Mrs. Vonus seemed more Methodist, Presbyterian, and/or Baptist than anything else was irrelevant. Leonard had met so many Jewish mothers who acted Presbyterian, and so many Baptist mothers who acted Jewish, that he'd come to the conclusion that they were all interchangeable.

"The only mothers that out-Jewish-mother the Methodists, Baptists, and Presbyterians," he said to the ceiling, "are those Catholic Jewish-mothers, who on top of everything else get to complain about their swollen knees. And the only ones who out-Jewish-mother *them* are the sisters, who remain chaste out of shame that they were born to the goyim."

The disapproving face of Mrs. Vonus appeared above him, and

he choked on his own breath. He couldn't get used to her habit of materializing without warning. It might be that she was simply good at sneaking up on him, but he preferred to think that she had the ability to transform herself into a gnat.

"One of your most serious problems," Mrs. Vonus said, "is your apparent inability to comprehend the meaning of the word 're-spect.' "

You should talk, Leonard thought before he could stop himself. *I could've been naked in here, doing who knows what vile and perverted things in the absence of female companionship.*

Mrs. Vonus regarded him severely. "I have been placed over you as your teacher and guardian, and I shall do whatever is necessary to further your spiritual development. That includes confronting you when you do not expect it, which will train you to behave properly at all times."

"Oh, I see," Leonard said sarcastically. "Then I can wind up like Saint Whosis there and behave properly to the bitter end, huh?"

The corners of the Housemother's mouth twitched upward for only the second time since Leonard had come to the Home. "You have already had your 'bitter end,' Leonard. That you met it as you did is one of the reasons you are here."

Leonard turned onto his right side to face the wall. *I've already got a minus for today,* he thought miserably. *What more can she do to me?*

"What I am going to do," Mrs. Vonus said, "is allow you to do something you love."

All Leonard could think of were the two unsmiling candy-counter women and the various methods he wanted to use to teach them to laugh out loud.

"Don't be ridiculous," Mrs. Vonus said. "The non-fraternization rule shall never be broken."

Leonard turned back toward the Housemother and gave her a murderous look. "Then just what are you going to allow me to do, O Great Giver of Just Desserts?"

Mrs. Vonus's eyes narrowed. "Be in the Front Parlor in two minutes, or I shall do something I've never done before."

Have an orgasm? Leonard thought, and was immediately horrified at his stupidity.

He was dead now. He was definitely dead now.

Of course you are, schnook. That's the whole problem.

He expected something far worse than a minus for this transgression. He expected the Housemother to wave her hands and start his insides boiling like so much stew.

But what happened was that, for the first time, Mrs. Vonus looked upset. Her face flushed, and she averted her eyes. Her hands fumbled with the handkerchief she always carried.

Oh-ho, Leonard thought, feeling a bright bit of glee. *Methinks I've struck a nerve in this old yenta.*

The Housemother's discomfort, however, came and went in an instant.

"Be in the Parlor in two minutes," she said, "or I shall assign a minus a day in advance—something I have never considered doing to any other resident. How does it feel to be unique, Leonard?"

She turned and waddled out of the room.

If God placed her over me, Leonard thought, *why'd He build her to walk so funny?*

8

The furniture in the Front Parlor had been arranged in a circle and was occupied by thirty dour men and women, all dressed in stiff black clothing.

"What's this?" Leonard asked as Mrs. Vonus took his arm and pulled him into the center of the circle. "The Inquisition?"

The Housemother handed him a cordless microphone and then sat on a sofa with three unsmiling, horse-faced men.

Instinctively, Leonard spoke into the mike. "Hey, what's the scam?" he said, and was startled when his amplified voice emanated from the walls.

Mrs. Vonus waved a bony hand. "This is what you lived for. A performance."

Leonard's skin began to itch. His body was telling him to get out of there, but he knew better than to try. The carpet would hold him as it always did whenever the Housemother wanted him in a certain place.

He looked at the men and women in black. Their faces seemed to have been molded into perpetual frowns.

"Who are these people?" he asked. "Ex-lawyers?"

Mrs. Vonus gave him her almost-smile. "You spent a large part of your life claiming that you knew what your country stood for and that your judges did not. These are the founders of your nation. Perform for them, and see if they approve."

Leonard scanned the audience. "So where's George Washington? Ben Franklin? Tom Jefferson?"

"Those men came after," Mrs. Vonus said with a strong note of satisfaction in her voice. "These people came to escape persecution. . . ."

Realization hit Leonard like a splash of ice water.

Oh, terrific. She expects me to do my gig for a slavering pack of Puritans.

"Please begin," Mrs. Vonus said.

"Why? So they can tie me up and toss me into the pond out back to see if I float?"

"If you want to eat tomorrow," Mrs. Vonus said, "begin. I am curious to see just how funny they think you are."

Leonard wanted to fling himself onto the Housemother and beat on her head with the microphone, but instead he took a deep breath and let himself free-associate.

"Puritans, huh?" he began, pacing around the circle and shaking his head. "I hear you were really strict. 'If you don't work, you don't eat.' That was yours, wasn't it? Funny, I knew a rabbi who said it originated with Moses. 'Those crummy Pilgrims!' the rabbi used to say. 'They stole all our best stuff!' But, hey, I believe you, it's yours—you want the Ten Commandments, you can have those too.

"Don't get me wrong—it was a fine rule, although it might've been more effective if you'd made it 'If you don't work, you don't schtu—scht—'"

Leonard stopped pacing and glared at Mrs. Vonus. "How am I supposed to do my act if I've got half of my vocabulary blocked?"

"Do you think these people would find that portion funny?" the Housemother asked. "For that matter, would any decent person? If you feel you must be obscene to be funny, then you must not be too intelligent, must you? Shouldn't an intelligent person have better tools at his command?"

Leonard began pacing again, faster than before. "Y'know, I really don't get it with this obscenity hang-up," he said, the words starting to come rapid-fire. "I mean, obscenity is in the eye of the beholder, isn't it? You take this schlepper here—" He stopped pacing and pointed at an especially grim-looking Puritan. "What's a dirty word to you, Jim—how about 'toilet'? Now, of course that's not dirty to you, because you don't have the faintest idea what a toilet *is,* do you? I could stand here and tell you dirty toilet jokes all night long, and you wouldn't be offended because you wouldn't know what I was talking about. But suppose I started talking about witches—"

The Puritan stiffened in his seat.

"Ha, that got you, didn't it?" Leonard half yelled. "Now *there's* a dirty word. Hey, I've got one—when is a witch not a witch? When the broomstick she's riding belongs to Ye Reverend Pastor, Leader of the Flock. 'Cometh ye here, naughty witch,' he sayeth righteously. 'I'll put the fear of the Lord into you. Well, I'll put something into you, anyway, yea verily.'"

Leonard waited for a reaction, but it didn't come.

"Didn't quite catch that one, eh? You guys never were much for subtlety, except when it came to killing off the Indians. What you did was, you drowned, burned, or hung your witches, but only if they didn't have any social diseases. If they *did* have social diseases, you sent 'em to be social with the Mohicans, sort of your basic cultural exchange program. . . ."

The Puritans sat stone-faced.

Leonard zeroed in on a matronly woman.

"Excuse me, ma'am, but I'm conducting a survey. Have you ever, you know, had, um, *relations* with a Mohican? No, I thought not; you look unhappy. You don't follow the logic? Well, look at it this way—who has more stamina, a fat old preacher whose only exercise comes from turning pages in the Good Book"—he gestured at the man sitting next to the woman—"or a copper-skinned nature boy who wears a loincloth and wrestles bears for a living? 'Ugh, that tenth bear me wrestled today. Bring on fourteen white squaws; me got a few weeks vacation coming.'

"And speaking of Indians—or did you folks call them 'savages' or 'heathens'?—how about that Manhattan Island deal? Bunch of goyim similar to yourselves shelled out twenty-four bucks in beads for a prime chunk of real estate. The kicker, though, is that the savage who sold the island had bought it from God the week before for a sack of rocks, so he went away chuckling because he'd done so well on the deal. . . . 'Those white-eyed schlemiels with the funny hats! What a bunch of suckers!'

"Later on, of course, the white folks felt guilty for taking advantage of the poor ignorant redskins, so they threw in some good used blankets. Who knew the previous owners had died of smallpox?

"Speaking of disease, though, the Indians had the last laugh. They gave us tobacco in exchange for the blankets, and sooner or later all our lips are going to fall off. We're going to be up to our tuchises in lips, which, ultimately, is what we all want anyway, right? Who says white people are stupid?"

The Puritans were still unsmiling. They clearly understood no more than every fifth word, and that word invariably made their expressions even grimmer.

Leonard was getting no laughs. Ultimately, when he wound down, that would hurt. He would finally run out of things to say, and then he would stand in the center of the circle, drained and defeated.

For now, though, he wouldn't think of that. For now, he was high on his own patter, his own stream of consciousness.

For now, he was on a roll.

". . . and after you boys and girls came over, you discovered that this nation-building business was a real pain, so you imported black men and women to do it for you. You were awfully smart to do that, but not as smart as us Jews. *We* waited until the country was built, and *then* we came over. Meantime, of course, we were getting slaughtered wherever else we happened to be living, but we didn't mind, because we knew that eventually we'd get to go to the Promised Land—Brooklyn.

"Oh, I see what you're thinking, sir. You reacted when I identified myself as Jewish, and I know what you want to ask. The answer is Yes, we killed Him. Why? Because He refused to go to med school, that's why. . . ."

Calvin Coolidge looked down disapprovingly.

9

During his time in the pillory, Leonard began to think that he finally understood the true horror of the Home: It was exactly like being alive again.

It wasn't that being in the pillory was so bad—at least he was in the backyard beside the pond, which was the best place on the grounds to be if you were trapped in a pillory. Since the pond was near the "northeast" corner of the wooden wall that defined the "eastern," "western," and "northern" boundaries of the mansion's grounds, he not only had a good view of what Mrs. Vonus called "the east yard and arbor," but could see all the way to the road beyond the front yard.

What bothered him wasn't the punishment itself but the fact that he had been forced to perform for people who couldn't possibly understand him, and that the Puritans had been allowed to put him into the pillory simply because they hadn't liked him.

"Well, of course you don't like me, you idiots!" he'd yelled as they had carried him out through the East Doorway. "A caveman wouldn't have liked *you*, either! For that matter, neither do I!"

"I'm terribly sorry, Leonard," Mrs. Vonus had said as the Puritans had latched the pillory. "But you see, they wouldn't have agreed to hear you if I hadn't promised them the opportunity to punish you for your blasphemies. Rest assured that this is the worst I'll let them do. I'll release you in a few hours, after they've gone."

"Gone *where?*" Leonard had wanted to know, but the Housemother had already turned to waddle back to the mansion.

Then, as the sun had gone down, the Puritans had thrown overripe vegetables.

"Now, tell me, you bozos," Leonard had cried. "Would Christ have approved of this? Would Jesus have thrown the first cabbage?"

A moldy turnip had hit him in the eye.

Now, as he watched a pair of white geese paddle across the pond, it occurred to him that Mrs. Vonus had wanted to pillory him herself, but had let the Puritans do her dirty work. The black-clad fanatics had disappeared at sunrise, but it was midday now and the Housemother still hadn't appeared to release him.

None of the residents walking nervously about the grounds would offer any help. A few of them shrugged their shoulders as if to say, "Tough luck, but I've got my own tsuris, you know?" but most of them simply ignored him.

So Leonard waited as the sun rose higher, watching the geese and smelling the vegetable stuff baking on his face and hands. At least there weren't any flies.

After what felt like several more hours, he raised his eyes and looked past the mansion toward the road. If it were only possible to make a move without Mrs. Vonus knowing about it, someday he would cut a branch and try to pole-vault the ditch so he could run down the dirt road in the direction from which he had come. He wouldn't care where the road went, not even if it led back to the toilet he'd been sitting on when he'd died. He wouldn't even care if he died all over again, as long as it meant that he would ruin the Housemother's plans.

It was an impossible hope. Mrs. Vonus always knew what he was doing, and she always appeared whenever he was about to do something "against the Rules of the Home."

His crotch began to itch.

"Wonderful," he muttered, and rubbed his thighs together. It didn't help.

A flash of red appeared down the road, and then Leonard heard the sound of the International's chugging engine. After a few minutes the pickup truck emerged from behind the trees and stopped.

The passenger door opened, and a stocky, overweight man stepped out. He was wearing the standard brown suit.

"Go back!" Leonard yelled hoarsely. "Throw Ol' Pete in the ditch, hijack the truck, and go back before she's got you!"

The stranger peered in Leonard's direction, but didn't follow the instructions. He began to cross the narrow footbridge that had reappeared with the arrival of the International.

The pickup's horn blared, and the stranger flailed, nearly falling into the ditch.

Engager in filthy activity with sows, Leonard thought, wishing he could remember the words that really expressed what he thought of Ol' Pete.

He watched the newcomer totter across the footbridge and then look back, just as he had done. The truck had vanished.

Shaking his head, the stocky man stepped onto the walk that led to the front door.

"Hey!" Leonard yelled, trying to force his voice to overcome its hoarseness. "Don't go that way! Come on back here! Back here, schnook!"

The stranger paused.

"Yeah, I'm talking to you!" Leonard shouted. "C'mere and get me out of this thing!"

The stranger came toward the pond, and as he drew near, the puzzled expression on his broad, doughy face became more evident.

"I'm Leonard," Leonard said when the stranger was close enough to hear unshouted words.

"Uh, pleased to meet you," the newcomer said uncertainly. "I'm"—he peered at the copper band on his wrist—"John, I guess." His voice sounded like a combination of a baby's gurgle and an old man's cough.

"Well, that might be in your favor," Leonard said. "You're named after the Housemother's hero, sort of. Is 'John' all it says?"

John looked at his bracelet more closely. "Why? Should it say something else?"

Leonard tried to shrug, but the pillory wouldn't let him. "I've been trying to figure out if Leonard is my first name or my last, and nobody else will let me look at their bracelets. But if yours just says 'John,' it's got to be a first name."

"Who says? What about Elton John?"

"Is that who you are?"

John looked surprised. "Do I look like Elton John?"

Leonard tried to shrug again. "How should I know? I never heard of the guy."

"Where have you been the last fifteen years?" John asked, incredulous.

"Dead," Leonard said. "Get me out of this thing, will you? I got an itch. Find something to break the lock."

John squinted. "There isn't a lock. Just a latch, like on a toolbox, you know?"

Leonard was finding it difficult to be patient. His crotch felt as if a thousand crabs had settled down to lunch.

"So quit kibitzing and unlatch it already!" he yelled.

John reached for the latch, then paused and eyed Leonard suspiciously. "Am I going to get in trouble for this?"

"No!" Leonard shouted, not caring that he might be lying. "Now either get me outta here or scratch me where my pants are binding me!"

John raised an eyebrow in a way that Leonard supposed meant, "Hmm . . . interesting proposition," and then unlatched the pillory.

Leonard flung off the upper board, jammed his hands into his pants pockets, and scratched vigorously.

"That's disgusting," John said, and began to scratch himself in a similar fashion.

Leonard's first impulse was to snarl at the newcomer for mocking him, but then he realized that John's exaggerated mugging and scratching were *funny.*

"You should talk about disgusting," Leonard said. "You look like a sex-starved gorilla."

"I *am* a sex-starved gorilla," John said emphatically, and began lurching around the pond, waving his arms and screeching like a chimpanzee.

Leonard had a feeling that he was going to like this guy.

10

"I'll thank you not to bother our new resident," a thin, high-pitched voice said behind him.

Leonard's heart seemed to drop into his stomach and jump back up. Mrs. Vonus had sneaked up on him again.

He turned and glared at her. "I was merely making his acquaintance," he said. "He was kind enough to let me out of that Pilgrim peep show, which you promised you'd do a long time ago."

"I promised no such thing," Mrs. Vonus said.

"Bullsh—bull—," Leonard began, then gave up and fumed.

Mrs. Vonus waddled a few steps closer to the pond.

"Please come with me, John," she called. "We must begin your orientation. My name is Mrs. Vonus."

John, still an ape, screeched in happy mock-recognition and scampered to the Housemother.

Leonard grinned.

"That will be enough of that, John," Mrs. Vonus said.

John made ooh-oohing noises and began to probe Mrs. Vonus's blue-gray helmet of hair with his thick fingers.

Leonard laughed. It would probably earn him a minus, but he didn't care. He was getting to the point where he didn't miss dessert that much, anyway.

"Stop this instant, John," Mrs. Vonus said.

Her voice was so deadly cold that Leonard's laughter died.

John continued to search for lice.

"You have two seconds," Mrs. Vonus said.

Leonard started toward John, intending to pull him away, but he was too late.

John stiffened convulsively, and his eyes rolled back. Then he crumpled to the grass, landing on his side with a faint *whuff.*

Leonard knelt beside him and gently slapped his cheeks. He had to do something, because if he didn't, he would go for the Housemother's throat.

"He is quite all right," Mrs. Vonus said. "In any case, it is none of your affair."

I hate you, Leonard thought in a red heat. *I hate your scrawny guts, you miserable old yenta. You exist only to dictate rules, just like those self-righteous religion pimps back home.*

"Unless you wish to feel what John has just felt," Mrs. Vonus said, "I suggest you redirect your thoughts. I also suggest that you take a stroll about the grounds. Now."

Leonard stood stiffly and walked toward the back wall.

"Stand up, John," he heard the Housemother say. "There is a film I think you should see."

"A movie?" John's slurred voice said. "I love movies. I think I've been in some. . . ."

You can bet you'll be in this one, Jim, Leonard thought as he forced his eyes to stay focused on the wall that was too high to scale. *You'll goddamn sure be in this one.*

He stopped short.

He had just thought one of the forgotten, forbidden words.

He waited for the lightning to strike, but it didn't come. Then he tried to think of the word again, but it was gone.

No matter. The chink in the armor had been tiny, but it had been there. All he had to do was make it bigger.

To discover how to do that, he would need an ally.

The way to start, he decided, was to do something he knew was against the Rules of the Home.

He would wait until Mrs. Vonus and John were inside the mansion. Then he would follow and hide until the Housemother had finished showing the newcomer the portrait and the Progress Board. He would watch for his chance to sneak into the theater, and then—

He would watch the screening of John's death. Maybe he could find some way to use the film against Mrs. Vonus before she had a chance to use it against John.

I'm already dead, Leonard thought as he pretended to wander aimlessly about the backyard, *so what have I got to lose?*

When Mrs. Vonus and John were almost to the East Door, Leonard went to the pond and washed the dried vegetable stuff from his face and hair. It was time to prepare for battle.

11

Leonard waited in a shadow in the hall a few yards away from the entrance to the lobby. He saw Mrs. Vonus open one of the double doors and usher John into the theater, then watched as she went behind the candy counter.

For a moment he was afraid that he wouldn't be able to get in without her seeing him, but then she opened a panel in the wall and disappeared up a flight of steps. Apparently, her powers didn't include turning on the projector by telekinesis.

The two women behind the candy counter would be a problem, but Leonard decided to take his chances. He stepped into the lobby and strode across to the double doors.

"Excuse me, sir," the blonde said. "The main feature does not begin for thirty minutes."

Leonard didn't slow down. "Yes, I know I'm late, sorry," he said, then opened the right-hand door and stepped into the darkness. He sat in the back row, not wanting to find John until he had some idea of how to approach him.

After a half minute, the screen brightened and the House-mother's introductory spiel began. Leonard fidgeted in his seat, wanting desperately to shout an insult at the giant Mrs. Vonus image to see whether he could remember that word again.

When the death film began, Leonard experienced such a strong sense of déjà vu that he wondered whether he had known John in life. But as the film progressed, he realized that the feeling came from the fact that John's death was remarkably like his own.

In the same grainy black and white, John overdosed and died.

There were differences, of course: The camera-eye didn't remain stationary, but roamed from room to room, following John as he blundered through his final minutes. And there was a woman who gave him the injection, but she left before the end.

Finally, John lay on a bed, alone and still. Someone came into the frame and tried to revive him, then shouted angrily.

The final shot was a close-up of John's puffy face, the swollen tongue pushing out between dark lips.

The screen went black, and Leonard heard soft moaning noises.

191

Give the guy a few minutes of privacy, he thought. *Everybody ought to have a little time alone when they die.*

"I coulda," John moaned.

Leonard tried not to listen, but John's voice became louder with each syllable.

"I coulda," John said again. "I coulda gone back to New York. I coulda saved my stupid fat . . ."

There was a long pause, and then an explosive bellow:

"But *noooooooooooo. Nooooooooo,* I had to stay in *Hol-ly-woood* so I could get off on a speedball and be *cooool.*"

Leonard was impressed. Better to rail than to whimper and slide farther down in your seat.

The double doors opened, throwing a slanted shaft of yellow light down the aisle, and Leonard stood quickly so he could sit beside John before any of the others did. He didn't want the newcomer to meet anyone with jujubes before he had a chance to warn him.

12

Leonard found John in the same seat he had chosen on his own first day.

"Mind if I sit here?" Leonard asked, indicating the seat on John's right.

John looked at him through slitted eyes for a moment and then turned to face the screen again, shrugging his substantial shoulders.

Leonard sat down. "Whatever you do," he said, "don't take candy from these schmoes. It turns into bugs in the mouth of anyone except the guy who bought it."

John glanced at him. "Uh-huh."

"I'm serious," Leonard said. "The Housemother would rather you found out on your own, because she enjoys torturing schlimazels like you and me. I'm telling you in advance to save you the grief."

"Thanks," John said. "Now shut up. The movie's starting."

The screen was brightening, and Leonard closed his eyes even though he knew he wouldn't be able to keep them shut. He smelled popcorn somewhere behind him and hated whoever had been "good" enough to get the money to buy it.

"All right!" John yelped. "Jimmy Stewart!"

Leonard opened his eyes and shuddered. "You won't be so pleased after a while," he said.

"Are you kidding? *It's a Wonderful Life* is great!"

"Once, maybe, or even ten times if they're spread out over a few years. But not every afternoon for all eternity."

John shifted his bulk, jostling Leonard's elbow off the armrest. "What're you talking about?"

"Haven't you figured it out? Didn't Mrs. Vonus show you the Progress Board before she hustled you in here?"

"Yeah, but she's senile, isn't she? Hey—no more talk, okay?"

On the screen, the absurd nebulae-angels began discussing the poor soul who was about to take his own life.

Just once, Leonard thought, *I wish they'd let George croak himself. Let him leap into the ice-cold river. That's all, folks, thanks for coming. Frank Capra has suckered you, man.*

But it happened the way it always did—the ice-sledding accident, the distraught druggist, the swimming pool under the gym floor, the evil banker, the war-hero brother, the insufferably cute children, the bumbling, wingless angel named Clarence—

Leonard wanted to scream, but he didn't. He had, once, on Day 6, and had been served burnt gristle for dinner. He also knew better than to try to walk out. His seat wouldn't let him up until the last frame had whisked through the projector.

So he resigned himself to sitting through it again, miserable and thoroughly angry at John, who, despite his outburst after seeing his death, didn't seem to care that he was stuck here.

What was wrong with him, anyway?

For that matter, what was wrong with *all* of these schmendricks? Hadn't they ever considered the possibility that where one failed, many could succeed?

Or did Mrs. Vonus see to it that new residents arrived at long intervals, so she'd be able to break the spirit of each one before Ol' Pete brought the next?

It made sense, considering the nature of time at the Home. A hundred comedians might die in the same hour, but they'd arrive singly, one every fifteen or twenty "days," if that was the interval chosen by the Housemother.

Or by someone else?

If Mrs. Vonus chose the length of the interval, how could her failure to tame Leonard before John's arrival be explained?

Now that he thought about it, it seemed to Leonard that the previous night's performance for the Puritans and his subsequent imprisonment in the pillory had been the Housemother's last-ditch attempts to bring him into line before she had to concentrate on breaking in a newcomer.

That would explain how he had managed to remember that word: Mrs. Vonus had been preoccupied with John.

She was not omnipotent.

Leonard grinned. If he could enlist John's help before she sank her claws into him too deeply, they could bounce her back and forth between them like a Ping-Pong ball.

For what purpose? he wondered. *What good will that do me? Will it get me out of here?*

He brushed the questions out of his mind. Maybe running the Housemother ragged wouldn't accomplish anything; maybe he was bound here by forces beyond those she commanded. It didn't matter.

To rebel was to be doing something because *he* wanted to do it. That was enough.

13

"Punch him out, Jimmy!" John yelled, startling Leonard out of his thoughts. "Give the old fu—fu—"

John paused, and in the dim reflected light, Leonard could see an expression of confusion on the pudgy face.

"—the old fuddy-duddy a clop in the chops!" John concluded.

Leonard laughed.

"Sshhhhhh!" someone several rows behind them hissed. "Quiet, or I'll report you to the Housemother."

Leonard looked back over his shoulder.

"Dracula had his human henchmen, too," he said loudly. "Eat your flies and leave us alone."

"Fuddy-duddy?" John said, obviously bewildered by his own description of Lionel Barrymore. *"Fuddy-duddy?"*

Leonard leaned closer to him. "You beginning to get the drift? I had to deal with censorship in my life, and maybe you did in yours, but at least it was censorship you could see, censorship you could fight. Here they censor your *mind* so that you can't even think of what you want to say in the first place."

"How . . . how can they do that?" John seemed torn between listening to Leonard and watching the movie.

" 'How' I don't know," Leonard said, "but 'why' is no problem. Because this is hell, or maybe purgatory, where they punish you for your sins. And it's a rigged wheel, because they also decide what constitutes 'sin' in the first place."

"Who are 'they,' anyhow?"

"I don't know for sure, but they're represented by Mrs. Vonus. She's not known for excessive kindness to the recently deceased."

John made a derisive noise through his nostrils. "That little old lady? She's about as dangerous as a lobotomized gerbil."

"You forgetting what she did to you out back?"

"Sshhhhh!" the resident behind them hissed again.

"Somebody back there spring a leak?" John yelled.

"Pay no attention," Leonard said. "They're whining lackeys. Besides, they'll see this again tomorrow. That's the power of a lobotomized gerbil—whether you want to or not, you'll be here again tomorrow afternoon. She'll hook that invisible claw of hers into your brain and drag you here. If you try to resist, she'll send you to bed without dinner for a day or two."

John drummed his thick fingers on the armrest. "Let me get this straight. I have to come back here at the same time tomorrow. And I'm going to see the same movie?"

"Bingo, bubbie."

"Well, he—he—heck, then, I don't need to see the rest of it now. I've already missed too much listening to you, so I might as well go find something to eat."

John struggled to stand. When he finally gave up, he slumped like a chubby wrestler who had just lost a long, painful bout. Sweat glistened on his cheeks and forehead.

"See what I mean?" Leonard said. "If this doesn't qualify as Hell, I don't know what does."

"Certain portions of Utah," John said, panting heavily.

Leonard smiled. Mrs. Vonus would probably crush them both eventually, but he had a feeling that they were going to give her a run for her money.

That feeling grew stronger when John, having recovered from his struggle, straightened in his seat and began heckling the characters on the screen.

"Come on, you jerk!" John yelled. "Take an ax to the piano if it bugs you! Whop the kid up side the head!"

And later: "G'wan, jump! The water's dee-lightful!"

And still later: "You talk like a sissy, Clarence!"

Toward the end of the film, Leonard decided to get into the act.

"Merry Christmas, Main Street!" he cried. "Merry Christmas, old building and loan! Merry Christmas, old movie theater! Merry Christmas, old five-and-dime! Merry Christmas, old cathouse!"

John guffawed and then bellowed, "Merry Christmas, old

chuckhole! Merry Christmas, old dirty bookstore! Merry Christmas, old dog-frozen-to-the-fire-hydrant!"

"Merry Christmas, old social-disease clinic!" Leonard shouted.

By now, the scene of Stewart-as-George-Bailey running down Main Street was over, but Leonard and John didn't care. They were on a roll.

"Merry Christmas, old drunk in the alley!" John yelled.

"Merry Christmas, old bird-do on the sidewalk!" Leonard cried.

Something strange happened then, something Leonard never would have expected.

A few other dead comedians joined them in their heckling, and then a few more.

"Merry Christmas, old smashed cat in the gutter!"

"Merry Christmas, old rats in the sewer!"

"Merry Christmas, old tires at the gas station!"

Before long, the soundtrack was drowned out by the shouts. Leonard thought he even heard the voice of whoever had tried to quiet him earlier.

"Merry Christmas, old jokes on the john wall!"

"Merry Christmas, old strippers on the stage!"

"Merry Christmas, old scotch-and-soda!"

"Merry Christmas, and a Happy New Rear!"

"Merry Men, save Robin Hood!"

"Marry me, darling!"

"Mary, Mary, quite contrary . . ."

It degenerated into lunacy, and Leonard felt happier than he had at any moment since dying.

The movie ended as it always did, with the bell on the Christmas tree ringing and the little girl in Jimmy Stewart's arms expressing the opinion that some angel was getting his wings. This time, though, when Stewart said, "That's right," John shouted. "That's ridiculous!"

Leonard decided that was the perfect response, so he added his own "Yeah, that's ridiculous!"

Before the credits came on, the whole audience was chanting, "That's ridiculous! That's ridiculous! That's ridiculous!"

"Merely silly!" someone cried between chants.

Joy thrilled up in Leonard, giving him a greater rush than he'd ever gotten from horse. The Revolution, he was sure, had begun at last.

14

But the joy was more like the transitory ecstasy of a narcotic than Leonard had thought. As soon as the lights came up, the chanting stopped, and the other residents hurried out of the theater like frightened mice.

John stood up and yelled, "Any of you guys play the blues?"

A few of the residents glanced back, but none answered.

"Forget it, man," Leonard said sullenly. "I thought we might've put a spark into them, but they were just having flashbacks to when they had some guts, to when they were alive. She's got them under her thumb."

The last of the others disappeared beyond the double doors, leaving Leonard and John alone.

John's stomach growled so loudly that the sound echoed off the walls.

"This is the first movie I've ever sat through without at least a box of popcorn," he said. "Where can I get something to eat around here?"

"You can't," Leonard said.

"Whaddaya mean, I can't? I'm hungry, aren't I? I've gotta eat if I'm hungry, don't I?"

Leonard stood and moved toward the aisle. "The dinner bell rings a few hours or a few days after the movie, depending on your time sense. You get to the dining room by going through the Front Parlor. You know, Calvin's room."

John walked beside him toward the double doors. "Hey, I can't wait. I'm hungry *now.*"

"Me too. But I doubt that the Housemother'll let me eat today. I've been a bad boy."

"I didn't figure you were wearing a wooden collar to be stylish. But I'll get to eat, won't I?"

"That's up to her," Leonard said, pushing open the doors. "In all fairness, though—hanging out with me won't do you much good in that department. I'm on her excrement list."

"Don't you mean sh—sh—," John said as they stepped into the lobby. He stopped and frowned.

Leonard paused and studied John's face. The heavy eyebrows were angled and pushed together so that the frown seemed almost a parody of the expression.

"Weren't you listening to what I said about censorship?" Leonard asked. "Haven't you caught on yet?"

John seemed about to answer, but then his eyes shifted to the candy counter. His expression changed abruptly, and he nudged Leonard in the ribs.

"Women and junk food," he said eagerly. "I noticed 'em before, but the gerbil was with me." He headed toward the counter.

"You're wasting your time," Leonard said.

John looked back over his shoulder, raising an eyebrow. "I've got nothing *but* time, Jack." He turned toward the counter again.

Leonard considered heading for his room to avoid seeing John's coming humiliation, but there was nothing waiting for him there except the picture of the saint-about-to-become-chopped-liver.

He reached the counter at the same time as John. Together, they leaned with their elbows on the glass countertop and leered at the women.

John waggled his eyebrows lasciviously. "Helloooo," he said. "I couldn't help but notice that there are two of you ladies and two of us gentlemen. A convenient coincidence, wouldn't you say?" The women stared blankly.

"Arithmetic seems to be beyond them," Leonard said.

"I don't care if they can count," John said. "I don't even care if they can talk. I'll take the blonde, you take the brunette. Deal?"

"Sure. Just out of curiosity, though, how do you plan to convince them of the reasonableness of the arrangement?"

"Sheer animal charm," John said, and vaulted over the counter with far more ease than Leonard would have thought possible for a man of his bulk.

"Which animal?" Leonard asked. "An orangutan, maybe?"

"Maybe," John said, and grabbed the blonde around the waist, dipping her backward as if he were Rhett Butler and she were Scarlett O'Hara.

Leonard winked at the brunette and started clambering over the counter.

"Baby," John was saying in a bad imitation of Clark Gable, "you're for me."

"I suggest you release me immediately," the blonde said.

"Better turn up the animal charm a notch or two," Leonard said, swiveling on his belly on the countertop.

"I cannot release you, mon cher," John said, his lips less than an inch from the woman's. "We're bound together by invisible diamond chains of hot volcanic love."

Leonard landed heavily on the tiled floor inside the U of the counter, slipping a little on a slick of spilled popcorn butter. " 'Invisible diamond chains of hot volcanic love'?" he asked.

"Shut up," John said. "Can't you see I'm seducing this woman?"

"Release me now," the blonde said.

John planted his lips on hers in what appeared to Leonard to be the sloppiest kiss in history.

Leonard grinned at the brunette. "I'd hate to feel left out, wouldn't you?"

"You might find it preferable," she said.

Leonard moved a step closer. "Oh, I don't think—"

The rest of his sentence was cut off by John's scream.

Leonard whirled and saw his friend locked in an embrace with a catfish-woman.

She had arms and legs, but they were sickly gray, *slimy* arms and legs. Her head, although still covered with blonde hair, had transformed into that of a scaleless fish, complete with whiskerlike barbels.

John was writhing in the creature's embrace, spitting frantically.

"For the love of—pahhh!" he cried. "She tastes like rancid cat food!"

Leonard glanced back at the brunette woman, who still looked delectably human, and said, "Maybe some other time."

"I doubt it," she said.

John tore away from the catfish-woman, shoving her to the floor in the process, and lunged for the candy counter.

"Gotta get that taste outta my mouth!" he yelled, and grabbed several boxes of Junior Mints.

"That will be six dollars," the brunette said.

"Don't," Leonard said, grabbing John's arm. "They'll start crawling in your mouth."

John twisted away and ripped open the boxes, dumping their contents onto the countertop. Dozens of chocolate-coated mint-buttons rolled and slid across the glass.

"They don't look alive to me, bud!" John yelled.

Leonard stared at them. Maybe the thing with the cockroaches only happened if you ate candy that someone else had bought. No one had bought this stuff yet, so—

"Junior Mints, prepare to meet thy doom!" John roared, and squatted so that his mouth was at the edge of the counter.

The catfish-woman flopped on the floor and made a gurgling noise.

Leonard gave her a sidelong look. "No offense, sweetheart, but you've got an odor problem."

John began scooping the candies into his mouth with both hands, making small noises of pleasure as he chewed.

The scents of chocolate and mint overpowered the fish stink and filled Leonard's head, making him dizzy. He resisted for several seconds, but when he saw that nothing was happening to John, he decided to grab some candy before it was all gone.

He knelt beside his friend.

"I feel like a Catholic who just hit the Host jackpot," he said, and shoved a handful of mints into his mouth.

"You must stop immediately," the brunette woman's voice said behind him. The warning was accompanied by the sounds of the blonde's flopping and gurgling.

Leonard ignored them and concentrated on his feast. Even when Mrs. Vonus let him eat, the food was relentlessly bland, but this—this was smooth, creamy, minty, and luxuriously chocolaty. He reveled in it, filling his mouth with a huge blob of sweetness.

For a second, he thought he was no longer in Hell, but Heaven.

Then something squirmed out of the blob and tried to slither down his throat.

He gagged, and as he spun away from the counter he heard John give a strangled cry.

I knew better, Leonard thought as he saw the writhing mass he had spit onto the white tile.

Worms and slugs.

I knew better, and I did it anyway.

He felt nausea, but no regret.

15

"Yes, you did know better, Leonard," Mrs. Vonus said. "Why are you so self-destructive?"

He looked up and saw her standing over him. He wasn't surprised to see her.

John was crawling across the floor like an overweight dog. "Oh, mother," he moaned. "Bad acid. Bad, bad acid. I knew I'd get flashbacks, I *knew* it, but *noooooooooo*, I had to have three tabs, and six years later, here they are again."

Leonard stood and wiped his mouth on his jacket sleeve. "You're not flashing back. This is what's happening. And this"—he nodded toward Mrs. Vonus—"is who's doing it to you. She claims she's trying to mold us into perfection, but she really means to crush our spirits, not build them up."

"You're confusing 'spirit' and 'will,'" the Housemother said. "Will is the evil part of man and has always been his downfall. Only by denying the will can you be saved."

Leonard tugged on John's left arm, trying to pull him to his feet. To his surprise, the brunette woman grasped John's right arm and helped.

"That isn't necessary, Melody," Mrs. Vonus said sharply.

"Nice name," Leonard told the brunette as they brought John to a standing position. "Thanks."

Melody looked down. Leonard's eyes followed, and he saw that the blonde had flopped across the floor and was gulping the worms and slugs.

John was swaying back and forth and beginning to babble nonsense.

"—ponies jump sniff good hot mother don't needle ah yes Baskin-Robbins—"

Leonard couldn't tell whether it was an act or not.

"Come on, friend," he said. "Let's get out of here." He tugged John toward the narrow gap between the end of the candy counter and the wall.

"Another resident will show John to his room," Mrs. Vonus said. "I would rather you didn't have any further contact with him."

Leonard was maneuvering the chunky man through the gap with some difficulty; John's belly had folded over the countertop and didn't want to move.

"—tutti-frutti all over the redeye Louie Louie—"

"What are you gonna do?" Leonard asked the Housemother.

"Baby-sit him constantly so he doesn't meet me in the hall or the backyard? Well, that's fine with me, because if you're with him, you can't be nudzhing me. Here, he's all yours."

Leonard left John stuck in the gap and clambered over the counter again, kicking a few stray Junior Mints across the lobby.

It was only when one of the mints bounced off a resident's forehead that Leonard noticed eight other comedians standing in the mouth of the hallway.

"What are you guys doing here?" he asked. He had never seen anyone loiter in or near the lobby after the movie. "Enjoying the floor show? What'd you think of the amazing fish-faced bimbo?" He glanced back and saw that the blonde was in human form again.

"These gentlemen are my most advanced residents, and they aren't here for amusement," Mrs. Vonus said. "Four of them are being assigned as companions to John, and four are being assigned as companions to you. At least one will be near you at all times and will report any problems."

Leonard stopped in the center of the lobby and stared at the eight men facing him. They seemed so incredibly dull—as if they were all from Buffalo, New York—that he found it hard to believe that any of them had ever made it in comedy.

But they had, or they wouldn't have been brought to the Home in the first place.

Realizing that, he studied their placid faces and saw what Mrs. Vonus wanted to turn him into. He saw the truth of the Afterlife:

The way to move up the Hill, to get to a Better Place, was to resign oneself to an Eternity of white-bread complacency and ordinariness. To become a thing of flesh-colored clay.

To become a golem.

He backed away from them. "Oh no you don't. You don't transform four of these schmendricks into my shadows, lady. Where this Jewish boy walks, he walks alone. Or if not alone, then in the company of a good-looking chick."

"You have no choice in the matter," the Housemother said.

"Frederick, you shall take the first shift with Leonard. Albert, you shall take the first shift with John."

Two of the white-bread golems stepped forward.

Leonard held up a fist. "Who wants to be the first to sing soprano?"

"If you touch your companion," Mrs. Vonus said, "you will experience pain three times as intense as what you experienced for trying to alter the Progress Board."

John, who had been babbling quietly since getting stuck between the wall and counter, now shouted, "You useless weenies!"

Leonard turned and saw the fat man squeeze himself out of the gap like a cork out of a bottleneck.

"What are you, men or mothballs?" John yelled, pointing at the golems.

" 'Mothballs'?" Leonard said.

"Whatsa mattayou pimple-brains?" John bellowed, gesticulating so vigorously that his paunch shook like gelatin. "Don'tcha know when you're being walked all over? Are you just going to sit back and take it? Did Custer sit back and take it when the Japanese attacked? Did Joan of Arc let her religion stop her from eating her enemies raw without salt? Did Dagwood cower like a whipped dog when Mister Dithers hit him with a typewriter? You bet he didn't, boy! He went ahead and asked for a raise anyway, and when Mister Dithers hit him with another typewriter, he asked *again!* And here you are, standing like doofs with your elbows up your noses, afraid to—"

John turned toward Leonard and whispered, "What are they afraid to do?"

"Anything," Leonard said. "Everything."

John's face took on an expression of exaggerated disgust. "What a bunch of wimps," he said.

"Enough nonsense," Mrs. Vonus said. "Frederick, Albert— please take these gentlemen to their rooms. If they are reluctant, touch them lightly. Neither of them will be allowed to eat this evening. Lock them in their rooms until you've finished your own meals, then allow them the freedom of the grounds as long as they do not meet. You will be relieved in the morning."

The brown-haired, Presbyterian-looking golem named Frederick gestured to Leonard, and the brown-haired, Presbyterian-looking golem named Albert gestured to John.

"Sorry, friend," Leonard said to John. "Looks like I got you into trouble after all."

John went into a sumo wrestler's stance. "Trouble? Ha! I'll show these guys trouble. Trouble is my middle name. I'm John T. Something-Or-Other. Let 'em at me. I'll eat their gall bladders. I'll stomp their toes. I'll move their kneecaps to their ankles. I'll put black dots on their teeth and play dominoes. I'll—"

The golem called Albert walked up to John and brushed his wrist with a fingertip. John sat down on the scarlet carpet.

"—do whatever you say," he mumbled.

Leonard charged at Albert. Before he could get there, a spear of heat stabbed from the top of his head to the soles of his feet.

He found himself kneeling before Frederick. He looked up at the white-bread face through a red-and-black checkerboard of pain and said, "I wish you were an enemy plane and I were on the USS *Brooklyn* so I could do horrible things to you with a five-inch deck gun."

The golem gestured for Leonard to stand. Leonard did so, after three tries, and was about to help John up, but stopped when Frederick shook his head.

"He won't make it without me," Leonard said.

Mrs. Vonus came around the candy counter and waddled toward the hallway.

"That's where you're wrong," she said. "He'll 'make it' perfectly well without you, and you without him. If you meet again, it will be because I have decided that there will be some benefit to both of you as a result. I do not expect that day to arrive for quite some time."

The Housemother entered the hall and was gone.

The brunette woman, Melody, came around the counter and

helped John to his feet. The blonde frowned at her but said nothing.

John looked pale and disoriented. As his eyes refocused, he stared at Melody as if seeing her for the first time. "Are you one of my groupies?" he asked, slurring the words.

Leonard noticed that Melody flushed slightly. He managed to smile at her, although it made his teeth hurt. "How'd a nice chick like you wind up working for the Gestapo Queen? I'd've thought you'd have gone to the Florence Nightingale Home for Knockout Angels of Mercy."

Melody returned to the other side of the counter. "I was given the opportunity to volunteer," she said. "How about you . . . sir?"

Leonard shrugged, even though that hurt too. "I was drafted."

Frederick gestured at him again.

"Gotta go now," Leonard said, waving to both John and Melody. "Command performance in my room. There's this saint about to be made into bratwurst who wants to laugh before she dies."

"A challenge!" John cried, a little weakly. "Did Magellan give up getting to the South Pole just because it was a challenge? Did Alexander Graham Bell throw out the penicillin just because it was a little moldy? Did Abe Lincoln stop being president just because he got shot?"

"Yes," Leonard said, and headed for the hallway. Each step sent a red rush of pain boiling into his head.

"Oh," he heard John say behind him. "Darn that Abe Lincoln, anyway."

Yeah, Leonard thought. *Darn it all to heck.*

16

Within five sunrises, Leonard was spending all of his free time in his room, coming downstairs only for mandatory activities—

sing-alongs (endless repetitions of the Doxology), meals (one out of every three dinners he was allowed to eat consisted of broiled liver and Brussels sprouts), and the daily movie (after a while, he was so bored that he even stopped wishing Jimmy Stewart would jump into the bush after the possibly nude Donna Reed).

At least one of his four guards, his golem for the day, was always with him. When he lay on his bed, the golem sat on a hard-backed chair beside the door. When he awoke in the morning, the golem accompanied him down the hall to the communal bathroom. When he went to the afternoon movie, the golem sat beside him.

None of the four would talk to him or do anything besides watch him. Leonard began calling them all "Fred," knowing he would be right at least twenty-five percent of the time.

"Hey, Fred," he said on the seventh evening, lying on his bed after eating a dinner that thankfully, blessedly, had not been liver and Brussels sprouts, "tell me a story."

Frederick sat on his chair, looking like an embalmed corpse in the weak yellow light given off by the kerosene lamp on the nightstand.

"Don't feel like it, huh?" Leonard said. "Okay, then, explain things to me. Explain why this place has electricity—you've gotta have electricity to run a movie projector, right?—but every lamp has a wick instead of a lightbulb."

Fred didn't even blink.

Leonard sat up. "You don't seem to understand," he said, the muscles in his throat becoming as taut as stretched steel cables. "I have to have a conversation. You won't let me near the candy counter, so I can't even say hello to Melody or the amphibious bimbo. I only see John at distances of twenty yards or more. And talking to Mrs. Vonus is like trying to chum up to my executioner. So here's the deal: I'm going to talk to you, and you're going to talk to me, or I'm going to take off your head, Fred."

Leonard searched the golem's face for some evidence that he was getting through—a muscle twitch, an eye movement, anything—and found nothing.

"All right," he said slowly, "if you're shy, I'll go first. The topic we'll begin with is Early Trauma: When I was in seventh grade, I stole money from my school's Red Cross drive so I could buy a pair of sneakers for gym class. I was caught, and my father, in addition to beating me up, never forgave me for the shame I had brought upon him. Your turn."

Frederick remained still and silent.

"C'mon, Fred," Leonard said, "surely you can remember something of your life before death, of life before servitude to an ancient and vindictive Daisy Duck."

A muscle in Frederick's left cheek twitched, but that was all.

"I'm going to count to five," Leonard said, pressing the balls of his feet against the hardwood floor and tensing on the edge of the bed, "and then I'm tearing out your esophagus. One, two, three, four—"

He paused, waiting for Frederick to do something, or at least to warn him again of the penalty Mrs. Vonus had imposed for touching a golem. But Frederick did nothing.

Leonard had no desire to feel the pain he knew he would feel when his fingers touched his guard's skin, but he had committed himself. He had told the golem he would attack, and to fail to do so would be to demonstrate that the Housemother had frightened him into obedience, that she had won.

"Five!" he yelled, and launched himself across the room.

In the instant before his hands closed on Frederick's throat, he saw the golem smile.

Then he fell into an inferno of blue-tinged pain.

When it faded, he found himself lying on his side looking up at the ecstatic saint. His shoulders throbbed violently, and his arms felt as if they had almost been torn off.

Groaning, he turned onto his back and saw Frederick sitting like God on Judgment Day, looking down on him with an expression similar to that of the *Mona Lisa*.

The throbbing subsided to a painful tingle, and Leonard pushed himself up to a sitting position.

"That made you happy, didn't it, Fred?" he asked.

Fred's expression didn't change.

"I'm glad," Leonard said. "If you're taking pleasure in my pain, that means I've broken your spirituality a little. They don't want sadists on the Hill, do they?"

Frederick's half smile faded, and Leonard was pleased to see that the golem actually looked distressed.

He hadn't been able to strangle the jerk, but he had accomplished something anyway.

With that realization, Leonard knew what he would do next.

What was the saying? That which does not kill us makes us stronger, wasn't it? And who had said it? Plato? Nietzsche? Teddy Roosevelt? John Wayne? The coyote from the Road Runner cartoons?

Doesn't matter, Leonard thought. *The point is, nothing can kill me, on account of I'm already dead. So pain can only make me stronger . . . in theory, anyhow.*

He struggled up to his feet. "Don't worry, Freddy boy. I'm going to give you another chance to turn the other cheek."

He took a deep breath and fell on the golem before he could change his mind. His hands closed around Frederick's throat, and a razor of pain slit his arms, shoulders, and head.

He felt his eyeballs boiling, his teeth shattering.

But he held on.

A second razor followed the first, and he thought he screamed. He wasn't sure, because he couldn't hear anything except a thundering rush of white noise.

But he held on.

Then came the third razor, and the red-and-black checkerboard pattern flooded in.

But, until the last half second of consciousness, he held on.

When he came to, Leonard knew that he had not been out long. He was on his knees beside Frederick's chair, and the golem was looking down at him with something in his eyes that might be fear.

Forcing a grin, Leonard stood shakily, staggered to the bed, and sat down.

"I'm going to rest a few minutes, Fred ol' buddy ol' pal," he said, surprised at the strength of his voice, "and then we'll try it again."

"I will report," the golem said. The three words were the first that any of the guards had spoken.

"So go ahead," Leonard said. "Let's see what she comes up with this time. Variety is the spice of life." He chuckled, and winced at the pain in his chest. "Or, in this case, death."

When the pain subsided, he walked across the room and jabbed his right index finger into Frederick's shoulder. The jolt sent him stumbling backward, but he didn't fall.

He jabbed the golem again. And again.

It hurt horribly, but after several more jabs he began to think that he might be able to get used to pain, just as he had gotten used to the tattoo he'd had in life.

"You can hit me back if you like," he said as he continued to jab.

Frederick didn't answer, but now Leonard was sure that the look in his guard's eyes was fear.

When he finally lay on his bed again, exhausted and half-paralyzed with pain, Leonard winked at the saint on his wall.

17

Mrs. Vonus called him down to the foyer two nights later, and he had to restrain himself from laughing when he saw that John, without his guard, was there too.

He had to restrain himself because laughing was extremely painful.

"Frederick, you may leave until I call for you," Mrs. Vonus said as Leonard and his guard left the stairway.

The golem turned to go back upstairs.

"See you later, eh, Freddy?" Leonard said, punching the golem in the shoulder. His arm felt as if the skin were being flayed off, but he only grinned and tried to keep his mind blank. He wanted the Housemother to think he didn't feel a thing.

Frederick, looking distraught, retreated.

John whistled admiringly. "How'd you do that? I tried to get Prince Albert in a half nelson once and thought I was gonna split open like Humpty Dumpty."

Leonard shrugged, barely keeping himself from wincing, and said, "Looks like you've lost some weight."

John's expression switched from admiration to unhappiness. "That'll happen when you're only allowed to eat every other day."

Leonard glared at Mrs. Vonus. "You starving this kid?"

The Housemother seemed perturbed. "He is overweight, so I have put him on a diet."

"Diet, schmyet," Leonard said. "He's dead, isn't he? You've got powers, don't you? Why don't you just hocus-pocus the excess baggage away?"

Mrs. Vonus sighed. "I've told you before: Here you must learn the things you did not learn in life. John was a glutton in life, so he must learn to avoid that sin before being allowed to—"

"Yeah, yeah, yeah," Leonard interrupted. "Before he goes skipping up the Hill like a good little angel, tra-la-la, whoop-de-do. Bullsh—bull— Nonsense." The word was far too weak. "The truth is that you still want to punish him for the trouble he got into on his first day. You made up this 'diet' scam as an excuse to hurt him."

John's eyebrows shot up, and he spun to face Mrs. Vonus. "Is that true? I've been good except for the half nelson, haven't I? I paid for that mistake as soon as I made it, didn't I?"

The Housemother pursed her lips. "You mustn't listen to Leonard. I'm afraid he hasn't progressed beyond the point where he'll say anything to cause difficulty for me."

"Hey, John," Leonard said, "am I the one who gave you a two-legged electric eel for a playmate?"

John opened his mouth to answer, but Mrs. Vonus spoke before he had a chance.

"Enough of this," she said. "Leonard, you are dangerously close to losing dinner privileges for three days in a row. Kindly be quiet and come with me, both of you." She turned and waddled into the Front Parlor.

Leonard leaned close to John and whispered, "She's scared, man. Why else would she crack enough to let us get together again?"

John edged away and followed the Housemother.

Leonard hurried to catch up. "What's wrong? I got a disease or something?"

John paused at the entrance to the Parlor. "Nothing personal," he said softly. "It's just that I'm dying from lack of food, and I don't want to tick her off. You've only been downstairs two minutes, and you've already made me gripe at her."

Leonard felt dazed for a moment, then angry. "You're a coward."

"No," John said, "I'm hungry." He followed Mrs. Vonus into the Front Parlor.

Leonard stood in the entranceway, debating whether to finally try to escape.

"The front door won't let you out," Mrs. Vonus called. "And if you hesitate any longer, the floor of the foyer will become hot enough to burn the flesh off your feet."

Leonard went into the Front Parlor and saw that the furniture was arranged in a circle again.

This time, the audience consisted of forty Orthodox rabbis wearing phylacteries, tallithim, and yarmulkes.

John and Mrs. Vonus waited in the center of the circle. The Housemother was holding two cordless microphones.

"You're slipping," Leonard said as he walked sideways between two chairs to enter the circle. "These guys aren't going to slap me into a pillory."

"Perhaps not," Mrs. Vonus said, handing him one of the microphones. "But can you make them laugh?"

Leonard considered that.

With the Puritans, he had known what to expect. But with this audience . . . How could he predict how they would react to him? It would depend on where they were from, who they knew, in which decade they had died. . . .

"Sure I can," he said, hoping that the Housemother wasn't reading his mind.

Mrs. Vonus turned toward John. "And you? Can you make these good men laugh?"

John looked nervous. "I, uh . . . what am I supposed to do?"

"Why, what you did in life," the Housemother said. "Be funny." She handed John the second microphone and went to sit beside one of the rabbis.

"You want to go first?" Leonard asked John.

John's face looked waxy. "I—," he began, whispering hoarsely, and swallowed. "I can't do stand-up. I'm a sketch player. Besides, I need some . . . some stuff."

Leonard nodded. "Sometimes I needed a little taste, too. But no matter what I did to get ready, I always needed to throw up before going onstage. Three good upchucks, and I was fine."

"I heard that about you," John said.

Leonard was taken aback. "You know who I am?"

John licked his lips. "I think so, but I can't remember your name. It's as if it's one of those words we can't say here."

Leonard grinned. "Sounds right." He looked around the room at the rabbis, most of whom were stroking their beards in an irritated fashion. "Tell you what. I'll start, and if you think of something, jump in."

John swallowed again, his Adam's apple jerking as if it were trying to escape his throat. "Don't count on me. I feel like barfing."

"There'd be something wrong with you if you didn't," Leonard said, and brought his microphone up to his lips.

18

"Shalom aleichem, gentlemen," Leonard said, his voice booming from the walls, and waited for the rabbis' response.

They said nothing.

"What's this?" Leonard said in mock surprise. "Rabbis unwilling to wish a fellow Jew peace? Have you been hanging out with Baptists or what? Oh, not that I blame you—you probably don't consider me a proper Jew. I was foulmouthed, disrespectful, unobservant, and irreverent. Besides which, I had a tattoo and consorted with so many shiksas that you'd all drop dead if I told you the number—if you weren't already dead, that is."

"Shame," one of the rabbis said severely.

"This is funny?" said another.

"*Oy, Gottenyu!*" moaned a third.

Leonard turned to gesture at the portrait of Calvin Coolidge. John was standing to one side of the fireplace, looking pale and sick.

"Now there," Leonard said, indicating Coolidge, "was a good Jewish boy for you. He was clean, reverent, chaste, temperate, and so polite that he often seemed to be in a coma. Not to mention that he grew up to be president. Why is it, rabbis, that all of the really good Jewish boys turn out to be goyim?"

As he asked the question, he brought his gaze down from the portrait and saw that John's eyes were wide with terror.

Leonard turned quickly and saw that all of the rabbis had become smooth-shaven Catholic priests.

They've been waiting for this chance ever since Chicago, ever since I started doing the Religions, Incorporated bit, he thought. *Now they can keep me in a hostile courtroom until the universe disintegrates and each of them puts a spot of the ash on his forehead—*

He saw that Mrs. Vonus was smiling more broadly than she had at any time since he'd come to the Home.

—and Miss Self-Righteous Daisy Duck gave me to them.

"Are you going to tell us your confession or aren't you?" one of the priests asked sternly.

"Confession?" Leonard asked. "That's only for the faithful, isn't it? Do I look faithful? Let's try a test: 'Hail, Mary, full of grapes—' What the heck, you didn't wanna hear my confession anyhow, pops, er, Father. It's pretty messy, particularly the part where I dress like a priest and con middle-aged women into giving me loads of cash for a South American leper colony, keeping half for myself. But hey, you can understand that. You put on a stiff white collar, and anybody who's carrying around the smallest shred of guilt—meaning everybody—feels compelled to give you money, all of it tax-free. It's almost worth giving up sex, and it's definitely worth *saying* you'll give up sex."

The priests' faces became more than grim.

"Heretic," one said, almost growling.

"He should be burned at the stake," another said, and turned toward the Housemother. "We can do that, can't we?"

Mrs. Vonus nodded. "Keep in mind, however, that he won't die."

"As long as he hurts," the priest said.

Leonard stared at the Housemother. "But—when the Puritans put me in the pillory, you said—"

"You've made no progress since then," she said. "More serious measures are in order."

Every muscle in Leonard's body knotted with his outrage. "Hypocrite!" he screamed, and his voice shrieked from the walls with a sound like grinding metal. "You think you've fixed us so we can't say dirty words? Well, you forgot *hypocrite*. A hypocrite lies to the people she claims to be saving, and when she's caught in the lie, she says, 'That was then; this is now; you haven't been good enough.' "

Mrs. Vonus's smile disappeared. "You could have listened to me. You could have tried to understand why you have to change—"

"But *noooooooooooooooo!*" John cried, bounding up to stand beside Leonard. "You had to be an *individual.* You had to indulge your *self.*"

Leonard couldn't tell whether John was being sarcastic or serious, but he chose to believe that the other comedian had found some courage.

"I know, I know," Leonard said melodramatically, closing his eyes and placing the back of his left wrist against his forehead. "How could I have been so unreasonable as to believe in the sanctity of anything so despicable as individual freedom?"

"REPENT!" fifty voices shouted.

Leonard opened his eyes and saw that the priests had been replaced by evangelical preachers in three-piece suits. They were all standing, waving heavy black Bibles and pointing at him.

"THE DAY OF JUDGMENT IS UPON YE!" they cried.

John touched Leonard's arm. "What's going on?" he whispered. He was still holding his microphone to his mouth, and the whisper hissed through the room like a gust of wind.

Leonard felt dizzy. He was afraid to see what the preachers would turn into next.

He lowered his microphone and spoke into John's ear. "She's pulling out all the stops," he said. "She wants to make an example of me."

"So why am I here?" John's whisper roared from the walls. "I've been good—"

"An example's useless without a 'beneficiary,' " Leonard said.

Mrs. Vonus, still seated, smiled up at the preacher standing next to her.

"Proceed," she said.

The preachers raised their Bibles higher and moved a step closer to Leonard and John.

"HE HATH APPOINTED A DAY, IN THE WHICH HE WILL JUDGE THE WORLD," the preachers roared.

"Holy sh—sh— What are they doing?" John said tremulously, his voice vibrating from the walls.

217

"I'm not sure," Leonard said, trying to squelch his fear, "but I think we're about to be bludgeoned with the Good Book."

"DEPART FROM ME, YE CURSED," the mass preacher-voice bellowed, "INTO EVERLASTING FIRE, PREPARED FOR THE DEVIL AND HIS FALLEN ANGELS."

John dropped his microphone and fell to his knees. "They're going to burn us!" he shrieked, and covered his face with his hands.

Leonard felt heat on his neck. He looked behind him and saw flames leaping in the fireplace.

"God damn," he said. He wished he had time to enjoy having said it.

He turned to face the preachers again, hoping to find a gap in the cordon.

The preachers had become blue-uniformed police officers. The Bibles had become billy clubs.

"YOU'RE UNDER ARREST, SCUM," they chanted. "YOU CAN'T SAY THAT IN A PUBLIC PLACE."

"I'm sorry, I'm sorry, I'm sorry," John was sobbing.

Leonard's teeth clenched. It was the cops or the fire.

He raised his microphone as if it were a blackjack.

"Come on!" he yelled. "This time I'm not gonna try to fight you with the Constitution! This time I'm giving back what I get, you bas—bas—"

"SCUM," the cops said.

John was crying hysterically.

The cops became judges in black robes; the billies became gavels.

"GUILTY," the judges said.

Leonard sucked in a breath that scorched his lungs.

"You *bastards!*" he shouted, and swung the microphone.

His head exploded in agony as the gavels rained down and transformed.

Now his attackers were lawyers; now priests; now cops; now Puritans; now nuns; now rabbis; now preachers; now SS troops; now judges.

After a while, Leonard didn't know whether he was being beaten with billy clubs, or Bibles, or whips, or rosaries, or briefcases, or gavels, or phylacteries. He didn't know whether the liquid on his tongue was sweat, saliva, blood, or wine.

19

It lasted until he hurt so much that he wished he could die again.

Then until he wished he had never died at all.

Then until he wished he had never been born.

Finally, when he had been beaten so long that he no longer knew what it was like not to be beaten, he wished he had never done anything against the Rules of the Home.

It stopped.

The priests, the judges, the rabbis, the cops . . . all were gone. Leonard's vision cleared, and he saw his hands pressed into the carpet, yellow and orange flickers dancing across the skin. The microphone lay a few inches beyond the fingers of his right hand. He smelled blood.

He stared at his hands and the microphone for a long time, trying to understand which was a part of him. He flexed his fingers, and the carpet fibers prickled his palms.

Gradually, he began to hear a sound that was unlike the sound of clubs striking flesh. Someone was crying.

He knew it wasn't him. He had gone beyond crying centuries ago.

"You may stand," a brittle voice said.

Slowly, Leonard pushed himself up until he was resting on his knees alone.

A small, elderly woman stood before him.

"I——," he began, and then coughed because he was unaccustomed to using his voice. "I remember you."

The woman nodded. "I am Mrs. Vonus."

The crying had not stopped. Leonard turned his head and saw a chubby man crouching next to the mantel, hiding his face against wooden cherubim.

"John?" Leonard said tentatively.

John twitched and turned away from the mantel. His face was tear-streaked. "They didn't kill you?" he asked tremulously.

This struck Leonard as funny, although he wasn't sure why. "No, they couldn't do that."

John blinked and then wiped his nose on his necktie. "I guess not," he said, his voice half-muffled by the fabric.

Mrs. Vonus walked toward John, extending her right hand. "Come along. The remainder of Leonard's lesson will be private."

A nugget of panic pulsed in Leonard's chest. "Are they coming back?"

Mrs. Vonus helped John to his feet, then smiled at Leonard. "Not unless you want them to. Someone else is here to see you, though."

Satan, he thought. *Satan has come to throw me into the lake of fire.*

"No," Mrs. Vonus said, tugging on John's arm. "Not unless you want him to."

Leonard crawled to a chair and used it as a brace to help himself stand. By the time he was fully upright, Mrs. Vonus and John were going through the wide doorway.

"Don't leave me alone," Leonard said.

"I won't," the Housemother answered.

John looked back. "Sorry I let you down," he said weakly.

Then they were gone. Leonard tried to follow, but his legs wouldn't carry his weight. He collapsed into the chair.

He found himself facing the fireplace, where a small fire was burning. Standing in front of it was a slender woman wearing a cream-colored evening gown. Her face was hidden in shadow.

"Melody?" he said hesitantly. It was the only woman's first name that he could remember.

The woman walked toward him. "Who's that?" she asked. "One of your girlfriends?"

Her voice was like music with a sharp edge.

"No," he said, not knowing whether he was lying. "I don't . . . have any girlfriends."

"Better not," the woman said.

She sat in a chair beside him. He could see her clearly now— her smooth, fair skin; her incredibly long red hair; her penetrating blue eyes. Her expression was a combination of disdain and pity.

Leonard felt as though someone had stuck a knife in his throat.

"How have you been?" he said hoarsely.

"You cut out on me," she said.

He tried to swallow. "I didn't mean to."

"There were a lot of things you didn't mean to do," she said. "You did them anyway. You hurt me. You hurt everybody."

Leonard felt a small stirring of anger. "You hurt me too."

"We didn't wallow in it. We weren't so obsessed with truth that we forgot about caring."

His anger drowned in a wave of remorse.

"I never forgot," he said, almost whispering.

"You did," she said. "You forgot about everything except your tapes and transcripts, your affidavits and judgments. We wanted you to stop. But you kept after it until you killed yourself. Until you left us."

Leonard reached for her. He wanted to caress her hand, her arm, her cheek.

She was sitting right next to him, but his fingers found nothing but air. She was so near that he could smell her perfumed skin and hair, and she was much too far away to touch.

"I didn't do it on purpose," he said desperately, stretching for her. "They did it. They killed me."

The woman's eyes narrowed. "Who?"

"The lawyers, the judges, the priests, the councilmen, the cops—"

The woman shook her head. "If you had only tried a little, they would have left you alone."

"I had a right—"

"Which you exercised at our expense." The woman stood. "I didn't expect you to change entirely, not when I wasn't able to myself. But it wouldn't have hurt you to try."

She turned her back on him and walked toward the fireplace.

Leonard wanted to go after her, but he couldn't even stand.

"Don't," he pleaded. "I need to be with you."

The woman paused before the hearth. "It will have to be on the Hill," she said. "You'll have to change. Otherwise, this is good-bye."

She stooped and entered the fire, which flared and consumed her.

Leonard wanted to cry, but he still lacked the ability. Of all the things that had been taken from him, that was almost the worst.

Almost.

But he couldn't remember what else was missing. He couldn't remember ever having had anything to lose.

All he knew was that he was tired. He would do anything, anything at all, for just a little . . . peace.

He sat alone in the Parlor. The countenance of Calvin Coolidge half smiled down on him, and Leonard imagined that it was conferring a blessing. A benediction.

20

In the days that followed, Leonard sometimes saw John in the theater, or at dinner, or sitting by the pond in the backyard. John always turned away as if afraid, but that was all right with Leonard. He knew that he and John weren't good for each other.

Everything else, though, was perfect. The season was always spring, and the trees and grass were always green. He accepted the Housemother's word as law, and he even began to understand the value of seeing *It's a Wonderful Life* over and over again.

He began to accumulate a long string of equal signs on the Progress Board.

He said hello to the women behind the candy counter every day, but while an impure thought occasionally crossed his mind, he no longer considered attempting a seduction. The price, he knew, would be too high to pay.

Strangely, the brunette, Melody, was getting lines around her eyes that made her look sad. Leonard couldn't imagine why, but he tried to be especially friendly toward her. It didn't seem to make any difference, so he decided to pray for her.

He ate his meals silently and reverently. He sang the Doxology at house meetings. He polished the woodwork in the foyer and Front Parlor. He dusted the glass cases that lined the long hallway. He threw bread to the geese and breathed deeply of the warm air. He was polite and respectful to his fellow comedians and to Mrs. Vonus. Occasionally, he was even allowed to escort the Housemother to dinner.

Once he saw a new arrival throw a roll at another resident, and he shuddered in revulsion. How could anyone be so ungrateful, wasteful, and rude?

Day followed day followed day, and at last the afternoon came when Leonard passed by the Progress Board on his way to the theater and saw a plus sign in his most recent box.

He stopped and stared at it, unable for a moment to comprehend what it meant.

"It's a pleasant feeling, isn't it, Leonard?" Mrs. Vonus asked.

She had appeared beside him out of nowhere, but he didn't flinch. He was used to it.

"I don't know," he said. "I don't know what to feel."

"You should feel fulfilled," Mrs. Vonus said, "but not proud. Pride is the downfall of mankind, you know."

"Yes, ma'am," Leonard said.

The Housemother extended her right hand toward him and opened it. Instead of a balled-up handkerchief, a thick silver coin lay in her palm.

Leonard began to reach for it, then stopped himself. "I owe the Dessert Fund," he said. "I owe two dollars for every minus."

Mrs. Vonus smiled so broadly that Leonard saw for the first time that her teeth weren't all the same color. Some were a brilliant white, while others looked grayish.

"I may have neglected to tell you," the Housemother said, "that every plus received while paying off a debt to the Dessert Fund automatically becomes an equal sign." She nodded at the Progress Board. "All but the first few of your equal signs actually started out as pluses. Your debt is paid, and this dollar is yours to keep."

She took his right hand into her left, pressed the coin into his palm, and closed his fingers over it.

Leonard gazed at the arc of silver that extended beyond his fingertips, then looked again at the Progress Board. The box at the end of his row contained the numeral 1.

"I have a long way to go," he said.

Mrs. Vonus patted the hand holding the coin. "You'll be surprised at how quickly it will pass," she said. "Now that you've discovered the way of obedience and serenity, you'll be on the Hill in no time."

Leonard wondered if that could be true, then decided it must be. The Housemother had said so.

"You've learned well," Mrs. Vonus said, and waddled down the hall toward the foyer.

Before going on to the theater, Leonard looked at the total at the end of John's row and saw that his friend had two pluses. He briefly hoped he would see John at the movie so he could congratulate him, but then he decided he'd better ask the Housemother first to make sure that was proper.

At the candy counter, he said hello to the blonde and bought a box of Milk Duds from Melody, who still looked sad.

"Be happy," he told her. "You have a wonderful job in a wonderful place." He smiled. "It's a wonderful life. Or should I say afterlife?"

For some reason, she looked sadder than ever.

When he sat down in his usual seat and put a candy into his mouth, he found it so sweet that one was all he could eat. He was used to simpler fare—the beets, potatoes, beans, and bread that were the staples at dinner. It felt unnatural and sinful to eat chocolate and caramel.

He dropped the nearly full box into the lobby's trash can after the movie.

That evening, he was served his first dessert—a slice of cherry pie with a scoop of vanilla ice cream on top. He couldn't eat it, but he didn't feel that he had lost anything.

The other residents at his table looked at him strangely.

The next day he received another silver dollar, and he asked Mrs. Vonus if he might give it to a less fortunate comedian. She told him that was a fine impulse, but that it would be impossible to act upon. If given to one who was undeserving, the coin would crumble into sand.

So Leonard began stacking his silver dollars on the floor of his room, building a shrine to the saint on the wall. He didn't know her name, but he could see that she was a great and righteous woman.

Day after day, he studied the rapturous look on her face. Eventually, he decided that he knew just how she felt.

21

The little silver shrine was nothing more than two three-inch columns when Leonard stopped counting the coins and looking at the Progress Board. He was no longer so vain as to keep track of his status. Instead, he was content to spend his time praying for guidance.

The shrine consisted of ten five-inch columns arranged in a circle on the day that Mrs. Vonus appeared in his open doorway and asked him to escort her to the movie.

Leonard was surprised. In his memory, the Housemother had never gone to see *It's a Wonderful Life*. But he didn't question her; he extended his right elbow, and she slipped her left hand into the crook.

They walked downstairs at the head of a large group of residents. Leonard saw John, but he didn't speak to him. It would be rude to talk to the others while serving as the Housemother's escort.

When they were halfway down the hall to the theater, Mrs. Vonus stopped before one of the glass cases, and everyone stopped with her.

She took her left hand away from Leonard's arm and unballed the handkerchief that was in her right. Inside the handkerchief was a small key, with which she unlocked the case.

As Mrs. Vonus swung open the glass door, white light spilled out and blinded Leonard for a moment. When the Housemother closed the door again, though, he was able to see despite the green spots that swam in front of his eyes.

Mrs. Vonus held five golden medallions in her left hand, each on a loop of fine chain.

She turned to face the residents.

"Frederick, Theodore, Albert, John, and Leonard," she said. "Step forward."

Leonard didn't move, since he was already separated from the main group, but the others came up to stand with him. John stood immediately to his right.

"These will enable you to see the sign you must see," the Housemother said, "and to go where you must go."

She placed a medallion around each of their necks, beginning with Leonard. While she was giving the others their own medallions, Leonard took his between his right thumb and forefinger to examine it.

It was a gold coin with a hole near the edge for the chain. In the center of the coin was the face of a laughing clown. Leonard knew from the shape of the mouth that it was the same face that had been beaten smooth by the front door's knocker.

Forming an arc around the clown's face were block letters that said GOOD FOR ONE FREE RIDE.

"We'll continue now, Leonard," Mrs. Vonus said when she'd distributed the other four medallions.

He offered her his arm again, and they continued down the hall toward the theater.

22

When they reached the lobby, Mrs. Vonus told the medallion winners to wait while the other residents went into the theater ahead of them.

Leonard smiled at the women behind the candy counter. The blonde smiled back, but Melody turned her face away.

After the main group of comedians had disappeared beyond the double doors, Mrs. Vonus lined up the five special men and stood in front of them, clearly pleased.

Leonard saw her teeth for the second time. They reminded him of piano keys.

A shadow seemed to flicker across the Housemother's face.

"Today you will be leaving us," she said. "I have every confidence that you will all do well on the Hill."

"Pardon me, ma'am," Leonard said. He hadn't known that he

was going to speak, and the sound of his voice startled him. "Perhaps I shouldn't ask, but . . . what will happen to us on the Hill?"

The other medallion winners—except John, who kept his eyes averted—looked at him as if he were foolish to ask such a question.

Mrs. Vonus pursed her lips and then said, "Good things, Leonard. Prayer. Contemplation. Fasting. Worship. All the things you have learned to do here at the Calvin Coolidge Home."

Leonard nodded and lowered his eyes. "Thank you, Housemother. Forgive me for asking."

"That's quite all right," Mrs. Vonus said with an odd strain in her voice.

Leonard looked up again and saw that Melody was bent over beside the cash register, hiding her face in her hands. Her body was trembling as if she were crying.

Why should she cry? he wondered. *Perhaps because she's not going up the Hill, too?*

He noticed that the blonde was standing well away from Melody and had her nose wrinkled in an expression of contempt.

"I must say farewell," Mrs. Vonus said. "Enjoy the movie. Then go where you must, and be obedient and humble."

Leonard shifted his gaze from the candy counter to the Housemother, and he thought he saw another shadow crossing her face.

"Aren't you going to watch the movie with us, Housemother?" he asked.

Mrs. Vonus sighed, then said, "I've seen it."

"Oh," Leonard said. "I'm sorry, Housemother. It's just that when you asked me to escort you to the movie, I thought that perhaps someone else would start the projector, and—"

"I understand," Mrs. Vonus said, interrupting him. "Go on, now. Go to your destiny."

Leonard nodded. "Yes, Housemother," he said, and turned to enter the theater.

As he pulled open the double doors, he thought he heard Melody sob. He didn't look back to see for certain.

But he wondered.

23

"*Should auld ac-quain-tance bee for-got, a-and ne-ver brought to miiiind? Should auld ac-quaint-tance be for-got, a-and daays of Auld Lang Syne?*"

As *It's a Wonderful Life* ended with the triumphant song of a houseful of friends, Leonard felt moisture on his lower left eyelid. He reached up to rub it away, but as his thumb touched it, more came to replace it.

Tears.

How long had it been since he had shed actual tears?

More importantly, why was he shedding them now, when he should be happier than he had ever been before?

Maybe they were tears of joy.

As the music and credits faded away, he tried to examine his emotions and found that he had no idea what he was feeling. He had been content for so long that he'd forgotten what any other state of being was like.

It must be joy. How could it be anything else, when I'm going up the Hill?

The screen went white, and then the houselights came up. The unmedallioned residents began leaving.

Leonard waited. Mrs. Vonus had said that he and the other medallion wearers would see a sign. . . .

It was a few yards from the lower right corner of the screen, and it had never been there before:

A glowing red sign that said EXIT.

The last unmedallioned resident went through the double doors, leaving the privileged five alone. Leonard stood and shuffled to the aisle.

He couldn't feel his legs as he walked down the aisle and across to the slitted velvet curtain that hung below the sign. He couldn't even feel his thoughts. He was an automaton, doing what he had to do.

The others were ahead of him. John was immediately in front of him, and Leonard wanted to touch his friend's shoulder to get his attention. When he had done that, he would ask John what he was feeling, and whether he had cried at the end of the movie.

But Leonard's arms were as heavy as bars of lead, and he couldn't lift them.

The first three comedians went through the slitted curtain quickly, as if unable to contain their eagerness to reach the top of the Hill.

John paused at the curtain and seemed about to turn around, but then he went through also.

Leonard took a last look at the theater and wondered if he would miss Jimmy Stewart.

Then he stepped forward and found himself in the backyard, which was the same as it had always been except for the tulip-lined gravel path along which he and the others walked. Looking ahead, he saw that the path led from the northeast corner of the Home to a golden door set into the wall at the northern boundary of the grounds.

Leonard knew then that the path, the multicolored tulips, and the door in the wall had been there all along, as had the EXIT sign and the curtained doorway in the theater. But without the GOOD FOR ONE FREE RIDE medallion, he had been blind to them.

Pretty tricky, he thought, and then wondered if that was impious.

No matter. He had the medallion. The decision had been made. He was going to the top of the Hill, and Glory.

As he walked behind the others, he looked up at the pure blue

230

of the sky and breathed in the delicious scents of spring. It was wonderful to be outdoors after being cooped up in the movie theater.

He lowered his gaze slightly and squinted at the half-hidden golden buildings that were his destination. He hoped the worship, obedience, and-so-on-and-so-forth in which he would participate there wouldn't prevent him from getting out into the sunshine occasionally.

A distant noise brought him out of his reverie.

He paused, listening, and the noise grew louder.

It was the sound of the red International pickup's engine.

"Do you hear that?" he said to John's back, and turned around to look at the road.

The truck was just pulling up beside the again-visible footbridge. The driver's side faced the Home, and Leonard could see Ol' Pete's profile.

"Hello!" he cried, waving his arms. "Mr. Pete! I made it!"

Ol' Pete didn't seem to hear or see him.

Leonard took a deep breath, planning to shout as loud as he could, but let it out silently when he felt a touch on his arm.

He looked over his shoulder. John was right behind him, a troubled look in his eyes.

"Come on," John said nervously. "The others will leave us behind."

Leonard saw that the first three comedians had reached the wall and opened the door. He glimpsed a gleaming staircase beyond.

"Go ahead," he told John. "I'll catch up. I can open the door as long as I'm wearing my medallion."

John shook his head. "You don't know that. The Housemother sent us out as a group. There's no telling what might happen if we split up."

Leonard turned back toward the International. "I just want to see if I recognize the new man. If he's someone I know, I want to tell him not to be afraid, that he can make it to the Hill if he tries—"

The pickup's passenger door slammed, and Leonard felt a tension in his abdomen he didn't understand.

A slim, mustached black man walked around the front end of the truck, talking loudly and punctuating his words by slapping the hood.

"—kind of deal is this, motha—motha—," the black man said, and then pounded on the hood with both fists. "That rips it! You can mess with my clothes, you can mess with my name—"

The black man shook his left arm, and Leonard saw the wristband flash.

"—you can even mess with my memory, but when you mess with my *mind* so that I can't even talk like me, then you've ticked me! I want an explanation, and I want it *now.*"

Leonard found himself grinning at the thought that Mrs. Vonus was going to have a tough time with this one.

That's terrible. I ought to be ashamed of myself.

"—get across the ditch when I'm good and ready, and that ain't gonna be until I get answers. Say what? Well, I'd better, man. I got your license number—"

Leonard laughed, and was shocked at himself.

What's funny about this? That man has no idea of the rewards of obedience, of the blessing of contentment. . . .

The black man was halfway across the footbridge when Ol' Pete blared the International's horn.

The newcomer didn't flinch. Instead, he turned around with his arms akimbo.

"You think that's cool? How cool you think it'd be if I come back and beat your head on the gearshift, huh?"

The International's engine revved, and the pickup vanished. A small spray of dust swirled down the road.

Leonard couldn't see the black man's face, but he knew the newcomer was staring at the empty air.

John grasped Leonard's right arm with both hands and pulled hard. "They're through!" he cried, panic charging his voice.

"They're going up the Hill! We're going to be left behind if we don't go *now!*"

Leonard stumbled backward.

The Hill. That's my goal.

Why? What's there that's so important?

"A few more seconds," he said, bracing his feet. "I want to see what he does. . . ."

The black man turned around and, with incredible slowness, resumed crossing the footbridge.

"Motha—," the man said. "Motha—"

Come on, Leonard thought desperately, not knowing what it was that he was urging or why he wanted it. *Come on, come on, come on . . .*

The black man had reached the end of the bridge and was about to step onto the brick walk that led to the Home's front door.

"Motha—," the man said, hesitating.

Leonard wrenched forward, tearing his arm from John's grasp.

"Come on!" he screamed.

"He can't hear you," John said, beginning to sob. "He's not like us; he doesn't have the coin. . . ."

The stranger's right foot touched the brick walk.

"You've gotta come now," John said. "Please, please, you've gotta—"

"Motha*fuck,*" the black man said.

Leonard felt himself teetering, as if standing on a wire over a canyon. He could actually see the wire and the empty air surrounding him.

The Hill. That's my goal. . . .

He looked down at the jagged, multihued rocks of the canyon.

They were a lot more interesting than the slick golden mountain where the wire was anchored.

"Leonard" never did feel right. . . .

He stepped into space, into another name.

"Lenny!" John cried.

233

The black man started up the walk, and Lenny turned to face his friend.

"I'll help you if you stay," he said. "I promise."

John, almost crying, shook his head and looked down at the gravel. "No, I . . . No. All I ever *wanted* was to be happy."

Lenny nodded slowly. "I hear you can get that up there. Happiness by the barrelful."

Without raising his eyes, John turned and walked toward the golden door.

Lenny watched until his friend stepped over the threshold. Then he turned and ran back down the tulip-lined path.

Yelling like Johnny Weissmuller, he burst through the red velvet curtain, charged up the aisle, and straight-armed the double doors. They swung open with a *whooshing* sound, and Lenny leaped into the lobby, landing in front of the candy counter.

Melody and the blonde woman gaped at him. The blonde's mouth opened and closed repeatedly.

Lenny yanked the medallion off his neck, breaking the chain, and held it across the counter toward Melody.

"You can tie a knot in the chain," he said.

Melody held out her left hand, and Lenny dropped the medallion into it. Then he closed her fingers over it and held on for a moment.

"What you do is your business," he said, looking into her eyes, which were a much darker brown than he'd ever realized before. "Personally, though, I hope you stick around. I still wanna take you on a picnic."

He saw the beginnings of a smile at the corners of her mouth.

Then he was running again, out of the lobby and down the long hallway.

As he shot by the Progress Board, he yanked the felt-tipped marker from its string. A blue knife of pain stabbed up his arm, but he didn't fall.

Aching, elated, he dashed to the foyer.

Mrs. Vonus was there, facing the front door.

"Hey, Daisy Duck!" Lenny yelled, sprinting into the Front Parlor. "Glad the new guy's not in yet—I've got something to show you!"

He bounded over a divan, then grabbed a chair and dropped it in front of the fireplace.

Looking back into the foyer, he saw Mrs. Vonus staring at him, her slack mouth giving her face a most un-Housemotherlike expression.

"Ah, you're confused, madam," Lenny said grandly. "Allow me to explain: Happiness and contentment are fine things for some, but for me they're just *boring*. So bring on the Puritans, because I've thought of a Thanksgiving bit that'll knock 'em on their asses."

He jumped onto the chair, uncapped the marker, and carefully drew an elegant mustache on Calvin Coolidge.

Thunder shook the blue-paisley walls.

The comedian glanced over his shoulder and grinned.

"Pardon me, Housemother," he said, "but don't you think you should answer the door?"

To the memory of Leonard Alfred Schneider.

We Love Lydia Love

Introduction to

~

"We Love Lydia Love"

There's an old adage that says writers (or artists or musicians) should write (or paint or sing) only about things they know first-hand, and I've met a number of writers (etc.) who take that adage to heart. Their chain of logic is as follows: 1) Writing (etc.) is about life. 2) Life at its purest involves suffering and confusion. 3) I must therefore suffer and become confused. And 4) Hey! Drugs and destructive liaisons could be a fun way to accomplish 3)!

My own philosophy differs. My drug of choice is Ben & Jerry's Coffee-Toffee Crunch, and I've been married for seventeen years. In other words, I don't think you have to be hip or degenerate to be creative . . . just so long as you live in a *place* that serves that function for you.

And that brings me to Austin, Texas, which (with the Hill Country) provides the setting for "We Love Lydia Love."

I've lived in and around Austin since 1988, and I can assure you that it's a stunning city of beautiful hills, wooded glades, vibrant neighborhoods, and sparkling creeks.

I can also assure you that it's an urban armpit of hideous overpasses, God-awful architecture, allergens that could choke a cyborg, and traffic that sucks beyond belief.

Austin is an isolated bastion of progressive thought in a conservative state. It's also the state capital.

It's a city where country music rules, rock 'n' roll will never die, and blues is king. It's the Live Music Capital of the World—but there's a strict noise ordinance, so don't let a whisper of that live music seep into a residential neighborhood after 10:00 P.M.

Its natives are fierce defenders of everything Austintatious: barbecue, Barton Springs, slackerdom, salamanders, Sixth Street, free movies, live oaks, the O. Henry Pun-Off, salsa, bare chests, bad poetry, worse tattoos, chicken-fried steak, and armadillos. And some of the fiercest native defenders have Yankee accents.

This was the home of Madalyn Murray O'Hair until she vanished in 1995. (One theory suggests it was the Rapture.) It's still the home of American Atheists, a passel of pagans, and the biggest Baptist church I've ever seen.

It's also the home of James Michener, and of the Butthole Surfers.

In short, Austin may be the most schizophrenic city on the planet. It's a joy and a trial, a pain and a pride.

It's perfect, and I never want to live anywhere else.

We Love Lydia Love

⟨~⟩

She knows me, and she's happy, and she's not asking how or why. She's clutching me so tight that I can't keep my balance, and my shoulder collides with the open door. The door is heavy, dark wood with a circular stained-glass eye set into it. The eye, as blue as the spring sky, is staring at me as if it knows I'm a fraud.

From down the hill comes the sound of the car that brought me, winding its way back through the live oaks and cedars to Texas 27. Daniels didn't even stay long enough to say hello to his number one recording artist. He said he'd leave the greetings up to me and the Christopher chip.

Stroke her neck. She likes that.

Yes. She's burying her face in my shoulder, biting, crying. Her skin is warm, and she tastes salty. She says something, but her mouth is full of my shirt. Her hair smells of cinnamon.

"Lydia," I say. My voice isn't exactly like Christopher's, but CCA has fixed me so that it's close enough. She shouldn't notice, but if she does, I'm to say that the plane crash injured my throat. "I tried to get a message to you, but the village was cut off, and I was burned, and my leg was broken—"

Not so much. We're the stoic type.

The whisper sounds like it's coming from my back teeth. I've been listening to it for two weeks, but that wasn't long enough for me to get used to it. I still flinch. I told Daniels that I needed more time, but he said Lydia would be so glad to see me that she wouldn't notice any tics or twitches. And by the time she settles back into a routine life with me—with Christopher—I'll be so used to the chip that it'll be as if it's the voice of my own conscience. So says Daniels. I'm not convinced, but I'll do my best. Not just for my sake, but for Lydia's. She needs to finish her affair with Christopher so she can move on. The world is waiting for her new songs.

And as a bonus, they'll get mine. Willie Todd's, I mean. Not Christopher Jennings's. Christopher Jennings is dead.

You are Christopher.

Right. I know.

She's looking at our eyes. She thinks we're distracted, and she wants our attention. Her lips are moist. Kiss her.

You bet. I'll concentrate on being Christopher.

Being Christopher means that Lydia and I have been apart for ten months. She has thought me dead, but here I am. She kisses me hard enough to make my mouth hurt. Her face is wet from crying, and she breathes in sobs. The videos make her look seven feet tall, but she's no more than five-four. Otherwise, she is as she appears on the tube. Her hair is long, thick, and red. Her eyes are green. Her skin is the color of ivory. Her lips are so full that she always seems to be pouting. I would think she was beautiful even if I hadn't admired her for so long.

I meaning me. Willie.

You are Christopher.

To Lydia I'll be Christopher. But to myself I can be Willie.

You are Christopher.

"I didn't believe it when Daniels called," Lydia says. She's still sobbing. "I thought he was mindfucking me like he usually does."

Say "That son of a bitch." We hate Danny Daniels.

"That son of a bitch." It seems ungrateful, considering that Daniels has just now returned us to her.

She's trembling. Hold her tighter.

A moment ago she was crushing me, but now she seems so fragile that I'm afraid I'll hurt her. It's as if she's two different women. And why not? I'm two different men.

Carry her to the bedroom. When she gets all soft and girly like this, she wants us to take charge. You'll know when she's tired of it.

She weighs nothing. I carry her into the big limestone house, leaving the June heat for cool air that makes me shiver. When I kick the door shut I see that the stained-glass eye is staring at me on this side too. I turn away from it and go through the tiled foyer into the huge front room with the twenty-foot ceiling, the picture windows, the fireplace, the expensive AV components, and the plush couches.

No. Not in here. When she was a child, she went to her bedroom to feel safe. So take her to the bedroom. It's down the long hall, third door on the right.

I know where it is, and I've already changed direction. But the chip's yammering makes me stumble, and Lydia's head bumps against the wall. She yelps.

"Jesus, I'm sorry," I say, and think of an excuse. "My leg's still not right."

"I know," Lydia says. "I know they hurt you."

Who are "they"? I wonder. There was a plane crash, and—in this new version of Christopher's life—a village. A war was being fought in the ice and snow around the village, but all of my injuries were from the crash. The villagers did their best for me, but there was no way to get me out until I'd healed, and no communication with the rest of the world. The soldiers had cut the telecom lines and confiscated the radios, but had then become too busy fighting each other to do anything more to the village. So if the soldiers didn't hurt me, and the villagers didn't hurt me, who are "they"?

There is a "they" in Willie's story, but while what they did to me was painful, they did it with my consent. Getting my album recorded and released is worth some pain. It's also worth being Christopher for a while. And it's for damn sure worth having Lydia Love in my arms.

On the bed. Pin her wrists over her head.

That seems a little rough for a tender homecoming, but I remember that the Christopher chip is my conscience. I let my conscience be my guide.

I still worry that she'll know I'm not him, but it turns out all right. If there's a difference between the new Christopher and the old one, she doesn't seem to be aware of it. The chip tells me a few things that she likes, but most of the time it's silent. I guess that at some point, sex takes control away from its participants—even from Lydia Love and a computer chip—and instructions aren't necessary.

She's sweet.

And here I am deceiving her.

But this pang is undeserved. In any respect that matters to Lydia, I *am* Christopher. I will live with her, recharge her soul, and give her what she needs before she sends me away. And then, at last, she'll rise again from the ashes of her life to resume her work. Willie can be proud of that.

You are Christopher.

Lydia and I have spent most of the past six days in bed. It's been a repeating cycle: tears, sex, a little sleep, more sex, and food. Then back to the tears. According to what Daniels and the Christopher chip have told me, everything with Lydia goes in cycles.

But this particular cycle has to be interrupted, because we've run out of food. Despite her huge house, Lydia has no hired help; and since no one will deliver groceries this far out in the Hill Country, one or both of us will have to make a trip to Kerrville. But Lydia isn't supposed to leave the estate alone without calling CCA-Austin for a bodyguard . . . and if she were to go out with me, the hassle from the videorazzi would be even worse than usual. The headlines would be something like "Lydia Performs Satanic Ritual to Bring Boy-Toy Back from Beyond the Grave." I don't think she can handle that just yet.

But if I slip out by myself, I tell her, I'll be inconspicuous. Christopher Jennings is an ordinary guy. Put him in his old jeans and pickup truck, and no one would suspect that he's the man living with Lydia Love. I have the jeans, and the pickup's still in Lydia's garage. So I can hit the Kerrville H.E.B. supermarket and be back before the sweat from our last round of lovemaking has dried. It makes perfect sense.

But Lydia shoves me away and gets out of bed. She stands over me wild-eyed, her neck and arm muscles popped out hard as marble.

"You just got back, and now you want to leave?" Her voice is like the cry of a hawk. She is enraged, and I'm stunned. This has come on like storm clouds on fast-forward.

She's waiting for an answer, so I listen for a prompt from the Christopher chip. But there isn't one.

"Just for groceries," I say. My voice is limp.

Lydia spins away. She goes to her mahogany dresser, pulls it out from the wall, and shoves it over. The crash makes me jump. Then she flings a crystal vase against the wall. Her hair whips like fire in a tornado. All the while she rants, "I thought you were dead, and you're going out to die again. I thought you were dead, and you're going out to die again. I thought—"

I start up from the bed. I want to grab her and hold her before she hurts herself. She's naked, and there are slivers of crystal sticking up from the thick gray carpet.

Stay put. We never try to stop her.

But she already has a cut on her arm. It's small, but there's some blood—

She always quits before she does serious damage. So let her throw her tantrum. It's a turn-on for her. She expects it to have the same effect on us.

Lydia looks down and sees herself in the dresser mirror on the floor. She screams and stamps her feet on it. The mirror doesn't crack, but she's still stamping, and when it breaks she'll gash her feet. I have to stop her.

No.

This isn't right. But if Christopher would let her rage, then I must do likewise if I want her to believe I'm him. Even now, as she attacks the mirror, she's looking at me with suspicion inside her fury.

She expects arousal.

Having trouble getting aroused in the presence of a naked Lydia Love was not a problem I anticipated.

She stops screaming and stamping as if a switch in her brain has been flipped to Off. The mirror has cracked, but it hasn't cut her feet. She leaves it and comes toward me, moving with tentative steps, avoiding the broken pieces of crystal. Except for the nick on her arm, she seems to be all right. The rage has drained from her eyes, and what's left is a puzzled fear.

"Christopher?" she says. Her voice quavers. Her ribs strain against her skin as she breathes.

She is looking at my crotch.

What did I tell you?

This was the one area I hoped the surgeons wouldn't touch, and to my relief they decided that it was close enough as it was. Christopher had an average body with average parts, and so do I. So they didn't change much besides my face and voice.

But the surgeons couldn't see me with Lydia's eyes. And now she's looking close for the first time. She's realizing that I'm someone else.

No. She's only confused because we're not excited.

Lydia stops at the foot of the bed and shifts her weight from one hip to the other. Her tangled hair is draped over her left shoulder. Her lips are even more swollen than usual.

245

"I'm sorry," she whispers.

Oh. Well.

Maybe I'm more like Christopher than I thought.

You are Christopher.

Shut up. I can do this myself now. Whoever I am.

Later I take Christopher's beat-up white Chevy pickup truck and head for the H.E.B. in Kerrville. Lydia worries over me as I leave the house, but she doesn't pitch another fit. She gives me a cash card with ten thousand bucks on it, kisses me, and tells me to come home safe, God damn it. As I let the truck coast down the switchback driveway, I glance into the rearview mirror and see that both Lydia and the stained-glass eye are watching me. Then the trees obscure them, but I know they're still there.

As I reach Texas 27, a guy in a lawn chair under the trees on the far side of the highway points a camcorder at me. He's probably only a tabloid 'razzo, but I wait until the driveway's automatic gate closes behind me before I turn toward Kerrville. After all, Lydia Love has more than her share of obsessive fans. That hasn't changed even though she hasn't recorded and has hardly performed in the three years since Christopher Jennings came into her life. But I guess her fans know as well as I do that the phoenix will rise again.

And it will rise thanks to me. To Willie.

You are Christopher.

Thanks to both of us, then.

The pickup doesn't have air-conditioning, which says something about Christopher's economic situation before he met Lydia. I roll down both windows and let the hot breeze blast me as I follow the twisting highway eastward alongside the Guadalupe River. Kerrville, a small town with a big reputation, is just a few miles away.

Its big reputation is the result of its annual folk-music festival, but I stopped going to the festival two years ago. It seemed as if almost everyone was using amplifiers and distortion, trying to be Lydia Love. She's my favorite singer too, but some of these kids can't get it through their heads that if Lydia didn't make it big by trying to look and sound like someone else, they shouldn't try to look and sound like someone else either.

Like I've got room to talk. It's only now that I *do* look and sound like someone else that I have a shot at a future in the music business.

The supermarket's the first thing on my left as I come into town. After parking the truck, I find a pay phone on the store's outside wall, run the cash card through it, and punch up Danny Daniels's number in Dallas. Daniels is an L.A. boy, but he says he'll be working at CCA-Dallas until he can get a new Lydia Love album in the can. If he wants to stay close to her, he'd do better to relocate to CCA-Austin—but when I pointed that out, he gave a theatrical shudder and said, "Hippies." I guess Dallas is closer to being his kind of scene.

He comes on the line before it rings. "You, Christopher," he says. "Except for that minor bout of impotence this morning, you're doing peachy keen. Keep it up. And I mean that."

Unlike the original Christopher, I know that I'm being observed while I'm with Lydia. But there ought to be limits.

"You don't have to watch us screw," I say. "Sex is just sex. It's the other stuff that'll break us up."

"But sex is part of 'the other stuff,' Chris," Daniels says. "So just pretend you're alone with her. Besides, if everything continues going peachy keen, I'm the only one who'll see it. And it's not like I'm enjoying it."

How could anyone not enjoy seeing Lydia Love naked? I wonder. Or is that Christopher?

You are Christopher.

Not when I'm on the phone with Danny Daniels.

You are Christopher.

Let me think.

You are Christopher.

"The chip's talking too much," I tell Daniels. "It's getting in my face, and Lydia's going to notice that something's not right."

247

Daniels sighs. "We put everything we know about the Christopher-Lydia relationship into that chip, so of course it's gonna have a lot to say. I've already told you, just think of it as your conscience."

"My conscience doesn't speak from my back teeth."

"It does now," Daniels says. "But it won't last long. The shrinks say that Lydia would have given Christopher the heave-ho in another six weeks if he hadn't been killed, and now they tell me that she won't stay with the resurrected version for more than another three months. Then you'll be out on your butt, she'll do her thing, and everybody'll be happy. Including Willie Todd."

What about me?

You'll be happy too, because I'm you. Isn't that what you keep telling me? Now back off. Daniels sounds like he might be pissed off, and I don't want him pissed off. Not at me, anyway.

Why? You scared of him?

No. But I know where my bread's buttered.

"Thanks, Danny," I say. "We just had a bad morning, that's all. Sorry I griped."

The phone is voice-only, but I can sense his grin. "No problem. You need a pep talk, I'm your guy. And if you feel like chewing my ass, that's cool too. After all, you're Christopher now, and Christopher once told me that he wanted to rip off my head and shit down my neck."

"Why'd he—I mean why'd I—"

We.

"—do that?"

"Because I told him he was fucking up Lydia's creative process," Daniels says. "Which he was. But I shouldn't have told him so. She was going to dump you anyway."

Or maybe I would have dumped her. Smug asshole never considers that.

I remember Lydia's rage this morning. No matter how beautiful and talented she is, that sort of thing can wear a man down. "I think she might be about half crazy," I say.

Daniels laughs. "The bitch is a genius. What do you expect?"

Well, I guess I expect her to dump me, have her usual creative burst, and for the world to be in my debt. And for my first album, *Willie Todd*, to be released on datacard, digital audiotape, and compact disc.

You are Christopher.

Yeah, yeah.

"Guess that's all, Danny," I say. "Just figured I should check in."

Why? He's watching us all the time anyway.

"Glad you did, Chris," Daniels says, and the line goes dead.

I head into the ice-cold store, and now that I'm off the phone, I have a moment in which all of this—my new voice, my new face, my new name, my place in the bed of Lydia Love—seems like a lunatic scam that can't work and can't be justified.

But CCA has the psychological profiles, the gizmos, and the money, so CCA knows best. If it makes sense to them, it makes sense to me too. And what makes sense to CCA is that Lydia Love's creative process has followed a repeating cycle for the past eleven years:

At seventeen, after graduating from high school in Lubbock, Lydia had a violent breakup with her first serious boyfriend, a skate-punk Nintendo freak. Immediately following that breakup, she went without sleep for six days, writing songs and playing guitar until her fingers bled. Then she slept for three days. When she awoke she drained her mother's savings account, hopped a bus to Austin, and bought twelve hours of studio time. She mailed a digital tape of the results to Creative Communications of America and went to bed with the engineer who'd recorded it.

The recording engineer became her manager, and he lasted in both his personal and professional capacities for a little over a year—long enough for Lydia to start gigging, to land a contract with CCA, and to buy a house in a rich Austin suburb. Then her new neighbors were awakened one night by the sounds of screaming and breaking glass, and some of them saw the manager/boyfriend running down the street, naked except for a bandanna.

The sound of breaking glass stopped then, but the screaming continued, accompanied by electric guitar.

The next day, Lydia's debut album, *First Love,* was released at a party held in the special-events arena on the University of Texas campus. The party was supposed to include a concert, but Lydia didn't show up. She was in the throes of her second creative burst.

The music that emanated from her house over the next three weeks was loud, distorted, disruptive, and Just Not Done in that suburb. The neighbors called the cops every night, and at the end of Lydia's songwriting frenzy, one of the cops moved in with her.

The cop suggested that Lydia take the advance money for her second album and build a home and studio out in the Hill Country west of the city, where she could crank her amplifiers as high as she liked. He supervised the construction while Lydia toured for a year, and when she came home they went inside together and stayed there for a year and a half. Lydia's career might have ended then had it not been for the fact that both her tour and her second album had grossed more money than the rest of CCA's acts combined. So between CCA, the tabloid papers and TV shows ("Lydia Love Pregnant with Elvis's Siamese Twins"), and the continuing popularity of her music, Lydia's name and image remained in the public eye even if Lydia didn't.

Then the ex-cop showed up at an emergency room in Kerrville with a few pellets of bird shot in his buttocks, and the county sheriff found the alleged shooter making loud noises in her basement studio. CCA rejoiced, and the third album sold even better than the first two.

Lydia's next boyfriend lasted almost as long as the ex-cop had. He was your basic Texas bubba (Lydia seems to go for us common-man types), and he and Lydia settled into a happy routine that could have ruined her. But then he went to a rodeo and was seduced by two barrel racers. The photos and videos hit the stands and the tube before the bubba even got out of bed. When he tried to go back to Lydia's, he found the driveway blocked by a pile of his possessions. They were on fire.

Creative Burst #4 followed, and that resulted in the twenty-three songs of *Love in Flames,* my favorite album by anybody, ever. Lydia followed that with a world tour that took two years of her life and made CCA enough money to buy Canada, if they'd wanted it. And it was while Lydia was on that tour, Daniels says, that CCA bugged her house. The corporation wanted to be sure that they could send help fast if she hurt herself in one of her rages.

When Lydia came home from the tour, she discovered that a hailstorm had beaten up her roof. She hired an Austin company to repair it, and Christopher Jennings, a twenty-four-year-old laborer and semiprofessional guitarist, was on the crew. When the job was finished and the rest of the crew went back to the city, he stayed.

Christopher and Lydia had been together for almost eighteen months when Lydia agreed to do a free concert in India. They went together, but Christopher took a side trip to Nepal. On the way back to New Delhi, his plane detoured to avoid a storm, hit a worse one, and went down in a mountainous wasteland claimed by both India and Pakistan. The mountains, frequent storms, and constant skirmishes between the opposing armies made the area inaccessible, and all aboard the airplane were presumed dead.

Lydia remained in India for two months before coming back to Texas, and then CCA rubbed their collective hands. They figured that with Christopher now a corpse on a mountainside, they'd soon have more Lydia Love songs to sell to the world.

But six more months passed, and the studio in Lydia's basement remained silent. Death and grief couldn't substitute for betrayal and anger. CCA, and the world, had lost her.

Then one night a scruffy day laborer and aspiring singer-songwriter named Willie Todd was playing acoustic guitar for tips in a South Austin bar, and a man wearing a leather necktie approached him.

"Son," the necktied man said, "my name is Danny Daniels, and I sign new artists for CCA. How would you like to record your songs for us?"

To a guy who grew up in a Fort Worth trailer park with six

brothers and sisters, no father, and no money, Daniels looked and sounded like Jesus Christ Himself. I'd been trying to break into the money strata of the Austin music scene for five years, and I was still lugging junkyard scrap by day and playing for tips at night. But with just a few words from Danny Daniels, all of that was over. He took me into a studio and paid for my demo, then flew me to Los Angeles to meet some producers.

It was only then that I found out what I'd have to do before CCA would give Willie Todd his shot. And although it sounded weird, I was willing. I still am. As Daniels explained, this thing should have no downside. After the breakup, I get my old face and voice back, Lydia's muse gets busy again, and CCA releases great albums from both of us.

So here I am in the Kerrville H.E.B., buying tortillas and rice for Lydia Love, the biggest Texas rock 'n' roll star since Buddy Holly . . . and for her most recent boyfriend, a dead man named Christopher.

You are Christopher.

But I'm not dead. Dead men don't buy groceries.

Dead men don't sleep with Lydia Love.

It's my seventh week with Lydia, and something I didn't expect is happening. As I've settled back into life with her, I've begun to see her as something other than the singer, the sex symbol, the video goddess: I have begun to see her as a dull pain in the ass.

Her rage before my first grocery run hasn't repeated itself, and I wish that it would. She's gone zombie on me. Sometimes when she's lying on the floor with a bowl of bean dip on her stomach, watching the tube through half-closed eyes, I wonder if she was the one who decided to end her previous relationships. I wonder if maybe one or two of the men made the decision themselves.

Why do you think I took that side trip to Nepal?

She has a gym full of exercise equipment, but she hasn't gone in there since I've come back. So I've been working out by myself to take the edge off my frustration, and I'm heading there now while she watches a tape of a lousy old movie called *A Star Is Born*. A run on the treadmill sounds appropriate.

Even the sex has started going downhill.

We could look elsewhere. I was starting to, before the plane crash.

No. Forget I said anything. Lydia's just moody; that's part of what makes her who she is. It would be stupid of me to mess up a good thing.

Isn't that what you're supposed to be doing?

I don't know. Are we talking about Willie or Christopher? According to CCA, Willie is here to give Lydia someone to break up with, but Christopher ought to be here because he cares about her. So which one am I?

You are Christopher.

All right, then. We can't just let things go on like this, so let's try something. Lydia hasn't picked up a guitar since I came back, and neither have I. Maybe if she and I played together—

She's too critical of other guitar players. We don't like being humiliated.

In front of whom?

Ourselves. And the people behind the walls.

But CCA's already agreed to put out my album. They already know I'm good. What difference will it make if Lydia and I play a few tunes together?

CCA is putting out an album by Willie Todd. You are Christopher.

I don't care.

So I hop off the treadmill, and as I start to leave the gym, Lydia appears in the doorway. She's wearing the same gray sweats she wore yesterday and the day before. Her skin is blotchy, and she looks strung out. It occurs to me that she might be taking drugs.

Of course she is. When things don't go her way, she takes something. Or breaks something.

"I'm going to kill myself," Lydia says. Her voice is a monotone.

Oh shit.

Don't worry. this is old news. She craves drama, and if she doesn't get it, she invents it. Ignore her.

She's threatening suicide. I'm not going to ignore that.

I would.

Well, Willie wouldn't.

Sure he would. CCA wouldn't pick a new Christopher who didn't have the same basic character traits as the old Christopher.

Shut up. I've got to concentrate on Lydia.

But she's already disappeared from the doorway. I zoned out, and she's gone to kill herself.

No, she's gone to eat or get wasted. Or both.

Fuck off. Just fuck off.

That's no way to talk to yourself.

I run down the hallway, yelling for her. She's not in any of the bedrooms, the kitchen, the dining room, the front room, or the garage. Not out on the deck or in the backyard. But she could be hidden among the trees, hanging herself. She could already be dead, and it would be me that killed her. Just because I wanted a break, just because I made a deal with CCA, just because I flew off and died on a mountainside, leaving her alone and unable to write or sing.

And at that thought I know where she is. She's where her music has lain as if dead all these months. She's gone to join it.

So I find her down in the studio, sitting cross-legged on the floor. She's plinking on a Guild acoustic, but the notes are random. She's staring at the carpet, paying no attention to what she's playing. I sit down facing her.

She looks like a toad.

No, she's beautiful. Look at her fingers. They're slender, but strong. Dangerous. Can't you see that?

Sure. But seeing it isn't enough.

She's still alive. That's enough for me.

"I don't think you should kill yourself," I tell her. The gray egg-crate foam on the walls and ceiling makes my voice sound flat and unconvincing.

"Why not?" she asks without looking at me. Her hair is tied

back, but some of it has come loose and is hanging against her cheek, curling up to touch her nose. I'm close enough to smell the sweat on her neck, and I want to kiss it away.

If you touch her now, she'll go ballistic.

"Why not?" Lydia asks again.

"Because you wouldn't like being dead," I say. "It's boring."

"So's being alive."

She has a point there.

Quiet. "It doesn't have to be."

Lydia's shoulders hunch, as if she's trying to shrink into herself. "Yes, it does," she says. "Life and death are really the same thing, except that life is more work."

She's still plinking on the Guild, but I notice that the notes aren't random anymore. They're starting to punctuate and echo her words. They sound familiar.

It's the progression for "Love in Flames," but she's playing it a lot bluesier than on the album.

It sounds good, though. It gives me an idea.

"I think you should do some gigs," I say.

Lydia looks up at me now. Her eyes are like stones. "I don't have anything new."

And except for the India concert, she's always refused to perform unless she has new material.

Well, there's a first time for everything. "So play your old stuff," I say, "only do something different with it, like you are now. Play it like it was the blues. See if it gets your juices flowing—"

I'm just able to duck out of the way as she swings the Guild at my head. Then she stands up and smashes the guitar against the floor over and over again.

I could have told you that she doesn't like being given advice.

So why didn't you?

Because I thought it was good advice.

Thanks, Christopher.

You are Christopher.

255

Whatever.

When the guitar is little more than splinters and strings, Lydia flings the neck away and glares down at me.

"I'll call Danny Daniels and have him schedule some dates," she says. "Small clubs, I think. And then I'm going to bed. See you there." She goes out, and the studio's padded steel door swings shut behind her with a solid click.

Now you've done it. When this doesn't work out, it'll be our fault. She likes it when it's our fault.

I thought you said it was good advice.

But good advice isn't enough. Nothing is. Not for Lydia Love.

Apparently not for you either, Christopher.

You are Christopher.

We're at a blues club on Guadalupe Street in Austin on a Wednesday night, and it's jam-packed even though there's been no advertising. Word spreads fast. I'm in the backstage lounge with Lydia, and it's jam-packed back here too. The cigarette smoke is thick. We're sitting on the old vinyl couch under the Muddy Waters poster, and I'm trying not to be afraid of being crushed by the mob. CCA has sent a dozen beefy dudes to provide security, and I can tell that they're itching for someone to try something.

But Lydia, dressed in faded jeans and a black T-shirt, doesn't seem to be aware that anyone else is in the room. She's picking away on a pale green Telecaster, eyes focused on the frets. The guitar isn't plugged in, so in all of this cacophony she can't possibly hear what she's playing. But she plays anyway. She hears it in her head.

A spot between my eyes gets hot, as if a laser-beam gunsight has focused on me, and I look across the room and see Danny Daniels in the doorway. He's giving me a glare like the Wicked Witch gave Dorothy. When he jerks his head backward, I know it's a signal to me to get over there.

He's got our career in his pocket. Better see what he wants.

Why? You scared of him?

Up yours.

That's no way to talk to yourself.

I lean close to Lydia and yell that I'm going to the john. She nods but doesn't look up. Her music matters to her again, so screw CCA and their shrinks.

I squeeze through the throng to Daniels, and he yanks me toward the fire exit. My new black-and-white cowboy hat gets knocked askew.

Out in the alley behind the club, I pull away and straighten my hat. "You grab some guys like that," I say, "and you'd get your ass kicked."

Daniels's face is pale in the white glow of the mercury lamp on the back wall. "You haven't been doing your job," he says.

I take a deep breath of the humid night air. "How do you figure?"

As if we didn't know.

I'll handle this. "I'm supposed to be Lydia Love's boyfriend, right? Well, that's what I'm doing."

Daniels tugs at his leather necktie. "You're supposed to behave as Christopher would behave so that she'll go berserk and kick you out. But you're obviously ignoring the Christopher chip's instructions."

I can't help chuckling. "The chip hasn't been handing out many instructions lately. It's been making comments, but not giving orders. So I must be behaving as Christopher would. After all, I'm him, right?"

Daniels shakes his balding head. "Not according to CCA's psychs. Christopher wouldn't reason with Lydia when she goes wacko. He gave up on reasoning with her a long time ago."

Never really tried.

Guess you should have.

Guess so.

"If the chip's lying down on the job," I say, "that's not my fault. I'm holding up my end of the contract."

Daniels grins.

257

Watch out when the son of a bitch does that.

"Our contract," Daniels says, "is with Willie Todd. But if you were Willie, you'd be behaving more like Christopher even without the chip. That's why we picked Willie in the first place. You, however, seem to be a third party with whom CCA has no arrangement whatsoever." He sighs. "And if Willie has disappeared, there's no point in releasing his album."

This is bullshit.

"This is bullshit."

Daniels shrugs. "Maybe so, Willie-Chris, Chris-Willie, or whoever you are. But it's legal bullshit, the most potent kind."

My back teeth are aching. "So if I have to be Willie for you to honor his contract," I say, "how can I be Christopher?"

You can beat his ugly face into sausage, that's how.

"Chris and Willie are interchangeable," Daniels says. "Both are working-class dullards who think they deserve better because they know a few chords. Any superficial differences can be wiped out by the chip. So I say again: Listen to the chip as if it were your conscience."

If I listened to the chip, Danny, you'd have blood running out your nose.

If he was lucky.

"I know you're getting attached to Lydia," Daniels continues, his tone now one of false sympathy, "but sooner or later she'll dump you. That's just what she does. It wasn't until Christopher's death that we realized she trashes her boyfriends for inspiration, but then it became obvious. So we brought Christopher back to life so she could get on with it. The only variable is how long it takes, and that's up to you. If you drag things out until CCA loses patience, Willie's songs will never be heard. And he won't get his own face back, either, because we won't throw good money after bad. He might not even be able to regain his legal identity. He'll have lost his very existence."

There are worse things.

"Willie's existence wasn't much to begin with," I say.

Daniels puts a hand on my shoulder, and I resist the urge to break his fingers. "Something is always better than nothing, Christopher. And if you go on the way you've been going, nothing is what you'll be."

Big deal.

"So what do you want me to do?" I ask.

"Only what the chip and I tell you," Daniels says. "If you don't like my conscience metaphor, then think of CCA, me, and the chip as the Father, Son, and Holy Ghost. Mess with any one of us, and you get slapped down with heavenly wrath. Mess with all of us, and you go straight to hell." He gestures at the club's back wall. "See, this kind of crap can't continue. Neither Lydia nor CCA makes real money from a gig like this. So your current directive from the Son of God is as follows: Go and spend thee the night in a motel. You still have that cash card?"

"Yeah, but—"

Daniels gives me a shove. "You, whoever you are, talked her into doing this gig. So she'll expect you to be here for it. But you won't be. So saith the Son."

No. We can't leave now. Not with Lydia about to go on stage for the first time since India. She'd hate me. Us.

Yeah. But that might be what she wants. She thrives on being treated like dirt. That's why she goes for guys like us. But we've been too nice lately, and it's screwed her up.

That's sick.

That's Lydia.

"All right," I tell Daniels. "I'm going. But I don't like it."

Daniels grins again. "Shit, neither do I. But it's for her own good, and yours too. If you weren't fucked in the head right now, you'd know that."

Come on. Let's get out of here.

I turn away from Daniels and walk off down the dark alley, abandoning Lydia to herself. My boots crunch on the broken asphalt. A bat flies past my—our—face, coming so close that we feel a puff of air from its wings.

Is Daniels right? Am I fucked in the head?
In the soul, Christopher. In the soul.

The stained-glass eye has become an open mouth surrounded by jagged teeth. Blue shards cover the front step, and they make snapping sounds as I come up to the door. I smell something burning. The stereo in the front room is blaring an old thrash-metal number about a murder-suicide. My back teeth begin to ache again.

As I cross the foyer into the front room, I see what Lydia has done. The picture windows have been broken, and the walls are pockmarked with holes. Some of the holes seem to be the results of shotgun blasts, and some have been punched with free-weight bars from the gym. The bars are still sticking out of some of these.

All of the furniture has been torn to pieces. The only things left intact are the AV components, which are stacked on the floor in front of the fireplace. But the cabinet that housed them is with everything else from the room—with everything else from the entire house, I think. Everything has been broken, shredded, crumpled, melted, or twisted, and then piled in the center of the room. A misshapen pyramid reaches three-quarters of the way up to the ceiling.

Lydia, wearing the jeans and T-shirt from last night's gig, is sitting atop the pyramid and using a fireplace lighter to burn holes into white cloth that used to be drapes. She doesn't notice me until I cross the room and turn off the stereo.

"Christopher," she says, glancing at me with a distracted expression. "You're back." Her voice is thick. I wonder if she's taken pills.

No. Her eyes are clear. She knows what she's doing. If the shotgun's handy, she might kill us now.

"I'm sorry I left last night," I say, trying to think of a lie to explain myself. "Daniels told me it was my fault that you were playing a joint instead of an arena, and I was afraid that if I stuck around I was gonna pop him. So I went for a walk, but when I got

260

back, you and the truck were gone. I tried to call, but my card wouldn't work. And I couldn't find a cab that would bring me out here at night. So I stayed in a motel."

Too much. She won't buy it.

"I thought your card didn't work," Lydia says.

We're meat.

Not if you back off and let me deal with this.

"It didn't work in the phone," I say. "But the motel took it."

"So why didn't you call from the motel?"

Told you.

Piss on it, then. I'm going to tell her the truth, including who I am.

Who's that?

"Don't answer," Lydia says. "Just turn on the VCR and watch the monitor."

So I do as she says. The monitor flashes on as the tape starts, and there I am, doing it with a brown-haired girl I've never seen before.

Yee-oww. Where was I when this was going on?

This never went on. I know that's the motel room we stayed in last night, because I recognize the bent corner on the picture frame over the bed. But I don't know that girl. So that can't be me.

Looks like us.

So it must be you. It's Christopher before the crash.

You are Christopher.

Yeah, but I'm Christopher after the crash.

Check out the hat on the floor. We were wearing it last night. We're wearing it right now. And it didn't belong to Christopher before the crash. It's brand-new.

But I don't have a chance to figure out what that means, because Lydia has succeeded in setting the white drapery on fire. She waves it like a flag, bringing its flames close to her hair, so I move to yank it away from her. But she tosses it away before I can reach for it, and it snags on a chair leg sticking out of the pyramid. To my relief, the flames start to die down.

Lydia is staring at me now. "Tell me what happened last night,"

261

she says. "Tell me where you found that girl while I was sweating in front of all those people. Tell me whether you started with her while I was singing, or whether you waited until you knew I'd be on my way home. Tell me whether she can suck the chrome off a trailer hitch." She points the fireplace lighter at me. "Tell me the truth, Christopher."

I look at the video monitor. The brown-haired girl and I are still going at it. The clothes on the floor are the ones I'm wearing now. The stamp on my left hand is the one that was put on at the club last night, the one that's still here on my skin. But that man is not me. I didn't do those things. We're watching an imaginary past with false faces and artificial voices.

Whoa. Sounds familiar.

Danny Daniels. CCA.

"Where'd the tape come from?" I ask, turning back toward Lydia. But if there's an answer I don't hear it, because the fire, instead of dying, has jumped to some paper and plastic in the pyramid. I can still smother it with the drapery if I hurry.

But Lydia jumps down partway and jabs her lighter at my face, stopping me. The yellow flame at the end of the barrel is two inches from my nose. The brim of my hat scorches.

"Tell me the truth," Lydia says.

A wisp of black smoke rises to the ceiling.

All right, then. The truth. Or as close as I can get.

"I've never seen that girl before," I say. "Daniels faked that tape to split us up."

Just doing his job.

Right. This is the way things are supposed to be, and I'm supposed to help them along.

But I don't want to anymore, and I don't care if it costs me my album or my face or my name. Looking at her now, I realize that I only care about one thing: I love Lydia Love.

I know. So do I. But loving her isn't enough.

Lydia's upper lip pulls back from her teeth. "Why should Danny care who I'm with? He doesn't have a thing for me." The flame waves before my eyes.

"No," I say, "but CCA does."

"What—" Lydia begins, and then a deafening buzz buries her words.

It's the smoke alarm. The pyramid shudders with the sound, and Lydia loses her balance and pitches forward. My hat gets knocked off, and Lydia's flame burns across my cheek as I catch her and fall backward. We hit the floor as pieces of the pyramid crash down around us.

The video monitor is right before our eyes. The brown-haired girl's lips are forming a name over and over again.

Christopher, she says. Christopher, Christopher.

But that's not my name.

No. You are Willie.

But we are Christopher.

Sprinkler nozzles pop out of the ceiling hissing and begin drenching us. The fireplace lighter sputters out, and Lydia drops it. Then she pushes away from us, snatches up a pump shotgun from behind the AV components, and runs from the room. The fire in the pyramid dies, but the alarm keeps buzzing and the sprinklers keep spraying.

We struggle up and go after her. The door to the studio slams shut as we come down the stairs. A glimpse before it closes shows us that the sprinklers aren't on in there. We try the door but it won't open, so we pound on it and try to shout through the noise of the alarm. The door isn't padded on this side, and the steel is cold and hard. We tell Lydia our names and the truth of why we put on this face and came back to her. We tell her about CCA wanting to get its money's worth, about the surgery and the chip, about everything we can think of. The burn on our cheek stings as the water hits it.

She wouldn't believe anything we said now. Even if she could hear us.

But we have to try. She has the shotgun. And last week she said she was going to kill herself—

The alarm stops, and we shout Lydia's name as loud as we can. There are two quick explosions, and circular patterns of bumps appear in the door's metal skin. From the other side, Lydia's muffled voice tells us to go back to the dead where we belong.

Then comes the sound of an electric guitar, and of a scream fueled by betrayal and anger.

Lydia Love is writing songs again.

And we know what that means. It means that our name, or whether we even have a name, doesn't matter anymore.

We are—

Shut up. It doesn't matter.

No. We guess not.

We sit down to soak in the artificial rain.

On the day after our return to Austin, Danny Daniels called us at the motel and asked when we wanted to have the surgery to remove the chip and to return Willie's face and voice to their pre-Christopher states. We'd had a night to calm down, so we didn't accuse him of using the sex video to give our relationship with Lydia a shove over a cliff. Of course he had done it. But his job, and ours, was to get Lydia Love to start producing again. We had a contract, and all he did was help it along.

And he lived up to his end of the bargain. We got Willie's face and voice back, more or less, and the chip was removed from our jaw. The doctors made a point of showing it to us after the operation.

As if a conscience could be removed so easily.

Quiet. Willie can't shake hands, think, and listen to Christopher all at the same time.

So let Christopher take over the social duties. Crush a few knucklebones.

Deal.

Today our album, *Willie Todd,* has been released on datacard,

DAT, and compact disc. Just in time for Christmas. And thanks to Daniels, three of its tracks are already in heavy rotation on the audio and video networks. He even arranged for this release party at the Austin Hyatt Regency with a whole shitload of CCA big shots and performers in attendance.

We asked Daniels if one performer in particular would be here, and he winked. But we don't see her anywhere.

The son of a bitch can lie without opening his mouth.

Daniels has done a lot for us, but we still don't like him.

Wait. There she is, by the waterfall, talking to a couple of CCA execs.

She might not want to see us.

Sure she will. We don't look like Christopher anymore.

There's a touch on our arm. It's Daniels. Our well-wishers melt away until we're alone with him beside the fake creek burbling through the atrium.

"Your hat's crooked, Willie," he says, giving us that alligator grin of his. "You want to make a good impression on her, don't you?"

"It's all right if I meet her?" we ask.

Daniels raises his eyebrows. "None of my business."

What a load. It's exactly his business.

"You've finished her sessions?" we ask.

He straightens his necktie. "Yup. Got the last four tracks in the can yesterday. She wants to call the album *Go Back to the Dead,* but we're trying to talk her into something more upbeat. My coproducers like *Once More with Love,* but I'm partial to *What Goes Around Comes Around.* We've gotta decide soon, because it has to be out by Valentine's Day."

"Valentine's Day?"

Cute.

"Yeah, her tour kicks off in New York on February fourteenth," Daniels says. He nudges our shoulder. "How'd you like to be the opening act?"

Opening act. Right. You know what kind of act he wants us to be.

Should we refuse?

Like we could.

We turn away from Daniels and start toward her.

"Attaboy," Daniels says behind us.

The CCA honchos move away from her as we approach. Her hair is even longer now, and her skin is smooth and healthy. Her eyes are a bright green, like sunlight shining through emeralds.

"You're Willie Todd," she says, extending her right hand. "I'm Lydia Love. Congratulations on the album. It's good work."

Our fingers touch hers with a snap of electricity. We jump, then laugh.

"Danny Daniels played me some songs from your own new album," we say. "They sound okay too."

She smiles at the understatement. "Gee, thanks." She tilts her head, and her hair falls over one eye. "Did he mention that I'd like you to open for me on the tour? Your music makes you sound like a guy I could get along with."

For a while, maybe.

But a while is better than never. A while is all anyone ever has.

"Maybe we could talk about it after the party," we say.

"Maybe we could," Lydia says.

And so the cycle comes back to its beginning. But now Lydia isn't the only one who can play the phoenix game.

Across the atrium, Daniels raises his glass to us.

Like the man said: What goes around comes around.

Or "Once more with Love."

So we might as well plan ahead. What name shall we go under next time?

One we can use for both of us. It'll avoid confusion.

If you want to avoid confusion, you're in love with the wrong woman, Christopher.

My name is Willie.

Whatever. She's looking at our eyes. Her lips are moist. Kiss her.

We let our conscience be our guide.

A Conflagration Artist

.

"A Conflagration Artist"

I love Austin, but wherever you choose to live as an adult, you can never truly escape the place where you spent your childhood. So time and again, I find my stories pulling me back to the Great Plains and to the people and ghosts who haunt that land. Here's another one now.

All of the stories in this book harassed me into writing them, but some of them literally gave me nightmares until I set them down on paper. One of these was "A Conflagration Artist." I kept dreaming about three small children and their parents—and as I watched them, I knew what was going to happen to each of them. It was awful. And they wouldn't leave me alone. More than once, I woke up thinking I could smell something burning.

Even so, I balked at writing the story. One reason was that the weird Czechoslovakian Franz Kafka had used a similar conceit in his classic "A Hunger Artist." And although I myself am descended from weird Czechoslovakians on my mother's side, who am I to mess with an author who (metaphorically speaking) could turn me into a cockroach?

Another reason I balked was that this story gave me the creeps. But in one way or another, they all do that. And a guy's got to get a decent night's sleep. So I did it. It's the shortest piece of fiction I've ever published, and it still troubles me out of all proportion to its length.

"A Conflagration Artist" reminds me that, despite my flip comments about creative types who seek out turmoil, not every artist willingly chooses his or her own talent or medium. Sometimes those things are bestowed upon you like blessings . . . or forced upon you like damnations.

And when you don't have a choice about what you do, you might as well make the best of it. You might as well do it right.

You might as well light that fire where the whole world can see it.

A Conflagration Artist

꙳

The Amazing Evelyn emerges from the one illuminated door and walks toward the tower at the center of the arena. Her two female assistants, who have been talking with me, fall silent. The other workers who have been milling about fall silent as well. The only sound is the soft crunch of the Amazing Evelyn's slippers on the gritty floor, echoing from the distant, invisible walls.

For her so-called practice dive she is wearing a costume similar to the one she will wear tomorrow: a blue swimsuit dotted with silver spangles, white tights, and a silver cape tied at her neck. Her arms are bare. As she approaches I can see the pink ridges and puckers that mar her skin. Or perhaps, in her view, they perfect it. They cause me to look up for a moment at the tower's apex, at the yellow flame burning on the platform there. I am struck again by the incongruity of the television term, *conflagrationary performance art*. Surely this is inappropriate. A "conflagration" is a fire that affects all, wounds all. But here, the Amazing Evelyn will burn alone.

Then I look down from the flame, all the way down, to the surface of the water in the tank beside me. The water is only as deep as my shoulder. I reach over the rim to touch its cool surface with my finger, and the ripples dance across the reflections of the arena lights, splintering them into shards of white.

I look at the Amazing Evelyn again and see that her eyes are focused on me as she comes around the tank. Her hair is amber stubble, a faint shade on her scalp. It is the same color as her eyes. I have seen photographs of her when her hair was long, as have we all. She was one of the most beautiful women in the Midwest then. But today, despite her scars—or because of them?—she is the most beautiful woman in the world.

She stops before me. Her scent is acrid and compelling. I am so surprised that I almost forget to look for a sheen of protective ointment on her skin. I do not forget, though. Her beauty and scent are stunning, but I am here as a journalist, and I will do my job. I look her over and see no ointment. Perhaps, then, her costume is impregnated with a flame-retardant chemical. But I do not dare to reach out and touch the fabric. That would be testing a goddess.

Of this, however, I am now certain: Her arms, shoulders, neck, and head are unprotected, as are the tops of her breasts. Her scars bear witness.

"You will not be allowed in the arena tomorrow," she says. These are the first words she has spoken to me. Her voice is like the touch of a feather.

I tell her that I do not understand why she has said this.

"You have been gawking at me all week," she says. "I have allowed it because my management made the agreement, but we are under no obligation to allow you to attend the performance tomorrow."

I point out that anyone with a hundred dollars may attend the performance tomorrow.

"Anyone but you," she says. "I am not a freak to be gawked at."

But the people who will come tomorrow will do so precisely because they do consider her a freak to be gawked at. I do not speak this thought aloud. I do not say anything at all. She knows as well as I do why they are coming. But she needs their money, and so will prostitute herself for them in order to do as she pleases for another year. I am told that she dives at least once a month, sometimes twice a month, for no audience but her assistants and a video camera. But there is no money in that, and she and her assistants must live. So she signed the contract that requires her to dive once a year for a live audience and pay-per-view television. It is clear that she often regrets the arrangement; but she is a woman of honor, and will fulfill her obligations.

She steps around me and walks to the base of the tower. There her assistants attempt to remove her cape, and she stops them.

"We have to give our journalist a good show," she says.

Her voice is bitter, and I am ashamed. She believes I am here to exploit her, and I suppose that I have not given her reason to believe otherwise.

But I know her better than she thinks.

She was married for seven years and gave birth to three children. Her husband's given name was Zachary. The oldest child, a boy, was named Ezekiel; the girl, two years younger, was Emily; the baby, another boy, was Ezra. They lived in a farmhouse in north-central Kansas, where Zachary tended fields of wheat and soybeans.

Their lives seemed neither bleak nor mysterious to their neighbors. Nor would they seem so to anyone who could view the Super 8 movies shot by Evelyn. In one of these films, the family has a picnic beside a tree-shaded creek. Zachary eats a chicken leg and winks at the camera; the children's faces become smeared with potato salad. Then the scene shifts to an arched stone bridge that spans the creek, and the children race across it toward the camera. But Ezekiel, who must be six years old, has eaten too much. He holds his distended little belly as he runs, and Emily wins the race. The toddler, Ezra, lags far behind, laughing and flapping his arms. Ezekiel staggers toward the camera, close to tears, and his mouth forms the words "I lost." Then Zachary comes into view and picks up Ezekiel to comfort him. Emily dances a victory dance, and Ezra spits up on his shirt.

It all appears sweet and normal, and perhaps it was. But Evelyn, serving as camerawoman, appears in none of the films. While the faces of Zachary and the children betray no darkness or despair, hers might have told a different story. We shall never know.

What we do know is that one summer evening during supper, Zachary and Evelyn argued. The argument itself, according to Evelyn's later testimony, was over the fact that Evelyn was serving pork chops too often for Zachary's taste. It seems more likely, however, that the real source of distress was the fact that they were losing the farm. The bank was about to foreclose.

But of human motivations, one can never be sure.

In the midst of the argument, Evelyn ran from the kitchen table and out of the house. (I imagine her wearing an apron over a blue cotton dress, crying as she runs.) She ran across the yard and down the dirt road that passed before their farm. Here there were no trees. The evening was hot and dusty. Evelyn ran almost a mile, and walked a mile farther. Then she started back.

When she drew near the house, she saw black smoke rising from the kitchen windows. She began running again, shouting for Zachary, but Zachary did not answer. Much later, he was found in his soybean field, smeared with dirt, speaking in tongues.

In the kitchen Evelyn discovered the bodies of her children lying on the table, burning. Evelyn beat at the flames with her hands and with a dishrag, and after some minutes, during which her arms blistered and her hair burned, was able to extinguish the fire. But the children were dead, and had been dead before they were set ablaze. Autopsies revealed that Zachary had stabbed each child in the chest before dousing them all with kerosene.

Such events do not bear much commentary. But of the events that followed, more can be said.

After Zachary's trial, conviction, and imprisonment, Evelyn vanished for over a year. No one who knew her, not even her mother or pastor, had any evidence of where she had gone or what she might be doing. Her mother feared that she had disappeared in order to commit suicide. Others, including her pastor, were more inclined to believe that she had left to begin a new life elsewhere under another name, thus wiping out the horror of her children's deaths at the hands of their father.

Then, the following autumn, Evelyn returned. She would not say where she had been or what she had been doing, but moved back into her and Zachary's house as if to resume her former life. By now, though, the bank had taken the fields, and the house would have followed soon had not Evelyn's pastor collected money for her.

It was on the day the pastor delivered the check that Evelyn's new vocation was discovered.

"I was turning into the driveway when I saw her," the pastor told me. "I wouldn't have thought to look up, but the fire caught my eye."

What he saw was Evelyn standing atop the windmill behind the house. As he watched, she dove off, burning, into the water tank at the windmill's base.

"But I couldn't see the tank," the pastor said. "I just saw her disappear behind the house. I thought she was dead. Then I drove back there, and she was coming out of the water. . . ."

The pastor's voice softened and fell silent, and I could not persuade him to describe any more of what he had seen.

"Of course we all thought that poor Evvy had gone crazy," her mother said. "Turned out to be crazy like a fox." She said this without any hint of a smile.

I asked more questions, but neither of them said anything else beyond what I had already learned. So the three of us relaxed in lawn chairs in the front yard of the Amazing Evelyn's house, waiting for her to arrive from California for a promised visit. The grass was dry and brown. The vanes of the windmill turned with rasps and squeaks. I sipped lemonade and believed that I had managed to develop a sincere kinship with the Amazing Evelyn's mother and pastor. After all, I had made it clear that I would not paint her as an object of amusement, as television did. It was my hope that their trust would convince Evelyn to trust me as well.

But then the telephone in the house rang, and the Amazing Evelyn's mother went to answer it. When she returned, she told me that Evelyn would not be coming home for a visit after all. She had heard that a journalist was lying in wait for her.

Those were her words: "lying in wait." As if I were a wild animal, hoping to devour her.

And as I watch her ascend, I wonder if she might have been right. My heart is racing, and the sensation in my belly has overtones of both hunger and sex. I do not want to watch her do this thing. I do not want to watch the Amazing Evelyn burn. And yet I watch anyway, as will thirty thousand people here tomorrow, as will millions more via television, as will you all.

She climbs the tower, never looking anywhere but upward, never acknowledging the existence of those of us below. She climbs until she is above the lights and we cannot see her except as a blue shadow in the darkness.

There is a movement beside me, and I am distracted for a moment. I glance to my right and see one of the Amazing Evelyn's assistants training a VHS camcorder upward. The other assistant stands beside her, head tilted back, gazing at the apex of the tower with an expression of beatific awe. She is in love with the Amazing Evelyn.

I look back up just in time. The blue shadow steps onto the platform and stands over the flame.

The flame leaps up, engulfing the shadow, and the Amazing Evelyn burns. She raises her arms, forming a fiery cross for an instant, and then dives. The sound is a roar. It is the sound of the wind rushing faster and faster, blasting all other sound behind, into the past, into oblivion.

She falls and burns forever. If her clothes are impregnated with anything, it is gasoline. Her head is the amber coma of a comet; her torso a blazing blue spike; her arms and legs orange flames. Halfway through the fall the silver cape explodes, and there is no longer even a hint of head, of torso, of arms, of legs. The Amazing Evelyn is not a woman; she is fire. She is a falling star, a rushing meteor, spearing downward to crush me, to consume me—

I cry out, cringe, and hide my face in my hands.

Then I hear a splash and a sizzle, and drops of water spatter on my neck. The water is hot.

I straighten, uncover my eyes, and stare at the wet ash on my sleeve. Then, slowly, unwillingly, I turn to face the tank. I have a question to ask, the one question that my editor insisted I must ask despite its obvious, pathetic triteness. And ask it I shall. But I have waited until the moment when I know she will be most vulnerable, until the moment when I know that I have some hope of obtaining an answer that is honest, that is true.

The first word leaves my mouth as I turn:

"Why—," I begin, and then I stop.

Her assistants are in the tank, going to her with the robe, just as they will tomorrow. But tonight she waves them away, swims to the ladder, and rises from the water without their help, without the robe. She stands on the top step, at the rim of the tank, and looks down upon me. Her scent is sweet and terrifying.

Her tights and cape are gone, and her swimsuit is a blackened rag over her right shoulder. She is hairless; she is blistered; she is perfect.

Her assistants come up behind her. There is a hush in the arena, as if no one breathes. The Amazing Evelyn looks down upon me, her skin steaming, her eyes glowing.

"Did you get a good tape?" she asks. She is not speaking to me, but to her assistants.

"I think so," the assistant who held the camcorder says.

The Amazing Evelyn nods. "Then you may send it to Zachary."

She descends the outer ladder to the floor, her eyes still on me. She knows that I too am in love with her.

Now she accepts the wet robe, puts it on, and turns to walk back across the arena to the illuminated door. Her assistants remain behind, as do I.

When she is gone, I touch the surface of the water in the tank again. It is warm. My finger comes up with a charred silver spangle, which I press to my lips. The assistants see me do this, but say nothing. They realize that I have finally understood: The Amazing Evelyn is indeed a conflagration artist . . . for when she burns, all who see her—who do not gawk, but *see*—burn with her.

"Why do you do it?" I was supposed to ask.

But having stood below her tower and watched her fall toward me, blazing through the black air of an empty arena, I know that the answer is as obvious as the question. She does it because it is her art.

She does it because it is her life.

Blackburn Bakes Cookies

"Blackburn Bakes Cookies"

Early in 1981, when I was twenty-two, I wrote a story called "The Violent Life and Death of James L. Krantz."

Some fellow students in the fiction workshop I was taking got into an argument over it. One said that my protagonist was only a sociopath. Another insisted that the character had ample provocation for his behavior.

Our instructor sidestepped the argument and said that the story was "a promising beginning—but *only* a beginning—of an important piece."

I didn't know from importance, but I had already realized that the story wanted to be a novel . . . a novel that I wasn't ready to write. So I put the story into a file cabinet. But I never stopped thinking about it.

In February 1988, I retrieved the story and knew right away that James's—Jimmy's—surname needed to be something more evocative of who he was in his soul.

I also knew that some of the story's scenes would become chapters in the novel. But I didn't want to start by writing one of those.

Instead, I had to create something from scratch to assure myself that I really knew Jimmy's life from beginning to end.

So I wrote an episode from the middle of the book, one that had no counterpart in "Krantz." I called it "The Murderer Chooses Sterility," and it told the story of how a man named Blackburn obtained a vasectomy, fell in love with a pipe-bomber, and killed some people.

My wife, Barb, read the story and didn't say much at first. Instead, she walked around frowning.

Then she came up to me and said, "That story bothers me because I agree with everything the guy is thinking and feeling—but what he *does* is *horrible*."

Okay, I thought. Now we're getting somewhere.

Over the next few years, I worked on *Blackburn* as often as I could steel myself to the things it required of me. I finished the manuscript in April 1991, and the novel was published in February 1993 . . . giving *Blackburn* a total gestation period of twelve years, which was just over a third of my life at the time.

"Was it worth it?" you may ask. (God knows *I* have.)

You tell me.

All I know for sure is that when I went to Denver in June 1996 to sign my novel *Lunatics* at the Little Bookshop of Horrors, Ed Bryant and the now much-missed Tomi Lewis met me at the airport with a sign that read JIMMY BLACKBURN.

But Jimmy Blackburn is dead.

Long live Jimmy Blackburn.

Blackburn Bakes Cookies

≈

Once he was dead, Jasmine's brother stopped showing up in her dreams. In life, he'd been there all the time. But after his execution, he stopped bothering her. In fact, when Jasmine dreamed at all now, it tended to be about work or sex. Or about taking a test she'd forgotten to study for.

But it was never about Jimmy.

She guessed that was because she thought about him so much while she was awake. Most days, he was the last thing on her mind every night, and the first thing every morning.

That became even more true a month before the tenth anniversary of his death—because that was when Jasmine began getting phone calls from someone she named "the Sicko."

She called him that because of what he said he wanted from her. Jasmine was appalled that he thought she would give it to him. Even a maniac should have known better. But whether he knew better or not, he called four or five times a week even after she changed her unlisted number. She came to expect it.

So as she lay in bed waiting for that call on a warm Wichita evening one week before the anniversary of Jimmy's death, Jasmine listened to her boyfriend snoring beside her and tried to kill time by remembering a happy moment from childhood. But the only thing she could think of, the only thing that even came close, was an incident that had happened when she had been ten and Jimmy had been fifteen.

In those days, Jasmine had hated her brother and Jimmy had ignored his sister, as was only proper for their ages and genders. He was a high school sophomore and she was a fifth grader, and they might as well have been living on different planets. But late one afternoon at the tail end of a long Kansas winter, Jasmine had been sitting on an old tire behind the garage, miserable, when Jimmy had come around the corner and found her.

And then, to her shock, he had helped her.

She could still see him standing there, stark and skinny against the slate sky. And she didn't have to dream to do it.

He was carrying a magazine that he stuffed up under his shirt. Clearly, he was hiding it so she wouldn't see what it was. But she didn't care what the magazine was or why he was bringing it back here. She didn't care about anything or anybody. She hated everyone. Daddy was gone all the time, and right now Mom was off shopping in El Dorado instead of staying home to comfort her. And Jimmy was a creep. She couldn't count on any of them.

"Go away!" she yelled.

But Jimmy didn't go away. He just stood there staring at her. So she got off the tire, picked up a rock, and threw it at him as hard as she could. It hit him in his hidden magazine with a *thwok* and dropped dead to the dirt.

Jimmy adjusted the magazine. "Something wrong at school?" he asked. "You didn't turn on the TV to watch *Major Astro* the way you usually do."

That took Jasmine by surprise. She hadn't thought Jimmy paid any attention to what she usually did. And he sounded as if he was really interested when he asked if something was wrong. The shock of that cut through her rage all the way down to how she was really feeling, which was awful, so she collapsed back onto the tire and cried.

"Tell me what happened," Jimmy said, and after a while Jasmine managed to tell him the whole story.

She told him about Lyle and Sarah, the sixth graders who waylaid her on the playground outside Wantoda Grade School every morning, and about how they always grabbed the sack lunch that Mom had packed for her. If there were cookies in the sack, Lyle and Sarah would take them. And if there weren't, they stomped on the rest. Most often, they stomped on the rest anyway.

This had gone on for three weeks now, and Jasmine couldn't stand it anymore.

"I want you to beat them up," she sobbed.

Jimmy didn't respond to that right away. Instead, he asked, "Have you told Mom? Have you told your teacher?"

Jasmine wanted to throw another rock at him, but she didn't have the energy. Her face was cold and her nose was running. She stuffed her raw hands into her lint-pilled coat pockets.

"No," she said bitterly. "That would be tattling. I don't tattle."

Jimmy nodded. "Good. Never tattle, because the grownups you tattle to will punish you at least as bad as the kids you tattle on. It's better to take care of the problem yourself. You know, like how I used my kite to get back at Todd Boyle that time he was torturing your Doll-Baby. Remember?"

Jasmine scowled. "No. I don't play with that old doll anymore. I don't even know where it is."

"I guess that was a long time ago for you," Jimmy said. "Anyway, my point is that you can take care of Lyle and Sarah yourself."

Jasmine rubbed her face on her shoulder. "How? They're bigger than I am."

Jimmy came over and squatted beside her. The magazine under his shirt crackled. "So don't fight them. Instead, just let them take your cookies tomorrow. It's the best way."

Jasmine was dumbfounded. "They do that *every* day, stupid.

Except when I don't have any. And unless Mom makes some tonight, I won't. They'll squash my sandwich the way they always do."

Jimmy stood, turned toward the house, and motioned for Jasmine to follow. "Come on, then. We'll make cookies ourselves before Mom gets home. She'll be gone awhile, because she left a note that I should take care of you."

Jasmine got up and followed him past the chicken coop and down the rock path to the house's back door. "I don't want you to help me make cookies," she said. "They'll just take them away again. I want you to beat them up."

Jimmy paused at the door, looked down at Jasmine, and smiled.

It was the first time that Jimmy had smiled at Jasmine in she didn't know how long. In fact, it was the first time he had smiled, period, in as long as she could remember.

"Sometimes beating them up is your only choice," Jimmy said, "and then you have to do it. But it can come back and bite you, just like tattling can. So it's better to let them do what they want— but fix things so that once they've done it, they really wish they hadn't."

Jimmy took Jasmine inside then, and after he stashed his magazine in his room, they turned on the oven and made chocolate chip cookies. But there weren't any chocolate chips in the cupboard, so Jimmy had Jasmine bring Mom's blue-and-white box of chocolate Ex-Lax from the refrigerator. They crumbled the squares into the mixing bowl, and Jimmy said that Jasmine could spit or blow her nose into it too, if she liked.

So she did. And then they mixed up the batter and baked the cookies, which smelled great.

Lyle and Sarah attacked Jasmine once again the next morning, but then they both went home sick in the afternoon. They didn't show up at all the next day. And the day after that, Lyle came by himself. He tried to grab Jasmine's lunch before school as usual, but he was pale and weak, so she knocked him down and pounded him. A few other kids joined in, and they hit him until he cried.

The day after that, Lyle was absent again. But Sarah showed up. Sarah didn't try anything, but Jasmine knocked her down and pounded her anyway. Once more, other kids joined in, and they hit her until she shrieked. But her shriek was drowned out by the first bell, so they didn't get caught.

Afterward, though, Jasmine felt terrible. What she had done to Lyle and Sarah didn't seem fair, somehow. So she prayed to Jesus to forgive her for it.

She never knew whether He did or not. But she did know that Lyle and Sarah never bothered her again.

The nightstand phone rang at a quarter to two, and Jasmine jerked awake knowing that it wasn't Mack calling, because he was in bed with her. That meant it was either a family emergency or the Sicko. So she stuck her head under her pillow and pretended that she didn't hear anything.

In the middle of the second ring, she felt Mack reach over her to turn on the lamp.

"I don't recognize the number on the caller ID," he said. The pillow over Jasmine's head made him sound far away. "But it's local. Should I pick up?"

"No," Jasmine said. She spoke into the mattress, but was pretty sure that Mack could hear her. "Let the machine get it."

The machine clicked on after the fourth ring. But several seconds passed after the beep, and the caller said nothing. So maybe it was a wrong number. A few more seconds, and the machine would click off.

Jasmine took the pillow from her head and rose to her knees. Mack's hand closed on her right shoulder, and she put her left hand over it.

"Little Sis," the answering machine whispered.

If she had stayed under the pillow, she might not have heard it. But it was too late now.

"I know you're there." It was the Sicko, still whispering. He didn't usually whisper.

Jasmine squeezed Mack's hand. "Do you have your cell phone handy?" she asked.

Mack got out of bed, but kept his hand on her shoulder. "It's in the living room," he said. His dark hair was sticking up in places, and his deep-set eyes looked worried. "I can call the cops, but they haven't been much help so far."

"I know," Jasmine said. "But that Detective what's-his-name, Holliman, said I should phone in the number from the ID the next time Sicko called. You know the right extension?"

"God, yes. I know all the cop extensions, thanks to the high class of clients I represent. But I'd better take another look at Sicko's." Mack leaned over and peered at the caller ID unit while sliding his hand down from Jasmine's shoulder and running his fingers over her breasts.

"Little Sis," the machine rasped. "Is your loverboy there? Is that why you won't talk to me? Are you too busy letting him corrupt you with his filthy little lawyer business? Is he grabbing that short, sandy hair of yours and looking for an alibi in those baby blues?"

Jasmine reached out and gave Mack's lawyer business a squeeze. "Don't listen to him," she said. "It's not that filthy."

Mack grunted. "Uh. Thanks." He frowned at the answering machine. "I'm starting to dislike this guy more than I do most Sickos of my acquaintance."

"That's because most Sickos of your acquaintance happen to be colleagues," Jasmine said. She released his business. "Now go call the police before he hangs up."

"He won't hang up," Mack said. "He never hangs up. He's a goddamn recording artist."

"Go."

Mack went.

"Pick up, Sis," the machine hissed. "Pick up, and I'll tell you why I'm whispering."

Jasmine sat on the edge of the bed and took a few deep breaths to calm herself. It didn't work. The Sicko's timing had been impeccable. She and Mack had gone to bed screwing like rabbits at about midnight, and then she had lain awake until a little after one. So she had been at just about the deepest point in her sleep cycle when the phone rang.

But she couldn't let him hear that she was rattled. She would have to channel her emotions so they came out as annoyance. She thought she could maybe do that.

Jasmine took another deep breath, then picked up the receiver. But she left the answering machine on in case the Sicko let something slip. Sooner or later, he had to let something slip.

"You know what I wish?" she asked as soon as the receiver touched her ear. "I wish I had *your* phone number. Then I could call *you* at some ugly hour."

"But I'm up all night anyway," the Sicko said. "I can't sleep until I have what I need. Now, don't you want to know why I'm whispering?"

"I suppose you think it's sexy," Jasmine said. She put as much sarcasm into her voice as she could muster.

The Sicko made a clucking sound. "Now, we don't have that kind of relationship. That would be incestuous, and the results would be three-eyed monsters. Besides, you're too short and skinny. I prefer taller gals with some meat on them. No, I'm whispering because of the Wichita Wranglers. They blew a two-run lead against San Antonio tonight even though they had an enthusiastic homestand crowd. So I yelled in frustration, and something in my throat blew out."

Jasmine was puzzled. "I hate to break this to you," she said, "but I happen to know that the Wranglers are on the road. I think they're in Tulsa."

"That's right," the Sicko said, "but I despise Tulsa for its liberal attitudes, so I refuse to pay that city any attention. In protest, I listened to a tape of an old game. I get them off the radio. I have a collection."

Jasmine perked up at that. It might be a clue.

"I didn't know you were such a baseball fan," she said.

The Sicko gave a phlegmy laugh. "You still don't. Who gives a damn about double-A ball? My throat's sore because I choked on a tablespoon of cayenne pepper, and I've never taped a thing off the radio in my life." The tone of his rasp shifted toward nasty. "And if you don't want me to keep on filling up your answering machine tapes, you'll give me what I want."

Jasmine forced herself not to react to his shift in tone. "Well, at least you aren't threatening me or my boyfriend with bodily harm this time."

The Sicko let out a long, soft hiss. It made Jasmine shudder.

"No, you didn't respond to that," the Sicko said. "And I figured out why. You're an accountant and he's a lawyer, so the damage you inflict on each other is worse than anything I could do. But your mother, on the other hand—I could do something to her that you'd notice."

Jasmine came off the bed as if stabbed by a live wire. It was all she could do to sound as if she didn't believe him, as if she didn't care.

"You're so full of shit," she said. "My mother doesn't even live around here."

"I know," the Sicko said. "She lives in Spokane, Washington, which is where you lived as well until you moved back here two years ago." He made a *hmmmmm* noise. "Let's see, this is Sunday morning. Mother's Day. When you call her this afternoon, you can tell her that she'll have a visitor driving in on Wednesday to help her celebrate Jimmy's birthday."

Jasmine's head began hammering. "You can't even make a decent threat. My mother died two years ago. That's why I was able to move."

The Sicko laughed again. "Give it up. Your mother is alive and bitching. However, her second husband, Gary, had a stroke four months ago. You flew up and spent a week with them before your responsibilities at work and in your lawyer's boxer shorts called you back. Gary will probably go into a home if he has another stroke, because then he'll need constant care. And your mother is too dotty to provide that."

Jasmine thought so too, and the fact that the Sicko had said it made her furious. "You're not one to be passing judgment," she said. " 'Dotty' doesn't even begin to describe you."

"What does, Little Sis?"

"Motherfucking crazy."

"It's against the law to talk like that on the telephone," the Sicko said in mock indignation. "Besides, I'm no such thing. Not unless it's motherfucking crazy to cut off an elderly woman's fingers and toes and stick them into her bodily orifices. Which is what I'll do if you don't give me Jimmy's ashes. After all, they're mine."

Jasmine hated him. "I keep telling you, I don't *have* Jimmy's ashes. But even if I did, they wouldn't be yours. And I still don't know why you think they are."

The Sicko gave a sandpaper sigh. "I've explained that. I'm his successor, and I have to incorporate his body into mine to make the transformation complete. Otherwise, I won't become the perfect serial killer he was."

Jasmine yelled into the phone. She couldn't help it. "What do you want to do, eat him?"

"Well, yeah," the Sicko said. He sounded surprised that Jasmine would ask. "He was my enemy, so if I consume his remains, I'll ingest his power. It took me years to figure that out, so I'm out of time to waste. That's why I'm only giving you two more days. If you don't deliver Jimmy's true ashes—not fireplace leavings this time—to his grave marker by Tuesday morning, I'm off to Spokane. You'll have to do it at night, though, without a flashlight. I'll be watching. And of course, no one else can see or know about it. Otherwise, chunks of your mommy will start showing up in cans of sockeye salmon. Bye now."

"Wait!" Jasmine shouted. "Wait a second!"

But the Sicko had hung up.

Jasmine slammed down the receiver. Then she picked it up and slammed it down again. Then she picked up the phone, the caller ID box, and the answering machine, and she tried to slam them all down. But the cords yanked them from her hands, and they tumbled back to the nightstand.

Mack came up behind Jasmine and put his hands on her shoulders. She turned and slugged him. His chest hair was rough against the side of her fist.

"Sorry," Mach said, staggering back. "I thought you knew I was there."

Jasmine blinked away tears. "Jimmy wasn't a serial killer."

"I know," Mack said. "I know he wasn't."

Jasmine couldn't stop. She had to make somebody understand. "He had reasons. They were the wrong reasons, but he wasn't just . . . just *sick.*"

"You're preaching to the converted," Mack said.

Jasmine turned away and went out to the kitchen. She switched on the light, sat down on the floor, and opened the cabinet under the sink. Then she yanked out bottles of Windex and Comet and crusty floor wax until she came to the urns. One of the urns was blue ceramic, and the other was stainless steel.

She brushed her fingertips over the ceramic urn and murmured, "Hi, Daddy. You poor diseased old thing."

Then she picked up the stainless steel urn, pressed it to her chest, and planted a kiss on its lid. The metal was as warm as if charcoal smoldered inside. Mack had once suggested the warmth might come from the faucet's hot water line, but Jasmine didn't think so.

"Sicko can't have you," she said with her lips against the steel. "You're my brother. Not his."

Mack came into the kitchen. He didn't say a word about the scattered cleaning supplies, but extended a hand to Jasmine and waited for her to take it.

Eventually, she took it, leaving the stainless steel urn on the floor next to the blue ceramic one.

Mack pulled her up and said, "May I have this dance, Miss Blackburn?" Then they danced back into the bedroom and held each other until the Wichita police called to say they had found the pay phone the Sicko had used tonight.

But there had been no one there.

On Tuesday morning, Jasmine was waiting at the gate at Mid-Continent Airport when her mother and Gary came off the 737. A skycap wheeled Gary from the ramp, and Mom came along behind, fussing.

"Don't roll him so fast," Mom said. "You'll dump him out and run over him. Young man, I said don't roll him so fast."

Gary looked up with watery eyes and gave Jasmine a grimace that she knew was meant as a smile. He probably shouldn't have flown so soon after the stroke. But at least he didn't look any worse than he had four months ago.

The skycap stopped the wheelchair in front of Jasmine. "These folks with you, ma'am?" he asked.

Jasmine nodded.

"This is as far as I go, then," the skycap said. "They need the chair five gates down. Can he walk?"

Mom stepped up, and she was wearing the pinched, persimmon-lipped expression that Jasmine knew so well. But for once, it wasn't directed at her.

"Young man," Mom said to the skycap, "I know that you Negroes are proud of your natural speed, but this man has had a stroke. You could've killed him."

Jasmine winced and gave the skycap an apologetic look.

"Can he walk?" the skycap asked again.

Gary was nodding and reaching toward Jasmine, so Jasmine pulled him up from the chair. He was lighter than she expected, and she stumbled back a few steps. But then she caught herself and put her arms around Gary to steady him. He smelled of Ben-Gay and peanuts.

"You see?" Mom said, pointing a finger at the skycap. "You see what you almost did?"

The skycap made a noise in his throat, then turned and left with the wheelchair.

"Wait," Jasmine said, struggling to support Gary and open her purse at the same time. "I'll give you a tip."

The skycap kept moving, and Gary plunged both hands into Jasmine's open purse.

"He's looking for a mint," Mom said. "Do you have any mints?"

Jasmine gently removed Gary's hands from her purse and then stepped back from him. He stood on his own.

"I don't think so," she said. "I have gum, though."

Mom's pinched look intensified, and now it was directed at Jasmine. "He can't chew. If he tries to chew, he'll choke. Are you trying to kill him?"

"No, Mom. I didn't know he couldn't chew."

"You would if you'd stayed in Spokane," Mom said. "And then we wouldn't have had to ride in that death trap. Air pockets, my eye. The wings were coming off. I could see them bouncing."

"I couldn't stay in Spokane, Mom," Jasmine said. "I have a job. The firm's letting me take my vacation days now so I can spend some time with you, but they're reserving the right to call if they need me. So it makes more sense for you and Gary to stay with me for a while." She hesitated, then pulled out a weapon borrowed from her mother's own arsenal. "Don't you want to visit me?"

Mom gave her a grudging smile, then a quick hug. Jasmine noticed that Mom smelled just like Gary, and that she seemed to have shrunk a few more inches since the last time they'd hugged.

"Of course we do, honey," Mom said. "We appreciate the tickets ever so much. It's a very thoughtful Mother's Day present, even if it is two days late. But the flights were too long, and changing planes in Denver was a nightmare. And we wish you'd given us more notice."

Jasmine linked arms with Mom, then held Gary's elbow in her free hand and began guiding them to the baggage claim area. "I'm sorry about all that," she said. "But Mother's Day snuck up on me. And these were the only bargain tickets available."

It was a lie. The tickets had been outrageous, but Jasmine's hope was that Mom would hear the word "bargain" and inquire no further. Mom understood bargains. But she might not understand that there was a Sicko out there who was going to cut off her fingers and toes if she stayed in Spokane.

"Oh," Mom said. "Well, I can see that."

Mom and Gary had just two pieces of luggage. The first was a garment bag that Jasmine snagged from the carousel with no trouble, but the second was a huge suitcase. It was a brown faux-leather behemoth that nearly dragged Jasmine away when she tried to pull it from the carousel. Mom had apparently packed it with sacks of wet flour. Gary shuffled forward, reaching out to lend a hand, but Jasmine managed to heave the suitcase off the carousel and onto the floor before he could come close enough to hurt himself. She could just see him tumbling onto the metal belt and chugging off around the bend while Mom went apoplectic.

"And what are we going to do now?" Mom asked. "How are we going to get these things to your car? And where is that—that *boyfriend* of yours? He could at least have come to lend a hand."

Jasmine winced. Mom said the word "boyfriend" as if it were a euphemism for "pimp."

"I told you when I called, Mom," Jasmine said. "He had to be in court today. They can't postpone criminal cases so the defense counsel can make airport runs. We'll rent a cart for the bags."

"Waste of money," Mom muttered. "Shouldn't be defending criminals anyway. Should be *prosecuting* them."

Jasmine thought that was a bit hypocritical, considering who Mom's other child had been. But she said nothing.

Gary tapped Jasmine on the shoulder. When she looked at him, he gave her his grimace-smile and held out a hand. There were four quarters in his palm.

Jasmine smiled back. Gary hadn't talked much before his stroke, either, so except for his frailty he seemed about the same as always. He was a good man. She wished that Mom had found him before Daddy and Jimmy had turned her into the bitter pill she was now.

If that had happened, though, then Jasmine might never have existed. But that would have been a small price to pay, as far as the world was concerned. Because then Jimmy would never have existed either.

"Thanks, Gary," she said, scooping the quarters from his hand. She glanced around. The baggage carousel was still surrounded by the passengers from Mom and Gary's plane, and a big security guard was keeping an eye on things. It was probably as safe here as it was at her house. "You two wait here, and I'll go grab a cart."

Mom muttered something negative, but Gary nodded. So Jasmine stepped away from the carousel, spotted a rental-cart rack a dozen yards away, and hurried over to it.

One of Gary's quarters jammed in the coin box, so she had to pound on the box and yank the cart back and forth for a minute. But at last the quarter dropped, the cart came free, and she turned to head back to the carousel.

As she turned, she saw Mom dragging the suitcase into the middle of the concourse. Gary was shuffling after her with the garment bag draped over his outstretched arms like a dead body.

And a dirty, longhaired man in a lime green bathrobe was coming up behind them.

Jasmine's heart seemed to freeze for an instant. Then a shriek leaped up from her chest, and she ran at the man in the bathrobe, shoving the luggage cart ahead of her.

People scattered and cursed. But the man in the bathrobe didn't. Instead, he stepped to one side so that Gary was between him and Jasmine.

For a moment, Jasmine thought about plowing right through Gary. But then she veered to one side and slid to a stop just beyond Mom, Gary, and the bathrobe man. She spun the cart around and aimed it at the bathrobe man again.

"For the love of Morton!" the bathrobe man cried. His ratty hair bobbed, and his tangled beard waggled. His voice was like the sound of balloons being rubbed together. He raised his hands, and a sheaf of black-and-white pamphlets flapped in one of them. "I'm just handing out free literature. Don't break a Commandment for no good reason."

His voice was wrong. But that didn't mean anything. He could have altered it for the phone calls.

"Get lost, Sicko," Jasmine said. Her voice was fierce. "Get lost and leave us alone. Jimmy's gone. There's nothing left of him. Not a speck, not an ash. So get lost."

The bathrobe man backed away. "Okay, miss," he said. "I just wanted to give you some information, that's all."

He took a pamphlet from his sheaf and let it fall. It fluttered away from him and landed on the luggage cart.

"And another thing, miss," the bathrobe man said. "You ain't got a lot of room to be calling other folks 'Sicko.' " He turned and trotted off down the concourse, his shower slippers flapping on the buffed tile, his pipe-cleaner legs flashing under the hem of his robe.

Jasmine watched him until he vanished down the broad hallway that led to the gates. Then she turned her attention back to Mom and Gary.

Mom had picked up the pamphlet from the cart. She was staring at it and trembling.

"These people," she said. Her voice quavered. "These people and their horrible lies. James didn't say any of these things. I know he didn't."

Gary teetered beside her, looking off down the concourse as if he might be thinking about trying to chase down the bathrobe man for upsetting his wife.

Jasmine reached toward her mother. "Give it to me, Mom."

"He was a good boy," Mom said. She looked up at Jasmine, and her eyes were wild with maternal fury. "He didn't do any of the things they say. He was innocent."

Jasmine was annoyed. Mom was constantly making backhanded

remarks about her daughter's sinful and wasted life, but Jimmy—no, Jimmy was her poor abused baby boy.

And the worst part of it, the part that rankled most, was that Jasmine agreed with her.

"Mom," Jasmine said. "Please. May I have that?"

Mom dropped the pamphlet and turned away. Jasmine caught the pamphlet before it hit the floor, and she was about to look at it when someone cleared his throat behind her. She turned around and saw the security guard glaring down at her.

"There seemed to be a commotion here," he said. "Can I be of assistance?" His tone made it clear that by "assistance," he meant chucking them out onto the street.

"No, thank you," Jasmine said. "We were just leaving." She opened her purse and stuffed the pamphlet inside, then grasped the handle of the suitcase and tried to heave it onto the luggage cart. But her arms and legs were shaking. She wanted to sit down and put her head between her knees before she passed out.

The security guard reached around her, brushed her hands away from the suitcase, and then tossed it onto the cart as if it were a box of Kleenex.

"Thanks," Jasmine said.

"No problem," the guard said. He was grim. "There's a cart rack out by the parking lot. You can return it there so you don't have to come back in."

That was all right with Jasmine. She didn't want to run into the bathrobe man again.

Mom gave the guard a disdainful glance. "I wish this man had been as helpful when he was rolling my husband at a hundred miles per hour."

Jasmine took the garment bag from Gary and flopped it over the suitcase. "Mom, it's not the same man," she whispered as she began pushing the cart toward the automatic doors.

Mom and Gary came along with her, but Mom looked back at the guard.

"Well, he's a Negro and he has a uniform," she said. "How do you expect me to tell the difference?"

"I don't expect anything, Mom," Jasmine said, squinting as they stepped out into the May sunshine.

"It was a Negro who did the crimes they accused your brother of doing," Mom said. "Five different witnesses said so. But by then it was too late."

That was all Jasmine could stand. Mom had been in Wichita less than twenty minutes, and it was already too much. Maybe it would have been better to leave her in Spokane for the Sicko to find.

Jasmine stopped the cart in the middle of the street between the terminal and the parking lot. Three cars squealed to a halt and honked, but Jasmine ignored them.

"Those 'witnesses' were all in the Texas Klan!" Jasmine shouted. "And two of them said that *Jimmy* was black. They were *liars*, Mom."

Mom had stopped in the middle of the street too. She looked at Jasmine and blinked against the sun.

"He was your brother," Mom said in a low voice. "And tomorrow would have been his birthday."

Jasmine closed her eyes, but opened them when another horn blared. She saw that Gary had gone on across and was now waiting for them in the parking lot.

"You're right," Jasmine said, pushing the cart toward Gary. "He was my brother."

They joined Gary, and Jasmine led the way to her Pontiac. The luggage cart rattled. Jasmine still felt shaky, and her chest ached.

"He was my brother," she repeated. "And he would have been thirty-nine tomorrow."

She spoke in her normal voice. But Mom and Gary were behind her, and she knew they couldn't hear her over the rattle of the cart.

"But that doesn't mean he didn't kill them," she said.

She remembered how unafraid and unashamed Jimmy had looked behind the thick glass in Huntsville.

"That doesn't mean he didn't kill them all."

Jasmine sat in the reading chair in her bedroom, waiting for Mom to get off the cordless extension in the kitchen so she could call Mack. Mom was talking to Mrs. Boyle, the only friend she still kept up with from the old days in Wantoda. Mom and Mrs. Boyle talked on the phone at least twice a month, and Mom always seemed surprised that Jasmine didn't also keep in touch with Mrs. Boyle or her children—especially now that Jasmine was only thirty-five miles from Wantoda.

But Jasmine barely remembered the Boyles. And what little she did remember indicated that they had been bullies and brats. Especially the boy. Not that he had been much trouble after Jimmy had gotten through with him.

Mom was already making noises about paying Mrs. Boyle a visit. But Jasmine would put that off as long as she could. She didn't want to go near Wantoda unless she was on her way somewhere else. Wantoda was a place where boys fought, dogs died, and men wielded fiberglass switches. Or guns.

And maybe every place was like that. But she hadn't had to grow up every place.

The pamphlet from the airport was on her lap. It was made from two sheets of photocopy paper folded together and stapled at the crease. On the first page, in large type, were the words:

The One True Gospel of
MORTON
Son of Stan
as revealed to his prophet
James
(later cruelly martyred)
in the wilderness of Palestine in the Republic of Texas
in May of the Year of Our Previous Lord
Nineteen Hundred and Eighty-Six

Jasmine was pretty sure now that the bathrobe man hadn't been the Sicko. The odds were that he was just a Mortonite.

She had heard of the First Church of Morton before today, of course. Jimmy had even mentioned Mortonism when she'd visited him in prison. But this was the first time that she'd seen one of them doing the Hare Krishna thing in an airport.

It might be that they were making a special effort to proselytize this month. After all, tomorrow would mark the tenth anniversary of the martyrdom of their chief prophet.

Jasmine hesitated, but knew she would turn to the second page. The words here were in smaller type:

> For lo, Morton, Son of Stan, having been born of the virgin-only-fourteen-times-removed Bernice in the city of Bethlehem in the state of Pennsylvania, didst appear to Blackburn the Righteous in the Wilderness of Palestine. And Morton and Blackburn didst wrestle two falls out of three, after which Blackburn didst drink of the Gatorade of Life and eat of the Cracker Jacks of Redemption. And yea verily Morton didst proclaim, Now shalt thou no longer be called by the name Blackburn the Righteous, but shalt forevermore be known as James the Prophet, lest I shalt knowest the reason why.

The rest of this page, and the next, contained more of the same. From the Church's perspective, Jimmy had killed ("sacrificed") Morton at Morton's request when the "centurions" approached so that the world might be saved by his wacko blood. And as he'd died, Morton had charged Jimmy with the responsibility of spreading the Conditional Gospel—which Jimmy had done until the State of Texas had stuck a needle in his arm. Jasmine suspected, however, that the .357 slug that had pierced Morton's heart had in fact been the result of something Morton had done to piss Jimmy off, and that Jimmy's spreading of the Gospel had been exaggerated.

She turned to the center of the pamphlet, and there, in large type again, were the Church's "Ten Conditional Commandments" as supposedly set down by Morton and revealed through Jimmy:

I. Thou shalt have no other gods before Morton (unless a better one cometh along [but what are the odds of that?]).

II. Thou shalt not make unto thee any graven image, or any likeness of any thing that is in heaven above, or that is in the earth beneath, or that is in the water under the earth; thou shalt not bow down thyself to them, nor serve them, unless they shalt incorporate something useful, such as alarm clocks in their bellies.

III. Thou shalt not take the name of thy Lord and Savior Morton in vain (but, again, what are the odds of that?).

IV. Remember the sabbath day, to keep it wholly, with a football game, picnic, or movie.

V. Honour thy father and thy mother, unless they beith abusive assholes.

VI. Thou shalt not kill, unless the guy deserveth it.

VII. Thou shalt not commit adultery, unless thou just canst not helpeth thyself, and then useth an appropriate prophylactic device.

VIII. Thou shalt not steal, excepteth in an emergency.

IX. Thou shalt not bear false witness against thy neighbour, but little white lies to spareth his feelings beith okay.

X. Thou shalt not covet thy neighbour's house, thou shalt not covet thy neighbour's wife, nor his manservant, nor his maidservant, nor his ox, nor his ass, nor any thing that is thy neighbour's, and—oh, just forgettith this one, for yea verily it beith impossible in the event that thy neighbour's wife beith a babe.

Jasmine wasn't sure. Some of it sounded like Jimmy, but some of it didn't. The lax Commandment about adultery, for example, didn't seem like one that her brother would endorse. If the circumstantial evidence was to be believed, he had killed at least two of his victims for committing that particular sin.

She was about to turn the page when the doorbell rang.

"Jasmine!" Mom's voice called before the ringing faded away. "Someone's at the door!"

Jasmine stood, tossed the Mortonite pamphlet onto her bed, and went into the hall.

The bell rang again. "Jasmine Leigh!" Mom yelled at the top of her lungs. "Someone—is—at—the—door!"

Jasmine paused at the kitchen and saw Mom and Gary sitting at the table. Mom had the cordless telephone pressed to her face.

"I heard the bell, Mom," Jasmine said. "You don't have to shout."

Mom looked hurt. "I'm sorry," she said. "I wasn't sure. You had your bedroom door closed. Although I don't know why. That boyfriend of yours isn't even here. But that might be him at the door, and I thought you'd want to know."

Jasmine muttered "Thanks" and then went to the front door. It wouldn't be Mack. He was working late tonight.

It occurred to her then that it might be the Sicko showing up at her home at last. Maybe he had decided not to drive to Spokane after all. She wondered whether she had been right in deciding not to buy a gun.

But guns had been Jimmy's thing. And Daddy's. And the fact that she kept both of those men under the sink didn't mean that she wanted to emulate them.

Besides, it wouldn't be the Sicko at the door. Sickos didn't ring doorbells.

She looked through the peephole, and at first she didn't recognize the man standing under the porch light. He was stoop-shouldered and tired-eyed, and had creases in his face that cut down from either side of his nose to his jaw. He was wearing a blue necktie and a ratty brown sport coat, and his formerly white shirt looked as if he'd fished it out of his dirty laundry that morning.

He held up a flat black wallet and flipped it open. There was a dented badge inside.

Jasmine unlocked and opened the door, trying to push down a surge of panic.

"Officer Holliman?" she said. Her throat was tight, and she had trouble getting the words out. "What's wrong?" All she could think of was that the Sicko had done something to Mack.

Holliman looked at her with dull hound-dog eyes. "Lots of things are wrong," he said. His voice was a low monotone. "For one thing, my back hurts. And of course there's that thing in Lebanon. And call me 'Detective,' please. I haven't been 'Officer' for seventeen years. I know it's all the same to you, but it's a matter of respect. Makes up for still getting lousy pay after three decades of selfless service." He flipped his wallet closed and stuck it into a back pocket, just behind the holster clipped to his belt. "And you can wipe the worry off your face. Nobody's been shot. At least, nobody you know. But I've been trying to get you on the horn for the past hour and a half, and your phone's been busy. So I figured I'd drop by on my way home. You ever think of getting call waiting?"

Jasmine was discombobulated. "I—what? Then Mack's all right?"

Holliman made a face that indicated he couldn't care less. "Far as I know. Mind if I come in?" He slapped himself on the cheek. "You got mosquitoes out here. You wouldn't think there'd be any, what with the dry spring. But there's been a rash of septic tank leaks in the area, so that might account for it."

Jasmine didn't see any mosquitoes. But she stepped back and let him in.

As Holliman came into the living room, Mom emerged from the kitchen with the cordless phone still pressed to her ear. She was talking into the mouthpiece as if nothing else were going on, but her eyes were fixed on Holliman.

"I see you have company," Holliman said. "And I also see why

I wasn't able to get you on the phone. But I'm glad you took my advice."

Jasmine frowned. "What advice?"

Holliman jerked a thumb at Mom. "Bringing your mother here. So the perpetrator wouldn't be able to find her in Spokane."

Jasmine didn't remember Holliman saying any such thing. Bringing Mom and Gary here had been her idea. But maybe he had said something to Mack.

Holliman was staring at Mom now. "Excuse me, ma'am," he said, "but who are you talking to?"

Mom stared back and put her hand over the mouthpiece. "I'm sure that's none of your business. I don't even know you."

Holliman's eyes narrowed, and Jasmine wished she hadn't let him in.

"I'm the police detective assigned to investigate the threats your daughter has been receiving," Holliman said. "In other words, I'm the guy who's supposed to look after you people even though you're next of kin to a cop-killing sociopath. Who are you talking to?"

Mom blanched. "I'll call you tomorrow, Nadine," she said, and turned off the phone.

"Nadine who?" Holliman asked.

A strange heat began building up behind Jasmine's eyes. She had the feeling that if Holliman didn't leave in the next few seconds, it might flare out and burn him to a crisp. He didn't have any right to be telling Mom about the Sicko's threats, or to be grilling her like this.

Jasmine stepped behind Holliman and opened the front door again. "I think you should leave," she said.

Holliman looked over his shoulder and raised an eyebrow. "Sorry, Ms. B.," he said. "It's my job to investigate. I came by to let you know that you ought to keep your phone line free in case we need to call you, and also to ask you a few questions because of a possible lead. So as long as I'm asking questions, I don't think 'Nadine who?' is unreasonable."

Jasmine glared. "What kind of lead?"

"Jasmine," Mom said. Her voice was small. "What's he talking about? What kind of threats? Who's been making them?"

Holliman turned back toward Mom. "That's what I'm trying to find out, ma'am. Your daughter's been receiving telephone calls from someone who wants to possess the ashes of your deceased psycho-killer son. He says the urn buried in the Wantoda cemetery isn't the real McCoy. Or rather, wasn't, since he already dug it up."

Jasmine slammed the door, and the house shuddered. Mom dropped the phone, but Holliman didn't even twitch.

"If you have to speak with me," Jasmine said, "let's go into another room."

Mom went to the couch and sat down. "It's too late for that now, dear," she said. Her voice trembled, but her tone was no-nonsense. "I want to hear what the officer has to say."

"Detective," Holliman said.

"As you wish," Mom said. Her voice seemed to be getting stronger. "What's this about James's grave being desecrated?"

Jasmine brushed past Holliman and sat beside her mother. "Mom," she said, taking her hand, "Jimmy's grave has been vandalized five times since he died. The third time, somebody actually tried to dig him up, so I—I had the urn removed and replaced with a fake. I thought that would give the grave robbers something to steal, and then they wouldn't come back. I did the same for Daddy, because they'd done things to his grave too. God knows why."

Mom looked at her, incredulous. "Why didn't you just take the urns and stones away, and give the plots to someone else? Then there wouldn't be anything to desecrate."

Jasmine was nonplussed. There was no bitterness or sarcasm in Mom's voice. She was serious.

"Well," Jasmine said after a moment, "because I thought you'd be upset. You visit the cemetery every year. So I thought I should keep the graves nice . . . for you."

Mom closed her eyes and shook her head. Then she put her arms around Jasmine and hugged her.

"Oh, honey," Mom said. "Graves and ashes don't matter to me. The only thing left of Jimmy that matters is what's in our hearts and memories. And as for your father, well, the only reason I've never desecrated his grave myself is because I thought it might upset *you.*"

Jasmine disengaged herself from the hug. She didn't feel comfortable with a display of affection while Holliman was peering at them.

"So why have you kept visiting them?" Jasmine asked.

Mom rolled her eyes. "I haven't. Not really. But Gary and I *have* gone to visit Nadine Boyle a few times, and since you're in Wichita now we've come to visit *you*—and it would seem wrong not to stop by the cemetery. As long as we're here."

Jasmine felt stupid. All these years she had donated money to the Wantoda Nazarene Church, which maintained the cemetery, to ensure that they would keep Dad's and Jimmy's empty graves presentable. And now it turned out that Mom hadn't cared one way or the other.

Holliman stepped in front of the coffee table. The furrows in his forehead had deepened. "Nadine Boyle wouldn't be the wife of the guy used to be the constable over there, would she? Fellow named Ted?"

"His name is Todd," Mom said icily. "He's her son. And he's still the police chief."

Holliman gave a derisive sniff. "Yeah, for a force of one. Unless he's hired himself a Barney Fife. Haven't talked to him in about eleven years, so I wouldn't know."

Holliman's voice sounded odd, and Jasmine didn't like it. "Why would you have talked to him at all?" she asked.

Holliman put his hands in his pockets and rocked on his heels. "Police business. After your brother was caught, we figured he might be responsible for some of our unsolved homicides here in Wichita. So I naturally called the lawman in the suspect's hometown for information. Guy said he knew the suspect when they were kids, and that the suspect was one foamy-mouthed puppy even then. But maybe it was genetic, on the father's side. No reason to blame yourselves for the family environment, which I'm sure was as wholesome as could be. Let's give you the benefit of the doubt and blame the boy's testosterone."

"You're very rude, Officer," Mom said.

"Only to the blood relations of cop killers," Holliman said. "I'm funny that way. And it's Detective."

Jasmine stood. She wanted to get Holliman out of there. "You said you had a lead on the person who's been harassing me."

Holliman took his right hand from his pocket and scratched his chin in what Jasmine thought must be a gesture copied from some TV or movie cop.

"Yeah, maybe," he said. "What I'm wondering is, have you ever had contact with any known Satanists? Any pagans, witches, Wiccans, Druids, Scientologists, yahoos like that? See, we got a tip that some local coven worships your brother, or possibly Jeffrey Dahmer. Our informant wasn't sure which. But your caller's expressed desire to eat your brother's remains like they were Grape-Nuts seems to tie in with that sort of thing."

Mom made a strangled noise. "Eat—oh, dear God."

Jasmine went past Holliman and opened the front door again. "We've never had contact with people like that," she said, struggling to keep her voice even. "The closest was a Mortonite who approached us at the airport this afternoon."

Holliman shook his head, sighed, and started toward the open door. "Nah, your perpetrator isn't a Mortonite. Those guys only eat Cracker Jacks." He stepped past Jasmine, but paused halfway out the door and looked into her eyes without blinking. "You want some advice, Ms. B.? Off the record?"

Jasmine didn't blink either. "There's a record?"

"Sure," Holliman said. "I write up everything we talk about. Part of my job. Except this advice, if you want to hear it. I would, if I were you."

"No shit," Jasmine said, lowering her voice so Mom wouldn't hear.

"No shit," Holliman said without lowering his voice at all. "And my advice is: Give this guy what he wants. After all, what do you lose? Sane people like you and me understand that ashes are nothing but dust. But this subgenius perpetrator wants them anyway. And I think he'll leave you alone if he gets them."

Jasmine felt her lip curling. "I have a better idea. Let's arrange a transfer with fake ashes, and when he shows up for them, you can do your job and grab him."

Holliman looked disgusted. "This isn't a kidnapping case, Ms. B. This is just some pissant necrophagiac jabbering over the phone. There hasn't even been any violence up to this point—and I don't think there will be, if you give him the ashes. And I mean the real ashes, not some barbecue-grill substitute. Just let him have 'em, and be done with it."

Jasmine started to close the door even though Holliman's foot was still inside. "That's a perverted suggestion, Officer Holliman, and I wouldn't take it even if I could. But as I've told you before, I scattered both Jimmy and my father in the Whitewater River after I had them disinterred."

Holliman smiled. It was repulsive.

"Yeah, well, I ran into your boyfriend at the courthouse the other day," he said, "and Mr. Legal Eagle let it slip that you keep the ashes here in your house somewhere. Don't be too mad at him, though. He tried to cover by saying he thought you just had the empty urns. But the boy's a lawyer, Ms. B. And you know how you can tell when a lawyer is lying?"

"No," Jasmine said, looking down at her feet. Holliman's foot was between them. "How?"

"His lips are moving," Holliman said. "But I'll give him this: The boy knows enough to call me Detective." He moved his foot away. "You consider my suggestion, now. Off the record, I truly do think it's the best solution to your situation."

Jasmine listened to him walk to the street, get into his car, and drive away. Then she closed the door and pressed her forehead against it.

Mom came up beside her.

"You've kept some bad secrets from me, haven't you?" Mom said.

Jasmine stayed against the door. "Whenever possible."

Mom gave her another hug.

"Thank you," Mom said. "That's really the way I prefer it."

Jasmine slumped on the couch with all of the living-room lights turned off except the television. She was watching David Letterman mug his way through the Top Ten list. It reminded her of the Mortonite pamphlet's Ten Conditional Commandments. Neither one struck her as funny.

Mom and Gary had retired to the spare bedroom an hour ago, and then Jasmine had called Mack to tell him about Holliman's visit. She hadn't mentioned his slip about the ashes. There didn't seem to be any point.

But she had told him about Holliman's suggestion that she just give Jimmy up, and Mack's response had made sleep unlikely for tonight.

"I can see where he might say that," Mack had said. "Because I'm beginning to think the Sicko might be a cop."

That hadn't occurred to Jasmine before Mack said it. But it made sense. The Sicko claimed that he and Jimmy had been enemies—and cops certainly qualified in that category.

She glanced over her shoulder and saw the little amber lights glowing on the security-system console beside the front door. If anyone tried to break in, the system would alert the security company, and the security company would alert the police. But what if the police were the ones breaking in?

Mom was right. The ashes weren't Jimmy. Wouldn't it be worth it to give them up if that would give her a normal life again?

Except that Jasmine's life had never been normal. Her father had been a cancer-ridden misanthrope, and her brother had been a multiple murderer.

Now Mack said he wanted to move in with her. But as long as those other two men were under the sink, she couldn't let him do that. It would be too weird. Even if ashes were only ashes, they were family.

As she thought about it further, she decided that she might be able to give up Daddy. If she had to.

But not Jimmy.

At first that struck her as odd, because she had spent a lot more time with Daddy than she ever had with Jimmy. She had even nursed Daddy through his final illness. But from the year she'd turned twelve to the year she'd turned twenty-two, she hadn't even laid eyes on Jimmy. He'd left home on his seventeenth birthday after killing his first man—Officer Johnston, the city cop of Wantoda.

Still, Jimmy was her brother. And that made him closer kin than Daddy. Jasmine had been only one chromosome away from turning out just like him.

The glowing face of the VCR atop the television told her that it was a few minutes before midnight. A few minutes before Jimmy's thirty-ninth birthday. A few minutes before the tenth anniversary of his execution.

She watched the dots between the numbers blink, watched the seconds count off. She thought about leaping up and yelling "Happy Birthday!" or "Good Riddance!" at the stroke of midnight. She thought about getting the steel urn out from under the sink and fitting it with a paper-cone party hat made from leftover Sunday funnies.

Then something creaked behind her, and she jumped up from the couch and spun around, grabbing the remote control from the coffee table. But as she cocked her arm to throw it, she saw that the creaking sound had come from Gary. He was at the mouth of the hallway, wearing an oversized white robe and leaning on an aluminum cane. The glow from the television flickered over him like reflected lightning.

Gary stopped where he was, gave her his crooked smile, and raised his hands in mock surrender. The cane swung from his right hand like a pendulum.

Jasmine replaced the remote control on the coffee table and let out her breath. "Sorry," she said. "I'm a basket case." She gestured at the couch. "Want to watch TV?"

Gary nodded, then grasped his cane at both ends and pushed. It collapsed into a foot-long tube, and Gary dropped it into one of the robe's big pockets. He walked the rest of the way to the couch on his own.

Jasmine grasped his arm and helped him sit down. "Couldn't sleep, huh?" she asked over the roar of laughter on the television.

Gary shook his head. Or maybe it was a spasm. Jasmine wasn't sure. Gary was looking at Letterman, and he made a noise that was almost like a chuckle.

"Nice cane," Jasmine said. "I've never seen one like it."

Without looking away from the TV, Gary pointed at his own chest.

At once, Jasmine knew what he meant. "Oh, you made it yourself?" she asked, and then was afraid that she'd sounded too surprised. Gary had spent most of his life maintaining the machinery at a salmon cannery, and had sometimes fabricated replacement parts himself. The cane would have been easy for him. Except that she couldn't imagine how he could have done it in his current condition.

Gary waved his hand back over his shoulder.

It took Jasmine longer this time. "You mean you did it before the stroke?"

Gary touched the tip of his nose. Bingo. He looked away from the TV then and, with obvious effort, gave Jasmine a wink. It told her that he had made the cane because he had guessed he might need it soon.

Jasmine had the sudden thought that she had just had a more meaningful conversation with Gary than she had ever had with her real father. And that included the years that she had spent taking care of Daddy while he was dying.

She wanted more. "Uh, Gary, I know you're watching the show. But would it be okay if I talk to you?"

Gary leaned forward and fumbled with the remote control on the coffee table until the TV volume went down to a mutter. Then he leaned back again and looked at Jasmine with a lopsided, quizzical expression.

"I guess you heard the whole thing with the police officer," Jasmine said.

Gary rolled his eyes and thumped his chest.

Jasmine managed a small laugh. "Right, sorry. *Detective.*" She rubbed her neck. "That guy hates me just because I'm Jimmy Blackburn's sister. Is it my fault that I'm the sibling of a notorious murderer and prophet?"

Gary shook his head.

"Of course not," Jasmine said. "But that doesn't matter. The sins of the brother are visited upon the sister." She slumped again. "I wonder if John Dillinger or Jesus had little sisters. I'll bet those girls got a raw deal too."

Gary opened his mouth, and Jasmine moved closer, anticipating a whisper that would be difficult to hear. But there was only a rasp of breath—and then the television winked off with a crackle of static, and the room was dark.

Jasmine was startled for a moment, then waited another moment to see if the power would come right back on. It didn't. Even the lights outside seemed to be off. The window shades were closed, but there still should have been a glow from the nearest streetlamps. And there wasn't.

She turned around to see if the security-system console's lights were still functioning.

They weren't. There was supposed to be a battery backup. But the console was dead.

"Gary, we might be in trouble," she said, reaching out for him. He wasn't there. She could feel the warmth on the couch where he had been. But now he was gone. She hadn't heard him, but he must have stumbled back down the hall to be with Mom.

At that thought, Jasmine felt as if an ice pick had been driven into her spine. She had fallen for the Sicko's bullshit about going to Spokane, and so had brought Mom and Gary right where he had wanted her to bring them.

The cops wouldn't help. The Sicko was one of them. That was why the security system was off.

Jimmy had been right. He had been right about cops and state troopers and everyone in authority. They were the enemy, and they had hated him for knowing it. So now they wanted what was left of him for themselves. They wanted the power that still burned in his ashes.

Jasmine heard glass shatter and knew that it was the window in the guest bedroom.

There was the beginning of a shriek. And then nothing.

Jasmine lurched up from the couch, banged her shins on the coffee table, and then dropped to the floor so she could crawl across the living room and down the dark hallway to the guest room. The Sicko and his policemen friends might not think to shoot low. Unless they had some of those night-vision goggles. And of course they would. They had everything. They were cops. They had guns and goggles and Mom and Gary and they wanted Jimmy's ashes and she didn't know why in God's name she couldn't just let them have what they wanted.

But she couldn't.

She wished Jimmy would come back and kill them all for her.

She ran into a wall and stopped there on her hands and knees, panting even as she tried not to breathe. This wasn't going to work. She didn't have a weapon. And she wasn't Jimmy. She needed help.

But the phone would be dead. She was sure of it. So she couldn't call Mack. And what could Mack do, anyway? Alert the police?

Jasmine stayed on her hands and knees, quaking and sweating, and tried to listen. She couldn't hear Mom. Couldn't hear the creak of Gary's cane. Couldn't hear anything.

She was in darkness, in silence. She was alone.

"Jimmy," she whispered, squeezing her eyes shut tight. "You jerk. Where are you when I need you?"

He had never been around. He had turned seventeen, killed a cop, and taken off. Jasmine had been left to endure being the daughter of a hateful father and bitter mother. And the sister of a homicidal maniac.

In high school, the only boys who had wanted to date her had been the ones who liked bragging that they had gotten some from a killer's sister. The others had all been afraid that Jimmy might come back someday.

And so he had. But not until years later, when Daddy was dying and Jasmine was stuck with taking care of him. And Jimmy had tried to fuck that up, too.

So the hell with him. And the hell with his ashes, too. Selfish little bastard. Why shouldn't she give him up? Hadn't he done the same to her?

A red blaze lit up her eyelids, so she opened them and found herself a few feet from the guest bedroom. The door was open, and hot electric light stabbed out and fell as a slanted knife-edge at her fingertips. The power was back on.

Jasmine managed to hold her breath and listen. There was still no sound. But she felt a puff of air against her face.

"Mom!" she yelled, and scrambled into the room. She hoped that the Sicko was still there so she could rip open his face with her teeth and fingernails.

But the Sicko wasn't there. Neither was Gary, and neither was Mom. The ceiling light glared, and the bedsheets sparkled with glass from the window. The window was open, and the breeze blew in and swelled the curtains.

Jasmine stood and went to the bed. She clambered across to the window and stared out at her small front yard and the street. She opened her mouth to shout again, then closed it. Shouting would do no good.

She got off the bed and stood in the center of the room. She had bits of glass stuck in the heels of her hands and in the knees of her jeans. She picked the bits from her hands and watched the blood well up. She imagined the strands of DNA tied up in helical tangles, floating there, waiting. Waiting for her to call on the part of her that was Jimmy.

If she could figure out how. And she had to. Jimmy was her only option now. Too bad he was dead.

When the telephone rang, she didn't even jump.

Instead, she walked to her bedroom, flicking on lights as she went. She didn't hurry. Jimmy wouldn't hurry. She even let the phone ring beyond the point where her answering machine would have picked up. But it didn't pick up this time, because it had to be reset after a power outrage. So she let the phone ring a few more times as she stood and stared at it.

When she finally brought the receiver to her ear, she didn't flinch at the sound of the Sicko's voice. He was trying to sound terrifying, but he was only trite. That was how Jimmy would think of him.

"Little Sis," the Sicko whispered. "I have your mommy. I have her old man. And I do mean old man. I'm concerned that I won't be able to cut on him for more than fifteen seconds before he croaks. So I'll probably begin with Mommy."

"You haven't already?" Jasmine asked. She was calm. Jimmy would be calm.

"Haven't had time. Got them trussed up like rodeo calves, though. Can't be too comfortable for old folks. But pretty soon we'll see what's what. Of course, I'd advise against your calling the police."

As if he'd had to tell her. "I'm not calling the police."

"Good deal," the Sicko said. "Because if I hear sirens, I'm going to take a tire tool and shove it through the womb that gave birth to Jimmy Blackburn. I might anyway. Do the world a favor."

Jasmine tried to think of how Jimmy would respond to that. "If you do," she said, "I'll never give you what you want. And I do have it."

The Sicko hissed, but Jasmine knew that to Jimmy it would sound like a cricket fart. So that was how she let it sound to her, too.

316

"I know you do," the Sicko said. "And I know you'll give it to me now."

"Yes." Jasmine didn't know whether it was a lie or not. "If no harm comes to my mother or stepfather."

"That sounded like attitude. You'd better not be giving me any attitude, Sis. My tire tool and I would frown on that. I got me a baseball bat too, autographed by two Wichita Wranglers."

Jasmine kept thinking of Jimmy. She could picture his face behind the glass in Huntsville. "I'm not giving you any attitude. I'm just resigned. I have to do what you want."

The Sicko chuckled. To Jimmy, he would sound like a dying chicken. "That's right. And I must say, it was easy. I wasn't sure you'd actually bring your mommy to Wichita."

Jasmine studied the beads of blood on her hands again. Some of them had smeared. "I didn't have much choice. You really would have gone to Spokane if I hadn't. And then you would have hurt her for certain."

There was a brief silence on the line.

"You've got a point," the Sicko said then. "But all's well that ends. And the end will take place about two hours from now. That should give you time to retrieve what's necessary from wherever it's hidden, and then to make a short drive. I'll expect you at the Wantoda cemetery at two A.M. Alone. You'll wait for me at your brother's false grave. But park your car several blocks away and walk to the graveyard. No weapons and no flashlight. The moon's at first quarter, and that'll be enough." He paused. "Be sure to bring his ashes, now. And they'd better be real this time."

"How can I prove they are?" Jasmine asked.

"Don't worry. I'll recognize the Blackburn smell."

Jasmine thought about that. "If you say so."

"I say so. Two A.M., big brother's grave. Any deviations—such as if you bring your boyfriend, or a steak knife—and that cemetery location will be real convenient. Bye now."

The receiver clicked. Jasmine waited a moment to be sure the

Sicko's voice didn't return, and then she replaced the receiver in its cradle.

She went out to the kitchen and looked at the clock on the microwave oven. It was blinking 12:00. So she looked at her watch. It was 12:11. It was Wednesday, May 14, 1997. Jimmy's birthday. Jimmy's deathday.

It was time to dispose of his earthly remains.

Jasmine figured that she had more than an hour before she would have to leave. Wantoda was only a thirty-five-minute drive away, and there was no point in showing up early. The Sicko would make her wait for him until 2:00. Leaving now wouldn't help Mom and Gary any sooner.

She brought out the urns from under the sink and held Jimmy's close to her chest with its smooth steel lid tucked under her chin. The metal was warm, as it always was.

"What would you do with an hour, big brother?" she asked.

An hour to kill.

And at that thought, Jasmine smiled.

She hadn't heard Jimmy's voice. It wasn't anything like that. She wasn't losing her mind. Despite the knot in her belly that kept tightening at the thought of what the Sicko might be doing to Mom and Gary, she was sane and rational.

No, Jimmy didn't speak. But Mom had been right: He was still in Jasmine's heart and memory. He lived in her blood and brain.

And so he had told her what to do. It was the same thing he had told her a long time ago.

Jasmine turned on the oven.

She left at 1:19 A.M. and drove fast, heading east out of Wichita on Kansas 132. Two Tupperware bowls, one white and one blue, were warm against her thigh. They were still warm twenty-eight minutes later when she slowed down to enter the dark little town of Wantoda.

"Home," she said, and then parked in the unlit gravel lot behind Nimper's IGA on Main Street.

The cemetery was eight blocks away, on the north side of town. Jasmine had a few extra minutes, so she opened the white Tupperware bowl and selected another cookie. It was her sixth. An even half dozen ought to be about right. She made this one last a full three minutes. It added to the warmth in her belly. The knot there had become a cluster of hot coals.

And then it was ten minutes to two. She picked up the blue bowl, got out of the car, and started walking.

Wantoda was asleep. Jasmine's footsteps were the only things breaking the silence of the tree-canopied streets, and that made her feel as if she owned the place.

It was the way Jimmy must have felt.

The cemetery gate was locked, but the stone wall was low enough for Jasmine to sit on it and swing her legs over to the other side. She hopped down onto soft earth and set out for the northern edge of the cemetery.

The weak moonlight didn't cast shadows, and the headstones were vague gray shapes. The cemetery was old, and the trees were tall and massive. Jasmine had never come in here as a child, and she hadn't visited too often as an adult. But even so, she knew her way around the place. Daddy's and Jimmy's graves had to be checked on twice a year. Otherwise, the groundskeeper would never bother to clean up the vandalism.

Jimmy's grave was next to the north fence, which was only barbed wire. This was the boondock area of the cemetery, where barbed wire was the only respect you got. Jasmine guessed that Daddy might appreciate that. His grave was right beside Jimmy's. He wasn't in it, but having his name carved on a piece of rock meant that something of him was here.

No grass grew on either grave. The dirt had been dug up enough that it had given up on supporting life. The headstone for Jimmy's grave was leaning, but Jasmine tried pushing it and found that it wasn't going to fall. So she placed the Tupperware bowl on the barren soil and then sat on the stone to wait. A cool breeze blew through just then, and a huge elm beside the graves rustled and moaned.

A dirt road lay beyond the fence, and beyond that were low hills of scrub pasture. Jasmine could barely make out their outlines, but she pretended that she could see past them to the place where she and Jimmy had grown up. The house was still there, three miles north of where she sat. She had sold it after Daddy's death, and she and Mom had split the money. She had driven by it just once since then, and had found that the guy who'd bought it had turned the place into a hog farm. It had smelled terrible.

That had upset her. The old homestead, as Jimmy had called it, had in many ways been an awful place to grow up. But at least it had smelled good. There had been trees and alfalfa and places to hide and think. It had just been the constant threat of rage and violence that had made things difficult sometimes.

It had only been as Jimmy's execution had drawn near that Jasmine had realized it hadn't all been his fault.

She wished she had paid more attention at the time. She wished she hadn't hated him so much.

Still, he shouldn't have killed all those people. He really shouldn't have. Then again, based on everything Jasmine had ever heard about any of his victims, none of their deaths had been any great loss to the world.

Except perhaps for Morton. And Morton had wanted to die. Otherwise, his followers could never have been saved. His death, then, had been a sacrifice on both his part and on Jimmy's. Because Jimmy might have escaped his own death if he hadn't granted death to Morton.

She wondered if Mortonism allowed women into the priesthood.

"Little Sis," a voice said.

Jasmine flinched, but didn't gasp or yelp. The voice came from right where she was looking, on the other side of the barbed-wire fence. So at least the Sicko hadn't crept up behind her as she had expected. And although he sounded hoarse, he hadn't whispered or hissed. That was something.

Not enough, though.

"Right here, Detective," she said.

The Sicko rose from the ditch, a gray specter against the black hills, and slid between the strands of barbed wire. It was only as he stepped close that Jasmine could make out the glint of the badge on his shirt, the bulk of the gun on his hip. He seemed to be a big man.

"You can just call me Officer," he said.

The hoarse voice did not belong to Holliman. And as the Sicko leaned down toward Jasmine, she could see that his face didn't either.

"Don't you know me?" the Sicko asked.

Jasmine smelled his breath now. He'd been eating peanuts.

The Sicko reached for his belt, and Jasmine tensed. But then he brought up a flashlight and turned it on under his chin so that it lit his face like someone telling a ghost story.

"Ooooh," the Sicko said. "Scaaary. But you still don't know me, do you?"

Jasmine studied his face. It was fleshy and unmemorable. Mid-western plain, like a clod of ruddy dirt. His hair was receding, and there was a pale stripe across his forehead indicating that he usually wore a hat. His eyes were small and ordinary.

She didn't recognize him at all. But she knew who he was.

"Todd Boyle," she said. "You're the Wantoda constable now."

Boyle flicked off the flashlight and replaced it on his belt. "Going on thirteen years," he said. "And I'm kind of sorry you remembered me. Now I suppose I'll have to bury all three of you. But at least they water the grass in here. This spring's been awful dry, and the ground'd be like concrete otherwise."

His tone was sarcastic. But Jasmine didn't know whether that meant he wasn't going to bury them, or just that he wasn't too upset about it.

Jasmine stood up from the gravestone. "I had assumed," she said, "that you'd already buried Mom and Gary."

Boyle stepped onto the grave and nudged the Tupperware bowl with his foot. "You assumed no such thing," he said. "If you had, you wouldn't have come. And you wouldn't have brought me what I want."

"Maybe I haven't," Jasmine said. "You don't know what's in the bowl."

Boyle took a breath and let it out with a whistling noise. "It smells of Blackburn," he said. "I recognize the stink."

Jasmine's muscles quivered, but she didn't think she was afraid. Fear might be in there somewhere, but what she was mostly aware of was anger. And contempt.

"If it stinks," she said, "then maybe you'd better not eat it. It might be too strong for you."

Boyle squatted beside the bowl and put his hand on the butt of his pistol. "I don't have a choice," he said, looking down at the bowl. "I have to consume him. He humiliated me when we were kids, and that made me a failure as a man. My old man hated me because of it. Even coming back to be constable didn't help, because he wanted me to be in the FBI. But they wouldn't take me, and it killed him. And now my mother just thinks I'm a bully."

"You *are* a bully," Jasmine said. She licked her lips and tasted sugar and sulfur. "You always were. I remember that much."

Boyle looked up then, and a sliver of moonlight gleamed in his eyes. "You sure got a mouth on you for a skinny woman in your position," he said. "I could pull out my .357 right now and put a hole through you that'd make you flat disappear."

Jasmine couldn't help smiling a little. She hoped Boyle couldn't see it. The moon was behind her, so her face ought to be hidden from him.

"So why don't you?" she asked.

Boyle looked back down at the Tupperware bowl. "Because you can't die until I'm sure you've brought me the stuff. I mean, it smells right, but that might be you. Maybe you stink just like him, and that's confusing me."

"I guess there's only one way you're going to know," Jasmine said.

Boyle reached for the bowl with his free hand, but Jasmine put her foot on the lid. Boyle glared up at her and unsnapped his holster.

Jasmine glared back. "I want to see Mom and Gary first."

Boyle stroked the butt of his pistol for a few seconds, then stood. "They're right here," he said. "Watching over us from above." He pointed upward.

At first Jasmine thought that Boyle meant he had killed them. But then she was able to make out the self-satisfied expression on his face, and she knew that he wouldn't look so delighted with himself if he had merely done away with them. No, he wanted Jasmine to look up into the elm tree. He wanted her to see how clever he was.

He wanted her to see how he had bested her brother.

So she looked.

All she saw for a moment were dark clumps of foliage. But then, twenty feet above, caught among the boughs, were the angular shapes of something else. The moonlight might have revealed them, but there were too many leaves and branches in the way. Jasmine saw only quick, pale flashes of hair, fabric, and flesh.

"Here," Boyle said. "Lemme help."

He unclipped the flashlight from his belt again, snapped it on, and aimed its beam at the shapes in the tree.

The spot of light played over first one shape and then the other. And now Jasmine saw that the shapes were enormous kites, one red and one green, and that Mom and Gary, still in their nightclothes, were strapped to the cross braces like Jesus being crucified. The kite's white tails snaked up and wrapped around their mouths.

"Got a winch on my cruiser," Boyle said. "Hook that up to a block and tackle, and bang. You got yourself a kite-eating tree."

Mom's and Gary's eyes were open, and they stared down at Jasmine. For a moment she thought they were dead, but then she saw her mother blink and turn her head from the light. Then Gary blinked too. And they were both trembling.

Something small and cold wriggled into Jasmine's chest, scuttled up into her skull, and began sucking blood from her brain.

Her poor old mother up in the tree. Dear sweet Gary up in the tree. And God only knew what else Boyle had done to them. All because Jasmine had been stupid. It was her fault they were there. Her fault.

Her knees crumbled, and she began to sink.

But then the knot of coals in Jasmine's belly reached up with a hand of fire and strangled the cold thing that was trying to pull her down. And when the cold thing was dead, the fire boiled through her brain and muscles and skin—and this time, she really did hear Jimmy's whisper.

Fix things, he said.

Fix things so that once they've done it . . .

Jasmine stood up straight, looked at Todd Boyle, and gave him a broad grin.

. . . they really wish they hadn't.

"Jimmy strapped my doll to a kite and made you think it was your baby sister," Jasmine said. "He told me about it. But I wouldn't think you'd hold a grudge over it this long. We were only kids, Todd."

Boyle sneered. "I guess you still think it's funny. But it wasn't. I was supposed to stay home with Tina, but she disappeared. And somebody left a note saying if I wanted her back, I'd better go to the water tower. So I did. And there was Jimmy Blackburn and his fucking kite. I could hear the baby crying when it flew away. But after I found it and saw that the baby was just a doll, I went home and got the shit beaten out of me because my old man thought I'd left Tina alone. She was back in her crib all covered in her own poop. Real funny. I did something brave and got screwed for it."

Jasmine suppressed a laugh. "You were the farthest thing from brave. You picked on me and all the other little kids. You were a prick. And since you've just taken out your grudge on a couple of helpless old folks, it looks like you still are."

Boyle's head jerked as if Jasmine had punched him. But then he brought the flashlight up under his chin again. "You've got it wrong," he said. "It's never been a grudge. It's been a learning experience. But I can't put it to use without surpassing my teacher."

He switched off the flashlight, clipped it to his belt again, and then kept his eyes fixed on Jasmine as he crouched down and opened the Tupperware bowl.

Jasmine didn't move. She concentrated on trying not to laugh. Jimmy would be patient. Jimmy would wait for his moment.

Boyle reached into the bowl and brought out a chocolate chip cookie. He held it up and stared at it.

"We are not amused," he said.

He stood and drew his pistol with his free hand. The moonlight shone from its barrel, and Jasmine could see that it was a Colt Python like the one Jimmy had used.

Boyle pointed it up at the kites.

"I thought you said you could smell him," Jasmine said as Boyle cocked the pistol.

Boyle hesitated, then sniffed the cookie.

"It's Blackburn, all right," he said, lowering the Python. He gave Jasmine a suspicious look. "In cookies?"

Jasmine shrugged. "Why not? You said you wanted to eat him. And I think he would have preferred it this way. He loved chocolate chip cookies."

Boyle took another sniff. "I don't smell anything wrong—but how do I know you didn't add rat poison or something?"

"Because I wouldn't do that to him," Jasmine said. She reached for the cookie. "Here. I'll eat that one."

Boyle pulled the cookie away and pointed the Python at Jasmine. "No. Just knowing that you *would* have taken a bite is good enough for me."

He brought the cookie to his mouth.

325

"Say good-bye, Little Sis," he said.

Jasmine almost wished she could stop it.

"Good-bye," she murmured.

Boyle stuffed the cookie into his mouth, chewed once, and swallowed. He took a sharp breath and stood frozen for several long seconds.

Then he gave a hungry growl, crouched, and began wolfing cookie after cookie. But he kept the Python pointed up at Jasmine's face.

"I've never killed anyone," he said around a mouthful of crumbs, staring up with eyes that had begun spinning with white light. "But I will. I can feel it." He swallowed hard. "Tell you what. If you stay right where you are, I might let your mommy live, because she and my mother are friends. But you and ol' Gary, now. You know what I think I'll do?"

He stuffed another cookie into his mouth.

Jasmine said nothing. She just stood still and waited. It was all she could do.

It was all she *needed* to do.

Todd Boyle had just swallowed the last morsel of the last cookie when his spinning eyes grew wide. An instant later, he grabbed his chest with his left hand and ripped open his shirt.

Then he toppled onto his side and began clawing himself bloody.

His right arm shook, and Jasmine could see his trigger finger starting to curl tight. The Colt Python was still aimed at her face.

"Bitch," he croaked. "Poisoned me."

Jasmine tensed, trying to anticipate the moment when he would squeeze the trigger. She might be able to jump to one side. The odds weren't good, but there was no point in getting upset about it. Jimmy wouldn't.

"I didn't put anything in those cookies that you didn't ask for," she said, watching Boyle's palsied right hand. "You wanted Blackburn's ashes so you could become what he was. And that's just what you got."

326

Now she laughed. "It's just too bad that my daddy died as a crippled, cancer-ridden old man."

Todd Boyle gave a strangled cry, and then he brought his left hand up from his chest and clasped his right wrist, steadying the pistol.

"*He* would have shot you too," Boyle said.

Jasmine's blood said *Now,* and she dove to her right and rolled. She came to a stop on her father's grave, looking across at Boyle lying on Jimmy's. She had miscalculated. He hadn't pulled the trigger.

So all she could do now was watch as he pointed the gun at her again. It was already cocked. The hammer would snap to the shell, and that would be it. Mom and Gary would be left dangling over a grave where she lay dead. Mom would no doubt be annoyed that the headstone had Daddy's name on it.

"Here it comes," Boyle said.

Except it didn't. Boyle was making her wait for it. He was trying to be cruel. But that wasn't like Daddy at all. Daddy hadn't had to try.

"Here it comes," Boyle said again, and this time Jasmine knew he meant it.

She closed her eyes. She supposed that Jimmy would be disappointed in her.

As if in answer, the next sound she heard was Jimmy's voice. And he wasn't whispering now.

"*Todd Boyle thought he was Boss Stud,*" Jimmy said. "*But he was a candy-assed thug, and he deserved what he got. Hell, they all did. Most of them just got a quick one in the head, so it's not like they felt it. And I'd do what I did to every one of them all over again. Sorry if that makes me a bad person. I guess we can't all be as good as you think you are.*"

This made Jasmine angry. She had never thought she was better than he was. Not even when she'd visited him in prison. And here she had just died for him, and he was talking to her like this. She opened her eyes so she could find him and bawl him out.

But she didn't see Jimmy. Instead, she saw Todd Boyle lying on Jimmy's grave, still holding a Colt Python that was pointed at her.

But Boyle no longer seemed to know she was there. His face glistened, and he twisted his head back and forth as if he were trying to see something attached to the back of his neck.

"Where are you?" he yelled. "Let me see you!"

"I only ever did one thing wrong," Jimmy said. His voice bounced between the tree trunks and headstones. *"I failed to punish someone that I should have. So I'm punishing myself for that. See, you may think you're going to kill me, but you're wrong. I'm killing myself."*

Boyle screamed and lurched up to his knees. He whipped the Colt from side to side, searching for a target.

Then a silver flash shot down from the sky and hit the dirt in front of Jasmine's nose. She was startled for a second, but then saw that the metal tube before her was Gary's collapsible cane.

Jasmine got to her knees and snatched up the cane, then lunged at Todd Boyle as she found the button to release the spring. The cane expanded with a snap, and the tip caught Boyle in the eye. He recoiled and tried to bring his pistol around, but Jasmine raised the cane and brought it down on his wrist. The Python spat blue flame and fell from Boyle's hand.

Jasmine's ears rang. But she hadn't been hit. She knew that because she was still on her knees on her father's grave. So she got to her feet as Boyle crawled across Jimmy's grave to retrieve his gun. She knew he wouldn't make it. Even before she cocked Gary's cane back like a baseball bat and swung it around into the bridge of Boyle's nose, she knew he wouldn't make it.

Boyle crumpled and lay back on Jimmy's grave with his head propped against the stone. He stared straight ahead and began clawing at his chest again.

And Jasmine knew what Jimmy wanted her to do next. So she raised the cane to drive it down through Todd Boyle's throat.

"Don't bother," a voice said in a monotone. "I think you got him."

328

Jasmine looked toward the barbed-wire fence and saw Detective Holliman stepping through it. She lowered the cane.

"I heard my brother," she said.

Holliman came closer until he was standing over Todd Boyle. Then he reached into his sport coat, pulled out a microcassette recorder, and pushed a button.

"Once I'm dead," Jimmy said, *"you'll never be rid of me."*

"Jimmy Blackburn's Greatest Hits," Holliman said, clicking off the recorder. "Otherwise known as a jailhouse-confession bootleg. Tape six of seven. I got the whole set from a colleague in Houston. Good beat, but only psychopaths can dance to it."

Jasmine pushed Gary's cane back into itself. "It sounded fine to me."

Holliman's eyebrows rose. "Yeah, well, like I said." He slipped the recorder back into his jacket, then took a revolver from the holster on his belt and pointed it at Boyle. "Only thing I hate worse than cop-killing loonies is some small-time dinky-dick tarnishing the reputation of law enforcement in general. So Officer Boyle, you have the right to remain silent and all that horseshit. I expect that even a podunk Andy Taylor like you knows the drill. Do you understand these rights as I've explained them to you?"

Boyle gurgled and clawed his chest.

Jasmine went over to Boyle, leaned down, and took his flashlight from his belt. Then she stepped closer to the elm tree and turned the flashlight beam upward.

Mom still looked wide-eyed and terrified, but Gary was smiling around his gag. He even winked. He had worked his right hand free and was now clinging to a branch.

Jasmine raised his collapsed cane in salute. He had managed to drop it to her just when she'd needed it. Not bad, she thought, for a guy who'd had a stroke. Not bad for a guy who wasn't even a Blackburn.

"You want to help me get my parents down, Officer—I mean, Detective Holliman?" she asked without looking back at him.

"Nah," Holliman said. "They must have a volunteer fire department around here. Cripes, what did you do to this guy, anyway? He looks like Linda Blair with male-pattern baldness."

"Just gave him what he wanted," Jasmine said.

Holliman grunted. "Guess he should have been more careful what he asked for."

"Guess so," Jasmine said, then called up to Mom and Gary. "Hang on. We'll have you down as soon as—"

She wasn't able to finish the sentence because of a sharp crack behind her. She spun around, ready to fight off Boyle again, but then saw that it wouldn't be necessary.

Boyle was lying on his back on Jimmy's grave with his mouth, eyes, and forehead wide open. A dark smear had splashed onto the headstone and was starting to slide back down.

Detective Holliman was holstering his pistol. "Jackass grabbed his gun," he said. "Blew his own brains out."

Jasmine glanced at the Colt Python on the ground. It was still lying where it had fallen when she'd clubbed it from Boyle's hand.

"I guess it flew out of his grip when it went off," Jasmine said. "Like a rocket."

Jasmine eyed the handgrip of Holliman's revolver. "Your pistol is a .38, right? And Boyle's is a .357?"

Holliman nodded. "Yeah. But nobody's gonna want to see if my piece has been fired, because you and I both saw what happened. Don't think your parents did, because you had that light in their eyes. Also, Boyle's shot went clear through his head into your brother's tombstone. And a .357 slug can look a lot like a .38 after it's been shot into granite. See what I'm saying?"

Jasmine dropped Gary's cane and started toward the fence. "Yes. And now I'm going to call for help to get my parents down."

"Good idea," Holliman said. "I followed you over, so my car's parked next to yours at the grocery store—but Boyle's cruiser is just down this road about a hundred yards. I already broke into it and turned on the two-way. All you have to do is press the switch on the microphone, and you should get the county dispatcher."

"Thanks." Jasmine paused at the fence and turned the flashlight beam back at Holliman. "You broke into my car as well, didn't you? And you ate some of the cookies from the bowl on the seat."

Holliman's eyes narrowed. "It was a justified probable-cause search conducted within the normal course of my investigation. And I only ate one. Tasted like a rotten egg. No offense, but I wouldn't be applying for any pastry chef positions if I were you. How'd you know I got into them?"

Jasmine started through the fence. "Just caught a whiff of something."

She jumped down to the road and ran to Boyle's Ford Bronco cruiser. She hoped that whoever responded to her call would hurry, because she wanted to make sure that Mom was coherent as soon as possible. Someone was going to have to break the news about Todd Boyle to his mother, and it might as well be someone who knew her.

Jasmine's mother and stepfather stayed with her until mid-July. So when Jasmine and Mack returned to her house after finally putting Mom and Gary on a plane back to Spokane, they fell into bed and made love for the first time in two months.

Afterward, while Mack went to the kitchen to look for something to eat, Jasmine fumbled on the floor for her purse and pulled out the cassette tape that the Mortonite at the airport had just given her. It had been the same longhaired, dirty-bathrobe-wearing nut as before, but this time he had been handing out tapes instead of tracts. He had appeared out of the crowd, pressed a cassette into her hand, and then scampered off on all fours, giggling.

Jasmine popped the incoming-message tape out of her answering machine, replaced it with the Mortonite tape, and hit Play.

"I pulled the trigger in the Wilderness because it was necessary for Morton to come into his glory," Jimmy's voice said. *"He would have done it himself, you know . . . except that would have queered the deal."*

It seemed that Detective Holliman wasn't the only one who'd

gotten hold of Jimmy's jailhouse-confession tapes. Wonderful. And according to *Newsweek,* the Mortonites were becoming more and more evangelical. They were even starting to go door-to-door like Mormons or Jehovah's Witnesses. So how the hell was Jasmine going to keep her mother from hearing this stuff?

She was just about to shut off the tape when Jimmy's voice gave way to an old play-by-play broadcast of a Wichita Wranglers baseball game.

Jasmine stiffened. She felt that ice pick in her spine again.

Then she heard Mack open the freezer door on her refrigerator. Heard the Tupperware pop open. Heard the crackle of aluminum foil.

She ran to the kitchen and slammed her shoulder into his ribs just as he was about to bite into the cookie. He fell back against the counter, and the cookie flew from his hand and skittered into the wall, where it shattered.

"Jesus H. Christ!" Mack yelled. "What was that for?"

Jasmine pushed him aside, then scooped up as many of the chunks and crumbs as she could find.

"I'm sorry," she said as she rewrapped the pieces in the foil that Mack had opened. "But these are bad."

Mack rubbed his ribs and glared at her. "Then why are you saving them?"

"And it looks like we're going into extra innings," the tape in the bedroom announced.

Jasmine replaced the packet in the Tupperware bowl with the others and snapped the lid shut. "Because it's a family recipe. So I can't throw them out. I can't."

Mack's expression softened, and he put an arm around Jasmine's shoulders. "I understand," he said, although she knew he didn't.

Back in the bedroom, the voice became Jimmy's again.

"Don't bother with the shackles," he said. *"I'm not going anywhere."*

"Damn," Jasmine said. "Damn, damn, damn."

"It's going to be all right now," Mack said. "The Sicko's gone, and your folks are on their way home. So just remember what all those posters said when we were kids: 'Today is the first day of the rest of your life.' "

Jasmine couldn't help giving a short, bitter laugh. She had just had a vision of the rest of her life as a runaway kite.

"In other words," she said, "one day closer to death."

Mack frowned. "That sounds like your brother talking."

Jasmine pulled away from him and picked up the Tupperware bowl. She put the bowl back into the freezer, then kept her hands against the closed door for a moment.

The metal was warm.

"I know," Jasmine said. "So let's try not to piss him off, okay?"

Afterword

⤳

Bradley Denton, fiction writer, died on _____ , __ ____ , of complications resulting from _____.
He was ___ years of age.

Bradley Clayton Denton was born in Wichita, Kansas, on June 7, 1958. (This was also the birthdate of The Artist Formerly Known as Prince, which has led to speculation that Denton and TAFKaP were the same person, or identical twins.) Denton grew up in suburban and rural Kansas, where he stepped on nails, played with dogs, and caught crawdads. He earned a B.A. in astronomy and English from the University of Kansas in 1980, and an M.A. in English from KU in 1984.

He married Barbara Eggleston in 1980, and the couple lived in and around Lawrence, Kansas, until 1988, when they relocated to Austin, Texas. This transition was smoothed by a friend who introduced them to everyone in the city and also taught them the appropriate colloquialisms for cursing idiot drivers.

Denton wrote short stories beginning at age five, and he made his first professional sale to *The Magazine of Fantasy & Science*

Fiction at age twenty-five. In addition to short fiction published in various magazines, anthologies, and collections, he was the author of the novels *Wrack and Roll* (1986), *Buddy Holly Is Alive and Well on Ganymede* (1991), *Blackburn* (1993), *Lunatics* (1996), _____ (____), _____ ! (____) (which was made into the film _____ ?), _____ / / _____ @ ___.___ (____), and others too numerous to mention. *Buddy Holly Is Alive and Well on Ganymede* won the John W. Campbell Memorial Award in 1992, and the limited-edition story collections *The Calvin Coolidge Home for Dead Comedians* and *A Conflagration Artist* won the World Fantasy Award in 1995. Several of Denton's other works were honored with the _____, _____, and _____ awards, each of which included a substantial honorarium.

Denton's artistic influences have been difficult to pin down, but in various writings and conversations he expressed admiration for the works of Mark Twain, Eric Clapton, John Kessel, Edward Bryant, William Shakespeare, Buddy Guy, B. B. King, Michael Bishop, Karen Joy Fowler, Sue Foley, Muddy Waters, Bruce Sterling, Steven Utley, Peter Townshend, Neal Barrett, Jr., George R. R. Martin, Little Walter, Charlie Watts, Joe Haldeman, John Cleese, James Gunn, Gene Wolfe, J. G. Ballard, Keith Richards, Caroline Spector, Victor Contoski, Buddy Holly, Steven Gould, John Lee Hooker, Howard Waldrop, Rory Harper, Walton Simons, Stevie Ray Vaughan, David McDowell, John Lennon, Sven Knudson, George Alec Effinger, Bill Hicks, Laura J. Mixon, Douglas Potter, Freedy Johnston, Joe R. Lansdale, Don Webb, Ax Nelson, Robert Crais, William Browning Spencer, Keith Moon, Lenny Bruce, Connie Willis, Warren Spector, Terry Bisson, and Etta James. Among others.

Denton's success during his lifetime was somewhat limited by his own hedonistic excesses (such as his premarital habit of dating actress-models who wore their underwear on the outside of their leotards—no, wait, that was TAFKaP). The success he did obtain was largely the result of support from the loved ones who now survive him.

He is survived by his wife, Barbara, . . . family (including Dentons, Kocis, Keitels, Snyders, Morgans, Egglestons, Booths, Prevedels, Sargents, etc.), . . . friends (including agents, editors, and everyone he ever met through KaCSFFS, FACT, conventions, bookstores, bands, owls, workshops, the Saturday Morning Breakfast Herd, etc.), . . . colleagues (including Howard Waldrop and Caroline Spector, critiquers beyond compare), . . . and caretakers (including Watson, Rufus, and Clarence).

Denton's body will be cremated, and his remains will be packed into one of those humongous Fourth of July mortars and blown up over whoever objects the most.

Memorial contributions may be made to whatever organization is dedicated to fighting whatever it was that killed him. (Not that it matters to *him* at this point.)

In lieu of a funeral service, friends and family are asked to gather wherever they live next Saturday morning and eat a big whopping breakfast. The cost of these meals is provided for in the deceased's will, unless he checked out before he got around to it (in which case mourners are advised to see if TAFKaP will pick up the tab).

And finally, booksellers around the world are encouraged to honor the literary legacy of Bradley Denton by jacking up the prices on all of his titles.

There. Now all you have to do is hang on to this book long enough, and you can fill in the blanks.

In conclusion, I'd like to thank you for taking the time to read these stories. I really do appreciate it, because time is one of the most precious things you have.

You know what I'm saying.

Unless, that is, you'd care to make a friendly wager.

	DATE DUE		